T0354807

A NIGHT
WITHOUT
STARS

SABRINA ALBIS

A NIGHT WITHOUT STARS

iUniverse books may be ordered through booksellers or by contacting:

iUniverse
1663 Liberty Drive
Bloomington, IN 47403
www.iuniverse.com
1-800-Authors (1-800-288-4677)

ISBN: 978-1-5320-0165-9 (sc)
ISBN: 978-1-5320-0164-2 (e)

Library of Congress Control Number: 2016910806

Print information available on the last page.

iUniverse rev. date: 08/12/2016

For my dear Aunt Donna, for believing in me
and encouraging me to follow my dreams

Prologue

Walking through the halls of her high school for the last time ever, Autumn Kingston felt nothing but joy. The school that had once brimmed with possibilities and hope seemed desolate to her now, like a vibrant picture drained of color.

She walked past the principal's office, past administration, through the front corridor. She passed by the cases of trophies, awards, and plaques that glinted in the sunlight streaming in through the large skylight.

Once upon a time, she had dreamed *her* name would be on the list of graduates beside the title of valedictorian. She never thought she would be leaving her home and that these halls would haunt her with such bad memories.

She could almost see herself now, the dark-haired girl with the big green eyes, walking into this school in September. It was her freshman year, and she could remember the feeling of terror and the knots in her stomach. She was a stranger in a new world, so when she went to her locker and was greeted by a friendly girl, she was overjoyed.

"Hey there. I'm Nicole Lancaster your locker neighbor," she said, outstretching her hand.

"Autumn Kingston," she took her hand, shaking it.

"A pleasure to meet you," she smiled brightly, exposing braces. "It's nice to see a friendly face around these halls."

Autumn smiled back. "I know the feeling. I am so unbelievably nervous."

Nicole popped her locker open. "My brother told me that high school was a breeze for him. You just need to find the popular kids and cling to them."

"I don't know about you, but I'm not so good at clinging," Autumn admitted.

Perhaps it was an understatement. Autumn was rather stubborn, and she wouldn't let anyone tell her what was wrong or right. She was her own moral compass. No one dictated how she should dress, how she should look or who she should be friends with.

"Ah. So you're a born leader then," Nicole said, fishing a notebook from her backpack. "That is really cool."

Autumn shrugged. "I know I am definitely not a follower."

Nicole nodded. "No worries. I would never follow my brother's advice. He spent his freshman year as a lackey for some jock dude," she paused. "Can I see your schedule?"

Autumn nodded, pulling it out from her knapsack. As she did, she felt a body bumping into her. She handed Nicole her schedule and turned to see a guy standing behind her. He was tall, well-built and had light blonde hair and hazel eyes. He smiled at her awkwardly.

"Sorry about that. This kid bumped into me, and then I bumped into you."

Autumn smiled. "I'll chalk it up to a bad chain reaction. It's all good."

She turned back to Nicole, who was scanning their schedules.

"We have most of our classes together," she began but the boy was still standing there.

He stared at Autumn, looking enthralled. She blinked at him. Were all high school guys this strange?

"Can I help you with something?"

"Your name," the boy said, grinning. "Do you have one?"

"Funny that. My parents gave me one at birth," she said lightly. "Autumn."

The boy nodded slowly. "Autumn huh? A beautiful name for a beautiful girl."

Autumn blushed, though she was trying to remain cool. "And you might be?"

"Kyle," he said, reaching out his hand to her.

"Nice to meet you, Kyle," Autumn said, shaking his hand.

He smiled. "So, is there any chance you might want to go out sometime?"

Nicole looked up from the schedules, a grin upon her face. Autumn's eyes went wide with disbelief. This guy didn't waste any time.

"I'm sorry?"

"On a date," Kyle began, but he recoiled after seeing her expression. "Too soon?"

"Considering we just met, I would say yes."

Nicole giggled as another boy came over and smacked Kyle on the back.

"Dude, we gotta go. Homeroom," he said, glancing at Autumn and Nicole. "Hello ladies."

The girls greeted him as Kyle turned back to Autumn.

"It was nice meeting you Autumn. I hope to see you around so we can get to know each other better."

"See you later," Autumn said as she waved. When they were no longer in earshot, Nicole jabbed her arm.

"The first day of school and you get asked out. I am so jealous!" she squealed.

"Don't be," Autumn said. "That guy is from another planet asking me out so soon," she paused.

"And he will probably be doing the exact same thing to the next girl he sees."

"Hey, Kingston!" A voice entered Autumn's reverie, pulling her from it. No need to check your reflection in the display cases Aut. You are still ugly."

The girl chortled, and Autumn turned, facing her. It was Nicole Lancaster, and she was looking at Autumn with her usual icy stare.

Autumn grimaced. She had never gotten used to the fact that her best friend hated her now. She did, however, come to accept it.

Normally, Nicole was flanked by her *pretties*. The flying monkeys she called *friends*. The two girls followed her around, groveling at her feet, thirsting for just a taste of her popularity.

However, today she stood alone, dressed in a leather mini skirt and a white blouse, her chestnut hair secured in a perfect ponytail.

She grinned wickedly, her braces gone, showing perfect teeth.

"What's wrong Kingston? No comeback?"

Autumn sighed. "Nicole, I know your brain is the size of a pea but are we really resorting to childish name calling again?" she paused. "Better yet, don't you have anything better to do than follow me around? Maybe you can go find a guy to sleep with? He can be lucky number fifty."

"Spoken like a true virgin," Nicole snorted, crossing her arms over her chest. "You keeping track?"

"Someone has to," Autumn said, hands on her hips. "Since you don't know how to count."

Nicole rolled her eyes and began tinkering with her ponytail.

"I didn't come here to engage in a battle of wits with you Kingston," Nicole said.

Autumn nodded. "I would make the obvious joke about you being unarmed, but I would rather just get to it."

Nicole smirked. "I came to say goodbye. Or maybe good riddance is the better word for it?"

"Good riddance is more than *a* word," Autumn said, unruffled. "But please, try again."

"I heard through the grapevine you are moving," Nicole went on. "We are going to be seniors next year, and you are running away to another school?"

Autumn glared at her, feeling her temper rise, like hackles. She didn't run from anything or anyone.

"You of all people should know that I don't run from things Nikki," she snapped. "My friend Rick needs my help."

"Rick?" Nicole said, looking confused. "Oh! The dumb guy you told me about?"

"I never called him dumb. I said he's a slacker," Autumn said, bitterly.

"Splitting hairs are you?" Nicole asked. "Either way, I want you to know you will be sorely missed if only because you are my favorite enemy."

Autumn rolled her eyes. "I hope you grow up Nikki. Because when you do, you are going to realize how pathetic you were in high school and how you squandered your time being the bitchy queen bee, when you could've been so much more."

Nicole looked at her, and for a second, Autumn thought there was sadness behind her cold eyes. However, like magic, it vanished, and she was the ice queen once more.

"Whatever Kingston. Enjoy your new life," Nicole muttered and she headed towards the cafeteria.

As she walked away, Autumn felt a little tug in her heart for her old best friend. For the Nicole who was sweet, caring and compassionate. The monster who had just been in her midst was no one her heart recognized anymore.

By the end of the day, the rumor mill had finished churning, and everyone and their brother knew of Autumn leaving.

She was at her locker, grabbing books, when Kyle walked by with Nikki. She had gotten used to the sight of them together, but it had taken her awhile. She had dated him for a year before Nikki had managed to manipulate him and eventually snag him for herself. It was her grade ten year when they had broken up. It was her first heartbreak, and because of Nikki, her first real betrayal. It seemed like cliché movie fodder, but it didn't make the knife cut any less deep.

Autumn thought she would never trust anyone again. Having your *best friend* steal your boyfriend does that to a girl.

As Kyle walked by her now, he hardly smiled at her, but she could see a hint of something, perhaps regret, maybe even sadness, in his eyes as he looked at her. She pushed the thoughts of him, the memories and the pain, deep inside and when he was gone, she went back to her locker, closing it.

"I can't do this!" Autumn heard a familiar voice from behind her, and she turned around to see her best friend, Kristin Roberts standing there.

Kristin, who was normally quite sanguine, wore a frown that looked out of place on her round face. Other than that, she looked the same as usual. She was wearing her black cat eye glasses and had her curly brown hair pulled into a bun atop her head. She was dressed in a plain grey T-shirt and jeans that highlighted her slight frame, and she had her arms crossed over her chest, reminding Autumn of a pouting child.

"I refuse to let you go Aut," she said, stubbornly.

Autumn smiled, amused. "Kris, don't do this. You know I have no other choice. Rick needs me or he won't graduate."

"So tell his parents to hire him a tutor!" Kristin said defiantly. "You told me they are loaded right?"

Autumn chuckled. "It isn't that easy. They have tried that but Rick doesn't focus. They think he would be better off with someone he knows then he wouldn't be as distracted."

"Wouldn't he be *more* distracted then?" Kristin offered weakly.

Autumn knew she couldn't win. There was no logical explanation she could give her friend now that would actually appease her. Kristin felt abandoned and Autumn knew if the situation was reversed, she would feel exactly the same.

"Kris, I am going to miss you, but we can still visit. I am only three hours away." Autumn paused as she saw Kristin's expression change. She looked like she might cry.

"I am going to miss you too Aut," Kristin said, and she lunged at Autumn, wrapping her into a hug.

Autumn could feel the tears in her eyes threatening to spill over. She knew today wasn't really *goodbye*. She would have a good chunk of summer vacation here before she was left. August was when she officially moved.

Still, she always thought she would be graduating from high school with Kristin.

This was home to them and while others tried their best to escape, she never wanted to leave.

Her parents were here, her sister, her family, Kristin, her roots and her memories. She felt like her seeds had been planted here, and she wasn't ready to move on. However, she wasn't selfish. She couldn't say no to her Aunt Katherine and Uncle James. She knew if they requested her help, it was serious. Rick really needed her.

Even though they weren't family by blood, Rick was her childhood best friend. She had always called Katherine her aunt and James her uncle. After all, James *was* practically a brother to her dad, Chris. They had grown up together and from her understanding, her grandparents had pretty much raised James as their own.

Knowing all these factors and having her father reiterate something *she* had been thinking sealed the deal for her.

"You can look at this as a fresh start sweetheart," her dad had said after asking if she was willing to do her senior year in Whitan. "You won't ever have to see Nikki or Kyle roaming the halls again. You want your last year to be your best year right?"

Autumn had to admit it. It was a tempting prospect, but could she really have her best year in another city?

Kristin pulled away from Autumn, tears visible on her face. She wiped them away with her arm.

"Alright. That's enough with the doom and gloom. We still have time together before you go. So let's make the best of it."

Autumn nodded, fighting the urge to cry. "My thoughts exactly."

1

On a train, headed for the town of Whitan, Autumn Kingston somehow managed to fall asleep. She was curled up on the seat, under a blanket she had brought from home. She had been anxious, after her parents had seen her off. There were many tears and hugs and her mom reminding her of things she might forget.

She went through the list as she watched the buildings and vast fields going by.

She had to call home as soon as she reached her destination, and she needed to thank Aunt Katherine and Uncle James for their hospitality.

When she was done with the list, the panic slowly set in. She was going to a strange place without her parents and best friend.

She would be at a new school with new kids and living in a new house. It hit her hard suddenly, overwhelming her.

She took a few deep breaths, trying her best to focus on inhaling then exhaling. The simplest thing she could do, because it came naturally.

Before long, the panic had given way to exhaustion, and she relaxed into her seat. She pulled the blanket over her legs and was lulled to sleep by the sound of the train cruising smoothly along on the tracks.

Dressed in jeans and a white T-shirt, Autumn was your typical seventeen year old girl. With her long dark waves, full lips and porcelain skin, she was strikingly beautiful.

When Autumn was young she was a typical tomboy. She wore her hair in a messy ponytail, and dressed in baggy shirts and jeans. She was often found playing road hockey with boys or kicking their butts at video games.

Back then, she lived only minutes away from her best friend Rick. Autumn and Rick were inseparable. Together, they watched movies, played board games and biked around the small town of Whitan. Her favorite childhood memory was of her and Rick riding their bikes to the park and spending the day taking turns pushing each other on the swings.

Autumn awoke as the train was slowing down. The conductor announced her stop, and she stood up, put her blanket into her large purse and stretched. Then she grabbed her luggage and headed for the exit doors. They slid open and she walked along the platform, trailed by a few other travelers.

It was a perfect summer day, warm but not sweltering. The breeze danced lazily across her skin as she lugged her suitcase along the platform.

She looked around. She hadn't seen Rick in years. She really had no idea what he would look like in person. They chatted online often and sent pictures to each other but a picture was never quite the same as the real thing. She imagined that Rick wouldn't recognize her either.

Last he saw her, she was slim, with no figure and her hair was short. Years later, she finally filled out and developed curves. Her dark hair was so long it touched her lower back.

Autumn looked around the train station more thoroughly as the train's doors glided shut and it pulled away. She began searching the small crowds of people congregated on the platform and was relieved when she finally spotted Rick.

Not only was Rick the only younger guy at the station but he still looked exactly the same.

Dressed in a T-shirt and ragged jeans, he was taller and more muscular, but he still had the brown ringlet curls and blue eyes she remembered from when they were kids. Rick, however, continued searching for Autumn in the crowd.

She walked towards him apprehensively and waved at him. Rick saw her and waved back, looking surprised but happy.

"Autumn?" he began unsurely, slowly walking towards her.

"Hey, Rick," she said, setting down her luggage to greet him. It took him a moment to react and for a split-second, he just gawked at her. Finally, he smiled at her, his familiar dimpled grin.

"Aut!" he exclaimed, running at her, arms outstretched. He scooped her up without effort and spun her around.

Autumn enjoyed this movie moment. She probably wouldn't have many in her lifetime.

"Ricky!" she squealed, sinking into him as he set her down. They hugged until Rick pulled back and began examining Autumn.

"You look so different," he said. "You don't have chicken legs anymore!"

"You look different too," Autumn said, beaming. "Except for these," she said, touching his ringlets playfully.

Rick smiled at her. "You were always pretty Aut but you are just stunning now."

"You turned out pretty adorable yourself there Rick," she said, blushing.

"I'm just in shock," Rick went on. "I've seen pictures of you, but it's not like *actually* seeing you."

"The last time you saw me in person was years ago," she pointed out. "I've grown up."

Rick nodded. "It's a good change you know, the curves. Some of the girls at my school look like all they eat is lettuce and they are so bitchy. I think it's because they're starving."

"That is terrible," Autumn said.

"Personally, I don't want to see my girlfriend's ribs but that's just me," Rick said, grabbing Autumn's luggage. "Follow me. I parked close."

When they got to Rick's car, he loaded Autumn's bags into the trunk as she hopped into the passenger seat. Autumn buckled up her seatbelt as Rick got in beside her.

As they drove, Autumn took in her surroundings, trying her best to remember the town but the Whitan she had known as a little girl was no longer. The small sleepy town had grown into a city though not quite as big as she had imagined. There were fewer fields and trees and many more buildings and houses. The streets were filled with joggers and dog walkers, and the road was jam-packed with cars.

"Welcome to suburbia," Rick joked, catching Autumn's expression of wonder.

"I just can't believe how many people live here now," Autumn said.

"The times they are a changing," Rick mused.

They had been driving for only a few minutes when Autumn noticed many other drivers were passing Rick.

Most of them looked annoyed and glared at him but Rick didn't take notice. Staring straight-ahead, with both hands wrapped tightly around the steering wheel, he went about his merry way.

Autumn looked from him to the speedometer which read, sixty.

"Rick, what is the speed limit on this road?" she asked curiously.

"Eighty," Rick replied nonchalantly.

"So, how was your train ride?" he asked, looking directly at her only because he stopped at a yellow light.

"It was good," Autumn said.

She smiled to herself. She couldn't resist a chance to tease Rick, for old time's sake.

"Ricky, you stopped at the yellow light?"

"Yes. I drive with care *always*," he said confidently.

"Yellow means caution," Autumn pointed out. "And while I think that safe driving is commendable, you could've gone through. The intersection was empty."

"Autumn, haven't you heard all those safe driving slogans? Driving isn't a race! I want to arrive alive!"

Autumn giggled. "Sorry Rick. You wouldn't have made it through the intersection before the light turned red anyhow."

Rick shot her a look. "Why not?"

"Rick, you drive sixty clicks in an eighty zone," she said. "Didn't you notice the other drivers going past you? I've never seen such angry motorists. And I swear a guy on a bicycle passed you."

Rick rolled his eyes. "If they don't like my driving they can go around me," he said stubbornly. "It is their right."

Autumn already knew Rick had a penchant for overly safe driving. Uncle James told her dad Rick was so meticulous that driving with him had become an ordeal.

Autumn chuckled. "*You* are like no teenage driver I've ever met."

"Why?" Rick asked, as the light turned green and the car began moving again.

"Teenagers aren't exactly known for their safe driving."

Rick shrugged. "That may be so but *I* don't want us to end up *dead*. And you will thank me for that when you are alive and well."

Rick and Autumn continued chatting and it felt natural. It wasn't like they hadn't spoken in years.

Autumn would call Rick at least once or twice a week and they emailed often.

He would talk about skateboarding with his best friend Nathaniel, and she would tell him about school and cheerleading. Still, Autumn had to admit she enjoyed talking to Rick in person much more.

Ten minutes passed before they finally arrived at Rick's house and when Autumn first saw it, she hardly recognized it.

It was very different from the house she had visited when she was a young girl.

The house she was remembered was smaller, with old rustic details and a tiny garden out front.

This house was huge, with a wraparound porch and an enormous garden encompassing it.

"Wow," Autumn managed as she was getting out of the car. "Did your parents do some remodeling?"

Rick got out and opened the trunk, grabbing Autumn's luggage.

"Yeah. It took them years to get the house how they wanted it. Man, they are perfectionists if you ask me."

As they strolled up the cobblestone walkway, Autumn examined the house. The garden was filled with an array of beautiful flowers and plants and the house itself had bay windows and a huge old-fashioned wooden front door.

Autumn heard the sound of the door opening and saw her Aunt Katherine standing there. She stepped out onto the front porch, smiling the familiar smile Autumn had grown to miss.

Seeing her again reminded Autumn of being a little girl. She had always thought her Aunt Katherine was so pretty.

Aunt Katherine was tall, with high cheekbones framed by a black bob. She always wore something classic like a pantsuit or an A-line skirt with a blouse. Today was no different. Though she was older and her skin crinkled when she smiled now, she was still beautiful.

It's so good to see you Autumn," she said hugging her tightly. "Come inside sweetheart."

As they stepped inside, Autumn remembered the sweet scent of baking lingering in the air as her and Rick played board games in the kitchen. Aunt Katherine always made cookies, brownies and squares on weekends.

"Aunt Katherine I missed you so much," Autumn said. As tears of joy filled her eyes she felt foolish thinking she would feel like a stranger here. This was like another home to her as a child and she could never forget that.

"You look so beautiful," Aunt Katherine said, tearing up as well. "Pictures don't do you any justice Autumn. You are just gorgeous."

"I don't see it," Autumn said modestly. "But thank you."

"Oh don't give me that," her aunt said in disbelief. "The boys must love you. You have an amazing figure."

"Mom!" Rick grumbled, rolling his eyes.

"Rick, what's wrong honey?" Aunt Katherine asked.

"Come on mom. You are embarrassing me!" Rick said, setting the luggage down in the front foyer.

"Am I?" she asked, grinning slightly.

"Yeah you are! Autumn is my best buddy and you are talking about her figure! It's really weird!"

"Well, you go ahead and take her bags up to her new room then," Aunt Katherine said looking back at Autumn. "I want to give you the grand tour sweetie. Things have changed a lot since you were last here."

Rick heaved the luggage off the floor and started up the stairs as Aunt Katherine began showing Autumn around.

She couldn't believe how different the house was on the inside as well. The kitchen had been expanded and modernized, with beautiful tile flooring and new white cupboards. All the carpet had been torn up and replaced by hardwood in the dining and living room and in the backyard there was a pool and a hot tub. The best part was the added on library where Autumn was free to peruse books whenever she wanted. She was in heaven.

After Autumn's tour, Aunt Katherine began making dinner, chicken and potatoes, and Autumn headed for her room to unpack.

When Autumn saw her new bedroom, she couldn't believe her eyes. She blinked once, in utter disbelief, before walking into it.

It was almost as big as her parent's master bedroom back home.

She sat her purse on the huge bed that was decorated with a white duvet and tons of fluffy pillows. The room smelt like a mix of vanilla and lavender and there was a window seat, a big bookshelf and a desk.

Mounted on the wall, across from the bed, was a large flat-screen television. Autumn was also excited to discover she had a massive walk-in closet.

She began taking her clothes out of her suitcase, eager to use her new closet, when she heard a tap on her open door. She looked up and saw Rick standing there.

"Unpacking?" he asked and Autumn nodded. "Come in."

"Do you need any help?" he asked, making his way over to the suitcases.

"I'm good, thanks."

"Oh, come on! I don't mind." Rick insisted.

He reached into her luggage, blindly grabbing a few articles of clothing.

"I'll just put these away for you," he began, but he stopped short.

Autumn looked up and saw to her amusement that Rick had a pair of her lacy underwear in his hands.

"I'm sorry," Rick mumbled, his face red as he gently set them on the bed.

"It's okay," she grinned. "They are just underwear."

"So you need help with school?" she changed the subject.

"I don't think so," he said bluntly. "I pass and passing is all that matters."

"That's what those drivers *passing you* said too," Autumn cracked and Rick groaned.

Autumn was already warned about Rick's passé attitude towards school. Her aunt told her that rollerblading, skateboarding and tinkering with his sword collection, took precedence over his academics.

"Well, according to your mom, you just barely passed last year, and if you fail this year *you* won't be graduating," she paused as she headed towards the mirrored dresser. "Hence, why I'm here."

Rick stared at her, puzzled. "Hence?"

"Exactly," she said.

Rick shrugged, looking bored. "Either way, I don't want to fail, so yeah, copying off you would be ideal."

Autumn chuckled as she put her shirts into the top drawer of her dresser.

"Oh no, we aren't going down that road Rick."

"Why?" he asked, pouting. "I'll pay you Autumn."

"Money can't buy me," she said firmly. "You need to pass your classes *honestly.*"

Rick rolled his eyes and slumped onto her bed, defeated. "Now you sound like mom."

"Sorry Ricky. Your mom and dad brought me here to help and if I let you cheat I wouldn't be helping you would I?"

"Is that a trick question?" he asked, narrowing his eyes at her.

A loud beeping sound came from Rick's pocket as Autumn continued putting clothes away. He pulled out his cellphone and grinned broadly.

"Sweet!"

"What's sweet?" she asked.

"My buddy is here. We skate together. Wait until you meet him," he said. "He's a really nice guy. We have been friends since grade nine. I'm sure I mentioned him to you before. His name is Nathaniel."

Autumn arched an eyebrow at him not missing a beat. "Is this a setup Rick?"

"No! Of course not! I wasn't setting him up with you *yet*. We hadn't seen each other in years. You could've been horrid in person," Rick said as he began texting.

Autumn looked at Rick incredulously.

"Thanks," she grumbled sarcastically.

"What? I said *could've* been," he said, looking up at her sweetly. "You actually turned out to be pretty."

"Wonderful," Autumn muttered.

Autumn had filled up two drawers in her dresser with clothes when a voice bellowed up the stairs.

"Rick? Dude? I'm here!"

"Dude, I'm in the guest room," Rick replied.

Minutes later, a guy about Rick's height and build, with ginger hair and light freckling on his face walked into the room. When he saw Autumn, his eyes went wide.

"Hello," Autumn said as she picked up more clothes to sort. She introduced herself as Nathaniel continued staring at her, mesmerized.

"I've talked about Autumn plenty. We grew up together. She is like family," Rick said proudly. "Our parents are tight man."

Nathaniel nodded slowly, not even looking at Rick before offering Autumn his hand.

"Nathaniel Abrams."

"Good to meet you Nathaniel," she said shaking his hand.

Autumn went back to sorting her clothes. Nathaniel studied her, his hand on his chin before turning to Rick.

"Dude, you said she might be horrid," he said loudly.

"I did, but it turns out I was wrong dude," Rick muttered.

"Yeah, you were," Nathaniel said, a grin on his face. "She is smoking hot."

Autumn felt her face growing hot. It was like she wasn't even in the room.

Nathaniel turned back to her. "So do you have a boyfriend back home Autumn?"

Rick rolled his eyes. "Even if she did, he lives far away now dude."

"I still have to ask man. It's procedure. Girls with boyfriends are off limits. You know that!" Nathaniel shot back.

Autumn sat patiently on her bed as they went on conversing like she was invisible.

"So do you?" Nathaniel asked again, shuffling his feet back and forth.

She thought about Kyle for a split second, but didn't let her mind delve too deep into the thought. She wasn't reopening that wound today or tomorrow. After all, she had her whole life to pine.

"Nope," Autumn said. "I did but we broke up."

Nathaniel nodded approvingly. "Awesome. And let me just say, any guy that let you go, is a complete moron."

Autumn smiled. "Thanks."

"So, are you staying for dinner man?" Rick asked Nathaniel, taking a seat at the end of Autumn's bed.

Nathaniel nodded. "Yeah, your mom already invited me downstairs."

"Good," Rick said. "You can ask Autumn all the questions you want instead of asking me."

Nathaniel smiled at Autumn sheepishly just as Aunt Katherine called them down for dinner.

As they made their way down the wooden stairs, Autumn could smell a medley of vanilla candles, roasted chicken and homemade mashed potatoes. When they stepped into the large kitchen, the table was set for five with fine bone china and in the middle sat a bouquet of fresh flowers.

"Autumn! You made it!"

Autumn was delighted to see her Uncle James by the fridge uncorking a bottle of white wine.

He put the bottle down and rushed over to hug her.

"Kiddo, you are a sight for sore eyes eh?" he said squeezing her tightly.

"Uncle James, how are you?" Autumn squeezed back just as firmly.

"Not bad for an old guy I guess," he jested.

Like her aunt, her uncle looked the same as he always had, albeit a little older.

He was short and stocky, with dark hair and eyes that usually had a mischievous twinkle in them. The one thing she remembered about Uncle James was he was always smiling.

Growing up, her father joked around with her but he was often somber. James, however, was always playing pranks on people.

Autumn had many memories of her Uncle James placing whoopee cushions on her chair or jumping out from behind walls and scaring her senseless.

As a child, he was heaven to be around because he was so silly and fun.

Even now, it was hard for her to imagine him in a business suit talking maturely with his colleagues.

"Katherine told me you were gorgeous, and she was right," her uncle went on. "You're smart and beautiful, so you obviously take after your mom and not your dad," he joked of his old friend.

When everyone finally sat down to eat, Autumn was famished. She hadn't eaten since leaving home due to her frazzled nerves.

After everyone was seated and situated, Katherine turned to Rick.

"Alright Rick, start passing around the chicken," she said.

Nathaniel took the serving plate from Rick and began putting chicken on his plate.

"Hey Nathaniel, do you like the breasts, legs or thighs?" Rick snickered.

Autumn rolled her eyes at his immaturity as Aunt Katherine shot him a look that made him stop laughing instantly.

"Rick," she said sternly.

"Sorry," Rick mumbled.

Nathaniel was trying his best not to crack up as he grabbed a piece of chicken.

"Here you go Autumn," he said handing her the serving plate.

She smiled and took it, placing some chicken on her plate. "Thank you."

"So Autumn, what do you think of your room?" Aunt Katherine asked as she started passing around the potatoes.

"It's beautiful," Autumn said, handing the chicken to her uncle. "You guys didn't need to go to all that trouble."

"Oh it was nothing," her aunt insisted.

Her uncle nodded in agreement.

"It was the least we could do knowing you have to tutor this knucklehead all year long," he ruffled Rick's hair affectionately.

"Guys, don't lie you went all out," Rick jumped in. "That room was just a single bed and a lamp before Autumn came here."

Autumn narrowed her eyes disapprovingly. "You are spoiling me."

"We only want the best for you," Aunt Katherine said, beaming at Autumn. "You should feel at home here."

"No need to worry," Autumn smiled. "I already do."

Autumn spent the rest of dinner catching up with everyone, while answering a bombardment of questions from Nathaniel.

She felt like she was being interrogated.

He wanted to know *everything* about her. Her favorite shows, bands and sports teams, how she felt about leaving home, if she liked skateboarding or video gaming?

It was late when she finally made it to her room. It had been a long day, filled with excitement and anxiety and despite her nap on the train, she was completely exhausted.

After taking a bath, brushing her teeth, and slipping into a white tank top and yoga pants, she collapsed onto her bed.

Her aunt and uncle stopped in to say goodnight and ask if she needed anything.

She told them everything was perfect.

A few minutes later, Rick showed up to say goodnight as well.

"Hey," he said. "Going to bed?"

She nodded at him. "I'm pretty tired. Traveling always exhausts me."

He smiled at her. "Alright. Night Autumn. Sleep well."

She smiled back at him. "Night Rick. You too."

When he was gone, Autumn climbed beneath the covers and turned out her lamp. Content, she snuggled into the warm and cozy down duvet. Her window was open and there was a cool summer breeze wafting in, and she could hear the sound of an owl hooting in the distance. She listened to it, slowly letting her muscles relax and her brain disengage, and before she knew it, she was asleep.

2

The next morning, Autumn was woken up by the sound of muffled voices downstairs.

The strong scent of cooked bacon drifted into her bedroom as she stirred, glancing at her clock. It was ten in the morning.

She yawned, lifting the covers to her chin, determined to keep sleeping when she heard a knock on her door.

"Come in," she said, sitting up and fixing her hair with her fingers quickly.

"Are you, like, decent?" Rick's voice said as he stepped inside her room with his eyes closed.

"If I wasn't, would I be telling you *to come in?*" Autumn asked.

"True," Rick said, opening his eyes. "Mom said to come down for breakfast when you are ready. It's better warm."

"Alright," Autumn said.

She got out of her cozy haven and stretched as Rick looked at her expectantly.

"What's up Ricky?"

"Nathaniel told me he *really* likes you."

Autumn pulled her hair into a bun, looking at him in disbelief.

"He doesn't even know me Ricky."

"He said you are hot."

"I'm glad he is basing his affection on something substantial," Autumn grumbled.

"He also said you are nice and smart," Rick went on, sliding his hands into his pockets.

"He's sweet," Autumn said cautiously. "Cute in an adorable little rascal sort of way."

Autumn began making her bed, eager to change the subject.

"You know my mom will do that for you."

Autumn stopped and looked up at Rick, her eyebrow arched. "Really?"

"She makes my bed every day," Rick said, looking proud.

"Back home, I made my own bed," Autumn said, fluffing her pillows.

"Besides, it's the least I can do."

When she was done with the bed, Autumn began making her way downstairs with Rick.

"So, if Nathaniel asked you out, would you say yes?" Rick asked.

Autumn sighed. "You don't mince words do you Ricky?"

"I don't think so," Rick said. "Just think about it okay?"

Autumn didn't need to think about it to know it was a bad idea. Nathaniel and her hooking up and breaking up, would make things awkward. And after Kyle, she barely dated.

"Rick, just give me some time to get adjusted then we can talk about this okay?" she said gently.

Rick nodded. "Sure. Okay."

When they finally made it downstairs Aunt Katherine, dressed in a white ruffled blouse and black slacks, was obviously on her way into work.

She was a secretary at a doctor's office downtown and according to Rick, Doctor Ronson, had been practicing in Whitan for thirty years. Since most of Whitan went to see him, he was beloved by the town which meant Aunt Katherine had a pretty cushy gig.

Autumn said good morning to her aunt who was clearly in a rush.

"Rick, make sure you take care of Autumn today. Show her around and make her feel at home," she said as she grabbed her purse.

Rick, who already began loading his plate with various breakfast foods, nodded.

"You got it mom."

She paused, taking Rick's face into her hands lovingly.

"Enjoy these last weeks of summer sweetheart because this school year *you* will be working your tail off," she said. "Autumn will make sure of that."

She winked at Autumn, who grinned, playing along. "Don't worry. I'll torture him Aunt Katherine. I promise."

"You guys are ganging up on me! Not fair," Rick grumbled as he grabbed three slices of bacon.

Aunt Katherine kissed him on his forehead and did the same to Autumn.

"Have a fun day you two," she said before leaning into Autumn.

"Just watch him please," she whispered. "A few weeks ago, we had to bring him to the hospital. He was riding his skateboard too fast and crashed into the neighbour's fence."

"I heard that mom!" Rick yelled as she left. "And I *meant* to hit that fence!"

The door shut, and Autumn looked at Rick in disbelief. "You meant to?"

Rick nodded, his mouth full of bacon. "Oh yeah. Totally."

As she packed food onto her plate, she couldn't help but be in awe of what her aunt had made.

A variety of eggs (hard boiled, sunny-side up and scrambled), bacon, sausage, hash browns and toast took over the table.

Autumn looked at Rick's plate, which was stacked with three of everything. Rick always had a rather large appetite.

Watching him inhale his breakfast made Autumn realize that some things never changed.

"So what are we doing today?" Autumn asked as she put some scrambled eggs into her mouth.

"I was thinking I could bring you to the skate park," Rick said, his blue eyes lighting up.

Autumn forced a smile. "Great. That sounds wonderful."

She would much rather have gone to the antique shop or a bookstore, but she didn't want to crush Rick's joy.

He looked at her suspiciously. Could he still see right through her like he always had?

"You don't want to go do you?"

"Yes I do," Autumn said as convincingly as she could manage.

Rick wasn't fooled. "I know when you aren't telling the truth Aut. When you were little, you would do the exact same thing when you lied. You have a *tell."*

Autumn looked at him incredulously even though she really wasn't surprised Rick knew her idiosyncrasies so well.

"Really," Rick said earnestly. "You get this twitch in your left eye."

Autumn sighed. "Rick, this is your town where you have lived your whole life," she said, taking a drink of orange juice. "I want *you* to show me around. Take me to the places *you* love."

"Well, I do really love the skate park," he admitted.

Autumn nodded, smiling. "Exactly. So take me there. It will be fun."

Autumn had promised herself when she came here she would try new things and embrace change. She wasn't going to be a killjoy, spending the rest of summer reading books in her air-conditioned bedroom. She wanted adventure and the only way to capture it was by going out and living.

Rick grinned excitedly and grabbed three more pieces of bacon for his plate.

"Awesome. I can show you my sweet jumps!"

"As long as you promise me you won't hurt yourself again." Autumn said sternly.

Rick waved his hand as if to shrug her off. "Relax Aut. I won't get hurt. I am a total pro."

It was early afternoon when Autumn and Rick finally headed to the skate park. Autumn, dressed in denim shorts and a flowing white tunic, had her long hair pulled into a bun.

As soon as she stepped outside, she could feel the heat on her skin. She could smell the scent of freshly cut grass lingering in the air, and she inhaled deeply. Back home, everything was smoggy and polluted on hot days. Here, the air was clean and pure.

Rick said the park wasn't far, and they decided to walk despite the heat.

Rick grabbed his board, and they were on their way.

It took them about ten minutes to get there and when they did Autumn immediately recognized Nathaniel on his skateboard puttering about in the parking lot.

"NATE!" Rick called out as they get closer to him.

Nathaniel looked up at them and began waving cheerily.

Autumn waved back and Rick looked over at her, nudging her gently in the side.

"Autumn, it's your secret admirer," he said in a singsong voice.

"It's not a secret now. You already *told* me," Autumn began, exasperated. "But you *didn't* tell me he was going to be here today."

"I only texted him a while ago and he wanted to come along. That way, you could see his sweet moves and maybe you'd want to hook up with him," Rick said, winking at her.

"Nothing gets me going like a guy jumping over things on his skateboard," Autumn said sarcastically.

"That's what Nathaniel thought," Rick said, not catching her sarcasm.

"What's up Rick?" Nathaniel called out. Today he was dressed in khaki shorts and a plain grey T-shirt. His ginger hair was messed up from the wind.

"Dude, not much," Rick said, and they exchanged a high-five.

Nathaniel looked at Autumn, a giant grin on his freckled face.

"Autumn. You look *exquisite* today."

"Thank you," Autumn said politely.

"I looked up that word on an online dictionary this morning. I thought you'd like it," Nathaniel said arrogantly.

Rick looked bewildered by this notion.

"There is a dictionary on the Internet dude?"

Nathaniel looked at Rick like he was absurd.

"Yeah dude. It's so much easier than flipping through all that paper with words on it."

"You mean a *book?*" Autumn offered.

Nathaniel cringed in response. "Yeah. One of those things," he said. "Now let's get going."

"So man, have you been practicing anything new on your board?" Rick asked as they all began walking. Autumn looked around. The park was pretty deserted for a summer day but she wasn't really surprised.

It was so hot that just walking made beads of sweat trickle unpleasantly down her back.

"Yeah. I looked up some videos this morning and there's this new move you can do on the rails. It's ridiculous!"

"You got to show me," Rick said excitedly.

Seeing Rick's smile, so childlike now, brought Autumn back to summer's they spent together as kids. Hanging out at the public pool, running through sprinklers, barbeques with their parents and eating ice cream in the hot sun.

"We're here!" Rick announced and Autumn was shaken from her thoughts.

In front of her eyes, in a large concrete area surrounded by green grass were different-sized ramps, half pipes and handrails. Back home, there wasn't a skate park. The kids just made do with curbs and pavement.

"Sweet right?" Rick said, catching Autumn's gaze. "It was a huge deal when they built this. Mostly, Whitan is getting bigger and people wanted a place to board and stuff."

"Yeah and the cops probably got sick of people skateboarding down the police station stairs," Nathaniel said smirking.

"Alright guys. I'll be here watching you," Autumn said, taking a seat on a nearby bench. "Have fun. Don't break any limbs."

"Alright," Rick said to her. "Let me know if you want to try my board out."

Autumn had an image of herself mounting the skateboard and wobbling on it feebly.

"I couldn't," she said.

"Seriously Aut. It's easy. We'll skate for a bit, and then you can try it out," Rick said encouragingly.

"Besides, you used to do ballet. That requires balance."

"Rick, I was five," Autumn said.

Rick shrugged her off. "I bet it's just like riding a bike."

Autumn sat on the bench watching intently as the guys began to skateboard. She really had no idea what they were doing. She was, however, impressed. They were flipping, sliding, pivoting and jumping all over. They were on the ramps, the rails and in the air. Autumn found herself holding her breath, only exhaling after the guys had landed safely.

"Hey Autumn! Check this out!" Nathaniel yelled at her.

Rick was also vying for her attention, calling out to her to watch his tricks.

They were like little kids competing, and she was the new toy they were fighting over.

As Autumn cheered them both on, she saw a group of guys approaching from across the field. They didn't look much like skateboarders. Dressed in polo shirts and khakis, they were all wearing red varsity jackets that had the symbol of a hawk on the chest.

She could hear them laughing and she thought they were going to pass her and be on their way, until one of the guys stopped. He said something to the others, and they all halted as he gestured towards her. A moment later, he was walking her way. As he got closer Autumn could see his features better. He was tall and built, with blonde hair, broad shoulders and grey eyes.

"Hello there," he said when he finally reached her. He smiled, exposing perfectly white straight teeth.

"Hello," Autumn began politely.

"Do you mind if I join you?" he asked, pointing beside her on the bench.

She shrugged. She didn't want to make enemies before school even began. "Sure."

She glanced up and saw his friends were watching them, smirks on their faces. Autumn realized that this was entertainment for them. They were clearly depraved.

"I haven't seen you in town before," the blonde said as he looked Autumn up and down.

"I could never forget someone as stunning as you."

"I just moved here actually," Autumn said, as placidly as she could manage.

He nodded at her. "What's your name sweetheart?"

"I'm Autumn."

He took her hand into his, squeezing it. "I'm Ben Mills. Maybe you've heard of me?"

Autumn pulled away, unimpressed. She had an overwhelming urge to smack the dunce, but she couldn't act on it.

"I told you. I just moved here."

"Well, word travels fast around here," he leered at her. "I think you might just be the prettiest girl in Whitan."

You would know, since you have probably dated most of the town, she thought as she tried her best not to roll her eyes.

Autumn noticed Rick and Nathaniel had stopped skateboarding and were watching Ben and her, looking perturbed.

"So *Autumn*," Ben went on. The way he said her name gave her chills.

"Are you going to Whitan High?"

"As far as I know, that's the only high school around here," she replied shortly.

"Oh yeah. I thought maybe you were in college though. You have this sexy maturity thing going on, you know?" Ben said.

Autumn felt like a fly caught in a spider's web but instead of the spider just eating her, he was boring her to death first.

Unfortunately for her, Ben couldn't take a hint.

"Autumn, why don't you come with us and hang? We have the best connections in town," he went on, shamelessly. "You walk in with our crew on your first day of school, and you will be set for the year."

Autumn arched an eyebrow in disbelief. "Really?" She was dumbfounded by the crap he was spewing at her.

"Yeah!" he chuckled running a hand through his blonde brush cut. "We all play football for the Whitan High Hawkes," he pointed at the symbol on his jacket. "We are popular and we can get you on the team."

Autumn nodded. "I appreciate the sentiment but I don't think I'd make a very good quarterback."

Ben guffawed. "No silly! I meant the cheerleading team. All of my buddies date cheerleaders, and I'm sure we could put in a good word for you."

"What makes you think I want to be a cheerleader?" Autumn asked.

"Truthfully?" Ben began and Autumn looked at him expectantly. "If you can manage it."

He shrugged. "You just have that *body* you know?"

Autumn crossed her arms over her chest. *"Do I?"*

"Curves that would fill out a tight uniform, and I bet you are flexible too," he ogled her.

"Listen up. I'm with Rick and Nathaniel," she gestured to them and saw with relief that they were on their way over. "So how about you and your buddies get lost."

Ben snickered. *"You* are with Rick Jacobs and Nathaniel Abrams?"

Autumn glared openly at him now. It was one thing to piss her off but attack anyone she cared about, and she would defend them like a bear protecting its cubs.

"Yes. Rick and Nathaniel are my *friends,*" Autumn said sharply. "Now get gone."

Ben leaned in, ignoring her scowl. "Just between you and me Autumn, those are *not* the people you want to be hanging out with. They are like the pariahs of Whitan High."

"Pariah? That's an awfully big word for you to use Ben," Autumn said. "Do you even know what it means?"

Ben shrugged, ignoring her jab. "They are *losers* Autumn!"

"Oh are they?" Autumn said cuttingly. "Funny that, I think you are a loser Ben."

Ben shifted uncomfortably, clearly taken aback.

"I'm just saying you are judged by the company you keep," he said.

"If that's the case, I sure as hell don't want to be seen with you," Autumn said, getting up. "Then people might think I'm an asshole too."

"Is everything okay Aut?" Rick asked, standing in front of her protectively. Autumn recognized this pose. It was Rick's defensive stance, even when they were kids.

"I'm fine Rick," Autumn replied, shooting Ben a glare. "We can leave now."

"You might be hot," Ben said to her, standing up. "But anyone who would associate with these two isn't cool in my books."

"Sorry to disappoint you but I really don't care what you think," Autumn snapped.

"Yeah well, come September you will regret that," Ben shot back.

"Don't you threaten her Mills!" Rick said heatedly.

As soon as Rick raised his voice, Ben's gang began heading towards them. Autumn felt her whole body clench up as the tension in the air grew thicker.

"Here come the cronies," Nathaniel muttered.

"You are pathetic Jacobs," Ben went on. "You too Abrams."

"You are the one hitting on a girl who obviously has no interest in you," Nathaniel piped up.

"*And* you are the one that needs your lackeys to back you up," Rick added in. "Can't you fight your own battle's Mills?"

"Is there a problem here?" A guy with dark hair stood beside Ben, eyeballing Rick and Nathaniel menacingly.

Ben's other buddies flanked him, and though they were big, Autumn wasn't worried. They had more brawn than brains. That much was evident.

"Why do people always ask that?" Nathaniel said to Autumn and Rick. "*Is there a problem here?* Obviously, there is or you guys wouldn't be rushing over!"

Ben cracked his knuckles. "Nothing that a good old-fashioned beat down wouldn't take care of Austin."

"Oh bring it on Mills!" Nathaniel shouted.

Ben sneered. "You asked for it Abrams!" And he raised his arm, ready to punch him.

"I wouldn't," Autumn warned.

Ben lowered his arm, turning to her. "And why wouldn't I *sweetheart?*"

Autumn said nothing. Instead, she pointed at the mother with two young boys approaching the skate park.

Ben saw them and rolled his eyes. He couldn't fight with people watching.

"This chick is a waste of my time," he said coldly. "And as for you two," he pointed at Rick and Nathaniel. "Your school year is going to be very long!" He turned to his friends.

"Let's jet."

Nathaniel snorted. "I am quaking in my sneakers."

Autumn shot daggers into their backs as they walked across the field, heading back the way they had come.

Rick's stance relaxed as they left. He looked at Autumn. "Are you alright?"

She smiled gratefully.

"I'm fine. Thanks for coming over guys. What an asshole he is."

"Yeah, and yet he's *still* the most popular guy at Whitan," Rick said disgusted. "When I saw him come up to you I knew it was trouble."

Nathaniel snorted. "Who wears their varsity jacket in this heat? What a bunch of jerks!"

"Mills took Autumn's hand!" Rick said through laughter. "He was *courting* her!"

"He thinks he's King freaking Arthur!" Nathaniel said between chuckles.

"Leave it to me to make enemies after only one day of living here," Autumn said, unable to hide her grin.

"Trust me. It's better to have Ben as an enemy then a friend," Nathaniel said as they headed back towards the centre of the park. "Ben is the type of guy who shoves kids into lockers."

"Yeah man. I remember when he did that to you freshman year," Rick said bitterly.

"He was all shoving you in there and his friends were yucking it up," Rick grimaced. "Losers."

Nathaniel's face turned pink from embarrassment as he turned to Autumn.

"Yeah. I was a lot smaller back then."

Autumn smiled, trying not to look at Nathaniel pityingly. "What a bully."

"Come to think of it Autumn, you might be the first girl to turn that sleaze down," Rick said proudly. "I think this is a momentous occasion. You have made history here today."

"Here here!" Nathaniel chimed in.

"I don't date guys like that," Autumn said. "He could never love someone else because he's too in love with himself."

Rick looked thoughtful. "One time in the locker room he was like, flexing his muscles in the mirror and kissing them. I thought he looked pretty lame making out with his biceps."

The three of them spent a couple more uneventful hours at the skate park before it began getting crowded.

True to his word, Rick helped Autumn learn to skateboard. It took many coaxing's to get her on it, but once she did he wasn't giving up on her.

Rick instructed her to put both feet on the board and practice balancing. Autumn tried this and almost immediately began wobbling. Rick put his hands on her waist, holding her steady until she got used to the board, but it felt like gravity was fighting against her.

Eventually, he began rolling the board, still holding on to her as he pushed it along. When he let her go, she coasted for a bit, actually managing not to fall.

Autumn could feel the gentle breeze in her hair and her stomach fluttering with anticipation. "Use your foot to push off!" Rick called out when she began losing momentum.

She did it and the skateboard moved smoothly and steadily along the pavement.

She was doing it. Something new, something she hadn't experienced before.

She was living for the moment, not thinking through every second, not worrying about falling flat on her face.

She had never felt freer in her life.

3

The weeks before school were generally relaxed and uneventful. Rick toured Autumn around Whitan, showing her different places to shop, eat and pick up her favorite books. There was a large chain bookstore that had just opened up and of course, the reliable public library. Most days, Nathaniel tagged along, attempting to work his magic on Autumn.

As the end of summer drew nearer, Autumn prepped Rick for a new regime of studying. She warned him that she wouldn't go easy on him just because they were friends.

Somewhere between the nights growing cooler and the increasing foliage, fall arrived with a bang and so did the first day of school.

Autumn spent a good part of her morning picking an outfit. Like most girls, she wanted to look put together and attractive on her first day.

She opted for a grey V-neck sweater dress that accented her curves and black leggings. She did her makeup and hair in a long braid and headed downstairs for breakfast.

As she made her way down the stairs, she had a terrifying epiphany. She would be the new girl today. It was petrifying, but she did have Rick and Nathaniel. That was more than most people had on their first day.

When she arrived downstairs, Rick was already seated at the kitchen table, eating like a ravenous animal.

His plate had four boiled eggs, three sausages and a pile of bacon on it. Autumn couldn't believe how much he ate and yet his body was still slim and toned.

"Morning Autumn," Uncle James said. He was dressed in a grey suit, looking rather dapper while reading a newspaper. He put it down and scanned her appraisingly.

"You look beautiful," he said. "You are going to knock 'em dead today kiddo."

"Thank you," Autumn said taking a seat at the table. "Morning Rick."

Rick looked up quickly from pigging out. "Hey Aut. Did you sleep okay?"

Autumn shrugged. "As good as to be expected before my first day."

Autumn was perpetually nervous on the first day of school, even back home. Ever since she could remember, she tossed and turned the night before school began and in the morning she had that sick feeling in her stomach. The relief came when the day was finally over and done with. After that, school was smooth sailing for her.

"Where's Aunt Katherine?" Autumn asked as she grabbed a boiled egg and a few slices of bacon.

"She had to leave early. She was behind on her paperwork," Uncle James replied, taking a sip of his coffee. "Are you excited for your first day?"

"I'm a little nervous," Autumn admitted.

Her uncle raised his hand as if to shoo away her fears. "Don't be nervous," he said. "You will love it there. Besides, you have Rick to help you out."

Rick nodded at her. "And Nathaniel."

After they finished eating breakfast, Autumn offered to drive Rick to school in her car. Her aunt and uncle were kind enough to lend her one of their four cars. It was older but it was well-kept, and as long as it got Autumn around, she wasn't too picky.

As they headed out the door, Autumn's uncle called from the kitchen.

"Have a good day you two!" he said. "And Rick, remember, if you need any help with school work ask Autumn."

"I hope we don't get any work today! It's the first day back," Rick said, looking genuinely terrified.

They loaded their backpacks into the backseat of the car and got inside.

As Autumn started to drive, Rick began tinkering with the radio as he explained how the first day worked.

"Our names are posted on a list on bulletin boards near the cafeteria. The list tells you where your homeroom is and that's where you'll get your full schedule."

"Do you think we'll have homeroom together?" Autumn asked hopefully, as she stopped at a stop sign. She never even considered that her and Rick might not have *any* classes together.

"I hope so," Rick said.

As they drove down the road, Autumn could see people filtering in. The clusters of teenagers walking and laughing, like an introduction scene for a teen movie. When she turned the corner, Rick pointed.

"It's up there."

In front of her eyes, was an average looking high school that was much smaller than her old one. She was first greeted by the side of the building. In front of it, people were congregated on the grass, talking and smoking cigarettes.

"The parking lot entrance is over there," Rick directed her.
She nodded and turned quickly, smiling at him. "Thanks."
Rick looked back at her panicked. "Eyes on the road!"
She sighed and turned into the parking lot, slowing her car to a crawl.

Golden letters across a sea of tan brick's spelt out the schools name: WHITAN HIGH SECONDARY SCHOOL. Underneath it was a white banner flapping in the wind: HOME OF THE HAWKS.

With some effort, Autumn managed to find a parking spot around the back side of the building. From there she could see a large track surrounded by bleachers, a baseball diamond, and a forest that the school backed onto.

Her nerves kicked in as she watched the flood of unfamiliar faces heading toward the school. Her stomach was doing summersaults.
She took a deep breath, cutting the car's engine.
You can do this! She coaxed herself. *Piece of cake.*

"Aut?" Rick broke into her thoughts. "Are you alright? You look a little pale."
Autumn caught her reflection in the rear-view mirror, and Rick was right. She was white as a ghost.

"I'm just anxious," she said quietly. "Everything here is new. I don't know anyone."
"You know me and Nate. Don't worry," he said, squeezing her shoulder comfortingly. "Besides, walking in with me makes you *instantly* cool," he grinned.

Autumn felt better as they grabbed their bags and began walking towards the back door.

She stepped inside a long hallway, and just as she suspected, people turned, looking at her.

She was like a caged animal in the zoo, and everyone was watching her.

She wished she didn't have such acute hearing because even through the chaos and noise, she could hear the whispers.

"Is she new?"

"I've never seen her here before."

"She's cute."

"I wonder how old she is."

"Is that Jacobs's girlfriend?"

"I doubt it. He could never get her."

As they made their way down the hall, Autumn felt hands grasp her waist from behind.

"Guess who?" Nathaniel asked jovially.

"Hey Nathaniel," Autumn said, grateful he was there.

"What gave me away?" Nathaniel asked, letting Autumn go as he followed her and Rick through the masses of people.

"Um, maybe it was your voice dude?" Rick said sarcastically.

"Good point. Next time, I'll talk in my British accent."

"Now she's definitely going to know it's you lemon head!" Rick said exasperatedly.

Autumn followed the boys down the hall as they headed towards the centre of the school where the cafeteria was.

Next to it, stood bulletin boards where students were lined up. The three of them joined the long queue.

"Man, I can't believe we're back here already," Nathaniel said miserably. "Summer went by so fast."

"Yeah but just think dude, one more year, and we are done with this place," Rick said happily. "Sweet freedom!"

"Yeah. If I can pass," Nathaniel said looking down at his shoes. "I'm not like you Rick. I don't have a pretty girl to motivate me."

"You can borrow her if you want," Rick offered. "I'm sure Autumn wouldn't mind." He looked over at Autumn and grinned.

"I think I'll have my hands full with you Ricky," Autumn said. "But if you need a little extra help Nathaniel, I would be happy to oblige."

"Thanks Autumn," Nathaniel said, looking pleased. "I just might take you up on that offer."

They stood in line for what seemed like ages. Every minute that passed, Autumn grew more anxious. The thought that she may not have any classes with Rick was unbearable.

Finally, when it was her turn, Autumn found her name on the board labeled *I J K*. She traced her finger across the paper. Her homeroom teacher was Mr. Brown.

Rick leaned over her shoulder anxiously looking for his own name.

"Sweet! We are in the same homeroom. We should have most of our classes together."

Nathaniel, who was at the *A B C* board, walked towards them, sighing dejectedly.

"I'm in Mrs. Parker's class. I hate my last name!"

"Well, we will have the same lunch at least," Rick said reassuringly.

As they walked away from the bulletin boards, Nathaniel and Rick began chatting about skateboarding as Autumn looked at her cell. They were going to be late for orientation in homeroom. She tugged Rick's arm.

"We had better go. I don't want to start the year off late."

Rick gave Autumn a nod and looked at Nathaniel. "See you at lunch dude."

"Bye Nathaniel," Autumn gave him a wave.

He waved back. "See you guys later."

As they walked through the clusters of students Autumn took everything in.

In her mind, she was comparing everything to her old school. The smell, the floors, how the kids dressed. It was sensory overload.

She took a deep breath and felt Rick's hand grasp hers.

Autumn looked at him, confused.

"Rick?"

"Sorry," he said as he pulled her along, weaving through a crowd of rowdy kids.

"You look nervous. When we were kids, when you were scared you liked it when I took your hand."

Autumn smiled. She couldn't believe Rick remembered this.

"Thanks," she said simply as they made their way past lockers and the library towards a small classroom at the end of the hall. Rick relinquished her hand and held open the door for her as she stepped inside.

As soon as she was in the room, everyone's eyes were on her.

Autumn looked at the sea of unfamiliar faces, and they all looked back at her.

She imagined they were wondering who she was and the fact that they didn't know, pleased her, just a bit.

She smiled to herself. She was finally getting the fresh start her parents said she deserved.

At the front of the room, a middle-aged man sat at a wooden desk, reading through paperwork. He was short and round with messy gray hair. His nameplate read: Mr. Brown.

"Good morning," he said as he looked down at his clipboard, scanning it.

"Rick Jacobs. I know you already." He looked to Autumn pleasantly.

"Your name please dear."

Autumn stated her name and after scanning the class register, the teacher looked up at her.

"You are the new student I presume?"

"Yes," she replied. She could feel all the eyes burning through her.

The man nodded. "Wonderful," he smiled then gestured to some empty seats. "I don't really have a seating plan. Make yourselves at home. After all, this is *home* room," he jested, and then he chuckled to himself.

As they took seats near the middle of the room, Rick leaned towards Autumn.

"One thing you should know about Mr. Brown is he makes horrible jokes and then laughs at them, like they are actually funny."

Autumn nodded. "Noted."

"If we have Mrs. Creeden for math, you will notice she is *obsessed* with her pet bird. It's like a parrot or something," Rick went on as they sat down. "She has a picture of it on her desk and one time she brought it to class and all it did was squawk and call us delinquents."

Rick sighed. "That bird knows bigger words then I do."

Rick went on, talking about more quirky teachers at Whitan High.

Mr. Belfour, who enjoyed dressing up as a woman every Halloween.

"He walks better in heels than a chick, which makes me think he's had lots of practice," Rick said.

Then there was Mr. Beachum, the gym teacher, who Rick suspected was taking steroids.

Ten minutes passed, and Mr. Brown began class.

"Good morning everyone," he started, just as the classroom door swung open.

Autumn frowned when she saw Ben Mills and one of his buddies sauntering in.

"Gentleman, how nice of you to join us," Mr. Brown said curtly. "Let me suggest you avoid being late again or you will be making up the time in detention. Now, find a seat."

Ben rolled his eyes and found a seat beside a tiny girl with red hair and brown eyes. She was wearing a clingy, white mini dress and too much eyeliner.

"Hey baby," Ben said, leaning towards the girl and giving her a kiss. Autumn cringed as some guys in the class wolf whistled. She was pretty sure she saw tongue and trace amounts of slobber.
"That is nasty," Autumn muttered and Rick nodded in agreement. "Who is she?"
"That's Candice Kincaid," Rick whispered. "Ben's girlfriend for the day."

Mr. Brown cleared his throat loudly.
"Mr. Mills, I don't believe I instructed you to kiss Ms. Kincaid. Enough shenanigans or I will send you to the office. After last year, you must be sick of that place."

"Sorry Mr. B," Ben muttered, a small smirk on his face.
Autumn watched Ben, repulsed. He saw her looking at him and winked, blowing her a kiss. Autumn made a gagging gesture with her finger before she turned away.

"Now, we can begin. Most of you already know me. I am Mr. Brown, and I want to welcome you all to grade twelve," he said. "This will be your last year at Whitan High. Unless you choose to slack off, in which case, I might be seeing you again next year."
Autumn who was sitting directly beside Rick saw him flinch at this, his eyes filled with terror.

"So, I urge you not to assume you will get through this year without any hard work. You are by no means home free yet," he tapped his fingers on his desk for emphasis.

"Now I'm going to pass out your schedules for the semester. If you have any questions, please talk to me or your guidance counselor. If you are wondering *who* your designated counselor is, it will be written on said schedule."

Autumn and Rick received their schedules and began comparing. Autumn was relieved to see they had every class together, minus last period, which was their elective.

"You took English," Rick said. "Reading and writing. No surprise there."

Autumn looked at Rick's elective. "Video communications Ricky?" She smirked.

"Yeah. I like filming things and besides, how hard can it be?" Rick said. "I bet it's a bird course."

Mr. Brown went on to read the daily announcements.

After he was finished, class was dismissed and Autumn and Rick headed to math class with Mrs. Creeden.

After Rick's tale, Autumn couldn't help but picture her wearing an eye patch, pet parrot on her shoulder, calling them all scallywags.

She wasn't like that of course.

Mrs. Creeden was a slender lady, who looked to be in her early fifties. She had long blonde hair and wore a bright yellow peasant dress.

"Look at her desk," Rick whispered when they had taken their seats. Autumn looked and sure enough there was a huge picture of a multi-colored bird. Its wings extended majestically and its beak open. The picture's frame was heart shaped.

Mrs. Creeden, who was bubbly and excitable, did roll call and like Mr. Brown, she welcomed Autumn to the school.

She talked about the year's curriculum (Equations, fractions and algebra, all forms of torture) and handed out outlines to everyone. Autumn, who was good at math but hated it, knew her sister was right. She had pointed out that math was probably the language in hell.

Near the end of class, Mrs. Creeden started a discussion about summer break.

"I hope you all had a fabulous holiday," she said, smiling brightly.

"Does anyone want to share what they did with the class?"

A few of the students raised their hands and began talking about what they did over break.

"I had a very relaxing summer myself," Mrs. Creeden said, her eyes lighting up. "My pet bird Ruffles and I, went to visit my mother out in the country. Ruffles loved the fresh air and watching the other animals roam about."

Rick's face went slack. "Here we go," he muttered.

Mrs. Creeden went on, saying she was teaching Ruffles math.

"He has quite the vast vocabulary like many Macaws, but he's not the best with numbers."

One of the students raised her hand. "Yes dear," Mrs. Creeden said.

"Can birds really do math?"

"Of course dear," Mrs. Creeden replied. "I'm sure not *all* birds can do math, but my Ruffles is exceptionally sharp."

Rick leaned into Autumn. "I feel sorry for Ruffles. I can't learn math with *my* human brain can you imagine what it would be like with a bird brain?"

Autumn giggled as the bell rang.

When math class was finished, Autumn and Rick went to their assigned lockers. Autumn plugged in her combination and opened her locker up, shoving her math book inside.

"Dude, that was brutal," Autumn looked over to see Nathaniel.

Rick shut his locker, which was a few over from Autumn's. "Did you get homework already?"

"Hell's no. However, all this talk of *learning*," Nathaniel held his head in pain. "It's giving me a migraine."

"We can go skateboard after school," Rick said excitedly. "Right Aut?" He looked at her expectantly.

"Nope! I've already made an ass of myself on a skateboard once. I'm out. Besides, you might have homework. The day isn't over yet," she grinned mischievously.

After they had dropped off their belongings, Rick, Autumn and Nathaniel headed to the cafeteria for lunch. Rick opened the doors, unleashing noise that was overwhelming. Sitting in rows upon rows of tables, were hordes of students, chattering and eating.

Autumn was nervous, seeing all the strangers that filled the room. It was asinine to feel so panicked with Rick and Nathaniel by her side, but the sea of unknown faces and the foreign surroundings, made her uneasy.

Autumn was deep in thought when she felt someone bump into her gently.

"Sorry," she murmured. When she looked at the culprit, she saw a rather handsome specimen before her eyes. He was tall, with long dark hair and brown eyes that met hers, only for a split second.

"You could say *excuse me* King!" Nathaniel scolded him as he went past.

The boy turned to looking back at them, smiling coyly before disappearing into the clusters of students.

"That kid is so weird," Rick muttered when he was out of earshot.

"His name is King?" Autumn wondered aloud.

He did look a little *peculiar,* but he was cute based on the quick glimpse she got of him.

"No. *Eric* King," Nathaniel said. "No one really talks to him and *he* ignores everyone. It's a win win."

Autumn looked at Rick, perplexed, hoping for more information as they began moving towards an empty table.

"Basically, people are scared of him," Rick went on as they sat down.

"All these rumours went around about him. That he's evil and stuff like that."

Autumn looked at them both in disbelief, trying her best not to laugh. "Evil? Really?"

"Yeah well, just because he doesn't wear a shirt saying he's evil, doesn't mean he isn't," Nathaniel said, looking somewhat offended by Autumn's skepticism.

Autumn shrugged. "I thought he was kind of cute."

Nathaniel and Rick exchanged troubled looks. "Autumn, my parents are pretty liberal, but if you bring home Eric King, I think they might worry about you."

"I never said anything about bringing him home," Autumn reassured him. "He's cute. That's all."

"Nathaniel is a far better choice," Rick went on. "He's funny and he can skateboard! Plus, I've already brought him home so you don't have to worry about that part."

Changing the subject, Rick began digging in his lunch bag, only to be letdown by its contents.

"Only three ham and cheese sandwiches and an apple?" He looked disappointed.

Autumn pulled out her one ham and cheese sandwich and rolled her eyes.

"Rick, have you ever considered you might have a tapeworm?"

Rick was already devouring his feast. "What's a tapeworm?"

"It's a parasite and it basically feeds on everything you eat, and you never feel full," Autumn explained.

"Dude! That totally sounds like you!" Nathaniel exclaimed.

Rick's face went white, and he stopped chewing: "You really think I have that?"

"No Rick," Autumn said. "I was joking. Relax."

"That was mean Aut," he said sternly and went back to stuffing his food down.

When lunch was over, Autumn and Rick said goodbye to Nathaniel and went into the gymnasium for gym class. Though they entered the room together, they were quickly separated. Girls were seated at one side and boys at the other.

"Good luck," Rick murmured as Autumn went to join the other girls on the bleachers.

Autumn sat down, smiling at everyone genially. A few minutes later, a woman came through the gym's double doors. Dressed in a grey tracksuit, she was tall, lean, and had her brown hair pulled into a ponytail.

She gave the girls a sidelong glance before smiling.

"Good afternoon," she began. "Some of you may already know me but for those of you who don't, I am Ms. Baxter."

"Now, first thing is first. I have your uniforms here. I want everyone to come up and pick their size then go into the change rooms and get suited up. When everyone is done, I will take attendance, and then we can commence."

Autumn, who was first in line to get her uniform, immediately went to the change room and quickly slipped into a dark tank top that had the school logo on it and the matching shorts.

She made her way out to the gym and awaited the rest of the class. When they were all congregated, Ms. Baxter did roll call. Afterwards, she said they would be starting class with light sprinting.

"Would it be fair to assume you have all heard the tale of the tortoise and the hare?" She began, standing in front of them, hands on her hips.

Most of the girls nodded.

"The moral of the story was, slow and steady wins the race," Ms. Baxter said matter-of-factly. "But the truth is, that quick little hare is in shape! That slacking tortoise?" She paused, her face deadpan. "It will be dead by a hundred. So let's push it out there!"

As Autumn began stretching, she looked over at the other side of the gym. Rick was already in uniform and doing drills with his teacher.

Autumn tried her best not to laugh when he waved at her excitedly. She waved back at him, smiling.

Rick's gym teacher was scary.

He had broad shoulders, a shaved head and wore a red polo shirt with the symbol of the school hawk on it. His muscles bulged out from the sleeves, looking monstrous and unnatural.

He never stopped pacing and was constantly yelling out commands.

"Hey! You! Pass the ball to your teammate!"
"I told you ten reps not five!"
"Boy, tie your shoelaces! You could fall and die!"

When gym class was done, Autumn couldn't have been happier. Her body felt warm and alive after her burst of exercise. She quickly showered and headed to English.

Ever since Autumn was a child, she was had been in love with books. While most kids watched television, Autumn preferred curling up with a good book.

Rick was waiting for Autumn outside the change room when she came out. When he saw her, he grinned.

"You looked so cute jogging," he teased. Autumn nudged him playfully.

"Please. I looked like a total spaz."

"That's not what some of the guys were saying," Rick began and Autumn gave him a withering look.

"I will pass on hearing the macho locker room talk."

Rick looked at her incredulously. "If I heard them saying *anything* disrespectful about you, do you think I would allow it? They were just saying how pretty the new girl is."

Autumn flushed. "They're clearly delusion."

Rick walked Autumn to English before jetting off to his class. Before she stepped inside, Autumn ran her fingers through her hair and took a deep breath.

Then she opened the door and stepped inside, heading for the desk closet to the back of the class.

Once she was seated, she began looking around the room, scanning for people she might recognize from her previous classes.

She was still looking around when he walked in.

Tall, dark, handsome and apparently strange, it was Eric King.

She got a much better look at him this time, and he was wearing grey jeans, a T-shirt and a black trench coat. Her heart raced a little when he sat beside her.

Not long after Eric came in, a petite lady with shoulder-length red hair arrived.

With her porcelain skin and bright blue eyes, she reminded Autumn of a classic doll.

She took attendance quickly and then sat on the edge of her desk.

"Good afternoon everyone. I'm Mrs. Reid and this is advanced English," she said, looking around the room.

"For those of you who enjoy literature, this is going to be an interesting class. We will be delving into everything, from Shakespeare to Anne Rice. You will quickly learn that I shy away from the traditional high school reading lists. This is because I like diversity and originality," she went on. "However, there are always classic books on my list."

Mrs. Reid asked the class to make a list of their top five favorite books.

Autumn pulled out her pen and notebook and began.

She was so caught up in thinking about her list that when the bell rang, she couldn't believe an hour had passed. When she turned to say something, *anything*, to the cryptic Eric, he was long gone.

Autumn walked to her locker with a smile on her face. She had made it through the day. At her old school, there was always at least one Nikki-related incident but here it was all smooth sailing. The freedom of having a clean slate, in a place where no one knew her, was enough to make her euphoric.

When she arrived at her locker, Rick was leaning against it, looking miserable.

"Excuse me sad sack, I need in there," Autumn said teasingly. Rick moved lethargically, eyes on his sneakers. "Fine."

"What's wrong with you?" she asked, as she began spinning her lock.

"I got video communications homework," he said unhappily. "On the first day of school, I got *homework!*"

"And you are blaming me?" Autumn asked, putting her books away.

"You cursed me!" Rick replied. "You said I *might* get homework and boom! I did!"

"So? What is it?" Autumn asked as she shut her locker door. "That class is your elective. It can't be that bad."

"I have to video record something interesting to show the class," Rick said as they began walking away from the lockers.

"And it's due tomorrow?" Autumn asked.

"In two weeks," Rick said. "And it has to be ten minutes long, minimum."

"So? You have time to work on it," Autumn said reassuringly. "Nate and I can help you."

Rick brightened at this idea.

"You would help me?" He asked.

"Of course Ricky," Autumn said as they headed towards the back doors to meet Nathaniel. "I am your tutor."

When they arrived at the back doors, Nathaniel was already there, looking like he was ready to escape.

"Hey!" he said urgently. "I thought today was never going to end! Let's go!"

"And just think, we only have until June, and it's all over," Autumn teased.

Nathaniel groaned. "Buzz kill."

"Did you get any homework man?" Rick asked as they made their way out the doors and towards the back parking lot.

"Nope," Nathaniel said grinning. Then he paused, looking grim. "Why? Did you dude?"

Rick nodded. "I have to record something interesting for my video communications class."

Nathaniel looked thoughtful. "Something interesting?"

"Yep and it has to be at least ten minutes long."

After a few seconds of silence, Nathaniel's eyes lit up.

"Dude! I know! Record Autumn."

Autumn looked at Nathaniel, bewildered. She didn't like the sound of this.

"She's pretty and most of your class is dudes right?"

Rick shrugged. "There are a few girls but *none* of them are hot."

"Bummer," Nathaniel said sympathetically. "Still even more reason to use Autumn. You can give the class some eye candy to gaze upon."

"No way!" Autumn said, looking at her car in the distance. "Not happening."

"Why not?" Nathaniel asked.

"Because for one, the camera hates me."

"That's not true," Nathaniel said, getting a glazed look in his eyes. "Mrs. Jacobs showed me pictures of you from last summer. You were wearing this little white sundress. You looked photogenic to me."

Autumn shot Nathaniel a glare. "You are an animal."

"I just can't go around recording Autumn," Rick said. "I need a reason Nathaniel."

"Because she's hot!"

"I don't think my teacher will go for that."

"Well, here's my car!" Autumn announced, eager to change the subject.

"Any more ideas?" Rick pressed as he got into the back seat.

"I'm still thinking dude," Nathaniel said as he got into the passenger seat next to Autumn.

They all buckled up, and Autumn began pulling out of the parking lot.

It was a few minutes later when Rick finally lost his patience. "Dude, I can smell the rubber burning! Hurry up!" he said.

"I got it! You could document Autumn's life as a teenage girl," Nathaniel said excitedly. "You could highlight all the differences between you and her!"

"Are we still on me?" Autumn sighed deeply.

"Highlight our differences? You mean physically? You want me to, what? Record her naked?" Rick said, looking scandalized. "You're sick man!"

"No! I mean, like her daily routine. Film her doing her makeup, picking out her clothes for the day. You could call it: *Men Are from Mars, Women Are from Venus!*"

"That is a great title!" Rick exclaimed.

"John Gray thought so too," Autumn chimed in. "He wrote the book. It's a bestseller."

"Oh damn! I knew that was too clever to be my idea," Nathaniel said sadly.

Autumn rolled her eyes as she turned a corner sharply.

"I love the idea Rick," Autumn began, grinning impishly. "You can film *all* my womanly things. My bras, my underwear and my *tampons.*"

Nathaniel cringed. "That was so hot up until you got to tampons."

"Aut, it isn't a terrible idea," Rick said gently. "The class *is* full of guys and they all love a pretty face."

"No way!" Autumn exclaimed. "I don't want to be filmed while putting on my makeup! That is private. It would be like me recording Nathaniel in the shower. Would you like that?" She looked at Nathaniel.

"Yes," Nathaniel replied quickly.

Autumn groaned.

"No! This is out of the question!" she said stubbornly before turning another corner sharply.

Rick winced.

"Alright!" he said, defeated. "Just stop the reckless driving please! Gentle turns!"

"What if he films you skateboarding Autumn?" Nathaniel asked, looking hopeful.

"Because filming me wobbling on a skateboard is far *less* humiliating than the first idea," Autumn jested.

Autumn needed a way to shift the attention away from her. Then it hit her. It was perfect.

"What if I film *you guys* doing all your boarding tricks at the skate park?" Autumn offered. "I watched you guys skate this summer. You are both really talented."

Nathaniel raised his fist triumphantly. "That *is* a cool idea. We can show off and stuff."

"That's a sweet idea Aut!" Rick said excitedly. "And we *always* skate longer than ten minutes so that's perfect."

Autumn smiled. The boys were satisfied and anything that kept the camera off her was just icing on the cake.

When they arrived at Rick's, Autumn pulled into the empty driveway. She put the car into park, killed the engine and they all piled out.

"I am going to get my board Nate!" Rick said eagerly before he turned to Autumn.

"We are going to practice at the park before we film. Do you want to join us?"

Autumn shook her head. "No thanks. I have some reading to catch up on."

"Aw come on Aut. It will be fun," Nathaniel pressed but Autumn wasn't budging.

"Nope. I'm all good. You two have fun."

After the boys had taken off, Autumn went into the empty house. She heard the newly familiar noises of the house that were once foreign to her. The sound of the fridge humming gently and the clock ticking, slowly and steadily. The noises that comforted her, that announced to her, *this is my home.*

She grabbed a water bottle from the fridge and headed upstairs where she set her bag down. She went to her book shelf and picked out a book.

She flopped onto her bed, took a sip of water and began reading.

An hour had passed when her mind began to drift.

Her first day was done and it had been rather uneventful, just the way she liked it.

No rivalries, no drama and an addition to the equation, the enigmatic Eric King.

She didn't believe rumors. Her parents had taught her not to judge someone based on hearsay. She liked to form her own opinions.

Eric seemed mysterious and the fact that he was taking English too was a sign. They had that in common and it would be the perfect ice breaker.

She shook her head, as if to shoo the thoughts away.

She didn't want romance did she? She was here to help Rick and to start over, but boys weren't part of her plan.

But the more she tried to force Eric from her mind the more he lingered, taunting her, daring her to find out more about him.

Eventually, she succumbed to her imagination and it wasn't long before she had fallen asleep, still holding her book in her hands.

4

The next morning, Autumn awoke to her cell phone alarm going off. She thought about hitting snooze, but instead she sleepily rolled over and shut the alarm off completely.

Still half-asleep, she rolled out of bed, grabbed clothes and headed towards the bathroom.

She cursed early mornings just as the bathroom door abruptly flung open.

Autumn stopped in the hallway as Rick came out, followed by a bunch of steam.

"Morning Aut," he said cheerfully, a towel wrapped around his hips. Autumn looked at his bare upper body and wondered how he ate so much and still stayed in shape.

"Morning," Autumn said groggily. "Are you done in there?"

"Definitely. The shower is all yours."

Autumn stepped into the bathroom, then turned to Rick.

"Is there any hot water left?" she asked over her shoulder.

"Yep. I was only in there five minutes," Rick replied as he sauntered into his room.

Relieved, Autumn shut the door behind her and slipped off her tank top and yoga pants.

She showered quickly, although she was tempted to stay in the encompassing warm water all morning.

She dried off, pulled on dark jeans and a black sweater, brushed her teeth and hair and headed downstairs for breakfast.

As per usual, her aunt had a buffet-style breakfast laid out for them.

Eggs, bacon, waffles and home fries were all par for the course. Rick already had a full plate when Autumn grabbed eggs and bacon and settled in beside him.

"Morning dear," Aunt Katherine said as she grabbed her purse and keys off the counter hurriedly. "I'm so sorry. I have to get going early. We are all booked up today. Fall weather always brings the colds. Have a good day."

"You too," Autumn said as her aunt rushed out the front door.

Rick mumbled some form of goodbye and went about wolfing down his meal.

"This is so delicious," Rick said between mouthfuls.

He glanced at Autumn. "Are we driving in today?"

Autumn looked at him while eating her eggs. "As opposed to *flying* in?"

"No," Rick said, looking at her like she was being absurd. "Sometimes I skate into school."

"On your skateboard?"

"Sometimes, but usually my rollerblades," Rick said. "I stuck my head outside, and it's pretty gorgeous out there."

"So what's the plan? You rollerblade and pull me along in the wagon we played with when we were kids?"

Rick smiled fondly at this memory. "I remember that wagon! It was red and shiny, and you used to make me pull you around town on the *hottest days.*"

"Remember the one time I pulled you around for like two hours and nearly got heatstroke? My mom called your mom and told her."

"My mother still tells me that one," Autumn said recalling the incident. "Apparently, your mom told her I made you fan me with these giant plant leafs and feed me berries from that tree in your backyard. I said I was a princess, and you were my prince."

Rick was chortling now.

"And the next time you came over to visit, the wagon was *mysteriously* missing."

Autumn was laughing hard when she looked at the time.

"If we aren't driving in, we had better head out now," she said, gathering hers and Rick's plates. She walked them over to the dishwasher, placed them inside then looked at Rick inquisitively. "You still didn't tell me how *I'm* getting to school, and if you say on your back, I will smack you."

"*My* bike," Rick offered. "It's a racing bike. You will love it."

Autumn sighed. "Alright. Let's get to it."

Rick and Autumn quickly finished cleaning up, grabbed their lunches and headed out.

They stood in the driveway as Rick adjusted the bike seat for Autumn's height. He was right. It was a gorgeous day out. The sun was shining brightly and there was a perfect mix of warmth and a light, cool breeze.

Autumn inhaled the fresh air. It was invigorating, and it woke her up.

"You were right Rick. It is amazing out here."

"When am I *not* right?" he teased as he tested the seat's stability by sitting on it.

"There you go Aut. It's all yours. Fit for a midget."

Autumn, who was a rather tall 5'4 in her opinion, rolled her green eyes and tried the seat herself. "Perfect," she said.

"Awesome," Rick said as he finished strapping his blades on.

"You ready?" He looked at her eagerly. "Like old times?"

"Yep! Let's go," she said excitedly. Rick was right. It was like old times. It took Autumn back to when she played with Rick as a child.

Autumn had always fancied herself a bit of a tomboy. Though she still had the distinct qualities of a girl. She feared bugs, often wore pink and could cry at the drop of a hat, but she could still rough and tumble with the best of them.

She was no stranger to biking with Rick all summer long, while her sister stayed home and sunbathed.

"I know the best way there! Follow me!" Rick announced and they set off.

As Autumn expected, Rick was quite fast on his rollerblades, having no trouble keeping up with her. She was surprised how quickly she became accustomed to Rick's bike.

As they glided together, Rick broke the silence.

"You should try out for the cheerleading team Aut," Rick said as they moved effortlessly along. "The videos your mom sent of you at those football games," he trailed off. "You were amazing."

Autumn had all but blocked out her days of cheerleading alongside Nikki.

The days when things between them weren't volatile. The good days were always harder to remember than the bad days were.

"Thanks for the vote of confidence but I don't think so Ricky," Autumn replied. "I don't want to get mixed up with that crowd again."

Rick nodded understandingly at her. "Alright then."

"I know I am being judgemental and maybe even a hypocrite," she began.

"You aren't being judgemental at all," he said, waving his hand.

"Most of those popular people are pretty harsh. They used to pick on Nathaniel really badly until we became buddies."

"Really?" Autumn was stunned. She couldn't imagine anyone picking on someone as outspoken as Nathaniel, and she certainly couldn't see him putting up with it.

"Yeah. He was a lot smaller in grade nine. Shorter and skinnier. Ben and his lackeys would shove him around. That's how we met actually," Rick said as they made their way up a hill.

"They had him cornered in the locker room before gym class. It was Ben and three other jocks. They were going to beat him up just because they could. So, I defended him."

"What did you do?" Autumn knew that Rick was quite capable of protecting himself. He had taken martial arts up until he was sixteen.

"I used some of my martial arts training and put Ben into a hold. I didn't hurt him, but I made sure they knew I *would* if they bothered Nathaniel ever again."

Autumn's heart swelled. She was so very proud of Rick. He was fearless and moral. It was something she had always envied about him.

"You are a good friend Rick," she said gently. "He is lucky to have you."

"That's what Nathaniel said," Rick said, beaming as they stopped in front of the school.

Rick helped Autumn lock up the bike. Then, he slid off his blades, and they began walking towards the entrance.

"Occasionally, they mouth off, but they know better than to try to bully us," Rick went on smugly.

"Poor Nathaniel," Autumn said as they made their way through the front doors. She was about to go on when she heard a voice from behind her.

"Poor me what?" Autumn looked over her shoulder to see Nathaniel walking a few paces behind her, brows furrowed in confusion.

"This is getting weird," Rick said as they walked into the front foyer together.

"What is?" Nathaniel asked.

"You just popping up randomly behind us at school," Rick said. "It's creepy dude."

"I *do* go here too you know," Nathaniel said, then he looked from Rick to Autumn suspiciously.

"Why? What were you two talking about just now?"

"Nothing," Rick said awkwardly, averting his eyes. Even as a kid, Rick couldn't lie worth a damn and that obviously hadn't changed.

"Don't lie to me! You look guilty Rick! I can read you like a book!" Nathaniel said, pointing at Rick accusingly.

"You don't even read books dude!" Rick exclaimed as they headed to their lockers.

"That's true dude but Autumn was saying *poor Nathaniel* and as far as I know, I'm the only Nathaniel you both know," he said.

Then he paused, looking uncertain. "Aren't I?"

Rick shrugged his shoulders. "Maybe you are."

Autumn looked at Nathaniel's confused expression and felt instantly sorry for him.

She nudged Rick, grimacing. "Rick. Come on."

"Fine," Rick said, surrendering. "I was telling Autumn the story of how we met."

Nathaniel's confusion faded, and his face filled with realization.

"The story of how we met? Gee man, it sounds like *we're* dating! No wonder Autumn won't go out with me!" he said, looking annoyed.

"Sorry. Aut was saying Ben and his friends seem mean. I was just confirming it," Rick said as he opened his locker.

"Yeah and?" Nathaniel pressed.

"I told her they picked on you a lot until I came along," Rick said warily.

Nathaniel's face went many shades of red. "Oh my hero!" He grumbled. "That is so embarrassing!"

Autumn began examining the inside of her locker, trying her best to appear busy. She didn't want Nathaniel feeling any more awkward then he already did, and if she listened in, it would make everything worse.

"No way! It's not embarrassing dude! You sound like a guy who *was* a wimp but isn't anymore," Rick said matter-of-factly.

"Much better!" Nathaniel said sarcastically. He sighed, looking to Autumn.

"Autumn, do you think I'm a weakling? Be honest."

Autumn knew Nathaniel was many things. He was a flirt, a jokester and a slacker, but he *wasn't* cowardly.

"Of course not," Autumn said, looking into his hazel eyes with sincerity. "You stood up for me at the skate park."

"I did?" he looked thoughtful.

"You don't remember? Ben was bothering me and you came over to defend me," Autumn said.

"Oh yeah I did!" Nathaniel said, instantly cheering up. "I was like your white knight!" He puffed out his chest proudly.

"You were quite brave," Autumn agreed, touching his shoulder meaningfully.

"You are touching me," Nathaniel said, eyes wide as he stared at her.

"That is gross," Rick said, not missing a beat. "You are salivating like an animal dude."

"Sorry," Nathaniel snapped out of his stupor.

Autumn grimaced. "Boys. Always with their minds in the gutter."

Nathaniel smiled at her deviously just in time for the bell to ring.

"For whom the bell tolls," Autumn said and she grabbed Rick by the arm. "Later Nate!"

"Later!"

Autumn waved as her and Rick headed to homeroom.

"Good morning Ms. Kingston and Mr. Jacobs," Mr. Brown said. He looked up at them, smiling genially, from his desk.

"Morning," they both replied in unison.

"Here! Take a newsletter!" he said animatedly handing them both one. "There is a list of extracurricular activities and upcoming school events."

Autumn and Rick both took a copy and headed towards their desks.
"Ms. Kingston."
Autumn turned back to look at her teacher. "Yes?"
"May I have a word?"
Autumn nodded. "Sure."
"I saw your transcripts and I couldn't help but notice that you were the head cheerleader at your old high school for a year," Mr. Brown began.
"I *was*," Autumn said putting emphasis on the past tense. "You should try out here," he said encouragingly. "The girls are always looking for fresh talent."
Autumn had been put on the spot, but she gained her composure quickly.
"I will think about it," she fibbed. "Thanks."

Mr. Brown nodded, satisfied, and went back to his business. Autumn had no intention of considering cheerleading. As she walked to her desk, she caught a glimpse of Candice, Ben's girlfriend. Dressed in a tight white V-neck T-shirt and jeans, she was giving Autumn a dirty look. She whispered something to the girl sitting beside her, and both girls glared at Autumn disapprovingly. Autumn resisted the urge to clock them with her backpack, instead sitting beside Rick.

"What did Brown want?" Rick asked curiously.

"To *remind* me about the cheerleading tryouts," Autumn muttered. "And recommend I partake. He knows I was the head cheerleader at my old school."

"How does he know that?" Rick asked, his brow furrowed.

"My transcripts."

"Did you tell him you don't want to be a cheerleader again?" Rick asked.

Autumn shrugged. "Nope. He doesn't really care if I try out. It's his job to encourage students to join teams."

"Teacher's pressure is the new peer pressure," Rick muttered as he began skimming the newsletter, looking quite bored.

Autumn read through it herself, seeing if anything piqued her interest. She wasn't big on extracurricular activities, and it seemed as though nothing had changed.

Yearbook committee, basketball tryouts, cooking club, all things she wasn't into pursuing.

Autumn felt Rick nudge her.

"You elbowed me?" she joked.

"Check this out. It's a dance," he said, pointing at the paper.

Autumn glanced at it.

COME ONE, COME ALL!

IT'S THE "WELCOME BACK STUDENTS AND TEACHERS, FALL SEMI-FORMAL DANCE"!

MUSIC, FOOD AND FUN! DON'T MISS IT! IT WILL BE THE EVENT OF THE YEAR!

Autumn looked at Rick, unsurely.

"You want to go to the school dance?"

Rick shrugged. "Maybe. I have *never* been to a dance, and it's our last year as fancy-free high school students."

"*You* might be fancy-free," Autumn muttered. "The rest of us study."

Autumn recalled *the rules* back home. Dances or parties chaperoned by parents were strictly forbidden. Nikki wouldn't have it.

"So what do you think?" Rick asked.

"I think it might be fun." Autumn admitted. "If I could get a date."

"If?" Rick gave her a look.

"Yes if," Autumn repeated.

"I know for a fact, there are tons of guys here that would love to ask you out Aut," Rick said.

Autumn patted his arm appreciatively. "Thanks but I don't really know any guys here."

"Yeah you do," Rick said, a small smile coming across his face. *"Nathaniel Abrams* is a guy you know."

Autumn looked at Rick, her face deadpan. "You want *me* to go with *Nathaniel?"*

"I know he'd take you in a heartbeat."

Autumn pondered it. Nathaniel was a safe choice. She trusted him, and he wasn't going to pressure her to do anything she didn't want to.

It was settled. She would go with him, but she needed a little safeguarding first.

"Alright, I'll go with Nate," Autumn said cautiously.

"You will?" Rick asked excitedly.

"Yes but," she paused.

"Why is there always a *but?"* Rick asked.

"But," she said poking Rick's arm. *"You* have to come too."

"Me?" Rick whined. "Why?"

"A buffer," Autumn explained. "That way if things get awkward you are there. Plus, then it's not an official date."

"But I'll be a third wheel," Rick moaned.

"Well, you can always ask a girl if you want," Autumn said playfully. "Then you can be a fourth wheel instead."

"Fine," Rick said, relenting. "If it helps Nathaniel out, I'll go with you guys."

Morning classes flew by and before Autumn knew it she was walking to her locker with Rick to meet Nathaniel for lunch.

When they arrived, Nathaniel was already there, leaning against a locker, his nose buried in a comic book. When he saw them approaching he looked at Autumn, a toothy grin on his face.

"Hello there Autumn. Aren't you a sight for sore eyes," he said.

Autumn shot Rick a withering look. "You told him about the dance didn't you?"

"Sorry, I had to text him," Rick replied guiltily. "It's good news!"

"Yes it is my friend," Nathaniel said, his hands in the air. "Hallelujah! Praise the Lord!"

"You little stoolpigeon," Autumn muttered. "Don't ever get in with the mob Rick. You'd sing like a canary!"

"So about this dance," Nathaniel began.

Autumn popped her locker open, threw her books inside and turned to Nathaniel.

"I will gladly go with you Nathaniel *but* Rick told you my condition right?"

"Mint?" Nathaniel replied smartly.

"You're comparing me to a comic book? How romantic," Autumn grumbled.

"I know the deal. Rick's coming along to chaperon me and stop me from touching your goodies," Nathaniel said flatly.

"I didn't say that exactly," Autumn said as she closed her locker. "But I think it's best if we all go together as friends."

"Friends is cool but can I still get you flowers?" he asked, looking hopeful.

Autumn couldn't help it. Her heartstrings pulled and she melted just a little at Nathaniel's attempts to romance her.

"I love flowers," Autumn admitted. "So, please feel free Nate."

"Sweet," Nathaniel said. "Now Rick just needs a date and we are all good."

He patted Rick on the shoulder. "Don't worry dude. We will find you someone."

Rick's eyes narrowed. "That is what worries me."

Nathaniel was obviously eager to pawn Rick off on *anyone*, so he'd be occupied at the dance. It didn't take him long before he began pointing out girls in the cafeteria, trying to help Rick find his match just as promised.

"What about her?" Nathaniel asked as they took seats near the middle of the cafeteria. Autumn looked at a slender girl with platinum hair and vibrant blue eyes.

"Too skinny," Rick replied. "She needs a burger."

"Her?" he tried again, this time with a tall, statuesque, brunette.

"No boobs."

"What about that one?"

"Her ears are too pointy."

"And her?" He pointed at a girl with black hair and olive skin.

"*She* has sideburns," Rick said sharply.

Autumn looked at Rick in disbelief. "Sideburns? That's one I've definitely never heard before."

"Yeah man! You are too picky," Nathaniel said grumpily.

Rick glared at him. "If you think she is so hot, why don't you take Elvira out then?"

Nathaniel rolled his eyes. "I am already going with Autumn, duh. You know that dude!"

Nathaniel persisted pointing out girls to Rick to no avail. Eventually, a frustrated Nathaniel threw in the towel when Rick became enthralled with his lunch.

"I can't believe this burger mom made me!" he gushed. "Bacon, onions and cheese! It is perfect."

Nathaniel shot him a glare. "You can't take that burger to the dance Rick."

Rick shrugged, indifferent. "Dude! I have to tell you about this new skating move I saw online!"

As the talk of boarding began, Autumn's mind and her eyes began to wander. She glanced around the cafeteria, hoping to spot Eric, when instead she saw a girl at the table next to hers, eating alone. She looked familiar and Autumn soon realized she was in her homeroom.

She was tiny, had a dark pixie cut, delicate features and huge brown eyes. Dressed in jeans and a black tank top, she wore an expression Autumn easily recognized as loneliness.

Autumn felt compelled to talk to her. It wasn't so long ago, her friends had abandoned her and she ate her lunch alone in the cafeteria, until that became too humiliating and she opted to eat in a washroom stall.

She didn't want anyone to eat in a place that smelt like urine and feces, so she turned to the girl, eager to spark up a conversation.

"Hey there," Autumn said, looking in the girl's direction.

She was chewing so it took her a moment to reply.

"Hey."

Autumn smiled, her best welcoming grin, and introduced herself. She stated that she thought they were in the same homeroom.

The girl smiled slightly and put down her sandwich. "Yeah we are. I'm Mandy Jensen."

"I thought I recognized you," Autumn replied. "Did you want to come join us?"

Mandy nodded, looking relived. She grabbed her belongings and sat beside Autumn, putting her lunch tray on the table.

Autumn was surprised to see she had an even bigger lunch than Rick.

She had never seen a girl eat that much, and she considered it a sign. Maybe this girl was Rick's soul mate.

"Dude, are you going to eat all that?" Rick looked at Mandy, dumbfounded.

The girl looked at her tray and back to Rick. "Yeah, of course. What else would I do with it?"

"Man, you are a beast," Rick said bluntly. "I can't even eat that much, and I'm *me.*"

"Thanks," Mandy said, frowning. Autumn sighed. Rick was going to blow it.

I will just have to take matters into my own hands, Autumn thought. She needed to draw Rick's attention to Mandy.

She tried everything. Bringing him into the conversation, talking about movies, music, *anything* they might have in common, but Rick wouldn't bite.

Nathaniel and he went on like Mandy wasn't even there. They discussed ramps, jumps and when they were hitting the skate park next.

Eventually, Autumn became frustrated. She whistled trying to get the guys attention.

"Hey! Frick and Frack!"

Nathaniel and Rick both looked up at her blankly. "What?"

"This is Mandy Jensen," Autumn said.

"Rick Jacobs," Rick said, reaching out and shaking Mandy's hand.

Nathaniel grinned foolishly at her. "I'm Nathaniel."

"Dude, you are supposed to say your last name when you are introducing yourself," Rick scolded him.

Nathaniel put his hand on his chin thoughtfully. "Oh yeah."

He smiled again at Mandy.

"Last name, Abrams," he said abruptly. Then he turned back to Rick, and they began chatting among themselves again.

Stunned, Mandy didn't say anything. She looked at Autumn, perplexed.

"How do you know him?" she asked, pointing at Rick. "Is he socially inept?"

"Childhood friends," Autumn said. "And yes, sometimes."

Mandy nodded and began mowing down her sandwich. "And the other guy?"

"He's Rick's best friend."

"Ah yes. I can see that," she said. Autumn looked over at the two of them as they animatedly demonstrated a skateboarding move.

"They have their own guy lingo going on," Mandy observed. "I could definitely sense a bromance."

"Yeah. When you learn to decipher all the grunts and *dudes,* you can almost understand them," Autumn joked.

When Autumn arrived for gym class, she was excited to find out it would be outdoors. Hearing birds singing and basking in the welcoming warmth of the sun, made her yearn for an endless summer.

As she resisted the urge to lounge out on the bleachers, she saw Ms. Baxter approaching.

"Good afternoon ladies," she began, glancing at her clipboard. "Today, we will be running the track. I *know* some of you are smokers, so I would recommend you warm up those lungs first. Start with some stretching, then walk around the track a few laps," she grinned impishly.

"Now get to it!"

"She is mighty frightening," Mandy said when Ms. Baxter was out of earshot.

Autumn chuckled. "Yep. She's the cliché hard-ass gym teacher. Something tells me my "PMS cramps" notes, aren't going to fly with her."

Mandy laughed as they began stretching.

"So, who was your gym teacher last year?" Autumn asked Mandy.

Mandy stretched her leg out and looked at Autumn. "Actually, I just moved here this semester. My dad got a job at Cesus Corp, so we had to relocate."

Autumn nodded. "My uncle, *well,* not my real uncle, but Rick's dad, James, he works there too. He has been with the company for quite some time."

"A lot of people around here seem to be employed by them," Mandy said, switching legs. Autumn followed her lead.

"I wouldn't know. I am new here too. I just moved down in August."

Mandy puckered her lips sympathetically. "Being uprooted in your last year too? What is your excuse?"

"Rick," Autumn said and Mandy's eyes widened.

"Oh. He is the *reason,*" she grinned wickedly.

Autumn giggled at what she accidentally insinuated.

"Oh no! Nothing like that! He needed help with school. I am his last-ditch attempt at graduating."

"Ah the saving grace," Mandy said.

Suddenly, her eyes left Autumn's, distracted. Autumn followed her gaze and saw the boy's gym glass piling out from the gymnasium doors.

Autumn scanned the crowd and spotted Rick's mop of curls and Nate's ginger hair with ease.

"Let's hear it for the boys," Mandy jested.

Autumn arched an eyebrow. Nathaniel wasn't in Rick's gym class *yesterday.* Then she remembered Rick saying he had skipped it. How typical.

"He's so freaking cute," Mandy said, staring dreamily at the guys as they approached. "You are really lucky to be close with him Autumn."

"Rick is cute *and* sweet," Autumn agreed as she stretched, touching her calf. "And he has an infectious laugh and the bluest eyes ..."

"I *meant* Nathaniel," Mandy said, her eyes trailing him as he stretched against the bleachers alongside Rick. "I love gingers."

Autumn's mouth was agape. Nathaniel *was* very cute, but she still wasn't expecting Mandy to be interested in him. *Her* mind was so set on *Rick and Mandy* as a couple that she hadn't even considered Nathaniel.

"Oh *Nathaniel.* He's single," Autumn said brightly.

Mandy turned to Autumn, her eyes lighting up. "Really? Do you think you could put in a good word for me? I understand we just met and everything …" she trailed off.

Autumn realized this was her opportunity to help Mandy *and* play cupid for Nathaniel.

"I can do one better," Autumn said confidently. "How would *you* like to go with him to the fall dance?"

Mandy looked even more excited now. "I would love to but I don't really dance," she admitted.

"That's okay neither does he," Autumn reassured her. "And we can all go together."

"You have a date *already?*" Mandy asked. "Though it doesn't surprise me really. You are so pretty."

Autumn blushed. "Thanks but I don't have a date per say. Nathaniel and I are going together. Just as friends, of course."

"Oh, I couldn't intrude," Mandy said embarrassedly. "He obviously wants you to be his date."

"It's not a date," Autumn said truthfully. "Rick is even coming along with us."

"With his date?"

"Nope. He's going solo," Autumn said. "So please, let me talk to Nathaniel."

"Alright," Mandy gave in. "But don't force it. I don't want to impose."

"Trust me. You aren't imposing," Autumn reassured her.

"Alright girls, stretching time is over!" Ms. Baxter bellowed. The brutish gym teacher stood in the middle of the field, blowing her whistle. "Take your positions on the track!"

Autumn and Mandy headed to starting positions, just as Mr. Beachum began playing drill sergeant with the boy's gym class.

"HEY ADAMS, I SAID TO GIVE ME TWENTY, NOT TEN!"
"IF THERE IS NO PAIN, THERE IS NO GAIN, AND *YOU'RE LAME!*"
"FEEL THE BURN BOY! IT'LL MAKE YOU A MAN."

As Autumn and Mandy exchanged perturbed looks, Autumn couldn't help thinking that both Mr. Beachum *and* Ms. Baxter had too much testosterone.

Autumn couldn't have been more thankful to see gym class end. She took a quick shower, got dressed and headed to English.

When she got to class, she took the same seat she had yesterday and pulled out her binder.

She glanced around the room. Mrs. Reid hadn't arrived yet and from the looks of it, neither had Eric King.

Autumn decided now was the perfect time to start writing Kristin some snail mail. Emails were convenient but there was something extra special about a handwritten letter. So she pulled out a piece of crisp paper from her binder and began writing.

She only wrote a few lines, when she heard a voice from above her.

"Are you actually writing a letter?"

Autumn looked up and saw Eric King standing in front of her desk.

Today he was wearing dark jeans and a navy blue T-shirt with the name of a band on it.

Up-close, his eyes were chocolate brown and his skin was lightly tanned. He tucked his ear-length hair behind his ears, looking at Autumn inquiringly.

"Yes. I am," Autumn began and Eric chuckled slightly.

"What?" Autumn asked confused.

"Sorry," Eric said, taking a seat at the desk beside hers. "I thought letter writing was extinct, much like the dinosaurs."

Autumn smirked and introduced herself.

"A pleasure to meet you Autumn. I'm Eric King," he said.

"So I've heard."

"Ah. My reputation precedes me does it?" he grinned. "It's good to hear that years later I am still the talk of the town."

"Or just the school," Autumn teased.

Eric winked at her. "Obviously, you haven't been around town yet."

Autumn was quiet, thinking of what to say next when Eric spoke up.

"For the record, I have heard about you too Ms. Kingston."

Autumn arched an eyebrow.

"Oh really?"

"Really," he said, leaning towards her. "The saying is 'if these walls could talk' and around here, they never shut up."

"Now I *am* curious," Autumn admitted, running a hand through her dark hair anxiously.

"Let's see. According to my *intel*, you moved here to tutor Rick Jacobs, your childhood best friend. The general guy consensus is you get nine stars out of ten in the hotness department, though personally, I would give you a shining eleven."

Autumn was stunned. It took her a minute to regroup. How did he know so much about her?

"Ok? So are you a stalker or did you shakedown Rick at some point?"

"I have connections," Eric said, smirking.

"Connections?"

"A good reporter never reveals his sources sweet pea," he smiled and turned away just as Mrs. Reid entered the room.

She greeted the class, but Autumn wasn't done yet. She poked Eric's arm.

He looked back at her appraisingly. "Yes?"

"Seriously. How did you find all that out?"

Eric shrugged, beaming. "All in due time sweetheart."

He put a finger to his lips. "Now hush. Class is starting."

5

The bell rang indicating the end of English. Autumn grabbed her backpack swiftly as Eric walked over to her.

She gave him a disapprovingly look. "Let me guess. You know my blood type too?"

Eric leaned across her desk, looking mock hurt. "Hey! It's high school. There is a grapevine."

"A very long, nosy one," Autumn grumbled as she began walking out the door.

It was unnerving knowing so little about someone who already knew so much about you.

"Hey wait!" Eric called after her just as Rick came strolling down the hall.

He said nothing, but he didn't look pleased. Autumn knew what he was thinking. That his best friend was talking to Eric King, the demon worshiper.

For some reason, the thought made her want to laugh.

"I feel rather misunderstood," Eric said. "I was going for charming. Not creepy guy who watches you through your bedroom window. So can we start again?"

Autumn looked at him. He was rather charismatic and mysterious. She smiled. "Sure. We can do that."

"Perfect. Why don't we start with this?" he handed her a black envelope.

"What is it?" she asked.

"An invite to my party Friday," he said. "Invites to my manor are exclusive," he grinned.

"So this invite makes me special?" Autumn said, failing to hide the hope in her voice.

"Or cursed, depending on who you talk to," Eric joked. "Now," he reached out touching her arm gently. "Tell me you will come."

Autumn glanced over at Rick. Though he appeared to be giving her space to talk to Eric, he was still watching them like a hawk.

"I will, if you can swing an invite for my friends."

Eric looked hesitant. "How many friends?"

"Three," Autumn said.

Eric looked over at Rick, who was giving him the evil eye, then he turned back to Autumn.

"Sure. They can come, but based on the way Rick is looking at me, I don't think he'll show," Eric said, as he reached inside his bag and handed her three more envelopes.

"So this seals the deal? You are coming?" he asked, looking excited by the prospect.

"Yes. I will be there," she smiled.

"I look forward to it," he said. "See you tomorrow." He winked at her and headed down the hall. As he walked past Rick, he nodded cordially.

"Rick."

"Eric," Rick said sharply.

When Eric was gone, Autumn went over to Rick. "Hey there."

"What the hell was that?" Rick asked, his eyes narrowed.

"What was what?"

"Don't play dumb Aut! You and The Demon King. You guys talking with him touching your arm! That was truly a sight!"

Autumn rolled her eyes and headed to her locker. "You act like you caught us making the beast with two backs Rick!"

"The what?"

"Having sex!" she snapped.

"Ugh," Rick grimaced. "Just stop. That thought is enough to make me hurl."

Autumn sighed. She didn't want to fight.

"Rick. He isn't a bad guy. A little odd? Maybe. Arrogant? Definitely."

"Well that's a winning combination," Rick muttered as he followed her.

"But he seems quite nice. He even invited us all to his party."

She held up the black envelopes.

Rick gave her a withering look. "Great. And I suppose I have to go because you are."

"You don't have to …" she began, but he raised a hand to object.

"Yes I do. I have to protect you from him Aut. When you find out he makes voodoo dolls out of human hair, I need to be there."

Autumn shot him a daunting look. "Rick, just give him a chance. You aren't like everyone else. You don't judge people by the rumors that swirl around about them do you?"

Rick's shoulders slumped. "No."

"Perfect. I will invite Eric to sit with us at lunch tomorrow so we can all get to know him better."

She handed Rick the invitation and smiled. "For you."

Rick stared at the black envelope. "How festive," he muttered sardonically.

"Autumn, just face it! You are going to be eating my dust!" Rick bellowed.

"Funny that Rick. Aren't *you* dining on *my* dust as we speak?" Autumn called back to him.

Rick and Autumn were racing home, and Autumn was currently in the lead. She swerved around a fallen branch in the road and began pedaling as hard as she could. For a moment, she flashed back to her childhood, when racing was the epitome of summer fun. Her sister never cared much for it, but Autumn loved it.

"Girls don't sweat Autumn." Audrina had told her. "It isn't attractive."

Autumn didn't care. She wanted to be included in everything Rick did. In her mind, anything Rick could do, she could do too.

Riding along, her movements flowed seamlessly, and she sped across the pavement, with ease and grace. She looked behind her.

Rick was gaining on her.

She welcomed the challenge, pedaling just that much harder, pushing her body, willing it to be faster. As she came up a small incline, she spotted a figure in the distance. Something about him caught her eye, though she wasn't sure what.

As she got closer, she saw he was sitting in the grass, under a large oak tree. He was an older man, probably in his mid-thirties, and he wore a tattered hat, a ripped suede jacket and grass stained jeans.

Autumn knew right away. He was homeless.

She didn't know why, but she felt an overwhelming urge, to help this man. It was like gravity was tugging at her to do *something*, so she pulled over near the park.

"Hey! Why are you stopping? The race isn't over until we get home!" Rick yelled.

Autumn ignored him and began slowing down.

Rick pulled over behind her, looking confused.

"What's wrong? Is it the bike?"

"No," she said quietly. "Look." And she tilted her head discreetly in the man's general direction.

Rick studied the man for a moment then turned back to Autumn.

"Yeah I know. That's my future if I don't graduate. I've heard this speech from mom before."

"No!" Autumn said. "We should give him some money."

Rick didn't argue. Instead, he shrugged his shoulders. "Okay. Let's go."

Autumn jumped off her bike and began walking it towards the man. Rick followed behind her on his blades.

The man, who was playing with the blades of grass unsuspectingly, looked up at them as they approached. As they got closer, Autumn noticed he had attractive features underneath all the grim. He had brown hair and dark eyes, and beyond the initial stress and dirt on his face, she could see hints of youth and exuberance.

"Hey there," Autumn said, approaching the stranger cautiously.

The man looked at them, confusion in his eyes. "Well, hello there."

"Are you drunk sir?" Rick asked capriciously. Autumn shot him a glare and elbowed him in the ribs.

"OW!" Rick yelped.

"Me drunk? Nope, sorry," the man replied in a raspy voice. Then he grinned.

"Sorry. It's just been a long time since someone referred to me as *sir.*"

"Oh," Rick said, looking down at his rollerblades. "I can call you *dude* if you want."

The man chortled. "That *would* be more appropriate I guess."

The man straightened up a little and stretched his legs out.

"So what brings you two kids over here?"

"We wanted to give you something," Autumn said, suddenly feeling a little sheepish.

The man eyed up her bike, looking excited.

"Is it the bike?"

"It most certainly is not!" Rick replied sharply.

"Oh," The man said, frowning.

"Actually," Autumn said, looking at Rick, annoyed. "We have some money for you." And she reached into her backpack, grabbing her wallet. She opened it, pulling out two crisp ten-dollar bills.

Rick, who got a rather large allowance, gave him a twenty.

They handed the man the money, but he didn't reach out to take it. Instead, he hesitated, looking at them suspiciously.

"I don't know if I can accept your money," he said warily.

"Why?" Autumn asked confused. "We want you to have it."

"Sorry," he said, looking at them guardedly. "Most kids who give me money hand me change, maybe a five if I'm lucky. Which makes me wonder," he paused, putting a hand to his scruffy chin. "What kind of jobs do you two have?"

"We don't have jobs," Autumn admitted.

"I see. You aren't bullies are you?" he asked, eyes narrowed. "You know. Shaking down people for their money?"

"Nope," Rick smirked.

"Petty thieves?"

"Nope."

"Just *borrowing* money from mom's purse every week?"

"Just take the money please!" Autumn insisted holding it out to him again.

"Yeah dude," Rick chimed in. "We want you to."

The man looked to be pondering this. Eventually, he sighed and reached out his hand.

"Alright. I'll take it."

He grabbed the money hesitantly and slid it into his jacket pocket.

"Thanks kids. I appreciate it. Most people aren't as generous as you two are," he said. "I'm Stuart by the way."

Autumn and Rick introduced themselves, and Stuart smiled.

"Nice to meet you both," he said jovially. "You two a couple?"

"No," Autumn said. "Best friends."

Stuart nodded. "I see. Maybe one day," he grinned at them. "Thanks again for the cash. I think I'm going to go get myself some pie from the diner up the road. Lemon Meringue. My favorite."

Looking quite excited about the pie, Stuart stood up and dusted himself off.

"You kids have a good day," he said. Then he tipped his hat to them and headed on his way.

Autumn and Rick made it home just in time.

The sky had suddenly become overcast, and rain had started pouring just as they got into the house.

Autumn could hear the claps of thunder and the torrential rain pounding on the windows as they stepped into the kitchen.

"Damn it," Rick said, as he looked at his cell.

"What's wrong?" Autumn asked, as she set her bag down on the floor.

"Mom just texted me. She's going to be late tonight."

"Is something wrong?" Autumn asked, alarmed. Aunt Katherine was hardly ever late coming home.

"No. Mom is fine. She is just overloaded with paperwork. *I'm going to starve!*" Rick said, eyes wide. He ran to the fridge and opened it, looking inside frantically.

"We need to cook Autumn! I don't cook! I just eat!" he cried.

"Why don't we go out for dinner?" Autumn suggested. "We can go to that diner you and Nathaniel took me to this summer."

Rick's panic swiftly disappeared and was replaced by joy.

"Good idea Autumn! Now we don't have to cook anything! You are a freaking genius!"

He reached out and hugged Autumn tightly with both arms.

"Oh, don't get too excited," Autumn said grimly.

Rick pulled away slowly. "Why's that?"

"Before we go, I believe *you* have some homework to attend to?" she said, grinning.

Rick's happiness dissolved almost instantly. "Oh yeah. I forgot."

"Come on. I'll help you," Autumn said, as she led a begrudging Rick to the kitchen table.

6

The rest of the school week flew by and before Autumn knew it, Friday night had arrived. She was in her room, getting dressed for Eric's party while talking on the phone with Kristin.

"Wear your low-cut black dress with the jewels along the straps," Kristin said, sounding remotely envious. "Though your cleavage might give the poor guy an aneurysm."

Autumn giggled. "You are hilarious."

Kristin had an amazing sense of humor. It was what Autumn liked most about her. Suddenly, she was overwhelmed by sorrow.

"I miss you Kris."

"I miss you too Auttie," she said. "Things haven't been the same without you here. I am pretty sure even Nikki misses seeing you roam the halls."

"I doubt that," Autumn said, crashing onto her bed. "So how have things been with the ice queen?"

"She is too busy planning what to wear to prom to harass me," Kristin replied, sounding bored.

Autumn sprawled out, feeling tears forming in her eyes. "I told you Kristin. Anytime you want to come up Katherine and James offered to pay your way. You can stay here and meet the infamous Rick."

"I will definitely take you up on that offer, but I swear, with all my advanced classes and extra credit courses, I will be lucky to sleep let alone travel," she said. "But when school is done, I am more than willing to come up there. I mean, look at you! You're the new girl and you already have an invite to some hot guy's party."

Autumn's cheeks flushed. "Eric is my type, that is for sure."

"Let me guess: tall, brooding and undeniably charming?" Kristin teased.

"He looks broody at first but as it turns out, he is actually quite the joker," Autumn admitted.

"A prankster is he?" Kristin pressed. "Or is he just really funny?"

Autumn turned onto her stomach. "Let's put it this way. When it comes to the battle of wits, he is armed to the teeth."

When Autumn was finished chatting, she showered and put on the black dress Kristin had recommended. She brushed her long, dark hair and pulled it into a sleek ponytail. Then she adorned her vibrant green eyes with plum eyeliner and added the finishing touches: jet black mascara and pink lip gloss.

She was studying herself in the mirror when she heard a knock at her door.

It was Rick, so Autumn directed him to come in. When he did, she couldn't believe her eyes.

He was actually dressed up. He looked rather dapper in a white dress shirt with the cuffs rolled up and khakis. Even his curls looked less wild as he appeared to have tamed them with hair gel. Rick stared back at Autumn, looking just as stunned as she did.

"Wow," he murmured and Autumn bowed dramatically.

"Really? I think the cleavage is a little much."

Rick shook his head. "Take it from a guy. It isn't."

"Typical male," Autumn rolled her eyes. "What did you need? Are we running late?"

"No. I just need help with this," he held up a skinny black tie. "Usually, mom or dad helps me, but since they are out tonight I thought you could."

"No problem," she said, walking over to him. She slipped the tie around his neck and began knotting it.

"Have you given any thought to who you might want to take to the dance?"

"Nope," Rick said, his blue eyes meeting her green ones. "You look amazing by the way."

She beamed. "Thanks. You don't look too shabby yourself there Ricky."

After she slipped the tie through the knot and tightened it, she stepped back admiring her handwork.

"As perfect as a sailor's knot if I do say so myself."

Rick looked down, loosening the tie a smidgen. "Thanks Aut," he said, holding out his arm to her.

"Are you ready?"

Autumn took one final look in the mirror, fixing any stray hairs and straightening her clothes until she was satisfied. Then she linked her arm into Rick's. "Lead the way," she said, and they headed for the door.

"Rick, please! We want to get there *today!*"

Autumn was sitting shotgun in Rick's car, an old black Cadillac. Mandy and Nathaniel were in the back.

"I am just saying! If any of us make it out of Eric's house tonight *alive* it will be by some small miracle!" Nathaniel griped.

"What the hell are you saying?" Mandy huffed.

"I am saying, this whole *party* is a cover-up and we are actually being sacrificed to Eric's demigods!" Nathaniel said sharply.

Autumn glared at Rick. He glanced at her but had his eyes back on the road in a split-second.

"What? I am driving at the pace I am comfortable with," he said. "The speed limit!"

Autumn rolled her eyes. She wasn't giving Rick a death glare because of his driving. It was the fact that he *obviously* hadn't talked to Nathaniel about dating Mandy. It was evident Nathaniel was still holding out for Autumn, even though she wasn't interested.

She looked out the window, taking in her surroundings. They definitely entered the wealthier part of Whitan. The houses were larger, the grass greener and lusher and the parks more clean and well-kept.

"Are we there yet?" Nathaniel groaned and Autumn flung around in her seat to scowl at him.

"Are you going to start kicking my seat next?"

"We are getting close," Mandy said, looking at her cell. "It should be around this bend here."

The car turned and suddenly they were driving uphill. Autumn could see many cars parked on the road already, lined up like colorful blocks along the street.

"Looks like Eric has lots of friends," Mandy said, sounding impressed. "I find it hard to believe he is an outcast." She looked at Nathaniel accusingly.

"The question becomes, how much does he pay them?" Nathaniel sniggered and Autumn barely resisted the urge to sock him.

They drove for a little while longer, traveling along a winding cul-de-sac, until they reached an end. Beyond it, on a vast property, surrounded by nothing but trees and field, was Eric's house.

Hidden behind a large wrought-iron gate (that was closed at the moment) was a gorgeous Victorian style mansion. Autumn wasn't materialistic, but even she could appreciate the beauty of this home. The mix of vintage elements and modern touches, made it unique and striking.

"Autumn you didn't tell me your boyfriend was loaded!" Mandy squealed.

"He isn't her boyfriend!" Nathaniel snapped.

"Not yet," Mandy said. "But give the girl time."

"I don't really know anything about Eric," Autumn admitted.

"And yet here we are," Nathaniel muttered as Rick pulled the car up and began parking along the side of the road.

It took Rick time to park, as he cautiously maneuvered between two vehicles. When he was finally satisfied with his parking job, he turned to Autumn.

"I parallel parked. I *hate* parallel parking so don't say I never do anything for you."

Autumn smiled and planted a quick kiss on his cheek. "Thanks Ricky."

"No problem. Now let's plow."

"I am just happy we didn't miss the party," Mandy said, as they began stepping out of the car.

"We were going so slow."

Rick opened his mouth to retort but was cut off.

"Hey guys!" Eric called out. "Good to see you all!"

Autumn looked over to see him behind the gate, coming towards them. He was dressed in a crisp white button down, tailored grey pants and a red satin bow tie.

"A bow tie?" Autumn heard Nathaniel mutter under his breath. "Who is this guy?"

"Rick!" Eric called out, as he punched buttons on a keypad. The gates began opening.

"You could have parked in the driveway!"

"Dude, I would've," Rick said, putting his hands in his pockets. "But there was a giant gate in my way."

Eric considered this. "I guess *I* should have instructed you to buzz in. My mistake. By all means, the gate is open now. You can move your car if you like."

"I'm all good," Rick said confidently. "But thanks."

"Perfect," Eric said.

"Nathaniel nice to see you again and Mandy you look lovely."

Autumn thought Mandy looked amazing. She was wearing a leather mini dress with red Converse running shoes. Her pixie cut with spiked up, and her eyes were lined with heavy black liner.

Mandy flushed a little. "Thanks Eric. You look pretty smoking too."

"Why thank you," Eric said, tugging at his bow tie.

He turned to Autumn, smiling at her, his eyes wandering up and down her figure appreciatively. His dark eyes burnt into her green ones, and her heart pitter-pattered in her chest.

"You look stunning Autumn," he said. "Though words can't do your beauty justice."

Mandy let out a dreamy sigh while Nathaniel rolled his eyes. Rick shook his head, looking rather impressed.

"Smooth dude. Smooth."

Autumn's heart fluttered as Eric took her hand into his. Nathaniel grunted in protest and for a moment, she felt a stab of guilt. She didn't *want* to hurt Nathaniel, but she couldn't hide her feeling for Eric either.

"Shall we?" Eric said and he led her by the hand, past the gates, as the others followed closely behind. As they walked up the long drive, Autumn could see just how vast Eric's property was. Surrounding his house was a large garden with many different shrubs and flowers, some that weren't even in bloom. Near the gated perimeter, tall oak and willow trees provided more privacy. In the middle of the front yard, was a beautiful courtyard with a fountain spouting water, a bird bath, and chairs and tables for outdoor dining.

Autumn pictured herself sitting in a chair, reading a good novel, as the sun danced on her skin, and the birds played carelessly in the bird bath across from her.

"Dude, this house is big," Rick said bluntly and Eric chuckled.

"Yes, it is quite the house," he admitted, still holding onto Autumn's hand tightly. "I am very lucky."

As they got closer to the house, Autumn could hear the faint sound of music, a swelling concerto, filtering through the open windows.

The song was hitting a crescendo, and Autumn listened, enthralled. It was beautiful.

"Is that classical music?" Mandy asked, crinkling her nose.

Eric grinned. "Yes it is."

He turned to Autumn. "I hope your friends weren't expecting some crazy rager. That really isn't my style."

Autumn arched an eyebrow. "What kind of party is this then?"

"A party where we can chat, share stories and laugh," he said. "Not the kind we *forget* in the morning."

Autumn frowned. "You think we drink?"

"Speak for yourself," Mandy said, waving a flask in Autumn's face. "I came prepared with provisions."

She took a long swig from the flask. "Anyone else want some?"

Eric stopped dead in his tracks and let go of Autumn's hand. Then he turned to Mandy, looking displeased.

"Amanda, please hand me the flask."

Mandy looked at him, confused. "Amanda?"

"That is your name isn't it?"

"Yes, but no one calls me that," she grumbled.

"The flask," Eric repeated sternly. "I will need to confiscate it."

Mandy crossed her arms over her chest, looking appalled.

"Isn't this supposed to be a party *dad*?" she asked scornfully.

"Yes, but no drinking," Eric said firmly.

Autumn looked at the others. Rick was standing back, his body language indicating he wasn't getting involved and Nathaniel looked utterly bored.

"Call me square, but we don't need booze to have fun Mandy. So please, if you want to enter my home, give me the flask," he put out his hand expectantly.

Mandy, who looked like she might explode from anger, began to tremble. She looked at Autumn for support, but she just shrugged helplessly.

"I'm sorry Mandy. It isn't my house."

"Just give it to him!" Nathaniel snapped, obviously frustrated. "His house, his rules Mandy!"

Autumn knew Mandy hated authority. She hadn't known her long, but she could tell that Mandy didn't like rules. She marched to the beat of her own drummer, even if that meant pissing people off. In some ways, Autumn admired that.

"Fine!" Mandy said, relenting and handing Eric the flask. "But I want it back when we leave! It's a family heirloom!"

Eric took the flask, smiling. "Not a problem. Thank you for being so cooperative Amanda."

Mandy groaned, looking defeated. "Stop that! Only my parents can call me Amanda!"

They continued walking, until they reached Eric's front porch. As they approached, a man, who looked to be in his seventies, opened two glass doors. Handsome, with silver fox hair and blue eyes, he was dressed in a tuxedo. He smiled at them warmly.

"Greetings everyone," he said, and then he looked at Eric. "Welcome back Mister Eric."

"Thank you Simon."

Eric began the introductions. Simon was Eric's family butler and close family friend. He had been with the King family since Eric was seven years old.

Autumn reached her arm out, glad to meet someone so close to Eric.

"Nice to meet you Simon," she said, shaking his hand.

"Likewise, my dear," he looked to Eric, the ghost of a smile on his face. "She is just as lovely as you proclaimed Mister Eric."

"Isn't she?" Eric said, looking at Autumn admiringly. He looked back at Simon.

"Simon, I left the gates open. Would you mind closing them?"

"Of course Mister Eric," he said. "It was a pleasure meeting you all. Please, enjoy your evening."

When Simon had left, Eric grabbed Autumn's hand again. She looked at him, beaming. He looked much cuter when he was smiling, and right now she couldn't imagine anyone calling him the prince of darkness.

"I would offer to give you guys a tour," he began.

"But that would take all night," Nathaniel offered.

Eric smirked. "What I was *going* to say was I would offer to give you guys a tour, but I'm sure you are anxious to get to the party."

"And the food!" Rick added.

Eric chuckled lightly. "Alright then. Let's go," he said and he motioned for everyone to follow him.

Eric's house was just as detailed on the inside as it was outside. It was decorated with rich tapestries, sculptures and art work.

Autumn wondered for a moment if she would be meeting his parents tonight. The thought made her nervous, but she pushed it away. She would cross that bridge when she got to it.

"Dude, we would need like, a golf cart to get around this place," Rick said, stunned. "And I thought my house was huge."

Eric guided them down a long hallway with white carpeting at their feet. Along the walls were old-fashioned, wrought-iron sconces, filled with elegant white candles that were lit. They casted eerie and disproportionate shadows of everyone as they moved.

"I really love candles," Eric admitted, looking over at Autumn. "They create such a beautiful atmosphere in any room."

Autumn heard Nathaniel snickering from behind her, but she ignored him.

Finally, they reached a hallway, where the sound of chattering echoed from an adjacent room. The music that had been playing in the foyer wasn't playing here. This music was more modern, and beyond the clamoring of people, she could vaguely make out eighties hits playing in the background.

Eric led everyone through two huge wooden doors that were open.

"This way," he said and they followed him inside.

The massive room reminded Autumn of a vintage ballroom. It had glinting, polished wooden floors, huge crystal chandeliers hanging from the vaulted ceiling, large windows and a classic balcony.

Autumn was breathless. It was like something out of a movie.

Around the room, people were huddled in groups, chatting and dancing. She looked around, scanning the crowds for familiar faces, but of the roughly forty people in attendance, she didn't recognize anyone. This didn't surprise her. Eric was a lone wolf at school. It wasn't like he was seen talking to anyone other than her in the halls.

"This *is* a classy setup, King," Mandy said, impressed.

"Yes. The flask would've stood out a little don't you think?" Eric grinned.

Mandy looked down at her outfit. "Because the leather dress and red sneakers don't stand out at all."

"Please allow me to get you all refreshments," Eric said. "There is punch, water, soda."

"And food?" Rick asked excitedly.

"Ah yes. There should be waiters walking around with trays of hors d'oeuvres."

"Sweet," Rick said, scanning the room. "I see one!" And he rushed off towards the waiter giddily.

"Nathaniel, why don't you come and help me with the drinks?" Eric asked.

Nathaniel shrugged. "Sure. Why not?"

Eric gave Autumn's hand a squeeze. "Don't go too far." And they headed off to a long banquet table set up at the end of the ballroom.

When they were out of earshot, Mandy smiled at Autumn, looking like the cat that swallowed the canary.

"Well, he has really taken a shine to you hasn't he?" she said, watching Eric and Nathaniel in the distance.

Autumn flushed. Eric was being very affectionate with her so far. That it could be this simple, that she liked him, and he liked her, was shocking to Autumn. It was never easy with the guys back home. They played games and courted five girls at once to see who the best choice was. It was a contest, and Autumn didn't want to be included.

"He seems to like me."

"Seems?" Mandy said incredulously. "The guy has practically melded his hand with yours. I say you are a shoo-in."

"What's going on with you and Nate?" Autumn asked, eager to change the subject. "You guys have been bickering all night."

"Yeah, he's a little crusty about you and Eric," Mandy admitted, looking sullen. "Truth be told, the guy has it bad for you Autumn. I don't stand a chance."

"Don't say that Mandy!" Autumn scolded her just as Rick returned. "You need to give him time. He will eventually see that I am not interested and move on."

Rick, who had his mouth and hands full, looked at Autumn, perplexed.

"Who? Nathaniel?"

Autumn nodded.

"I don't know. He has that creepy shrine of you and your hair in a glass jar," Rick said, looking distracted.

"What?" Both Autumn and Mandy exclaimed.

Rick chuckled. "It was a joke! Relax!"

"Not funny!" Autumn snapped just as Eric and Nathaniel came back with beverages.

"Here you are," Eric said, and he began handing out the drinks. "I see you guys haven't been mingling."

"We don't really know anyone here but you," Autumn admitted and Eric nodded.

"Fair enough. Allow me to get things rolling."

Eric began perusing the room and it took him a moment to find who he was looking for.

"There she is. Give me a moment."

And he was gone, moving across the room swiftly to retrieve the mystery person.

She? Autumn thought, and she felt a pang. *Perhaps it was his mother?*

"She?" Nathaniel said, echoing Autumn's thoughts. "Maybe Casanova has a girlfriend already?" he looked at Autumn, but she didn't flinch.

"That is doubtful. He has been all over Autumn tonight," Mandy said sharply.

Autumn watched as Eric approached two people conversing. One was male and the other female.

The girl was *definitely* not his mother. She was far too young. Autumn couldn't make out too many details from afar, but she could see the girl was very attractive.

Eric whispered something to the girl, who smiled politely and exited the conversation.

As they began walking over, Nathaniel sized her up.

"She is pretty," he said brusquely. "But not as pretty as you Autumn."

"You're an asshole," Mandy muttered to Nathaniel. Then she looked at Autumn sympathetically.

"She has nothing on you Aut."

"Maybe she is just a friend!" Rick piped in between bites of shrimp.

Autumn smiled gratefully. "Thanks guys."

Should she be worried? Eric never mentioned a girlfriend, but why would he? She hadn't asked him if he was single.

Autumn's stomach knotted up. She took a sip of her punch, willing herself to relax as Eric and the strange beauty approached them.

Up close, Autumn could see that the girl was indeed stunning. Her eyes were violet, her skin was bronzed, and she had perfect auburn curls framing her heart-shaped face.

She was tall and dressed in a strapless, black, maxi dress, with an amethyst amulet dangling down her chest.

"Everyone, I want to introduce you all," Eric began.

"To your very lovely girlfriend?" Nathaniel said hopefully.

The girl looked at Nathaniel appraisingly. "To his *sister* thank you."

Autumn felt relief sweep through her. She was his sister!

The girl turned to Eric, her face humorless. "Where did you find this pinhead Er?"

"We go to school together," Eric said, smirking.

"Ah yes," she looked at Nathaniel, unpleasantly. "Proof the education system is still working *wonders.*"

Nathaniel shot her a dirty look as Eric introduced her as his older sister, Arabella King. Everyone introduced themselves and when she got to Autumn, she looked her up and down, obviously scrutinizing her.

"Eric has told me about you. You just met right?"

Autumn nodded. "Yes. In English class."

"Well, you are every bit as gorgeous as Eric said," the girl smiled warmly. "But watch out for this one. He is quite the heartbreaker," she teased, nudging Eric in the side playfully.

"There isn't a girl in this room he *hasn't* been with."

Autumn's eyes went wide. Eric didn't seem like the type to *date* a lot, but when it came down to it, she barely knew him.

"Whoa dude," Rick said, in awe. "At school, you are like a total loser but outside of the halls you are like a scoring machine?"

"She is *kidding!*" Eric said, tugging at his sleeves uncomfortably. "Aren't you Ara?" he gave her a warning look.

Arabella took one look at Eric's annoyed expression and crumbled.

"I'm joking. I'm kidding. Really Autumn, he could use a girl in his life," she said. "All he does is read books. He is really quite boring."

"Ha!" Nathaniel chimed in.

"Sadly, that sounds more like me," Eric said, as he grabbed Autumn's hand again.

"Well Eric, if Autumn ever gets bored with you, as they say, there are plenty of fish in the sea," Nathaniel said, smirking.

"How profound," Arabella deadpanned.

She took a sip of her drink and began scanning the room. "Ah Eric. It looks like the same-old crowd here tonight. Mom and Dad would be proud."

"I thought so," Eric replied.

Autumn was relieved when the conversation with Eric's sister flowed so naturally. Though Nathaniel had managed to annoy her, she was very friendly and talkative. The six of them all sat chatting for most of the night, with Eric and Arabella introducing them to many of their friends and family. Autumn was disappointed Eric's parents weren't anywhere to be found. She was dying to meet them.

It wasn't until late into the evening that a couple arrived, that Arabella didn't seem particularly pleased to see.

Eric was telling a story about him and his sister getting lost together at the mall when they were children when Arabella interrupted him.

"Great," she said sarcastically.

Eric looked over at her, following her line of vision. Two people had just walked in. A girl, with blue eyes and long blonde hair. She wore red lipstick and a tight white evening gown. Escorting her was a guy with the same matching blonde hair, though his was cropped. He was guiding her through the throngs of people, dressed in a pair of tan slacks and a navy blue polo shirt with a matching blazer.

Arabella's purple eyes flashed with rage when she looked at Eric.

"You invited Bonnie and Clyde?" she said sharply.

Mandy looked over at the couple who made their way towards them now.

"Bank robbers are they?" Mandy chuckled.

"No," Eric replied. "Those are my cousins. I rarely see them, though they live fairly close."

"I call them Bonnie and Clyde because they are *always* together," Arabella said, eyebrows rising with meaning. "Partners in crime, if you get my drift."

"Stop gossiping Ara. That is sick," Eric said, admonishing his sister. "They aren't actually *together.*"

"No, but it wouldn't surprise me if one day I heard they had done the deed," Arabella said flatly.

"And here they come!"

The boy was the first to speak, as he reached out and shook Eric's hand.

"Eric," he said. "It's been awhile cuz."

Eric shook his hand. "It's been too long Caleb."

Arabella, making no attempt at hiding her discontent, sighed exasperatedly while standing up from her seat.

"Renee," she said, and the blonde girl grinned and pulled her into an embrace.

"Oh how I missed your suffocating bear hugs," Arabella muttered and the blonde girl giggled raucously.

"You are my favorite cousin Bell," she cooed.

Arabella pulled away abruptly. "Huh. I was almost certain I came in second to Caleb."

Renee ignored Arabella's jab. "And who might these people be? We saw you guys sitting together, looking thick as thieves."

"Do people still say that?" Arabella chimed in.

Eric looked at his sister disapprovingly.

"They are friends from school," Eric said, introducing them all.

"Well, it is a pleasure meeting you all," Renee said as she and Caleb took a seat.

"Can I get you something Renee? Caleb?" Eric offered.

"No thanks," Renee said. "But we do have some news."

"Let me guess. You guys are having a kid?" Arabella said dryly.

Caleb looked at his cousin, his smile strained.

"Good to see you haven't lost the King sense of humor," he said.

"The truth is, we didn't come here only for your party Eric."

"An ulterior motive? Well color me surprised," Arabella said. Eric shot her a daunting look.

"What Ara means is, you guys usually pass on my party invites," Eric said, clearly trying to keep things light.

"I know Eric and we are truly sorry. We have been quite busy of late," Renee said, crossing her legs.

"You guys get a lot of stupid homework too huh?" Rick asked between bites of pastries he snatched from a waiter.

"No, we travel frequently," Caleb said, smiling. "We are rarely home."

"Dude, that is pretty cool," Nathaniel said, turning to Eric. "Is *anyone* in your family poor?"

Eric ignored Nathaniel and focused on Caleb.

"So what is the news buddy?"

Caleb and Renee exchanged glances. Autumn didn't know why, but the way they looked at each other and the grimness in their eyes, set her on edge.

"Eric, we came to tell you we're going to the caves," Renee said finally.

"You can't be serious," Arabella said cuttingly.

Autumn looked at Eric. He hadn't said a word but she could see the color had been drained from his face. She squeezed his hand, urging him back to her, but he had shut down.

The caves? She racked her brain. Had Rick mentioned them before? The better question was, why did talk of these caves send Arabella into defense mode and plunge Eric into silence?

She had a feeling she was about to find out.

"Eric, please let us explain." Renee pleaded.

"What is there to explain?" Arabella asked, lips curled into a sneer. "You two are stupid. No explanation required!"

"Excuse me?" Renee shot back, but Arabella wasn't backing down.

"Seriously! Do you two think anything through or do you make all your life-altering decisions by flipping a coin? Heads we live! Tails we die!"

"Whoa!" Caleb said defensively. "That isn't fair Arabella! Are you two the only ones allowed to be the martyrs in this family?"

"How dare you!" Arabella said, standing up now, her voice rising with her. "How dare you come into *our* home, to *Eric's* party and act like this is *your* God-given right Caleb!"

Autumn looked at Eric. He was still silent, his eyes saying something and nothing all at the same time.

"Should we leave?" Mandy whispered to Autumn, her shoulders rigid with tension.

"No!" Arabella barked, looking to Mandy. "You guys shouldn't have to leave! It's these two that should go!"

Renee stood up, her blue eyes stony. She stepped towards Arabella until their faces were inches apart.

"We just want to avenge them Bell. You know what they meant to our parents, to us."

"Why the hell should you avenge anyone?" Arabella was shouting now. "You aren't the ones that deserve the revenge or the closure and you sure as hell aren't strong enough to handle what lies inside those cave walls!"

Autumn looked around. Arabella was louder than the music, and almost everyone in the room was intently watching Arabella and Renee now.

"You have no idea what she is capable of!" Caleb said, fuming.

"Other than following you around like a flying monkey?" Arabella said. "You mean she can do something else?"

"You are a bitch Arabella you know that?" Caleb said, standing up. "So high and mighty because you are the most powerful right? You surpassed everyone else, and you think that makes you queen of the castle."

"Dude, calm down!" Rick said, getting to his feet.

Nathaniel watched on helplessly as Mandy and Autumn exchanged troubled looks. They both knew this wasn't going to end well.

Autumn felt Eric's hand slip from hers. She watched as he stood up from his seat, his calmness being replaced by defiance.

"Rick, I got this," he said, patting Rick's shoulder. Rick nodded and sat back down, his jaw tight with agitation. Autumn smiled to herself. Rick was so loyal and protective of his friends. It was one of his best qualities.

"Caleb, watch the way you speak to my sister," Eric warned him.

"So he finally speaks!" Caleb said, throwing his hands in the air. "I suppose you are going to warn us too? Tell us whatever tricks you two have up your sleeves so we won't go."

Eric eyes didn't leave Caleb's.

"I have no intention of putting a damper on your adventure. You know the implications of what you are doing, and you sure as hell don't need me to remind you. So, if you two want to be the family heroes and go into those caves, I say, it is your heads on the chopping block, not ours."

Autumn listened to Eric's words trying to put everything together. Nothing sensible formed in her mind, no logical answers only questions. What were these caves? What revenge were they speaking of? This was all a puzzle to her, and she didn't have all the pieces yet.

"We have been researching Eric," Renee said, lowering her voice. It was obvious she didn't like the attention they were garnering. "We have been practicing, honing our craft, and we are ready."

"It doesn't matter how ready you feel Ren," Eric softened to her. *"They* exceled above us. They were so much more than I can even *fathom* being and yet here we are. Why risk your lives on a whim? Why not wait for us?"

"We aren't waiting anymore!" Caleb snapped.

"Caleb please, calm down," Renee pleaded.

"You know we have waited long enough! It has been years!" Caleb looked at Renee, rounding on her now. "What happened to them was an atrocity. The fact that no one has tried to even the score makes our family look pathetic and weak."

Autumn noticed other members of Eric's family were standing guard in case things escalated. Renee seemed to be trying to calm Caleb down and diffuse the hostility in the air.

"We have a plan in the works, a solid one. You just need to be patient and let it all play out," Eric said firmly. "Don't be so impulsive."

Caleb took a long, deep breath before speaking again.

"Eric," he said, appearing calmer now. "We aren't budging on this. We didn't come here to seek your approval. We just wanted to give you a heads up. This is *our* mission."

"Yeah a suicidal one," Arabella added in harshly. She stepped closer to Caleb, her face inches from his, her eyes menacing.

"You will be meeting your maker if you do this Caleb. Just don't try to take me or Eric down with you."

Before Caleb could respond, Arabella stormed off.

"Always with the theatrics that girl," Caleb frowned before turning back to Eric.

"We are doing this Eric. There is no maybe, no possibility of us changing our minds. You have been informed."

Caleb looked at the group of them.

"It was a pleasure meeting you all," he said, and then he turned and began walking towards the exit door.

Renee watched him go, but she didn't follow.

"Eric, please. Give us your blessing," she said, touching his forearm. "It would mean so much to me."

Eric's face was stony but when she touched his arm, it softened. It was obvious to Autumn. He cared greatly for these two people, and he didn't want to see either of them harmed.

"I can't give you that Renee. I have known you since we were kids. I don't want you to risk your life for revenge," Eric said. "There is no glory in being a legend when you are dead. You are far too young to end up like them. You know this is dangerous."

Renee's eyes brimmed with tears. "I know," she took a deep breath, wiping them away. "I just can't let him go alone. You have to understand."

Her head turned towards the ballroom's exit door, where Caleb stood patiently awaiting her, his arms crossed over his chest, his expression unreadable.

Renee moved towards Eric and pulled him into a hug.

"Don't Ren," he whispered, hugging her back tightly.

"In case we don't see each other again," she said. Autumn watched as she reached into her purse and handed Eric something. Eric squeezed whatever it was tightly in his palm.

"Renee, I can't," Eric said.

"Just take it," she said, placing her hand over his clenched fist. "Goodbye Eric."

She looked at Autumn and the others, forcing a weak smile.

"It was nice meeting you all," she said. "Sorry about the circumstances. Usually, we aren't so dramatic."

Renee headed towards the door, and Eric watched her go, still clenching whatever she had given him in his palm. His eyes filled with sorrow as her and Caleb disappeared from sight.

Autumn put her hand on Eric's shoulder and leaned towards him.

"What did she give you?" she asked gently.

Eric opened his hand. In his palm was a small, shiny, silver talisman.

Eric chuckled lightly at the sight of it. "She gave me her good luck charm."

7

It wasn't long after the incident with his cousins that Eric announced the party was over. He told everyone he appreciated them attending, but he was no longer in the celebrating mood. No one questioned it. They all abided Eric's wishes. They said their goodbyes, some commenting on the quarrel. Most were in favor of Eric.

"Caleb is making a huge mistake," one tiny blonde girl said. "Renee should know better not to follow Caleb's lead."

"We all know what happened that night," said one of Eric's male cousins. "This isn't history repeating. It is blatant ignorance."

When everyone had filed out, Autumn asked the others to wait for her while she talked to Eric alone for a moment.

"Seriously, I think I might get lost on the way out," Nathaniel admitted, looking embarrassed.

Mandy rolled her eyes. *"Oh no.* You are not stopping her goodnight kiss from happening!" She grabbed Nathaniel by the arm. "We are going! Now!"

"Night Eric!" she waved.

Eric waved back.

"Thanks for coming you guys!"

"Good luck," Mandy said to Autumn. "Though I doubt you'll need it."

Then she pulled Nathaniel, practically kicking and screaming, towards the door.

"Let me go you little brute!" Autumn heard Nathaniel's voice fading down the hall.

Rick approached Autumn. "I am going with them. We will be waiting for you, okay?"

Autumn nodded. "Thanks Ricky."

Rick gave Eric a nod and headed out.

As soon as everyone was gone, Eric moved towards Autumn. She took a deep breath. She felt awkward, like she had just witnessed a very private moment she shouldn't have seen with Eric and his family.

"Eric, I had so much fun tonight," Autumn said as he approached and Eric smirked.

"You are a terrible liar Autumn," he said. "You get this twitch in your left eye. Your own tell. It's adorable."

Autumn crossed her arms over her chest defensively.

"Sorry. What did you want me to say? It was an amazing party until your cousin went berserk over something I don't even understand?"

"Fair enough," Eric said. "I have to say, this is not the impression I wanted to make on you tonight."

Autumn shrugged. "It wasn't your fault Eric. Besides, I have seen people acting worse. Trust me."

"Well, there is much more to the story than you heard," Eric admitted, hands in his pockets.

Autumn frowned. She could tell by Eric's tone he wasn't going to tell her what the fight was *really* about.

"You aren't going to explain it to me are you?" she asked.

"Not yet. I am going to let this one simmer," he grinned. "Keep the air of mystery and all that."

Autumn stepped closer to him, smiling.

"There is nothing more compelling," she teased and Eric leaned into her.

"I thought so," he said,and he touched her face with his hands. Gently he trailed his fingers along her jaw line, then her lips.

Autumn tilted her head up, beckoning him to kiss her. He didn't disappoint as he leaned down and pressed his lips against hers. Autumn was lightheaded, and she wrapped her arms around him to steady herself. He pulled her closer to him, his hands on her waist now as their lips moved in harmony.

Autumn's heart raced as she breathed him in, his scent of cologne and soap. He moved his hands through her hair and down her back, and she sighed feeling his mouth open against her own.

Minutes passed before they finally pulled away. Both were breathless and Eric looked at her beaming.

"Wow," Autumn managed. "That was ..."

"Wow indeed," Eric muttered. "So you are beautiful, smart *and* a great kisser. Remind me again why you are single?"

"I must have some horrible secret huh?" she joked.

Eric shrugged. "I doubt it but if you do, after that kiss, let me say, whatever you're hiding I can live with it."

Autumn wanted to stay in this state of bliss forever. She forgot about the post-kiss endorphin rush. She knew she was grinning like a fool, and her face was flushed. Eric was relaxed, but she could see through it. He was resisting the temptation to kiss her again. Instead, he grabbed her hand, linking his fingers with hers.

"I want you to know, I will explain everything to you in due time," he said. "I just need time to take in what happened tonight."

"I understand," Autumn said. "Take your time. However, I want you to know, you can talk to me when you're ready Eric. You can trust me."

Eric smiled at her, his teeth showing. This was a rarity, and it made her heart flutter.

"I know I can trust you Autumn. I wouldn't have kissed you otherwise sweetheart."

As they walked down the corridor towards the front door, Autumn looked around. On the walls were elaborate paintings of landscapes, ancient castles and hooded figures.

A nagging thought tugged at her brain, and she couldn't ignore it. Did Eric's family harbor a dark secret?

Who were the people being avenged? Retribution seemed like a notion made for movies or television.

Her mind ran wild with possibilities. One question led to another so easily that Autumn had to stop them from overrunning her mind. As Eric walked with her to meet her friends, her only thoughts were of him. She wanted to revel in this moment of happiness, not ruin it with confusion and doubt. What people said about Eric couldn't be true right? He wasn't really trouble was he?

Autumn said goodbye to Eric and went to meet up with Rick and the others. As soon as they were off Eric's property and safely in the car, the questions began. Everyone was talking at once, excitedly discussing everything that had happened.

"What the hell was that?" Mandy asked. "I cannot believe those cousins of Eric's! I mean sure, every family has their issues but causing a scene at a party? Awkward doesn't begin to describe it," she said. "Though I have to say, for an arrogant ass, Caleb was smoking hot."

Autumn turned from the passenger seat to look at Mandy, who was sitting in the back with Nathaniel.

"I think you are barking up the wrong tree there Mandy. Arabella was insinuating that Renee and Caleb are kissing cousins."

"I doubt that," Rick added, as he stopped at a yellow light. "But there *was* something definitely off about those two."

Autumn looked to Rick, who was steadfastly watching the road in the darkness.

"Rick you have lived here forever. What are the caves?"

"To be honest, I know very little about them Aut."

"They are haunted!" Nathaniel piped in. "That is what my brother Conrad told me. He and his biker friends go down there sometimes to drink and shoot the shit."

Mandy looked at Nathaniel in disbelief. "Conrad? *Really?*"

Nathaniel gave her a dirty look. "It is a family name."

"One of Conrad's buddies, Slick," Nathaniel went on.

Mandy smirked but said nothing this time.

"He said people go missing in the caves all the time. Even the cops are too scared to go near them."

"That doesn't say much dude. Most of the cops around here wouldn't step out of their clown cars if it meant facing any real danger," Rick muttered.

Autumn frowned.

"So Renee and Caleb are going there to do what exactly? To get revenge on the ghosts that apparently haunt these caves?"

"Who knows?" Rick said. "Now please stop fidgeting Aut. You are making me nervous."

"Dude! I just got an *awesome* idea!" Nathaniel said suddenly.

"Well there is a first time for everything I guess," Mandy deadpanned.

"What if we go to the caves and get footage *there* for your class project Rick?"

Autumn turned forward again and looked at Rick's face for a reaction. She saw nothing but an expression of intense concentration. He was focused on driving, and she couldn't blame him.

It was pitch-black out.

"I don't know man," Rick said finally, sounding hesitant. "All the legends about that place …"

"Are probably all myths and besides," Nathaniel said. "If we can get video proof of something out there we would be famous dude! And you would totally ace your project!"

Rick looked like he was pondering this. Autumn knew he didn't have much time left. The video was due soon and like most things, Rick had procrastinated filming at the skate park. He was probably getting pretty desperate.

"We don't even have to go into the caves. We will just roam around outside them," Nathaniel said, trying to sway Rick.

"So apparently we aren't going to heed Eric's warnings about the caves being dangerous?" Autumn stated the obvious. "He was pretty distraught about his cousins going."

"What does Eric King know?" Nathaniel said, grimacing.

"He is the prince of darkness, remember?" Mandy said sarcastically. "Come on Nathaniel. You are just jealous."

"That Eric looks better in black eyeliner than me?" he quipped.

"No you halfwit," Mandy said. "That he likes Autumn. I mean, he gave her a kiss on the forehead before we left."

"So? My mom kisses my forehead before I leave for school in the morning. It doesn't mean she likes me!" Nathaniel pointed out.

Mandy sighed, frustrated.

"Autumn's messy hair, the googly eyes Eric was giving her. You didn't see it? I'd wager Eric didn't just kiss her on the *forehead* Nate."

Autumn felt her face heat up and she was glad it was dark inside the car.

"Enough Mandy," Rick said, mercifully changing the subject. "I think going to the caves, as long as we don't go inside them, is fine."

Autumn didn't like this idea at all. "Is it even worth it Rick?"

"What do you mean?"

"Catching the supernatural on film isn't easy Rick. Most things that go bump in the night like to keep a low profile. Besides, you guys said yourself this is all hearsay, so if you leave with no footage, then what?"

"Then I go back to plan A. Filming at the skate park."

Autumn shifted in her seat, trying to get comfortable. "And why are we going with plan B if plan A is the safest bet?"

"Because," Rick said glancing at Autumn for a split-second. "I want to film something intriguing and something unique."

Autumn closed her eyes and took a deep breath. She knew trying to change Rick's mind was a fruitless endeavor. He was as stubborn as her when he set his mind on something.

"So it's settled. We will go tomorrow night," Rick said.

8

When Autumn awoke Saturday morning, it wasn't to the usual sound of her alarm blaring loudly. Instead, she heard birds chirping through her open window and rain drops gently pattering against the pane. She turned over and looked at her cell phone.

It was nine in the morning. She snuggled deeper in the blankets, enjoying two thoughts: She could sleep in all day if she wanted, and she had made it through her first week at Whitan High. Eventually, her mind drifted lazily to thoughts of Eric, the caves and last night's events.

Autumn wasn't even aware she had fallen back asleep until she heard a knock at her door. She sat upright in the bed, fixing her hair.

"Hello?" she said groggily.

"Hey Aut," Rick said perkily through the door. He had obviously been awake awhile.

"Can I come in?"

Autumn pulled the blankets up to her chest.

"Sure."

Rick opened the door slowly and stepped in.

"Hey," he said. "You were still sleeping?"

Today he was wearing a navy blue hoodie and jeans. He looked tired, like he hadn't slept well.

"It's Saturday. We didn't get in until late last night."

Rick nodded. "To be honest, I couldn't stop thinking about the caves all night."

As he walked towards Autumn, she noticed he was carrying a large black backpack.

She arched her eyebrows.

"We don't have school today."

"I know," he said as he sat the backpack at the foot of Autumn's bed. Autumn felt the mattress sink a little under its weight. "I spent most of the night researching online."

Autumn couldn't help it. She was stunned. Rick was voluntarily researching something? She blinked.

"Really?"

Rick rolled his blue eyes. "Don't look so surprised. Someone had to do it."

Autumn glanced at the black backpack again.

"So what the hell is in there?"

Rick's face lit up with excitement. "What *isn't* in the bag is the better question," Rick began unzipping it.

"Supplies for tonight of course."

"Supplies?" Autumn looked at him blankly.

Rick nodded, and Autumn watched as he started to pull out a few things. She had to admit she was intrigued.

Rick held up a variety of survival basics for her approval.

"A compass, flashlights, a map of the area, extra batteries," he began.

"Well, at least we'll be prepared," Autumn said.

"Oh, it gets better." He dug deeper in the backpack and pulled out a large bag of salt, jiggling it meaningfully.

"To keep the ghosts at bay," he said, his voice lowered secretively.

Autumn couldn't help herself. She chuckled. "Are we going to season them first?"

"I read it online. Ghosts hate salt," Rick frowned.

"Oh Ricky," Autumn said, as she got out of her bed and began stretching. "I doubt we are running into anything out there tonight."

Autumn said the words trying to convince herself, but she felt nagging doubt in the back of her mind when she thought of the fight Eric and his cousins had. If there *wasn't* something in those caves, why would Eric and his sister be so distraught?

"Better safe than sorry right?" Rick said as he reached back into the bag, pulling out a large Catholic bible.

"No matter *what* we run into, reading a passage from the bible always fights off the evil stuff in the movies."

Autumn patted Rick on the shoulder, grinning. "Well, you have all the bases covered Rick," she admitted.

He looked proudly at his stash strewn out on Autumn's bed. "I know. We also need to make a stop today at the church downtown."

Autumn scrunched her face. "What for?"

"Holy water of course," Rick said.

"Can Nathaniel even enter a church?" Autumn joked.

"Oh and I almost forgot," Rick said, pulling out two curved daggers. "Check these out."

They glimmered in the light shining through Autumn's window. The handles were slate grey, and the blades were razor sharp. Their harsh edges glinted menacingly.

"Most ghosts aren't corporal," Autumn said, examining the daggers.

Rick looked at her blankly. "Meaning?"

"Meaning, it may be hard to shank them Rick."

Rick nodded slowly. "They aren't for the ghosts. During my research, I found stories online. The ghosts weren't the only things people claimed to have seen in the caves."

He carefully handed Autumn a dagger. She took it hesitantly. A weapon felt foreign in her hands, almost uncomfortable.

"I have never used a dagger before," she admitted.

"It's simple. Just stab whatever attacks you." Rick pantomimed a stabbing motion with his empty hand.

Autumn stared at the dagger. She knew Rick had quite the intense sword collection in his basement, but she wasn't aware of him owning any other blades.

"Where did you get the daggers from?" she asked, handing the weapon back to him.

"Nathaniel," Rick said, his eyes gleaming with mischievousness. "He has connections."

Autumn looked at Rick in disbelief. "So you tried setting me up with a petty criminal?"

"No! It's his brother, Conrad. He's in a biker gang. They run a huge part of town. So getting weapons is usually pretty easy for him."

"That is *wonderful* to know," Autumn said sarcastically. "Anything else in the bag of tricks?"

"Nope. That's everything. Well, there is my camera. So I can record everything," Rick said. "I even have an attachment for it. I can mount it to my head. Mom and dad got it for me for Christmas, so I could record my skateboarding from every angle."

As Autumn was listening to Rick, apprehension suddenly came over her. Were they making a huge mistake thinking all the cave rumors were fiction? Were they foolishly walking into a trap?

Rick, who had begun packing up the supply bag, looked over at her, his brow furrowed. He could always tell when something was bothering her.

"Autumn, what's that look for?" Rick asked, scrutinizing her.

She sat down on the edge of the bed and watched Rick put everything back into the backpack.

"You heard Eric last night," she said. "From what I gathered, being anywhere near those caves is dangerous."

Rick didn't say anything. Instead, he continued putting items into his bag until he was finished.

Autumn sighed, standing up. She began pacing the length of her room, frustration overwhelming her.

Why wasn't Rick listening to her? She knew if Eric was here, he would be admonishing them both for planning to visit the caves.

"Hello? Earth to Rick! Aren't you even the least bit worried?"

Rick walked over to her and placed his hands squarely on her shoulders, effectively stopping her from moving. His blue eyes met her green ones.

"Nope."

"Of course not," Autumn said sardonically. "Why worry? It's only our lives on the line!"

"Autumn, I am not going to let anything happen to you," Rick began, his eyes fixed on hers.

"I can take care of myself!" Autumn said obstinately, and Rick laughed.

"You are still stubborn. Glad to see that hasn't changed."

"I just see this as our epic adventure," he went on. "Life is ordinary. So, if we can spend one night chasing *ghosts,* I say, we are only young once. Let's be a little reckless."

Autumn tried her best to be somber but she couldn't help but smile. Hearing Rick talk about the caves like they were harmless, made her worries seem a little silly. She couldn't forget Eric and Arabella's warnings to Renee and Caleb, but they weren't going *into* the caves. They would just be outside them.

"So, are we going to do this or what?" Rick asked hopefully. "Then we can look back on our adventures when we are old and grey and being reckless is lawn bowling after taking our medication."

Autumn chuckled at the image in her head. Rick with graying curls and her wearing a floral granny dress as they tried their best to knock over pins. It was quite the mental picture.

"Fine. We can go but we shouldn't stay long. We get some footage and go, no tempting the fates," Autumn reasoned. "And no going inside the caves. Deal?"

Rick nodded, looking relieved. "Deal. I really want to get an A on this first assignment," he admitted. "Besides, it could all be myths and legends right?"

Rick spoke optimistically but even his voice harbored uncertainty.

The logical part of Autumn's brain told her it was ridiculous.

Evil entities lurking in caves? It was preposterous.

People could be evil, evil of the worst kind; she knew *that* for a fact. There was nothing more real than the evil that resided in the hearts of mankind.

As for vampires, ghosts and werewolves being real? Those creatures were myths, and their stories were mere fables.

Supernatural creatures were a part of many things: fiction books, horror movies and tales spoken around campfires. The one thing they weren't a part of was real life.

"It could all be just tales or maybe not," Autumn answered Rick's lingering question. "But we'll see for ourselves soon enough."

9

utumn was relieved when Nathaniel arrived at around eight
to pick her and Rick up. She spent most of the day climbing
the walls, and she couldn't relax. Now her fears had been
pushed to the back of her mind, and her adrenaline was pumping.

She just wanted to get this excursion over and done with.

Eric sent her a text message around five o'clock asking her if
she was busy. She told him she was going to Mandy's for the night.
Instantly, she felt terrible for lying to Eric, but she knew she couldn't
tell him the truth. The caves were a touchy subject for Eric, and she
didn't want him worrying about her.

Autumn was pulling on a pair of boots when she heard honking
outside. She looked up at Rick.

"That's Nate," he said, strapping on his backpack.

Autumn glanced once more around the empty house. Rick's
parents were gone on a business trip, and she was grateful they didn't
have to explain what they were doing tonight.

There was a knock at the door, and Rick opened it just as Autumn
finished fastening her boots.

"Hey man," Rick said as Nathaniel stepped in.

"What's up dude?"

Nathaniel, who was dressed in a black hoodie and jeans, glanced at Autumn quickly before looking away.

It was apparent he was still annoyed with her for running off with Eric last night.

"Hey Nate," she smiled brightly at him, a peace offering. She pulled on her grey pea coat and began buttoning it. "How are you?"

"Ready for a night of adventure." Nathaniel said, eyes on the ceiling.

Rick looked to Autumn expectantly. "Ready?"

"Ready."

They all headed out the door, and the cool air hit Autumn like a ton of bricks. Fall was here, and summer was long gone. The chill indicated that much. She looked up the sky. It was starless, and the moon was barely visible. The image was almost foreboding, and it sent chills down her spine.

When they reached the driveway, they saw a strange vehicle parked there. It was a large, white, nondescript van.

"Where did you get the wheels?" Autumn asked Nathaniel, inspecting the tinted windows.

"Conrad. It was his before he bought his hog," Nathaniel said, looking proud.

"Well, at least it's inconspicuous," Autumn said encouragingly. "Shall we go pick up Mandy?"

"Your chariot waits," he said, gesturing to the vehicle.

Autumn waited as Rick slid the back door open for her, and she slipped inside. He pulled the door shut and hopped into the passenger seat next Nathaniel. Autumn fastened her seatbelt as Nathaniel adjusted his seat.

"Alright guys, let's roll out," Nathaniel said with his usual cheerfulness. He started the engine, turned around in his seat and looked to Autumn.

She blinked at him, confused. "Is something wrong?"

"Are you sure you wouldn't rather ride up front with me?" He winked at her, his eyes glimmering.

So he hasn't given up, Autumn thought to herself.

"I'm good back here but thanks for asking," she said, smirking.

Nathaniel sighed disappointedly and began pulling out of the driveway.

"Don't be down man. She just didn't want to spend the entire ride having her breasts stared at," Rick said, nudging Nathaniel in the side playfully.

Nathaniel let out a snort as he drove towards the main road.

"There's always the rear-view mirror buddy."

It took them ten minutes to get to Mandy's place. When they pulled up, they saw her waiting on the sidewalk in front of her house. She was wearing tight blue jeans, a black tank top and a brown bomber jacket. She walked over to the van and opened the sliding door.

"Hey all," she said, smiling.

Everyone said their hellos, and they were off again. As they trucked along, there was a piercing silence in the van. All Autumn could hear was the faint sound of the radio humming and traffic passing by. She wondered if everyone in the van was feeling as anxious as she was. Were their stomachs in knots? Did they feel the incessant tugging in their brains telling them this was a mistake?

"So, Rick do you have any idea what you are going to shoot?" Mandy asked, her voice slicing through the quiet.

"Shoot? I have no guns here Mand, only daggers," Rick replied absently.

"I meant with your *camera,*" Mandy said, her eyes wide. "Wait. You brought daggers with you?"

Rick looked at her like *she* was the crazy one. "Of course. I have a whole kit. Salt, holy water, crosses." He looked at her indignantly.

"Holy water?" Mandy said, bewildered. "You just happened to have some around the house?"

"No. Autumn and I went to a church today and got some," Rick said. "They were more than accommodating."

"Well, at least you have all the clichés covered Rick," Mandy muttered, looking to Autumn, her eyebrows raised.

For the next hour of their journey, Autumn watched out the window. They passed by huge fields with old wooden fences, rickety barns and lush farm land. Eventually, they came to a large area, on the right side of the dirt road. The parking lot near it was virtually deserted.

As they pulled into the lot, Autumn saw the blanket of darkness ahead of them. The only light was generated from the moon, which had finally come out and the streetlamps in the parking lot.

The van came to a gentle halt, and Nathaniel cut the engine. Without the humming of the motor, everything around them became more desolate and eerie. Autumn couldn't help it. She shivered as the sensations danced over her skin.

"What does *haunted* caves really mean?" Mandy spoke finally, her voice almost inaudible.

The atmosphere around the van was quickly changing. It felt like a hand was pulling them, beckoning them into the depths of oblivion. Autumn felt the sudden need to run. Was this her gut instinct kicking in? Was this her body warning her it wasn't safe here?

"The impression Eric and Arabella gave me is, whatever lurks in the caves is tangible," Autumn replied. Mandy's heart-shaped face was filled with uncertainty.

"Tangible?" Rick repeated.

"Physical," Autumn replied. "Something you can actually touch."

"Most ghosts aren't like that," Mandy added in. "Well, at least that's how the legend portrays them. As transparent beings we can only see."

"I'm not worried. We're prepared for *anything,*" Nathaniel looked at Rick and the two girls. "I like tangible. Tangible things can be stabbed."

A look of concern flashed across Rick's face.

"What if they *aren't* ghosts? What if they are zombies and they try to eat our brain's dude?" he looked at Nathaniel, eyes wide.

Mandy snorted. "They are going to be sorely disappointed with that buffet."

Nathaniel shot Mandy a glare. "I'll have you know *Mandy* that I happen to get A's in school."

Mandy rolled her eyes. "In gym you mean? Or Home Ec?"

"In many of my classes," he said haughtily. "That's right. *A's*. Like your bra size."

Nathaniel began guffawing and held his hand out to Rick for a high-five. Rick put his hand up and looked at Autumn, who scowled at him, unimpressed.

"Don't even bother Rick," she scolded him, and he put his hand down, looking mildly terrified.

"Sorry dude," he looked at Nathaniel helplessly.

Mandy grunted with anger as she unbuckled her seatbelt. Then she reached over and smacked Nathaniel sharply.

"OUCH!" he exclaimed, rubbing the back of his head while glowering at Mandy. "If you keep hitting me in the head you will knock the smarts right out of me Mandy!"

"That ship has long sailed!" Mandy barked. "Now, apologize!"

"Yeah, yeah, I'm sorry," Nathaniel said, massaging his own head.

When Autumn stepped outside, it seemed much colder than it had been earlier. Autumn shivered and snuggled into her pea coat.

She looked at the huge open field that spanned out miles ahead of her. On the left side of the field, she could see masses of pine trees clustered together, making up the forest Nathaniel mentioned at one point.

Everyone made their way from the parking lot into the field where Rick handed them flashlights from his giant backpack.

"Alright. We're all set," he said, adjusting the camera attached to his baseball cap. "Remember, everyone sticks together. Got it?"

Everyone nodded their approval, and they began trekking.

The first thing Autumn noticed as they moved through the tall grass, was all the obstacles at her feet. She was constantly avoiding rocks, wayward branches and other natural debris.

Autumn thought about Eric, and she couldn't help but feel a pinch of guilt that she was doing this behind his back. Eric had said the caves were dangerous and yet, here she was. In an attempt at clemency, she told herself that when she returned, she would be honest with Eric. He deserved that much.

They had been walking roughly fifteen minutes when Autumn felt an odd sensation. It took her a moment to realize that the hairs on the back of her neck were standing up.

She stopped dead in her tracks, so abruptly that Nathaniel nearly ran into her.

He looked around, searching for an explanation as to why she froze.

"What is it?" he asked. Mandy and Rick watched her on bated breath.

"I don't know," she said as she shone her flashlight ahead of her, trying to find a reason for her panic.

"I just had this awful feeling come over me."

Rick netted his brow with concern.

"Do you want to go back?"

Autumn knew how much filming here meant to Rick. Despite her doubts, she couldn't let him down. She had to push through her fears. They were irrational anyway, probably just nerves.

"We came all this way. We might as well keep going right?" she said, forcing a weak smile.

Rick put his hands on Autumn's shoulders, squeezing them reassuringly.

"Are you sure?"

Autumn nodded. "Let's keep going but if we see anything peculiar, we turn around."

Everyone began walking through the field again, with everybody on guard, looking for any strange activity.

After another ten minutes of trudging through the grass, they halted again. This time, it was Rick who stopped.

"What is it Rick?" Autumn began.

She saw the look of determination on his face and felt his arm shoot out in front of her protectively.

She followed his line of vision with her flashlight.

In the middle of the field sat the enormous, land traversing, cave.

The grey, jagged rocks that shaped it, blended into the pitch-black night, making it seem looming and endless. Around its edges were tangled vines and overgrown moss.

Autumn glanced inside the caves gaping mouth and saw pure darkness.

With her eyes, she could see the cave itself was harmless. It was just another part of nature, a benign patch of earth's mosaic.

It was the energy that radiated from inside it that sent shivers down her back. She couldn't ignore the feeling of doom washing over her. Alarm bells were ringing in her head, and she wanted to run but she stood there fixated, staring at the cave. She couldn't look away, entranced by it.

Rick's worried face was suddenly inches from hers.

"Aut? Hello?" he said, concerned. "Autumn, are you in there?"

Autumn felt her focus slowly shifting to Rick, like he was breaking a trance.

"Of course I am here. Where else would I be?"

"We were all talking to you and you just like, zoned out," Rick said, looking relieved. "Are you alright?"

Autumn looked around. Mandy and Nathaniel were on either side of her, looking apprehensive.

"I can *feel* the evil coming from inside the cave. Being outside it isn't even safe," Autumn said.

She was aware how foolish it sounded when she said it aloud, and immediately she felt ridiculous. She sounded like a raving lunatic.

"I know Autumn. I'm getting bad juju too," Nathaniel said, looking from her to the cave and back again.

"So it's settled. Let's go back," Rick said finally.

"What about your project dude?" Nathaniel asked, as they turned around and began retreating. "You wanted to have the best one in the class remember?"

"I will figure something out," Rick replied casually. He looked back at Autumn who shuffled along, trying her best to subside her panic.

"If Autumn says something isn't right, we should listen."

"Oh *now* we are listening to her!" Mandy said, rolling her eyes. "The poor girl has been warning us all night. Even Eric wouldn't set foot here, and that is saying something."

Autumn shivered as her body was racked with chills. Rick offered her his jacket.

"I'm fine, but thanks," she whispered, and he took her hand into his, smiling warmly.

"Nothing bad is going to happen to you Aut. I'm here with you," he reassured her. "Soon, we will be home, safe and sound."

He didn't let go of her hand as they all walked through the field, making their way back to the parking lot. The further they were from the caves, the more relaxed Autumn felt, like prey finally outrunning the predator. It was like freedom was on the cusp, so close she could touch it.

The wind began picking up rapidly, whipping around them, howling into the belly of the night. Autumn pulled her pea coat closer to her. She looked up at the sky again. The stars were missing, like a strand of lights with all the bulbs burnt out.

She didn't like it at all.

"You scared me. You weren't answering at first," Rick spoke suddenly, his voice trembling. "I thought maybe a cave ghost had possessed you."

Autumn quivered involuntarily at the thought. "Nope. I am still me."

The further they moved from the caves, the better it felt. The dread Autumn felt, slowly siphoned away.

It wasn't until they were almost halfway to the car that Autumn felt a shift. The energy around her changed and she became hyper aware of everything around her.

Her stomach clenched as the familiar terror gripped her tightly in its grasp.

She stopped and let go of Rick's hand.

"Guys," she said warily. She desperately looked around for the source of her trepidation, but she saw nothing. It was all blackness and patches of light from her flashlight.

"Why are we stopping now?" Rick asked evenly, but his voice betrayed him. He was worried. "We are almost there."

Autumn opened her mouth to reply, but the words wouldn't come. Her heart raced as panic ran rampantly through her. She didn't know *why* she was scared. The caves were long behind them now.

"Something isn't right," she said, her breath coming quickly. She felt beads of sweat trickle down her neck, despite the wind's chill brushing against her skin.

"Autumn, relax. We are safe now," Nathaniel said gently.

"She is sweating profusely and her face is white as a sheet," Mandy looked her over, her mouth a fretful line. "We need to get her to the van *now.*"

"Autumn, breathe," Rick said as he touched her back gently. Autumn did as she was instructed. She breathed in and out.

Again, she scanned the darkness anxiously, but saw nothing. The field was deserted except the four of them in the middle of it. The tall grass swayed, and the wind howled frantically like an alarm. She could feel a scream building up inside her throat, threatening to escape her lips.

"We are far enough away from the caves Aut. Nothing can hurt us now," Rick started but Autumn shook her head.

"It doesn't matter. As long as we are *here*, we aren't safe. We are being hunted."

They all stood there, terrified, uncertain and unable to move.

We are like sitting ducks, Autumn thought ominously.

"We need to keep moving!" Rick instructed.

Then Autumn heard it, piercing and loud.

Alien sounds, echoing in the dead of the night.

Guttural cries rang out, and they were close. So much so, they sounded like they came from beside them.

Autumn shone her flashlight around frantically but came up empty. All four of them looked around, but no one saw anything. It was dark and the night was a shroud, and Autumn knew what hunters would think of them.

Easy prey, she thought, and she didn't need light to know. It wasn't a person making the sounds. These noises were inhuman. Wild and frenzied, like a caged animal that was imprisoned and had just been set free.

10

"What was that?" Mandy asked, her eyes darting around. There was still no sign of anything in the pitch-black night.

Rick pulled Autumn closer to him as he reached into his bag of supplies.

"Nathaniel! Protect Mandy!"

"How misogynistic of you Rick," Mandy said, crossing her arms over her chest.

"Dude! What are you doing?" Nathaniel asked.

"I'm getting a weapon!" Rick said as he riffled through his backpack.

Nathaniel's eyes widened. "What kind of weapon? The salt, the holy water, or the daggers?"

"I don't know!" Rick said absently.

Finally, he decided on the daggers and handed one to Nathaniel.

"Where's mine?" Mandy asked indignantly, hands on her hips. "I can probably handle whatever is coming better than you two can."

"I didn't know you would want one!" Nathaniel said. "Besides, that's all my brother could get his hands on in such short notice."

Mandy looked from Nathaniel to Rick, her face red with anger.

"What did you think? Autumn and I wanted to stand back helplessly while you guys valiantly saved us?"

"Yes!" Rick said without hesitation. "That was the idea exactly! Now be quiet!"

They stood in silence, listening for more strange noises. Autumn looked around her and despite the fear dancing wildly inside her, she couldn't help but crack a smile at the image of Rick clutching a dagger.

It wasn't long before the noise sounded again, this time louder and more animalistic. Whatever it was, it was getting closer.

The panic inside Autumn reached a fever pitch, and she felt like she was trapped in a nightmare.

She commanded herself to wake up, but she couldn't.

She was stuck in a maze of horror and fear, and she couldn't escape.

"We should go," Autumn said through rapid breaths. "I don't want to see what's coming."

Everyone seemed to agree on this course of action, so they began moving swiftly through the field, towards the parking lot. The four of them sprinted, dodging the rocks wedged in the earth and plant limbs that were scattered throughout the grass.

As Autumn ran, she heard rustling sounds nearby. Flashlight still in hand, she glanced around her and saw nothing.

Rick grabbed her hand as they ran through the field with Nathaniel and Mandy. The wind whipped in Autumn's face, leaving her breathless and gasping for air.

She glanced up at the sky to see the clouds covering the moon menacingly. She could see the light coming from the parking lot in the distance. The white van beckoned to her, promising comfort and safety.

Then she saw something up above. It jumped over her, like she was a hurdle. It was so many feet above her that it wasn't even *close* to clipping her head.

"Guys!" she yelled and pointed at the sky. "Look! Above us!"

Everyone looked up to the heavens just as the figure cleared them, landing in their path, with a loud thump.

"Where the hell did that come from?" Mandy asked, sounding eerily calm.

"Behind us," Autumn replied. "It jumped over us."

"Holy shit," Nathaniel muttered. "What is it?"

"It has to be an animal," Mandy reasoned. "Right?"

"What kind of *animal* can jump that high Mandy?" Nathaniel asked.

"We need to move, now!" Rick ordered.

It was too late. The figure stood between them and freedom. It was crouched and ready to spring, blocking their escape. It growled menacingly, sounding like no animal Autumn had ever heard before.

Autumn tried to see its features, but the darkness hid its appearance. She didn't dare to use her flashlight. She didn't need to see its face, to know it wasn't peaceful. She knew instinctively they were all in serious danger.

The sudden movement of the figure made Autumn jump back.

Rick stood in front of her, taking his protective stance. Mandy joined him, and together they looked like trained martial artists.

With her tiny frame and pixie-like features, Mandy seemed harmless. However, there was something in her eyes that Autumn hadn't seen before. It was steely resolve. She would fight and win, at any cost.

"Let's see your face," Rick said, raising his flashlight and shining it on the ominous figure.

Autumn gasped. It was so horrific. She couldn't believe her eyes.

She felt a scream of pure terror escape her mouth.

It was something inhuman, something not even animal.

It was a monster.

The creature hissed wildly in the bright light. It had normal limbs but it was clearly deformed. Its yellow eyes were huge and bugling. Its skin was covered in pustules. It had no mouth. Instead, there was a giant gaping hole, encumbered with rows of razor-sharp teeth. Its hands and feet were webbed and clawed.

The way it moved was feral and Autumn could see its muscles tensing as it watched them, the veins in its arms protruding.

"What the hell?" Rick said shakily, not taking his eyes off the monster. "It can't be. It isn't human."

He glanced at Nathaniel, who shrugged his shoulders.

"Dude, I don't know *what* it is," he said, his jaw tense. "But I don't think it's a ghost."

The creature leapt closer to them, reminding Autumn of a frog trying to capture a delicious fly.

It watched them hungrily, its eyes darting back and forth quickly.

Autumn struggled to accept what was right in front of her.

She couldn't trust her own eyes.

Whatever this thing was, it wasn't of this earth. It was evil and dark, and she wanted no part of it.

"We need to go," Autumn stammered. "EVERYONE, RUN!"

And she was off, feet pounding on the ground, dashing across the field, as she attempted to escape.

Suddenly, the creature let out a deafening screech, and it began chasing her. She tried to outrun it, but it was no use. It was too quick. It wasn't long before Autumn felt its scaly hands grabbing her and pulling her in. Her body tensed as the creature snagged her in its grasp.

"Autumn!" She heard Rick bellow. She could see his face, and he was terrified.

The thing gripped her tightly in its arms, and she could feel its skin, slimy and cold against her. She looked down at her arms. She was cut where the creature had torn her coat with its sharp claws.

She was hardly able to breathe as it blew its hot, putrid breath on the back of her neck. It was strong but she squirmed anyway, trying to free herself from its grasp. It let out another ear-piercing screech.

Autumn shrieked and writhed, to no avail.

I'm going to die, she thought, resigning herself to fate. *I'm going to die then my friends will be next.*

She looked at Rick, perhaps for the last time.

He was furious. His eyes were cold, like a killer.

She didn't like it at all.

"LET HER GO!" he yelled as he trod closer to the monster with Nathaniel and Mandy flanking him.

"RUN GUYS!" Autumn screamed, unable to move now as the creature tightened its grip on her.

"GET AWAY FROM HERE! NOW!"

She couldn't bear the thought of Rick and the others dying with her. They could run now and never look back.

"Are you insane? We are *not* leaving without you Aut!" Rick snapped.

Mandy stood with Rick, unwavering. She stared the creature down, eyes full of rage.

"You don't scare me, you beast! I have relatives who are uglier than you! So let her go or I will kill you with my bare hands!" she growled.

The monster didn't seem to understand them. If it did, it wasn't responding.

Instead, it leaned towards Autumn's face, its tongue slipping out of its gaping hole tauntingly.

It was long and forked, and she felt it sliding across her cheek.

Rick watched in terror as the creature retracted its tongue and glared at him maliciously.

It growled and drew a single sharp claw down Autumn's chest. She screamed, feeling the hot, stinging pain as the blood trickled from the wound.

"You freak! Don't touch her!" Nathaniel snapped as he handed Mandy his dagger.

"Here, take this."

"Don't you need it?" she asked, examining the blade.

Nathaniel reached into Rick's backpack and pulled out a large hunting knife.

"No worries Mandy. I got bigger toys to play with," he grinned. "My brother got me this for my birthday."

Autumn watched her friends, her heart pounding. There was a chance the weapons wouldn't even hurt the creature, so stating they got close enough to use them.

She didn't want her friends to die saving her.

She couldn't. She *wouldn't* let that happen.

The creature's curiosity seemed to pique as the weapons were drawn. It tightened its grip on Autumn, its claws digging deeper into her flesh.

"I said, let her go!" Rick bellowed, and it dawned on Autumn that Rick was breaking. "Or I will *end* you!"

Nathaniel stood beside Rick, wielding his hunting knife menacingly.

"YEAH! END YOU!" he repeated.

He glanced over at Rick.

"We *can* end him right?"

"Yes we can," Rick said as he reached into his pocket and pulled out a bottle of holy water. He opened the lid swiftly and splashed it on the creature.

It shook off the liquid from its hide, clearly unscathed and growled loudly.

Rick glanced at Nathaniel. "It didn't work!"

Nathaniel watched the beast warily. "Nope. All you did was give it a bath dude!"

The creature, looking even more agitated now, bared its teeth and snapped at Rick, trying to bite him. Rick jumped back, avoiding the attack with ease.

Rick didn't hesitate any longer. He took his dagger and slashed the creature in the arm. It cried out in pain and tossed Autumn aside haphazardly before charging at Rick.

Autumn landed, rolling across the grass. Mandy rushed over to her as Rick went head-to-head with the creature, Nathaniel at his side.

"Autumn, are you alright?" Mandy knelt beside her, worry consuming her tiny features.

Autumn felt lightheaded but otherwise fine.

"Other than the fact that it licked me, I'm okay," Autumn said, wiping her cheek disgustedly.

"Yeah, what was with its tongue?" Mandy asked, helping Autumn up.

"I think it's part lizard or something," she replied as Mandy inspected her wounds. She had some cuts and bruises, but nothing too severe.

"All I know is, it's definitely not a phantom," Autumn muttered.

Mandy and her watched as the creature and Rick danced around each other. It leapt at Rick attempting to claw at his throat, but Rick dodged. Nathaniel moved in, slashing at the creature with his hunting knife and nicked the monsters arm.

The creature made a guttural sound and pounced on Nathaniel, clawing him before he could move out of the way.

Nathaniel looked at his arm, furious. "You son of a bitch!"

The creature went after Rick again, this time spitting liquid out of its maw. Rick dodged the thick brown substance narrowly as it hit the ground, burning a large patch of grass in its wake.

"It's hocking acid loogies at us now!" Nathaniel said breathlessly.

The creature was getting frustrated. It let out another feral cry and charged. Autumn felt her stomach drop inside her. Rick couldn't avoid this. He took a defensive stance and as the creature came at him, he adjusted his blade.

Autumn grabbed Mandy's arm and squeezed. She couldn't look. She closed her eyes, only for a moment, and when she opened them, she saw the blade of Rick's dagger going into the creature's chest. She watched as it clutched its chest, sputtering. Then it crashed into the ground, where it stopped moving completely, eyes lifeless.

The four of them stood frozen in the field, unable to move. Rick was shaking, his hand still holding the ghost of the dagger that was now lodged in the creature's chest.

Nathaniel's mouth hung open as he stared at the dead thing on the ground. Autumn was still clutching Mandy, neither daring to move a muscle.

The minutes slowly ticked by, like a clock with a dying battery. No one spoke or blinked, as though any movement might cause the beast to come back to life.

"It's really dead right?" Nathaniel was the one that broke the long silence.

Autumn let go of Mandy's arm, observing the creature cautiously. "It doesn't seem to be moving."

"I'll check," Rick said firmly, and he walked over to Nathaniel.

"What are you going to do?" Mandy asked dryly. "Check its pulse?"

"No," Rick said as he held out his hand to Nathaniel. "The knife please?"

"Uh yeah dude," Nathaniel said, handing it to him. "Are you going to stab it again for good measure?"

"No. I want to be armed just in case it's playing possum," Rick said.

"Rick, don't bother. Let's just get out of here," Autumn pleaded.

"It's okay Aut," Rick smiled at her reassuringly. "We can't take any chances right?"

Rick moved gingerly towards the beast, leaning over it slowly. Then he reached for his dagger, with Nathaniel's knife in his other hand. He grabbed it, tugging on it with force, and it slid out. The creature lie there, unmoving. Rick examined it more closely.

"It isn't breathing," he began, and then he looked at Autumn. She *was* in closest proximity to it.

"Did it *breathe* before?"

"Yes," Autumn replied, remembering its putrid breath upon her neck. She shivered. "Unfortunately."

"Well, it's not anymore, so yeah, it's dead," Rick said confidently.

He walked back over to Nathaniel and set the weapons down by his feet. Nathaniel looked at the dagger. It was covered in a mucus-like brown goo.

"Gross," he muttered wiping it on the grass as Rick rushed over to Autumn. He wrapped her into his arms.

"You scared the shit out of me Aut," he whispered into her ear as he squeezed her.

Autumn gripped him back tightly. "You saved my life Ricky."

"Hey, I helped too!" Nathaniel chimed in huffily. "I made an awesome speed bump between it and Rick."

Rick pulled away and began examining Autumn. "Your cut," he said as he took in the marks on her skin, tracing his fingers gently across the large one on her chest.

"They aren't deep," Autumn reassured him. "Nothing a first-aid kit can't fix."

"It's the *mental* scars that will never go away," Mandy added in lazily.

Rick had Autumn's face in his hands now. "I thought you were going to become that thing's meal," he said, his voice barely audible.

"I don't think it wanted to eat me," Autumn said thoughtfully. "Just *kill* me."

"Oh much better," Rick said sarcastically.

"I think," Nathaniel began as he picked up the wiped off weapons from the ground.

"You do?" Mandy cut him off.

He shot her an idle glare but went on.

"It was trying to procreate with her," Nathaniel said confidently.

Mandy shot Nathaniel a disgusted look. "Wow. A monster attacks Autumn, and his brain *still* goes straight to sex." She sighed. "Am I the only one that *doesn't* want to go round two with *another* beast? Let's get the hell out of here!"

"We can't just leave the thing out here in the open Mandy!" Rick said.

He had a valid point. A random dead creature in the middle of a field where people might pass by.

It would cause a panic.

"Well, what else are we going to do?" Mandy asked handing Rick back a dagger. "Bury it with the shovel you *didn't* bring?"

Rick sighed, as he put all the weapons into his backpack quickly.

"I just think leaving it here will cause a commotion. I mean, people do come out this way. Some camp in the woods or throw parties nearby. Imagine people finding this thing? Or worse, the cops?"

"It might do them some good," Autumn said, annoyed. "Maybe then they will deal with the problem instead of ignoring it."

Rick looked pensively at the creature.

"How about we go home, drop you all off, and I can get a shovel and come back alone and bury it?" Rick suggested.

"No way!" Autumn protested immediately. "No one is coming back here! Especially alone."

"Well, does anyone else have a better idea?" Rick asked, hanging his head with exhaustion.

"*I do,*" said a voice from behind them.

11

Autumn recognized the voice right away. She looked behind her, her heart clenching.

"Eric! What are you doing here?" she asked, unable to hide the surprise from her voice.

Eric was looking at the lifeless monster, his face expressionless or maybe even a little bored. He was wearing all black, a long trench coat and combat boots. His dark hair was messy from the wind.

Nathaniel walked over to Eric, hands in his pockets, a small smirk on his lightly freckled face.

"Well isn't this a *coincidence?*" he began, suspiciously. "A monster dies and Eric King shows up. Did you come to say goodbye to your brother King?"

"Nate," Autumn said, giving him a warning look.

"It's a little too late for goodbyes don't you think?" Eric said without humour as he walked past Nathaniel and over to the dead creature.

Autumn felt a small stab of hurt that Eric hadn't acknowledged her, but she knew why. She had lied to him about coming here tonight, and she deserved to be ignored.

Everyone watched as Eric crouched over the thing, lifting its limp arms as he examined it closely. He spent a moment or so looking over the corpse before he seemed to find what he was looking for.

"Who killed it?" he asked, standing up and looking at the group of them.

Everyone turned to Rick, who looked up from his feet and raised his hand. "It was me. Why?"

"Right through the heart. Your aim is dead-on," Eric said, obviously impressed. "You have skills Jacobs. Most people would crumble in the face of one of these *things.*"

"Eric?" Autumn looked at him, raising her eyebrows.

She had so many questions like, why Eric was here and *what* exactly did Rick kill?

"I can explain everything later," Eric said patiently. "What I want to know now is, can I trust you guys?"

Nathaniel snorted and Eric looked at him.

"What?"

"You are asking, if *we* are trustworthy?" Nathaniel said. "That's rich."

"Well, give the man a prize," Eric said sarcastically. "Seriously, all deep outrage aside, I need you guys to answer *now.*"

Autumn knew Eric wasn't playing games. She wondered if they were finally going to get the story behind Caleb and Renee's cave excursion.

Nathaniel crossed his arms over his chest defiantly.

"We will answer your question when we are good and ready King," he said smugly.

"Because that sounded like something an honest person would say," Mandy muttered.

Nathaniel looked at Mandy. "I just don't think we have to justify ourselves to him. We aren't his minions! We don't have to wash his dark ritual robes and tell him what a great evil mastermind he makes!"

Eric let out an exasperated sigh. "Allow me to sum it up for you Nathaniel. We don't know who or *what* might come wandering around next," he said. "So we need to pick up the pace. That or you guys can wait in the van while I deal with this," he gestured to the body.

Autumn knew she would never betray Eric, no matter what. She was loyal to a fault. She learnt that the hard way with Nikki.

"You can trust me," she said firmly.

"Says the fibber." Eric smirked.

"*I* offed the thing," Rick said proudly. "So trusting me is a given King."

"I didn't steal loot from your house," Mandy said plainly. "And trust me. I *could've.*"

Eric gave Mandy a disapproving frown then sighed, rubbing his temples.

"I guess this is as good as it gets," he said as he reached into his jacket pocket reluctantly.

"Let's get on with the show."

Eric pulled out a large vial of liquid, studied it for a moment and yanked the stopper from it.

"What is that? The blood of virgins?" Nathaniel said, still cracking jokes despite the tension in the air.

"Nope," Eric said as he poured the liquid around the beast in a circle. "Although if I ever need any, I'll be sure to ask you Nate."

Nathaniel's face went red with embarrassment.

"I'm not a virgin!" he snapped.

"Thou doth protest too much," Eric said apathetically as he continued dispersing the liquid around the monster.

All four of them surrounded Eric, watching him intently.

As far as Autumn could tell, Eric had definitely done this before. The thought both frightened and intrigued her.

"What is he doing?" Rick whispered to Autumn. She shrugged her shoulders. She wasn't too concerned. After what they had just been through, the night couldn't get any freakier.

When Eric was finished pouring the liquid, he stepped into the circle he created and began speaking in Latin.

He said the words slowly and precisely, as to not make a mistake.

"Creatura of nox noctis iam pulvis!" he exclaimed. "Vestri somes mos melt!"

Autumn's hair blew around her face, as the wind picked up rapidly. Eric went on with the incantation, repeating it over and over.

Autumn watched as the creature began to melt away, disappearing into the ground like dirt absorbing rain drops. When Eric was done, there was nothing left but the memory of its hideous body lying there.

Autumn was rendered speechless. What had Eric just done? Whatever he did, it seemed impossible. Though after tonight, she knew *anything* was possible.

Rick stared in awe at Eric. "You are like some kind of wizard King!"

"Yeah dude! That *was* wicked! It almost makes up for all your other bad qualities," Nathaniel said, astounded.

Mandy, who seemed to have had enough surprises for one night, plopped onto the ground, placing her hands under her chin.

"I don't think this night can get any weirder," she muttered.

Autumn knew Eric had secrets. Didn't everyone?

However, this was something she hadn't expected, despite all the tales about Eric circulating at school.

She looked at him, her brow furrowed.

"What was that Eric?" she asked, unsure if she really wanted to know.

Eric placed the empty vial back into his pocket.

"I told you I'd explain later, and I will," he said firmly. "Right now, we need to get the hell out of here."

Not needing any coaxing, the group of them headed back to the parking lot.

It was still empty, other than Eric's stunning red Camaro and Nathaniel's van.

As they stood around getting ready to leave, Eric assured them he would meet everyone at his house tomorrow to discuss what happened.

Everyone was far too tired to argue. Eric's promise seemed to mollify them, for the moment, even though everyone had many unanswered questions.

Everyone piled into the white van but before Autumn got in, Eric accosted her.

"Are you alright?" he whispered. He looked at her wounds and gently traced the ones on her arm with his fingers.

His brown eyes stared into her green ones, telling her what she already knew.

He was worried about her.

He still cared.

Autumn smiled gratefully. "I'm fine. It clawed me, but nothing too serious."

Eric ran his hands through her hair, tucking a stray strand behind her ear.

"I'm tremendously relieved to see you are *relatively* unscathed."

He leaned down to her forehead, kissing it gently.

She sighed softly. "Does this mean my fib is forgiven?"

"We all have our secrets. So yes, I suppose we can call it even." He grinned at her.

"When you get home, clean the wounds out thoroughly with this," he said, handing her a vial. "It will sting like you wouldn't believe at first, but it will flush out any infection and speed up the healing process."

Autumn took the vial. "Thank you Eric. For *everything.*"

The car ride home was silent and tense. Everyone was weary, and in shock and so many questions had been left unanswered. What was the creature? Why did Eric show up and how did he dispose of the dead body? Autumn couldn't help but wonder, who was Eric King?

When they finally arrived home, Autumn was both relieved and exhausted.

"We will all meet before going to Eric's," Rick suggested as the van pulled up to his house. "My parents are away so you guys can come here."

"Tomorrow is good," Mandy agreed.

"Yeah. It's been a long night. I'm not sure my brain can process much more," Autumn admitted as they opened the van door.

"Alright guys. I have to get Mandy home," Nathaniel said. "See you both tomorrow." He looked over at Autumn meaningfully. "You get some rest Auttie."

"Later," Mandy said, waving from the passenger seat. "Rick, help Aut with those cuts!"

When Rick and Autumn were safe inside, he helped her apply the liquid Eric had given her onto her injuries. Autumn screamed in agony as the liquid seeped into the cuts, burning like her skin was on fire.

Rick cringed at having to hurt her.

"It will be over soon Aut," he assured her. When he was finished, Autumn went to take a shower, then she slipped on a tank top and yoga pants and went into her bedroom.

She hopped into bed and as soon as her head hit the pillow she nodded off.

She awoke to find herself in a grassy field. The sky above her was on fire. She was alone and she sensed danger, thick in the air, so she fled.

She sprinted, trying to get back to the parking lot, to some semblance of safety, but before she could get there, she was surrounded.

Four hideously deformed monsters encircled her, bellowing their deafening, animalistic cries.

She glanced above her at the once inflamed sky. It was black now and when she looked back down, the creatures descended on her.

She let out one sharp scream and sprang awake.

When her eyes adjusted, she realized she was in her room, panting and covered in sweat.

"Autumn!" Her door flung open and Rick was standing there, looking concerned.

Autumn fought to catch her breath, her heart pounding against her chest. After she had calmed down, she looked up at him embarrassedly.

"Rick, sorry to scare you. It was just a nightmare. I am still seriously freaked out."

Rick ran a hand through his curls anxiously. "Yeah, that was pretty scary stuff," he said.

Then he moved towards her bed and looked at her apprehensively. "May I?"

"Sure," she replied shoving over.

Autumn was told that as you get older, your mind slips things out, replacing old memories with new ones, but she vividly remembered sleeping over at Rick's when they were younger. Now, it was visceral and natural to sleep with him.

Back then, if she had a nightmare, she would crawl into bed with Rick, and he would tell her funny stories to make her forget her bad dreams.

Then he would say: "I'm going to stay awake until you fall asleep." Autumn would ask him why.

"That way if anything bad comes, I'll be awake to protect you," he would say.

So Rick would watch over her, until she dozed off and only then would he fall asleep.

"Autumn," Rick said, breaking into her reverie. His low voice soothed her, making her panic dissipate.

Autumn looked at him. "Yes."

"Go to sleep, I'll stay awake until you fall asleep," he said, a small grin appearing on his face.

Autumn was amazed that Rick remembered.

For some reason, it made Autumn feel warm and tingly inside. They had a bond and it was unbreakable, even by time, a worthy adversary, to say the least.

He was her safe haven, and she prayed time would *never* change that.

"Thanks," Autumn murmured, feeling her eyelids getting heavy already.

Rick said nothing more and turned out the bedside lamp. Autumn pulled her comforter up to her chin and drifted into a peaceful sleep.

12

Sunday morning drifted by dreamily, with Autumn and Rick sleeping well into the afternoon. Perhaps it was her exhaustion, or Rick's soothing company but Autumn slept like a baby.

It was raining heavily and the sound of raindrops hitting the window and the warmth of her bed, made getting up a chore for Autumn.

When she finally stirred, she heard the soft sounds of Rick sleeping beside her. She rolled over and studied him. He looked so peaceful with his eyes closed and his curls sprawled on the pillow, just like when he was a little boy.

She could see him now. The same peaceful face, although smaller, his curls everywhere while lying beside her in his bed. She would look at him and watch him intently. She adored Rick. He would do anything for her, even then. He was only a kid, but he always protected Autumn, no matter what.

Nothing changed. She had seen him last night, his blue eyes filled with trepidation as a *real* monster held her in its clutches. He fought for her, risking his life. The only thing that *had* changed was they weren't up against the neighborhood bully. This wasn't just some kid trying to steal their bikes. They saw a monster last night, and she wouldn't soon forget it.

Monsters. It seemed ridiculous when Autumn thought about it. She was half expecting Rick to wake up and tell her it really *was* just a nightmare but the fading nail marks on her arms and the aching of her body, told her otherwise. She shivered at the thought of this and pulled the covers up to her chin.

She marveled at the notion that the world wasn't as it seemed. It was multifaceted and underneath the layers were creatures. Creatures beyond human, beyond animal and beyond the unfathomable.

The more she thought about the vastness of the world and the unknown yet to be discovered, the more it made sense. How arrogant were humans to assume they were the only beings walking the world?

Rick stirred, looking over at Autumn groggily and interrupting her contemplation.

"Morning," he said smiling, as he turned on his side to face her.

"Morning," Autumn said, returning his smile.

She was surprised that their smiles came so easily. After last night's traumatic events, she assumed they would never be the same again.

Right now, she felt content. She was safe, warm and secure. It was the world beyond her walls that was in disarray.

"How are you?" he asked. "Did Eric's medicine work?"

"I feel sore but the wounds are pretty much healed." She held out her arms to Rick, who looked for the claw marks. They were barely visible on her skin. Rick held her arms in his hands, observing them, tracing a finger across the faded wounds.

"So last night wasn't just a bad dream?" Rick frowned.

"I'm afraid not," Autumn replied.

They stared at each other for a moment. Rick shifted upright in the bed.

"When that *thing* grabbed you," Rick's voice was soft. "I knew I would do *anything* to save you. I never thought *I* could kill anything, but for you, I could, and I did. I didn't even think about it twice Aut, and that really scares me."

Autumn grimaced. She knew Rick made the right decision. It was a do-or-die situation. Still, she couldn't fathom the feeling of taking a life, even an evil one. Knowing your hands were capable of ending a life would change a person.

"You had no choice Rick. That monster was going to kill us all." She sat up beside him.

"You saved *everyone* last night."

Rick raked his hands through his hair anxiously.

"Mom always told me, there's a difference between braveness and stupidity."

"The only stupid thing we did was ignore Eric's warnings," Autumn said. "He said being near those caves is dangerous."

She looked at Rick, who got up and began stretching. She got out of bed and stood in front of him, looking into his blue eyes.

"Thank you," she said, her voice quavering. "For being so brave and selfless."

It was finally sinking in how *close* they might have come to death. She didn't think about death much. She was still too arrogant and naive to believe death could come at any time, for anyone. *The foolishness of youth,* her mother called it.

Last night, it was her first real encounter with the reaper, though his sickle missed her narrowly. She was certain that monster was going to tear her and her friend's limb from limb, had it gotten the chance.

Rick pulled her into his arms, holding her tightly against him.

"I would never let anything happen to you Autumn. You are my best friend."

Autumn was crying on his shoulder now, the tears flowing freely, her shoulders trembling.

"I know," she said through sobs. "I knew you would save me."

"Always," he whispered.

And she believed him.

Before Mandy and Nathaniel arrived, Autumn went to get ready and Rick headed to the nearest restaurant to pick up some food.

Autumn, decked out in dark jeans and a white dress shirt, her hair wavy and damp from the shower, came bounding down the stairs in time to see Rick in the kitchen setting up the takeaway. They ate quickly, with Autumn almost as ravenous as Rick.

The two of them had just finished, when they heard the doorbell ringing.

"I'll get it," Rick offered as Autumn began cleaning up. As she threw out the takeout containers, she heard Mandy and Nathaniel chattering in the hallway.

"That thing was a *snake* creature!" Mandy was saying, sounding frustrated. "Like a snake man!"

"No way Mandy! It was an iguana!" Nathaniel said firmly.

"What kind of *iguana* spit's venom?" she asked sharply.

"Good afternoon you guys! I'm so glad you came *together,*" Autumn heard Rick say sardonically.

She just finished cleaning up, when the trio finally made their way toward the kitchen.

Nathaniel rushed over to Autumn and encompassed her in a tight hug.

"Oh *Autumn,*" he said melodramatically.

"Hey Nate," Autumn said, patting his back awkwardly.

"How are you doing?" he asked.

"I'm sore but I'm fine," Autumn said pulling away. "Thanks for the concern though."

Nathaniel placed his hand on his chin thoughtfully. "I thought you might say that Autumn, so I planned ahead."

Autumn arched an eyebrow. "Oh did you?"

"Yes. Just to be certain you are indeed, *fine,*" he made quotations with his fingers. "I think *I* should go upstairs, strip you down and have a good, long, look at you."

Mandy rolled her brown eyes, a smirk spreading across her face.

Autumn fought the urge to smack Nathaniel and crossed her arms over her chest disapprovingly.

"Is that so?"

Rick looked at Nathaniel, frowning. "Dude, that was *weak.*"

"I ain't no doctor," Nathaniel said smugly. "But I can give her something to make her feel *much* better."

He looked Autumn up and down appreciatively. "Anytime you're ready sweetheart."

"Ready," Autumn smiled sweetly and quickly proceeded to punch Nathaniel in his arm *hard*.

"Ow, chick that stings!" he said, rubbing his arm sulkily.

"See? I'm one hundred percent better," Autumn said matter-of-factly.

"Oh Nathaniel, you are like endless hours of free entertainment," Mandy said through laughter.

Nathaniel continued to rub his arm and groan, as the four of them took seats around Rick's kitchen table.

Once everyone was seated, the carefree chatter died down and was replaced by ominous silence.

Now that they were all together and ready to discuss last night's events, no one knew where to begin.

After a few minutes of dreadful quiet, Autumn finally had enough of the four-way staring contest.

"Alright," she said banging her fist on the table dramatically.

Everyone stirred from their reveries and turned to look at her.

"A monster attacked us last night," Autumn said firmly. "We *need* to discuss what happened. Staring at each other blankly isn't going to help."

"With all due respect Autumn, what is there to talk about?" Nathaniel asked mirthlessly. "No amount of conversation is getting us any answers about what *exactly* we saw last night. Only King can help us now."

Mandy sighed. Up-close Autumn could see the bags beneath her eyes.

"Nathaniel, think of this as group therapy."

Nathaniel blew a raspberry. "Great. So now *I'm* crazy? You all saw the thing too."

"You aren't crazy," Mandy said, running a hand through her pixie cut. "Talking about it will make us *all* feel better."

She looked at Autumn. "Although I should warn you, I'm not the best at expressing myself. My go-to emotion is usually anger."

"Well that explains *everything,*" Nathaniel muttered.

"Alright so let's discuss," Rick said, as he pulled his chair closer to the table.

"Allow me to begin," Nathaniel said, cracking his knuckles. "The monster appeared. It was unpleasant, and now it's *dead.* We all lived, the end." He grinned. "I feel better already."

"It's not that simple Nathaniel," Autumn said, grimacing. "Eric said there are more of those *things* lurking around the caves."

"That may be so," Nathaniel said. "But why does that matter now? We went, we saw, we conquered."

"Because we know the truth now," Autumn began. "Are we going to be like everyone else? Are we just going to turn a blind eye?"

"That was the general plan," Nathaniel admitted.

"Coward," Mandy grumbled.

"Oh shut it pipsqueak!"

Autumn knew Nathaniel had a valid point. They made it out alive once, and tempting fate twice was like playing Russian Roulette. What exactly was she proposing? That they fight the monsters? That they become high-school students who moonlighted as vigilantes? As ridiculous and terrifying as the thought was, it was also exhilarating.

She couldn't deny it. Last night, her heart was racing and her blood was pumping through her veins at full speed.

It was a rush. Of course, she was terrified but underneath the surface, there was a thrill.

"I just think we saw that *thing* last night for a reason," Autumn explained. "It was like we lifted the veil, and now it would be wrong to look the other way."

"Ugh. Doing the right thing," Nathaniel said, crossing his arms defensively. "It always gets me into trouble."

Autumn looked at Rick. She could practically see the excitement in his blue eyes frothing and ready to bubble over. He felt the adrenaline too. They all had.

"I get what you are saying Aut," Rick said. "Instead of hiding, we could fight back."

"Exactly," Autumn said, straightening in her chair. She looked at Mandy and Nathaniel.

"What do you guys think?"

"Usually, I'm up for anything," Nathaniel said. "But we are teenagers and they are *monsters*. Freaky lizard monsters who spit venom! We don't stand a freaking chance!"

"Well, we would need to *train* dude," Rick said. "But it would be sweet. We would be like, vigilantes."

"Like superheroes," Nathaniel's eyes widened. "Known and feared by villains everywhere. We could rescue beautiful chicks, and they would reward us." He winked.

"Yeah dude! Exactly!" Rick replied.

"Or we could end up dead," Nathaniel said, his face suddenly going ashen.

Autumn shook her head. "No one will die. *I* would need the most training. Rick knows martial arts already."

"But you were a cheerleader back home, so you are probably quite fit and flexible," Nathaniel said gazing at Autumn longingly. "I mean, that's how I *imagine* you would be."

"Would get your mind out of the gutter?" Autumn gave Nathaniel a cautionary look then turned to Mandy.

"You know martial arts Mand."

"Yep. And I also have a secret skill," Mandy said proudly.

"Being able to hide in most cupboards?" Nathaniel offered. "Baking cookies with the other elves?"

"I am amazing with nunchucks," Mandy said, grinning wickedly.

"Really?" Nathaniel said, shifting uncomfortably.

"Yep," Mandy said. "I can pack quite a punch with them. It's how I kept my older brothers in line growing up."

"Man. I feel sorry for them," Nathaniel muttered.

"So that leaves you Nate," Autumn went on. "You can be our firearm's aficionado."

"*Aficionado?*" Nathaniel repeated. "That's good right? Should I be outraged?"

"It's good. It means you are our firearm's expert," Autumn said reassuringly.

"Oh yeah. I like busting caps," Nathaniel said throwing his shoulders back. "I'm like a regular cowboy with a gun. Just get me the hat and the chaps."

"And that is an image I will *never* forget," Mandy griped.

Autumn realized she was the weakest link when it came to fighting. She didn't want to be the damsel in distress. She wanted to fight alongside the others and be an asset, not a liability.

"I can't really fight," Autumn admitted.

Nathaniel rubbed his arm where she had punched him earlier. "I beg to differ."

"Well, anyone can use brute force," Autumn went on. "But to fight, you need more than that. You need technique, precision, timing and coordination."

"Not to worry Aut," Rick assured her. "I will teach you to fight. Think of me as your very own coach. Before you know it, you will be roundhousing monsters like a pro."

The four of them sat in the kitchen, continuing to hash out ideas about training, weapons and armor. Everyone knew this wasn't a decision to be taken lightly. They realized what they were undertaking was risky.

"Don't get me wrong. I love a good fight more than anyone," Mandy said. "But for once, Nathaniel has a point. Why are *we* going to fight these things? Why risk our hides when no one else will?"

"Because we can," Rick piped up. "Autumn is right Mandy. You and I can fight. Nate hunts and is a natural with guns. I can teach Autumn how to kick ass. Already, we are stronger than most people. Right?" Rick grinned. "I mean, can you picture Ben Mills out there fighting? Begging the monsters to let him live because he's a quarterback?"

"And don't forget, with my *contacts* we're going to be armed and dangerous," Nathaniel added in. "My brother Conrad can get his hands on some serious contraband."

Mandy, who was fiddling with the salt and pepper shakers on the table, frowned.

"So we are *somewhat* tougher than the average person, but that doesn't mean we're tough enough to contest hell beasts. Aren't we being a tad overconfident?"

"We just need to train more and learn to work together as a team," Rick replied. "I mean, I kicked a monsters ass, and I wasn't even trying." He puffed out his chest proudly.

Autumn raised her hand in the air.

"What's up Aut?" Rick asked her.

"Let's make a pact. We won't go back to the caves until *everyone* is in tiptop, fighting shape."

"I'm in," Nathaniel said, finally sounding keen about the idea. "As long as I'm packing heat, I'm happy to help."

"Count me in too," Mandy said.

Rick's blue eyes lit up. "Awesome! Now all I need is a cool nickname to go by, like Rick the Ripper."

Mandy chortled. "That just sounds like you fart a lot."

"You can be Miniature Mandy," Nathaniel interjected as Autumn went to get drinks from the fridge.

As she began searching for bottles of water, she heard the familiar jingle of her cellphone. She recognized the ring tone as Eric's.

She pulled her phone out of her pocket.

"Eric. How are you?"

On the other end, Eric was rambling, his words melting together, not making sense. He wasn't his cool and collected self. Feeling her stomach tie into knots, she asked him to repeat himself.

Autumn felt her heart drop when he spoke again, this time clearer and slower.

"Oh my God," she murmured.

Rick looked up and saw the expression of terror on her face.

"Autumn? What is it?" he stood up from his chair.

"We will be right there. Sit tight," Autumn said before hanging up.

"Autumn?" Mandy said, her brow furrowed. "What's wrong? Who was that?"

She looked at her friends worried faces and forced the words out.

"It was Eric. Renee and Caleb have gone missing."

13

As Nathaniel drove, the sound of Eric's rattled voice played over and over in Autumn's mind without refrain. She had never heard him so distraught.

"Poor Eric," Autumn murmured. "He is so worried."

"Eric *tried* to warn them," Mandy said flippantly. "But Caleb was so adamant about going to those wretched caves."

"Eric made a body *disappear* like voodoo," Nathaniel said. "Even I would think twice about crossing him."

"Like you know what voodoo looks like Nate," Mandy grumbled. "Either way he is obviously on our side," she went on. "He saved our hides, which you didn't have a chance in hell of doing." Mandy looked at Nathaniel, a smirk on her face.

Autumn was starting to realize squabbling was actually flirting for Mandy and Nathaniel. Still, she couldn't take any bickering now. She was relieved when Nathaniel rose above the bait to play verbal jujitsu with Mandy.

"I'm just saying, it's obvious that wasn't the first time he's gotten rid of a body," Nathaniel pointed out. "And that isn't normal."

"This from the guy who has a wall full of artillery in his basement," Autumn muttered as they turned down the long, tree-lined road that led to Eric's house.

"Nathaniel is just jealous because Eric is loaded, and he is broke ass," Mandy said, obviously trying to prod him further.

"I am not and *never* will be jealous of Eric King small fry," Nathaniel snapped back.

Mandy shrugged, ignoring his jab.

"It would be nice to have a guy who could afford to pay for my meals once and awhile. Take me out for steak instead of hot dogs and hamburgers."

Nathaniel snorted as he pulled in through the wide-open gates of Eric's home.

"If a guy had to pay for *your* meals Mandy, he'd go broke. You are a freaking bottomless pit."

"You wouldn't have the money *or* the manners to pay on a date Abrams!" Mandy barked, her face reddening with anger.

"I would pay for a lady, something you certainly are *not,*" Nathaniel shot back.

Mandy opened her mouth to retort, but Autumn cut her off.

"Can you two please stop?" she implored as she took off her seatbelt. "Usually, your sparring is endearing, but we need to focus on helping Eric. He needs us."

Autumn opened the van door and instantly felt the sun beating down on her. She looked up at the sky, admiring the crystal blueness of it, and when she looked back down, she saw Eric approaching.

He was wearing dark jeans and a black button-down dress shirt. His dark hair was messy like the wind had attacked it. He looked pale, and his brown eyes were ringed with darkness.

Everyone greeted Eric and Autumn couldn't help herself. She reached out and grabbed Eric, pulling him close. Eric hugged her back, squeezing her tightly.

"Oh come on," Nathaniel grumbled.

"They are freaking adorable," Mandy swooned, her cheeks pink.

"I'm so sorry about Caleb and Renee," Autumn whispered into Eric's ear.

"Thank you Autumn," he said gently. "You're truly a loyal friend."

Eric didn't let her go. He held her for a while longer, before finally pulling away.

"Let's go inside where we can talk more privately," he suggested to everyone. "It may not seem appropriate, considering the timing, but I want to give you all the grand tour."

Everyone delighted at the idea of snooping around the grand King mansion, so they all followed Eric inside.

Eric went on to tell them the house had ten bedrooms, seven bathrooms, a kitchen, a library, a study, a ballroom, three great rooms, a pool, a gym and a hot tub.

"My parents ensured the backyard is very private. There are tons of different trees and shrubs, which shroud the property. Almost like our own private little forest," he said wistfully. "It is my absolute favorite part of the house."

Eric continued leading them down another long, ivory carpeted, hall. Finally, they arrived in front of two giant mahogany doors which he pulled open without effort.

"This is the library," he said, gesturing for everyone to follow him inside. "I spend the vast majority of my time here."

Every part of the house Autumn had seen so far was astounding, but the library surpassed her expectations. The first thing she noticed when Eric opened the double doors, were the bookshelves. They were made of shiny cherry wood and were so tall they nearly touched the cathedral ceiling.

As Autumn got closer, she saw the array of books, all different sizes, styles and colors. Their bindings faced out, boasting so many titles. Autumn's head was spinning. Eric had every base covered, from classic literature to current bestsellers and beyond.

Mandy glanced at Autumn, a grin spreading across her heart-shaped face.

"Eyes glazed over, drool pooling around her lips. I think she's in heaven," she said to Eric, who chuckled lightly.

Nathaniel shuddered as his eyes passed over the rows of books. "Heaven? Try hell."

In the centre of the room, on a burgundy area rug, were three large recliners and two suede couches. Against the far wall, was an old-fashioned stone fireplace and a wet bar. Autumn saw a fire was already crackling, the orange flames dancing around wildly along the wood.

"You have quite the collection of books," Autumn said as she browsed quickly through the titles. Eric had every genre of literature. He had romance, history, fantasy and biographies. She really was in heaven.

Ever since she could read, it was Autumn's favorite pastime. Her mother taught her early on. She said that knowledge was power and reading gave you knowledge, in turn making you stronger. That and she loved getting lost in a story.

Her father always bought her a new book when he got paid every other week. Her sister Audrina didn't see the benefits of literature.

"Autumn can't be smart *and* beautiful," she had grumbled. "She is so greedy!"

"I'm an avid reader," Eric admitted as he pulled a tome off the shelf and ran his hand across its cover. "I actually collect antique books."

"I love to read. There is nothing like getting lost in a book," Autumn said. She continued to gaze longingly at the rows of books as Eric placed a hand softly on her shoulder.

"What is your favorite book?"

"I have too many to choose just one," Autumn said. "You?"

"The same," Eric said. "Well, if you would like to borrow anything, let me know."

"Thanks Eric. I will definitely take you up on that."

Eric was so mysterious and yet they had so much in common. This drew Autumn to him like a magnet. It didn't hurt that he had a gorgeous smile and dark eyes she could get lost in.

"Please everyone, make yourselves at home," Eric said, gesturing to the assortment of sofas and chairs. He took a seat in one of the recliners, while Nathaniel rushed beside Autumn on one couch and Mandy and Rick took the other.

The five friends sat in the library, glancing back and forth at one another. The air in the room was heavy with anticipation, as everyone waited for Eric to begin.

He took a deep breath, running a hand apprehensively though his dark hair, before he started.

"Would anyone like anything to drink or eat before we begin?"

"No thanks we just ate," Autumn began.

"Food?" Rick piped in, his blue eyes keen. "What do you have King?"

Autumn narrowed her eyes at her friend. Was he really delaying Eric's tale for another meal?

Eric couldn't help it. A small smirk came across his tan face. "I can have the cook whip us up sandwiches if you would like Rick," he offered.

"You have a cook?" Rick's eyes went wide.

Eric nodded. "I do."

"In your house?"

"Yes, in my house." Eric smirked again.

"You are so lucky," Rick said, scowling.

"Why are you so uppity?" Autumn asked, unable to hide her annoyance. "Your mother waits on *you* hand and foot Rick."

Eric pulled out his top-of-the-line cell phone. "Rick, I'll go ahead and text the cook."

"Your own servants," Nathaniel said, looking impressed. "You really are loaded dude."

"Actually, I call them my staff," Eric said as he began typing a text message. "And the huge house didn't give it away?"

After Eric sent the message, he shifted in his recliner, clearly trying to get comfortable.

"I don't see the point in wasting any more time," he said. "I'm sure you all want to know what happened last night. And what probably happened to Renee and Caleb."

Mandy, who was sitting, legs tucked up to her chin spoke bluntly, as usual.

"You saved our asses last night. If you don't want to explain yourself, we can't say boo about it."

Eric smiled indulgently. "As much as I appreciate the sentiment Mandy, I would *like* to explain but the words aren't coming as easily as I would've hoped."

Eric sat in the recliner, not saying anything more and for a split-second, Autumn thought he looked much older than his seventeen years. It was like he had aged before her very eyes.

Finally, after what seemed like an eternity, he spoke again.

"The truth is, I am not exactly as normal as I look."

"You *don't* look normal," Nathaniel piped in sarcastically. "Hence all the rumors at school."

Autumn nudged him sharply in the ribs.

"Ow!" Nathaniel winced.

"Fair enough," Eric smirked. "I guess the only way to do this, is to start at the very beginning."

"My parents moved to Whitan from Madrid when I was very young. I have basically lived in this little town my whole life. When we first arrived here, I couldn't even talk. Whitan has always seemed pretty normal, at least on the surface. Like most places, anything dark or abnormal is kept buried. The tales of the caves have been around for centuries that I know of.

However, through my extensive research, I have come to conclude that the caves aren't always brimming with evil activity. Nothing happens for years at a time and then suddenly the strange occurrences start again."

"And how do *you* know so much about the caves?" Rick asked, almost accusingly. "Most of the people in town don't believe the scary stories, but you obviously know they're true."

Eric put his hands together. "Well, to explain *that* I need to tell you all who *I* am."

"Uh Eric King," Nathaniel said flatly. "We already know that dude."

"Maybe I didn't phrase that properly," Eric said patiently. "I need to tell you *what* I am."

Nothing good could ever follow that sentence, Autumn thought as a chill tapped her spine.

"Are you an iguana in disguise?" Nathaniel asked warily.

"It wasn't an iguana!" Mandy snapped. "It was a snake man!"

"No," Eric said, ignoring the yelling. "Like my parents and my grandparents before them, I am a sorcerer."

The room was suddenly filled with thick silence. No one said a word. The only sounds were the ticking of an old grandfather clock in the corner of the room and the crackling of the fire.

Eric sat back awkwardly, awaiting his friends' reactions.

Autumn was surprised, but she wasn't frightened. If anything, she was relieved. This explained so much about Eric. His actions, his reputation and his need to distance himself from others.

"So you are a wizard," Autumn said, smiling.

"Like in the movies!" Nathaniel added.

Eric couldn't help but smile wryly at the comparison he most likely saw coming.

"Not exactly. Many of *my* spells require rituals to be performed although some of them are instantaneous. Oh, and I don't have a wand to shoot them out of, though that would come in handy at times."

"Eric, I knew you were … different," Autumn began, carefully choosing her words. "But I definitely didn't see this coming."

"Ever since last night, we haven't seen much coming," Mandy said dryly.

"Now you understand why I keep my distance from people at school," Eric said pensively. "Harbouring a secret like this, it's difficult and lonely. I have to keep people at arm's length."

He looked at Autumn. "But you changed that Autumn. When we first met, I knew I couldn't push you away. I wanted to trust you."

Autumn smiled, feeling a rush of affection for Eric. She had a sudden urge to hug him and never let go.

Now everything made sense. Why people feared Eric, why he was so peculiar. She felt special knowing she was the catalyst for him finally sharing his secret.

"I just approached you because I thought you were hot," Autumn teased.

Eric went on to explain that witchcraft was the King family legacy.

"The Kings have been sorcerers for generations," he clarified. "Both the men and women throughout our bloodline practiced magics. Kings have the innate ability to conjure magics. It's like a gift and a curse all at once."

"So you are like a *man witch,*" Nathaniel reasoned.

"I prefer, *warlock.* Women are enchantresses," Eric said. "I guess you could call me a man witch, if you really wanted, but I wouldn't like it."

"Then man witch it is," Nathaniel said gleefully.

"So your mother and father must be sorcerers too," Autumn said. She was both baffled and intrigued by Eric's lineage.

"Yes, they were," Eric said. He hung his head for a second and when he looked back up, he wore an expression of sorrow.

Were as in the past tense?

Autumn got a terrible feeling in the pit of her stomach.

Again, the room was thick with familiar silence and tension as Eric looked from his clasped hands, to the anxious faces surrounding him.

"My parents died," he said finally.

Nathaniel exhaled loudly. "So are dead parents like a must for people doing magic or what?" he asked crudely.

Autumn didn't hesitate. She shot Nathaniel a deadly glare before she elbowed him generously in the side.

"Ow Autumn!" he said then he looked at Eric apologetically. "Sorry man."

"Here's a tip Nate. Before you saying *anything*, double check if it's stupid or not," Mandy snapped.

"It's alright," Eric said graciously. "Everyone reacts differently when I tell them. It happened when I was young. Of course, it's not something you ever really get over, but I *have* learned to live with it."

"I'm sorry Eric," Autumn said gravely. She wanted so badly to comfort him, though she wasn't sure how.

"Me too Eric," Mandy said quietly.

Rick looked at Eric pityingly. Rick was close to his parents like no teenage guy Autumn had ever known. He of all people could understand how hard it would be without them. In fact, they all could.

"That's rough man. What happened?" Rick asked.

Eric didn't respond and Rick flushed, looking sheepish.

"Sorry. I mean, if you want to tell us …" he trailed off.

Eric nodded. "It's fine. I can talk about it now." He took a long, deep breath. "Simply put, my mother and father went to the caves, and they never came back."

"I knew very little of what happened when I was a boy. Everyone around me tried their best to protect me from the truth. It wasn't until I got older that Arabella told me. They were going to perform a ritual to permanently cleanse and seal the caves.

"After practicing the magics for months and preparing every small detail, they went to perform the ritual. My parents and my uncle went. His job was to hold off anything that attacked, while mom and dad completed the ritual.

They were all set up inside the caves and ready to go. About halfway into the ritual, the caves began to rumble and shake. The rocks began falling, the walls quaking, and my sister swore she saw thick, black ooze dripping from the cave walls."

As Eric spoke, everyone watched him, on the edge of their seats. He was definitely a natural storyteller, very eloquent and expressive. What made it all the more chilling was the tale wasn't fictitious. The story was true.

"Your sister was with them?" Autumn asked, surprised.

"No. She wasn't there, *literally*. She was what we call *scrying*, though she wasn't even supposed to be doing that," Eric said, shaking his head. "She was essentially watching what was happening through magics. Kind of like a crystal ball."

"Arabella said, at first, my uncle was having no issues. He was shooting off spells with no problems. He was a well-trained warlock and knew many instantaneous spells to fight off evil. Soon, the black ooze began spawning creatures.

My uncle was fending them off but ultimately the monsters began coming in droves. Creatures of all shapes and sizes attacked, trying their best to stop the ritual. He was overwhelmed. My sister was using the scrying bowl to try to heal people, but she couldn't keep up. Her magic wasn't powerful enough. She was far too young and inexperienced.

As soon as she healed someone they were injured again and in the end, the injuries were too serious for her magics to fix. So instead, she continued to watch on helplessly. My uncle died first. A monster bit into his throat. He bled out on the cave floor while listening to my parents struggling to survive.

With their guard down, my parents tried to abandon the ritual and escape, but it was too late. The exits were blocked with throngs of monsters.

Eric paused, obviously struggling to continue. Autumn couldn't resist anymore. She shot up out of her seat and rushed over to Eric. She leaned over and hugged him where he was sitting, and he held her back, tightly embracing her.

"Thanks Autumn," he murmured. "I needed that."

"I bet you did," Nathaniel muttered.

"If you can't go on, we would understand," Autumn said gently.

Eric touched her hand, squeezing it in his own.

"I want to keep going," he said firmly. "This is why you are all here, to learn about me and the caves. I need to tell you guys the whole story."

"Okay then. When you're ready, we're all ears," Autumn said as she took a seat in the recliner next to his. She looked around at her friends. They were all waiting for him to continue.

Eric cleared his throat.

"With no escape, and my sister unable to do anything but watch, my parents died in the caves. They fought until their last, gasping breath, but it was futile. Even the three of them, all-powerful and knowledgeable sorcerers, could not take on all that evil."

Autumn felt her heart wrench as tears escaped from her eyes. She couldn't imagine losing her parents, especially so young. She knew it then. Hunting and killing the cave monsters would be dangerous, but it *was* the right thing to do. The evil had to be contained. Someone had to finish what Eric's parents had started, or more innocent people would die.

"My parent's bodies were never found," Eric went on, his fists clenched into tight balls. "Arabella had stopped watching. After they were gone, she couldn't watch anymore."

"The terrible thing is, the caves were not always dark and evil. At some point, they were probably just ordinary, boring, caves. However, someone or *something* summoned the evil that thrives there."

"My parents were always convinced it was an evil sorcerer who awoke the darkness. They thought it was someone who had an ancient vendetta, or someone that loved chaos and death."

"If you look into the history, it just gets worse. It started out as little things, sightings and strange noises, and eventually it escalated into missing people and deaths." Eric said as he stood up and went over to the fireplace to tend to it.

"And now people are too terrified to do anything about it. They ease their fear by saying the stories aren't real, but most people know someone that can attest otherwise.

They think ignorance is the safest bet, but the problem is, people don't ignore those caves. Curiosity draws people there, and they keep dying and going missing. Like Renee and Caleb."

"So they knew about your family and still insisted on going there?" Mandy asked, eyebrows arched in confusion.

"They wanted to be the ones to gain the family acclaim. I told them vengeance would come in due time, but Caleb was never one for patience. Unfortunately, he dragged Renee down with him."

"We should go look for them," Autumn said finally. "If we can get them out alive ..."

"It's too dangerous Aut. I went there last night in hopes of tracking them," Eric said as he prodded the fire with a steel poker. "I think they went there Friday night after our big blow out. We would probably never find them. Best-case scenario, they are alive but not themselves anymore. Either way, they are beyond our help now."

Eric went on, telling them the creatures never ventured too far from the caves. It was assumed they needed the caves dark energy to flourish and with so many people visiting the caves, they had a constant stream of easy prey.

"What about the police?" Nathaniel asked hopefully. "Are they any help?"

"Some have tried," Eric said as he watched the fire. The flames flickered and began rising higher, licking the wood furiously. Autumn stared at Eric, one arm resting on the mantle, watching the flames as he spoke. This would be an image forever burned into her mind.

"They were foolish in the beginning. They let arrogance blind them, assumed the stories were folktales. They died and then more died, and eventually they avoided the caves at all costs. They gave their fair warning to the townspeople. The 'Please stay away from the caves' and when people didn't heed their warnings, it was hear no evil, see no evil …"

"Speak no evil," Mandy added wryly.

"Oh no! They speak of it," Eric said bitterly. "When they are safe, behind their desks at the precinct or in the comfort and warmth of their homes."

Autumn looked around. Mandy, Nathaniel and even Rick shared the same troubled expression. If trained police officers with loaded guns couldn't take out the creatures, how could they? When push came to shove, they were just *teenagers*.

Maybe they were being foolish. Maybe when they spoke this morning about being vigilantes and fighting the good fight, maybe they were still high on last night's adrenaline.

Now reality and logic, in all its ugliness, was setting in.

Still, there was that nagging thought in Autumn's mind. It tugged at her, pawed for her attention, washed away all reason and replaced her doubt with certainty.

We aren't them. We are different. She thought to herself.

She couldn't ignore it.

We were born for this.

Was this the arrogance Eric spoke of? The same arrogance that caused Renee and Caleb to go missing in the caves abyss?

Everything Eric had told them was still sinking in when Autumn finally spoke up.

"Eric, we want to help."

Eric, who had returned from the fireplace and was sitting back in his chair, looked at Autumn, perplexed.

"You want to help with what Autumn? I told you, the caves are too dangerous. I wouldn't ever put you at risk."

"We want to train and start kicking some monster ass!" Rick said. He didn't appear the least bit apprehensive now. He was moving full speed ahead.

The color drained from Eric's face. "Can you run that by me again?"

"This morning we discussed undergoing training and fighting the monsters ourselves," Autumn clarified.

Eric nodded slowly. "And what makes you think you guys are capable of fighting those things? My own parents, my uncle, couldn't handle what is inside those caves."

Rick threw his shoulders back proudly. "To be honest, I beat that lizard thing up without much effort," he said smugly. "And most of us are trained to fight in some form. Nathaniel hunts so he'd be our sniper. Mandy studied martial arts like me, and I can use a sword."

"And Autumn would be ..." Rick turned to Autumn, his brow furrowed in thought.

" ...the bait," Autumn offered.

"You would definitely play the part of the *beautiful* damsel in distress well Autumn," Eric said, giving her a half smile.

Then he turned to Rick. "You may have been victorious against one *lizard man,* as you call them, but as my family demonstrated, being faced with an onslaught is totally different. And if you went *into* the actual caves themselves, that would be a death sentence for everyone involved."

Rick, ever the optimist, was not the least bit deterred by Eric.

"Well I understand that," Rick went on. "Every good warrior knows his limits. That's why we aren't going back until we are all well-prepared."

"Dude, I think we would start on the outskirts of the caves and work our way towards the oozy monster infested centre," Nathaniel added.

"And if you are never ready Rick?" Eric prompted. "How will you know for sure?"

"I don't think we will ever know for sure. Does a police officer know when he gets a call over his radio to stop a robbery that he is going to get shot?" Rick said. "No matter how hard he has trained and prepared, he could end up dead. That is the risk he takes every day."

Eric sighed, rubbing his forehead. "That really didn't help your case."

Autumn knew Eric was hesitant, but she also knew how tempting having their help might be. His thirst for revenge would be palpable after what happened to his family. What better way to quench it than with a gang of friends at his side? He sat down, quietly pondering the idea.

"Truthfully, this town could use all the help it can get with the caves," he admitted.

"And I can't deny that I have been working on magic to banish the evil from the caves, for selfish reasons as well." He paused. "Revenge can be a powerful motivator."

"And have you come up with anything?" Autumn asked hopefully.

"There is a purification spell I have been working on, but I need more time," Eric admitted. "I can't take the risk my parents took. I am researching the spell, collecting the proper items and biding my time. The problem is, the longer I bide time, the more people disappear or die."

Everyone seemed to be weighing Eric's hefty words. Death was the end game for everyone. Autumn accepted that, but she didn't want her number to be up before she made it to thirty.

"So our vigilante idea is pretty outrageous?" Rick looked to Eric, shuffling his feet against the carpet. Autumn never thought she would live to see the day when Rick was seeking Eric King's approval.

"I think you guys are more courageous then most folks in this town are. I also think it's completely dangerous." Eric's lips formed his familiar mischievous grin. "But I am more than willing to help you guys if you'd let me. We can fight the evil together and save this town."

"Right on!" Rick said, throwing his fist into the air. "I didn't think you could fight Eric."

"He makes deals with demons," Nathaniel said, rolling his eyes. "He just gets them to fight his battles for him."

"I don't usually fight per say, but I can hold my own. I can cast spells, create barriers of protection and give you all healing potions."

"That would be awesome," Rick admitted. "Every team needs a medic."

Eric raised a hand in protest. "Now since we are being completely honest, I need to tell you guys something. If any of you get *seriously* injured, like say, a lizard man claws shank your heart, I can't help you. I can only heal minor injuries, nothing dire. Pulling you back from the brink of death is all dependent on how close you are to his doorstep."

Nathaniel's face was grim. "So if we die …" he trailed off.

"Dead is dead," Eric said simply. "I'm sorry to be so blunt about it, but what we plan on doing *is* risky. Life is precious, and we are gambling with it out there. You need to understand that. We *all* do. Even with safety nets in place, you don't always land in them."

"I don't have any potions or know of any spells that bring people back to life without serious repercussions. Otherwise," Eric trailed off. Autumn filled in the blanks for him.

Otherwise, he would've brought his family back.

Much to Rick's delight, the sandwiches arrived. An assortment of deli-style beef and cheese, ham, and salmon sandwiches were placed on the coffee table along with tea, soda and coffee. Eric and the others thanked Simon, and everyone grabbed a sandwich or two except Rick, who took a half a dozen to start.

As they ate, surrounded by the glow from the fire, Eric discussed his magic with them, specifically the spell he was working on to seal the caves. He said it would ideally banish the creatures, and cleanse the evil aura of the caves.

"The spell I'm working on now isn't the same one my parents attempted to use. Despite the short amount of time that has passed, magic has still come a long way. It is ever-changing and evolving. This spell is new and like nothing else. Those vile creatures won't know what hit them when I'm done with them." Eric smiled wickedly between bites of his food.

"I just wish Renee and Caleb had been patient enough to wait for the spell to be finished."

"Has Arabella been helping you out with the spell?" Autumn asked.

"She has been, even though she wants me to move on and be a *normal* teenager. She thinks revenge is a dangerous and foolish sentiment," Eric replied. "She has her own place but drops in every other day. I am a lone wolf here, other than Simon and the rest of the staff."

Autumn could see everyone looking at Eric with pity in their eyes. He was a seventeen-year-old boy living alone in a vast and boundless mansion. Was that a dream or a nightmare? Autumn imagined at first it might be fun, not being told what to do, not having any rules or boundaries. Then she thought it must get lonely.

"I know it seems very unorthodox." Eric began. "But it's not that bad. You adjust. You learn to enjoy your own company, to be your own best friend," he smiled crookedly. "To play games with the cook or share the details of your day with the maid."

"Especially if she's hot and wearing a sexy maid outfit!" Nathaniel piped in as him and Rick bumped fists.

Mandy grumbled, crossing her arms over her chest. "Misogynistic pigs."

"Doreen is actually in her sixties," Eric smirked. "She is a very sweet lady. She has been with our family a long time now."

Both Rick and Nathaniel exchanged disappointed looks. "*Oh.*"

After they finished eating, Autumn sat beside Eric on the cobbles of the fireplace, enjoying the warmth from the flames on her back and Eric's arm around her.

"I wanted to ask you something Autumn, though it never seemed like the right time," he said, taking a sip from his tea.

"Are you going to propose?" asked Rick, who had another sandwich heading to his mouth.

"No Rick," Eric said indulgently before facing Autumn again.

"I was wondering if you would attend the dance with me," he asked, taking her hand into his. "I have never gone to any of the school dances, but I haven't met anyone I wanted to go with, until you."

Autumn was excited, if only for a second, before she remembered she was already going to the dance with Nathaniel. From everything Rick had told her, this dance was the highlight of Nathaniel's life. She couldn't bring herself to break his heart, even if she would rather be on Eric's arm that night.

Before Autumn could politely decline, Nathaniel began his protest.

"Back off King! I'm already taking Autumn to the dance," he said sharply. "I asked her a long time ago. And I *met* Autumn first so she is *mine.*"

Nathaniel's words hit a nerve with Autumn. She was by no means a feminist, but she believed in being independent and not letting a guy define you. She wasn't a pretty decoration for anyone's arm, and she wasn't a prize to be won.

"I am not an object to be claimed Nathaniel Abrams!" she said, raising her voice. "When the day comes that I allow someone to call me *theirs,* they will know it. Until that day, I belong to me!"

Autumn turned to Eric, her eyes softening.

"Nathaniel *is* right about the first part. I am going with him Eric. He asked me first. It's only fair."

Eric seemed a little shocked by this admission and who could blame him? Autumn had never shown any romantic interest in

Nathaniel, and she had made it quite clear she wanted to be more than friends with Eric.

However, he took his loss like a mature adult, just like Autumn expected he would.

"I respect your choice. That is very gracious of you to honor your prior commitment Autumn," he said before he turned to Nathaniel, extending his hand.

"Nathaniel, I'm sorry. I wasn't aware you were taking Autumn to the dance. I wasn't trying to step on your toes. You are one lucky guy."

"That I am," Nathaniel replied arrogantly as he reached out his hand and shook Eric's skeptically.

Autumn glowered at Nathaniel. She would never understand men and their incessant need to have pissing contents over *everything*.

"Eric, come anyway. I'll save you a dance," Autumn urged. Even if she wasn't his date, she and Eric could still spend *some* time together that night.

"I would love that," Eric said.

"I would not," Nathaniel mumbled and Autumn resisted the impulse to get up and smack him.

"But one dance is fine. I *guess*," Nathaniel added in sulkily.

Autumn's mind began to wander, and she imagined the evening with Eric as her date. They were dancing together in the dark, smoky, gymnasium, their bodies close and their hearts thumping. He spun her, and her long, silvery gown coiled around her as they glided across the floor. Eric, in his sharp, tailored suit, laughed carelessly as he pulled Autumn even closer to him.

They moved together, light as air, cheeks touching, embracing one another. Eric dipped her, pulled her back up and began leaning in towards her. Her lips parted but before they could kiss, Nathaniel wedged himself between them, grinning foolishly, eyes wide and crazed.

When it was time to go, Eric walked the foursome through his extraordinary mansion and to the front door. Autumn was determined to get Eric alone and pulled Mandy aside in the foyer to request some teamwork.

"What's up?" Mandy asked, leaning in towards Autumn secretively.

"Do you think you could distract Nathanial? I could use a minute alone with Eric," Autumn asked.

Mandy's eyes went from Autumn to Eric, who was intently listening to Rick discuss his latest skateboard trick, and a sinister smile spread across her lips.

"Of course, I can help. What are friends for?" she said. "Besides, Nate has been annoying me all day. I would love nothing more than to foil his plans of being near you."

"Thanks," Autumn said, pleased.

Mandy didn't waste any time. She walked over to Nathaniel, and grabbed him by the arm forcefully.

"Come on buddy, let's go."

Nathaniel glanced down at his arm, puzzled, as Mandy began pulling him towards the front door.

"Mandy what are you doing?" he asked.

"I need to talk to you privately," Mandy replied sweetly.

Nathaniel grimaced. "About what?"

"I will tell you in *private* you dolt!" Mandy replied, as they moved out the door.

Rick watched Nathaniel being dragged away and shook his head in confusion before giving Eric a firm handshake.

"Thanks for the grub and for telling us about your past Eric. It's nice to know why you act so weird."

Eric ran a hand through his dark waves uncertainly.

"Rick. It has been a pleasure. Come back anytime."

Rick turned to Autumn, smiling knowingly. "See you in the van Aut."

When he was gone, Autumn turned to Eric, who was leaning carelessly against the door, smiling at her with his charming, toothy Eric grin.

"That Mandy. She doesn't beat around the bush does she?" he said, chuckling.

"She is a great friend," Autumn whispered as she moved in closer to him.

Suddenly, there was a heavy silence and anticipation loomed around them both.

In the hallway, the sconces filled with candles, glimmered through the darkness.

Eric touched Autumn's cheek, his long fingers tracing the curves of her nose, her eyebrows and then her lips.

She felt her heart hammering against her chest as Eric leaned into her. She wanted him to kiss her, to make her feel dizzy and alive, like he had before.

"So we are finally alone," he said softly, his voice a murmur.

Autumn tried to remember what she wanted to say to Eric, but her mind had gone wonderfully blank.

All she knew was her heart was pounding, and Eric's fingers were touching her. His hands moved from her lips to her hair as he moved closer to her. His face inches from her own, she tilted her head slightly, urging him to continue without words. Eric took the cue and pressed his lips against hers, softly and gently.

Autumn couldn't fathom that her second encounter with Eric, would be even better than the first.

"Eric," she began, her voice barely a whisper. She had her arms lazily draped over his shoulders now, and he was playing with her hair.

"Call me later," he said before kissing her on the forehead. "I love hearing your voice."

"Again, I'm so sorry about your cousins," she said. "I wish there was something we could do."

"Don't be," he said, his brown eyes meeting her green ones. "It wasn't your fault. They knew the consequences. For us to go to the caves half-cocked, would only ensure our demise. I am sure as hell not willing to trade your life for theirs."

Autumn felt her heart swelling. Eric truly cared about her. Of all the girls he had encountered over the years, she was the one he wanted, the one who got him to open up. He trusted her, enough to let her see the real him, the Eric King behind the mask.

"If you need to talk, you know where I am," she said, her hands on his chiseled cheekbones.

Eric nodded. "Thank you. I appreciate it sweetheart."

Autumn gave him a quick wave, and then she headed outside to meet up with the others.

14

The next week of school went by swiftly.

As promised, Autumn helped Rick with his video project. Though it was late, it featured normal, mundane footage of Rick and Nathaniel's skateboarding.

The same week, Rick began his training with Autumn.

She showed up after school in the home gym, dressed in a tank top and yoga pants, her hair in a ponytail, ready to learn anything Rick was willing to teach her.

When Rick and Autumn weren't at school or training, she was with Eric. There had been no news on his missing cousins, though Eric didn't really like discussing it much. Autumn knew he blamed himself. He thought he didn't try hard enough to protect them. Autumn knew there was nothing he could've done, short of tying them up.

It was a beautiful and wondrous time in hers and Eric's relationship. They were getting to know each other and when they weren't doing that, they were kissing. Autumn knew Eric was nothing like any guy she had ever dated. He made her feel safe and beautiful. He wasn't going to run off with some other girl like Kyle had. He wouldn't break her heart.

It was the Friday afternoon before the dance and though the day had begun bleakly, with heavy rain and a chill in the air, the sun bursted through the dreary clouds, and the sky was looking brighter.

Autumn and Mandy were holed up in Autumn's room getting ready.

They had their hair and makeup already finished, and they were lounging on the bed chatting.

The hooting and hollering Autumn heard from the next room, indicated that the guys were playing video games.

Autumn couldn't help herself. She stared at Mandy, who was almost unrecognizable.

She had her pixie cut adorned with a jeweled headband that swept her hair off her face. Though she rarely wore makeup, she had on mascara and eyeliner, highlighting her huge Bambi-like eyes.

Autumn had her long dark hair pulled into a sleek, elegant ponytail. Her eye makeup was violet, offsetting her green eyes.

They sat there together, reading tabloids, waiting for time to pass when Mandy looked up from her magazine.

"Rick is your best buddy Autumn," she began. "But he's kind of adorable. The curls and those blue eyes. Don't *you* think he's cute?"

Autumn had managed to persuade Rick into taking Mandy to the dance when Nathaniel wouldn't budge. He had made it clear it was a "friends only" type of invite, but Mandy was persistent.

Autumn looked up from the magazine she was skimming.

"Rick's cute. I'll admit it," she said, grinning. "So Nathaniel is finally driving you crazy?"

Lately, Mandy went from gazing at Nathaniel dreamily, to looking at him with daggers in her eyes. The usual 'Nathaniel is cute' comments, turned into, 'Nathaniel is so irritating' and recent interactions between the two seemed tense.

"He is a dope," Mandy grumbled as she stretched her legs out on the bed. "He has no idea how to treat a girl."

Autumn nodded understandingly.

"I can't say I have ever seen Rick around a girl he likes. He might be just as dopey as Nate."

Mandy frowned. "Has he ever had a girlfriend?"

"Nope. He was always too busy with his skateboarding," Autumn said, turning a page.

"But he would make a decent boyfriend. He's amazing with women and treats them like gold. His mom, me, even my stuck-up sister, if that's any indication."

"Some say it is," Mandy said as Autumn glanced up at the clock on her nightstand.

They had an hour and a half before the dance began and Aunt Katherine had been adamant about taking photos. The girls began changing into their dresses and when they were finished, Autumn was impressed by how pretty Mandy looked.

A few inches taller in her heels, the strapless, peach chiffon gown suited her skin tone perfectly. The hemline touched just above her knees. On her neck, she wore a delicate pearl necklace that her mother had given her for her sixteenth birthday.

"What do you think?" Mandy asked, spinning around. "Do I look girly enough?"

Autumn smiled. "You look absolutely stunning. Rick is going to be the luckiest guy there tonight."

Mandy, who rarely got embarrassed, flushed. "Oh I doubt it. I mean, look at you Autumn."

Autumn gave herself a quick look in the mirror. Clad in a long, white Greek-style gown that came into a deep V along her chest, the dress highlighted her soft curves. Her necklace, made of emerald stones, was a gift from her mom.

"You look so gorgeous." Mandy said. "Eric is going to see pictures of you in that dress and wish he decided to show up."

"Him and I both," she said flatly.

Eric had admitted he couldn't stand seeing her with someone else, so he wasn't coming tonight. He said she should enjoy her night and give Nathaniel her undivided attention. It *was* only fair.

As the girls made their way through the hallway, Autumn saw Rick, Nathaniel and her aunt and uncle, all standing in the front foyer chatting. Aunt Katherine had her digital camera and was taking some shots. Uncle James was next to her looking at Rick, every bit the proud father.

Even from above, Autumn could see how handsome the guys looked. Rick wore a white dress shirt, a black tie and black dress pants. Nathaniel opted for a less traditional navy dress shirt, grey dress pants and a red tie.

Mrs. Jacobs snapped a few more pictures as Rick's dad stepped forward, a huge grin on his face.

"Look at you son. Taking a girl to the dance." He paused, getting teary. "This is a big moment."

Autumn and Mandy, looking on from upstairs, exchanged bemused glances.

Rick looked at his feet. "Come on Dad. It's really not that big a deal."

"Really, it's not Mr. Jacobs. Mandy isn't even really a girl," Nathaniel said, trying to contain his laughter.

Mandy's face reddened. Fists clenched, she set off to attack Nathaniel but Autumn managed to restrain her.

Rick's dad looked at Nathaniel, puzzled, and shook his head.

"You boys know the rules," he began sternly. "About girls, that is."

"Don't worry about that Mr. Jacobs," Nathaniel cut in smugly. "I have the ladies eating out of my palm. Autumn is no exception."

Autumn grimaced, feeling the familiar urge to smack Nathaniel.

Uncle James stared down Nathaniel. His eyes squinted, and his arms crossed over his chest.

"Nathaniel, did you forget you are talking about my sweet, darling, innocent *niece* Autumn?"

Uncle James, looking freakishly calm, stepped closer to Nathaniel, until their faces were inches apart.

"Listen son. I'm not sure what you think is going to happen tonight," he began. "Actually, I *know* what you're *thinking*, but I want *you* to know that Autumn's dad and I, won't take kindly to you disrespecting her."

"I would never disrespect her sir!" Nathaniel said quickly, eyes filled with fear.

"Planning on *anything* but holding hands with Autumn, is disrespecting her, so if you even attempt any funny business tonight, you will have to answer to me. Do you understand?"

"But Mr. Jacobs you have known me forever," Nathaniel said, smiling weakly.

"And that's why I'm just *warning* you instead of hitting you," Uncle James said.

Then he smiled warmly and patted Nathaniel's lapel, before turning back to his wife.

"Now, where are the girls Katherine?"

Autumn and Mandy, who had been rooted to the ground watching the drama unfold from above, took this as their cue and began towards the stairs.

"Oh here they come!" Mrs. Jacobs said, sounding relieved as she got her camera ready.

Mandy went first, smiling nervously, as everyone watched her. She waved awkwardly and walked down the stairs, teetering a little in her heels.

"Dude," Nathaniel nudged Rick sharply.

"What dude?"

"She actually looks *pretty.*"

"She does," Rick agreed.

Mandy flushed and went to stand beside Rick and Nathaniel.

"You look beautiful sweetie," Mrs. Jacobs said as she took a few shots.

"Thank you Mrs. Jacobs," Mandy smiled. Then she turned to Rick. "You look handsome."

"Thanks. You look pretty Mandy. Peach is really your color, which reminds me," Rick said as he reached into his pocket, pulling out a peach corsage that he slipped on Mandy's wrist.

Rick's mom proceeded to snap more pictures of the trio as Uncle James watched on proudly. When a minute had passed and Autumn hadn't appeared, Nathaniel began pacing.

"Where is Autumn?" he asked, his eyes darting around wildly.

"She is coming Nate," Mandy said, rolling her eyes. "She didn't stand you up, though I would've."

Autumn, who was still at the top of the stairs adjusting her dress, heard her aunt calling out to her.

"Autumn dear, did you need help with anything?"

"I'm good thanks," Autumn said, and she took a deep breath and went down the stairs.

Even though she was surrounded by family and friends, she still felt uncomfortable with everyone watching her. When she finally reached the bottom of the stairs, Aunt Katherine put her camera down and hugged her.

"You look so beautiful Autumn."

As they embraced, Autumn could see tears forming in her aunt's eyes.

"My niece is all grown up and so stunning."

Uncle James nodded in agreement. "Your parents are going to be sad they missed this." Then he paused, smirking slightly. "Although, I think your dad would've made you wear a sweater over that dress."

"A sweater? Forget that! She looks smoking hot!" Nathaniel exclaimed.

Uncle James cleared his throat before shooting Nathaniel a glare.

"I mean, *beautiful*. You look very beautiful," Nathaniel said quickly.

"Thanks Nate," Autumn said, beaming. "You look handsome yourself."

He moved towards her, slipping a corsage of white flowers on her wrist.

"For you my lovely lady."

She admired it for a moment. It was breathtaking.

Aunt Katherine spent another fifteen minutes snapping photos before her and Uncle James bid everyone good night and disappeared up the stairs. When they had finally left, Mandy turned to Rick.

"Rick, are you alright?" she asked.

Autumn, who was chatting with Nathaniel, looked at Rick. He was staring at her, but something was different. She couldn't quite put her finger on it, but there was tenderness in his eyes that she hadn't seen before.

"Rick?" Mandy snapped her fingers in his face. He looked at Mandy, startled, as if awaking from a dream.

"Are you alright?" Mandy asked again, looking concerned. "You aren't going to heave on me are you? Because that's a deal breaker, buddy."

"No, I'm sorry. I'm just a little nervous," Rick said, looking away from Autumn.

"Dude, I know the feeling," Nathaniel muttered. "I hope I don't get the backdoor trots like this morning."

"And who said romance is dead?" Mandy muttered as Autumn put her hand on Rick's forearm.

"Ricky, calm down. It's just a school dance, not prom."

"I'm fine," Rick said, forcing a smile but Autumn could tell he was hiding something. Even when she touched him, he didn't look up at her, apparently more interested in his shoes.

"Well, if you are fine and everyone is fine, let's go dude," Nathaniel said eagerly. "I want to get my dance on!"

Mandy grabbed Rick's hand, attempting to lead him out the door.

"Mandy, can I borrow Rick for a minute?" Autumn asked.

Mandy nodded at her. "Sure, we'll be outside." And she and a perplexed-looking Nathaniel, headed out the door.

Autumn and Rick stood together in silence, when it suddenly hit her.

The silence felt *awkward*.

Never before had Autumn felt awkward around Rick. Silence, conversation, even quarrels were easy with him. He was like a song she knew by heart, a map she had memorized, a book she had read a hundred times.

He finally stopped examining his footwear and looked up at her. She remembered her own words, the ones she had spoken to Mandy earlier.

I can't say I have ever seen Rick around a girl he likes.

Was that what was wrong with him? Was he falling for Mandy?

The guy falls in love with the cute tomboy after her makeover? What a cliché, Autumn thought.

Unsure of what to say or do, Autumn reached out to Rick, wrapping her arms around him. For a moment, he was frozen stiff to her touch, but then he hugged her back.

When she pulled away, she cupped his face in her hands, smiling. His blue eyes met her green ones unsurely.

"You like her don't you?" she whispered, and Rick looked at her, eyebrows raised.

"Who?"

"Mandy," Autumn said. "That's why you are acting so strange. You realized you *do* want to be with her right?"

Rick shuffled uncomfortably. "No it's not that at all."

Suddenly, her face was in *his* hands. Then it happened, in slow motion but yet so fast.

Rick leaned in and kissed her.

His mouth pressed against hers passionately, and she didn't move. She felt her heart pounding in her chest and like it was the most natural thing in the world, she kissed him back.

Eric, her mind chided her, and instantly she pulled away. Unsure of where she stood with him, she couldn't keep on kissing Rick.

She had been blindsided, and her mind was mush now. She stared at Rick, her eyes wide and her body trembling. She was like a deer in headlights.

"You are gorgeous," Rick said, stroking her cheek gently with his fingertips. "The prettiest girl, I have ever seen."

"How could it have taken me so long to realize what I have known all along? I want you to be with me Autumn."

Autumn was speechless. Her knees were weak. Her breathing was erratic. She even had butterflies fluttering in her stomach.

It was bizarre, but in this moment, it was like she hardly knew Rick at all. Suddenly, he was a stranger to her. A stranger she had just shared a passionate kiss with.

"Rick, we need to go," she managed finally. "They're waiting for us."

"I know," he said, reaching out to take her hand into his.

"Shall we?"

15

It was a little after seven when Autumn and the others arrived at the school. As they pulled into the parking lot in Nathaniel's van, Autumn looked out the passenger seat window and saw rows upon rows of cars in the parking lot. The gym was going to be packed.

Though she was trying her best, Autumn couldn't stop thinking about Rick kissing her and his confession. She also felt guilty seeing as her and Eric had been spending so much time together. She tried to convince herself they were just friends, but she saw the way Eric would smile at her, with a mischievous twinkle in his brown eyes.

Like moths to flames, they were drawn to each other and when Eric held her, Autumn never wanted him to let go.

Then there was Mandy, her new best friend, who was on a date with Rick, yet minutes ago, he had just kissed *her*.

The whole thing made her sick to her stomach.

Another part of her, a selfish part, knew when Rick kissed her, she felt *something* and she wanted to explore that. Rick was the guy *she* grew up with, and if she hadn't moved away, they would've ended up together. It was fate, merely written in the stars.

Autumn looked in the rear-view mirror, trying to sneak a peek at Rick. His face always brought her back, like a lost ship finding its safe harbor.

Even his curl framed face and blue eyes couldn't placate her right now. The guilt would gnaw at her until she figured everything out.

Nathaniel found a parking spot for his oversized van in the far lot. He parked and jumped out, heading for the passenger side to open the door for Autumn.

"My lady," he said, reaching out his hand to help her out of the vehicle.

"Thanks," she said cordially, grabbing onto him as she stepped out.

She already made up her mind. She owed Nathaniel this night. She wouldn't mope. She wouldn't stew. She would dance and laugh and pretend everything was normal, even if it was a lie.

"The dance awaits," Nathaniel said, looping his arm into Autumn's.

"Let's get this over with," Rick grumbled as Autumn looked around.

Mandy was missing.

"Wait. Where is Mandy?" she asked.

"I don't know," Rick said, his eyes scanning the parking lot.

Autumn frowned. "I think she is still in the van Rick."

Rick rolled his eyes, looking annoyed. "Well, why didn't she get out?"

"I think she wants *you* to get the door for her."

Rick put his hands in his pockets nonchalantly. "They're sliding doors! I go out mine. She goes out hers! It isn't exactly rocket science."

"Neither is chivalry and yet here we are," Autumn said sharply. "Now, *go* get the door for her!"

"Fine," Rick said, puckering his lips into a pout. He rushed over to the van and slid the door open for Mandy.

"Dude, sorry," he muttered, reaching out a hand to her. "I didn't realize I was supposed to get your door for you and stuff."

Nathaniel leaned into Autumn, a smug expression on his face.

"Well duh. Even *I* knew that."

Mandy narrowed her eyes but still accepted Rick's outstretched hand.

"I don't know what is more delightful. You abandoning me in the van, or you calling me dude," she said sarcastically.

The couple walked over to join Nathaniel and Autumn, and they all headed towards the school entrance.

Autumn glanced up at the starless sky. It was foreboding. The heavens so pitch-black, the moon behind large draping clouds. Lately, the stars became an omen, a way of telling how the night might turn out.

A night without stars, she thought to herself wryly. It sent chills down her spine.

As the group of them approached the doors, Autumn noticed the swarms of kids entering the school. Girls in glittering dresses and stilettos, guys in dress pants, crisp button-down shirts and ties. All looking like they were playing dress up for the night.

Voices echoed throughout the vacant halls and reverberated off the white walls. From behind the gyms beige double doors, came the soft, distant thumping of bass.

As Autumn was taking it all in, a loud hooting sound garnered her attention. She looked behind her and saw Ben Mills snuggling with his date, Candice Kincaid. They were sauntering down the hallway, surrounded by their usual gang.

"Candice, you have had enough," Ben said stubbornly, pulling a silver flask towards his chest protectively.

"I need booze. Drinking is the only thing that makes school dances *fun*. Besides, you are already sloshed."

Normally, Autumn would challenge *anything* Ben spat out of his annoying mouth, but he appeared to be right about Candice. She was stumbling around, her eyes half-closed as she held onto Ben for dear life.

"I jusss want one more sipppp Bennyyy," she slurred.

"Back off Candy!" Ben snapped. "The rest is *mine!"*

As their voices faded into the distance, Autumn rolled her eyes.

"They're like a regular PSA ad."

Nathaniel chuckled heartily.

"I hope they get booted tonight," he said and Mandy snickered, looking pleased by the idea.

"Expelled would be even better."

When they finally arrived at the gym, Autumn was pleasantly surprised.

She had been imagining the traditional high school dance décor of rainbow-colored balloons, pastel streamers, signs made with markers and Bristol boards and a cliché smoke machine.

Instead, she saw tea lights were stationed all over. Some hung in fixtures along the walls, and others were placed on tables. They lit up the gym, casting a beautiful, dreamy haze. Tables draped in white lace tablecloths were spread out all over. In the centre of each, sat a vase filled with wildflowers. Another long banquet table housed the snacks and drinks. On a makeshift stage, a DJ was spinning. The floor beneath him was already filled with dancing students.

"Do you want a drink?" Nathaniel asked Autumn as he gestured towards the refreshment's table.

"Sure," Autumn said. "Water would be nice."

"Coming right up," he said, winking at her.

"Did you want anything?" Rick asked Mandy, obviously trying to be more attentive.

"Punch please," she replied and the two headed off to get the drinks.

When the guys were finally out of earshot, Mandy sighed, looking perturbed.

"Rick is acting funny!" she shouted over the music. "He seems distracted tonight! Did he say anything to you?"

Autumn was thankful for the dim lighting. She could feel the crimson rising up her neck and across her cheeks, giving away her guilt like a waving red flag.

"I think he's just nervous," she said, trying her best to sound normal. "The night is still young. Give him time to loosen up a little."

"I have to say Autumn, you were a total bitch when we met, but you do look scorching in that dress."

Autumn looked behind her to see Ben Mills smug face looking back at her. He had a large cup in his hand and he was staring at her, licking his lips disgustingly.

"Get lost you parasite!" Mandy ordered as Autumn glared at Ben, her hands on her hips.

"Ben Mills complimented me! I can finally die happy!" she said sardonically.

"Where is Candice Ben? I saw you come in with her. You ditched her to hit on Autumn? Classy," Mandy said snidely.

Ben, who was wobbling around, seemed to struggle with the question.

"Candice is probably puking by now," he guffawed and his cup shook, spilling punch all over his shirt.

He moved closer to Autumn, touching her hair with his hand.

"You are so hot," he slurred as Autumn jerked away from him.

"Mills back off!" Mandy snapped, stepping towards him, her face contorting with anger. "I may be wearing a dress, but I can still kick your ass."

"Listen! You little pipsqueak," he began, but before he could continue, Nathaniel and Rick had returned. With them was a man Autumn recognized as one of the school's guidance consolers.

Nathaniel's eyes swept from Autumn to Ben disapprovingly.

"Oh not *you* again," he muttered as he handed Autumn her drink.

"Good evening all," the consoler smiled before turning to Ben.

"Mr. Mills. So we meet again," he frowned.

Autumn looked around at the crowd that had gathered. Candice was one of the many faces she saw in the sea of students. She was watching, her mouth agape, as the fiasco unfolded.

"Mr. Garrison," Ben said, eyes heavily lidded now. "The coolest guidance consoler *ever* is here at the dance. Aren't we lucky?"

Mr. Garrison grinned in spite of himself. "That you aren't."

Suddenly, the consoler's expression turned grim.

"Mr. Mills, I was watching you chat with these young ladies over here and from what I gathered you seem to be, shall I say, rather inebriated."

"Sorry *Garrison*," Ben said belligerently. "I speak English not Spanish man. You should know that I'm failing that class. Nevertheless, I am acing Home Ec."

Rick snickered as the consoler looked at Ben, clearly unimpressed.

"I'm *Mister* Garrison," he corrected him. "You are obviously drunk Mr. Mills."

Ben's eyes closed and opened again as he rubbed his face.

"I am not drunk," he slurred again, stumbling as he pointed to Autumn.

"That girl, Autumn Kingston. I just came over to say hi and to see her nice rack." Ben began chuckling obnoxiously. Autumn felt her cheeks turn pink as the crowd looked at her. Rick jolted forward but Nathaniel held him back, shaking his head. It was a silent warning to let Mr. Garrison handle Ben.

Mr. Garrison crossed his arms over his chest. It was clear he was losing his patience and that Ben's big mouth wasn't helping matters.

"Mr. Mills, that is quite enough. You need to leave the gym immediately. We can't have you here like this. You can apologize to these two young ladies when you are back from your suspension and *sober.* Follow me."

"I can stay!" Ben began to argue, but Mr. Garrison was already ushering him away.

When the show was over and the crowd began to dissipate, Rick handed Mandy her drink.

"I leave you alone for a minute and Ben moves in like a vulture."

Mandy looked up at him from her drink, her brown eyes doe-like.

"*I* would've gladly beaten him to a pulp but then Mr. *Hot* Teacher showed up."

"He isn't a teacher," Nathaniel said, rolling his eyes. "He is a guidance consoler. Don't you listen?"

"Who cares?" Mandy said. "Did you see that authority? So sexy."

Fifteen minutes later, Mr. Garrison returned to the gym, *without* Ben. It was around this time that Nathaniel grabbed Autumn and dragged her onto the dance floor. Swaying with Nathaniel, Autumn looked over and saw Rick and Mandy dancing nearby.

She didn't know why, but even after encouraging Mandy to pursue Rick, she felt a stab of jealousy.

She couldn't tear her eyes away from the couple.

She could hear Nathaniel's voice in the background, but she barely *heard* his words. She watched, enthralled, as Mandy leaned towards Rick and pressed her mouth onto his.

Autumn's heart dropped inside her stomach. She felt like she might throw up.

Mandy was kissing Rick.

Her Rick.

She had never felt such jealousy.

She didn't even care how absurd her thoughts were, how petty and ridiculous. All she felt was betrayal and white-hot rage washing over her.

Autumn's expression must've changed because Nathaniel looked over at Rick and Mandy too.

"Whoa, she's like an animal!" Nathaniel said, his eyes bulging from their sockets. "She doesn't waste any time does she?"

Autumn didn't say anything. She could feel the tears building up, ready to crescendo at any moment. She mumbled some excuse about needing air, and then she ran. She didn't care where she went, as long as it wasn't here.

16

Autumn stood outside the gym, shivering in her white gown, the nights chill overcoming her. Her bare shoulders exposed to the icy air, she wished she had brought along a sweater. She knew she would have to go back inside eventually or risk freezing to death. Still, she wasn't ready to face anyone.

Not yet, not now.

She stared at the clouds, now perfectly parted to show off a glimmering moon set against a cobalt sky. She heard the muffled sound of music behind the doors, an owl hooting in the distance. She focused on these external things, hoping to avoid the feelings that raged war inside her.

The shame and the jealousy, dueled in her heart.

She blinked back the tears that threatened to spill over, but they didn't subside. They wanted to escape, and she let them.

As she sobbed, she imagined going inside and telling Mandy, Rick was *hers*.

Not so long ago she told Nathaniel *she* couldn't be claimed; now here she was, trying to do just that to Rick.

Rick was *her* best friend, *her* sanctuary for so long. She wasn't ready to give him up just yet.

The truth was this possessiveness wasn't new. If Rick even *mentioned* a girl in passing, she unleashed twenty questions.

To Rick, she was just being protective, but in her deepest heart she knew that wasn't the case.

The thought of some strange girl kissing the guy she had known her whole life, made her crazy.

She *was* jealous.

In some part of her mind, she had assumed her and Rick would end up together one day.

It was obvious she had never come to terms with her feelings for Rick. It was like the kiss they had shared tonight, opened a new page in their storybook. Then Mandy kissed him, effectively tearing that page out.

Images flashed in her mind, and she let her guard down, allowing the memories unfurl.

She and Rick were swaying back and forth on the swings in his backyard.

They were young and acting silly and rash by trying to use the swings to "fly."

"I can go higher!" Autumn said, giggling as the swing dipped to and fro. It made her stomach dance and flutter.

Rick looked up at her, with his big, blue eyes, even then, filled with adoration.

"I love you Autumn!" he announced as they swung together, in unison. "You are the only girl who doesn't give me cooties!"

Autumn looked back at Rick, smiling gleefully.

"I love you too Ricky!" she replied without a second thought. "You're my best friend!"

Another memory quickly went through her mind.

Autumn sent Rick a scanned image of her grade nine class photo.

Her long, dark hair framed her round face, and her green eyes were traced with thick black eyeliner. An attempt to look like some celebrity she idolized, no doubt.

"I look awful but it's the only recent photo I have," Autumn had said, feeling self-conscious. To her eyes, she looked awkward, boring and average.

"Are you blind?" Rick had asked her indignantly. "You are so beautiful Autumn. You would be the hottest girl at my school if you were here."

Upon hearing this, Autumn felt so delighted, that she wanted to leap up and dance.

Surely, that had been the first indication that his opinion meant something more to her.

She wanted Rick to desire her, to think she was pretty. Even then, she wanted him to *want* her.

The more she poured over her memories, the more she realized what she had already known deep inside her.

She had feelings for Rick.

Shoulders trembling, she sobbed, her tears like a catharsis.

Mandy had *every* right to kiss Rick. They were on a date, a date that Autumn had insisted on *and* set up. She was a terrible, selfish person.

Realizing this made her sob even harder.

"Aut," she heard Rick's familiar voice from beside her.

She felt the urge to run away, but instead she bravely turned, facing him.

As soon as she saw his face, his blue eyes, his curls, his smile, she melted.

Any hesitations she had were falling to the wayside along with any strength. She had to resist him.

"Why are you crying?" he moved closer to her, brushing the tears from her face.

Autumn shivered as a cool gust of wind touched her already-frozen shoulders.

"You are shaking Aut, put this on." Rick took his jacket off, quickly wrapping it around her.

He rubbed her shoulders as the jacket's warmth settled against her. It smelt like Rick, like his soap and deodorant.

"Thanks," Autumn said, smiling weakly.

"You're crying," Rick said. She felt his eyes on her, but she kept staring at the sky, determined not to look back at him. She feared the tears would come rushing back, along with all the feelings she tried to bury inside her.

"I was."

"Why?"

Because I'm your best friend, and I'm jealous you were kissing Mandy.

The words were there, lying in wait, but she couldn't bring herself to say them aloud.

"It's nothing," Autumn shrugged her shoulders.

"So you and Mandy looked like you were having fun," she began nonchalantly. "Seems you guys have more in common then you initially thought huh?"

She didn't want to sound bitter or accusatory. Neither Rick nor Mandy really did anything wrong.

"Aut, come on," Rick said, shuffling his feet, his jaw tense.

Was he nervous?

"I saw you guys kissing," she confessed as her eyes found the sky again. "That was quite a kiss."

Rick smirked slightly. Was he enjoying her jealousy or the memory of the kiss? She couldn't tell.

"*She* kissed me," Rick confirmed. "I didn't kiss her back. She wanted to make Nathaniel jealous. I pulled away but apparently," he touched her hand. "The damage was already done. Nathaniel said you stormed off. He was going to follow you, but I *insisted* I should do it."

She felt relief sweeping over her, as she looked at him.

Rick's eyes burnt into hers. The air was heavy with anticipation, like it was before their last kiss. She wondered if Rick felt it too.

"Ah so you were the pawn?" Autumn said, trying to lighten the mood. "The catalyst for Nathaniel's jealousy."

Rick nodded. "I never *agreed* to be, but yes, I guess I was."

"Was it everything you thought it would be?" Autumn asked, her voice barely a whisper. "The kiss I mean?"

"It meant nothing. Unlike *our* kiss," he paused, pulling her close to him so their faces were mere inches apart.

"Nothing can top *that* kiss. It was epic."

Autumn touched Rick's hair, finally exhaling. She hadn't realized it, but she had been holding her breath.

"Do you remember when we were young, how I used to play with your curls all the time?" Autumn said pensively. "I would run my fingers through them, twisting them in my hands."

The music in the gym faded even further into the distance, and it felt like everyone else was miles away. Autumn's heart raced, pounding rapidly in her chest as her lips longed to touch Rick's.

"I remember," Rick whispered. He touched her face with his fingers, tracing her jawline down to her neck. She sighed gently.

"Aut," he murmured. "You look so beautiful."

She tilted her head up, and her lips brushed against his tentatively. She felt like her breath was being pulled from her. They didn't kiss yet, both wondering if they should take the step that would change everything forever. Autumn could see the line drawn in the sand. She had stayed behind it for so long, but she couldn't anymore.

They were both crossing that line tonight. There was no turning back now.

Without words, they plunged into each other, kissing passionately. They were lost in each other, embracing so tightly and so longingly, like they couldn't get close enough.

The kiss quickly morphed from slow and tender into wild and ravenous and when they finally pulled away, they were both breathless.

They stared at each other, wild-eyed and gasping.

If there was ever any fear, that they might lack chemistry, this sealed the deal. They had it in spades.

Autumn opened her mouth to speak, but she saw someone coming.

The figure moved from the gym doors and into the light.

It was the guidance consoler, Mr. Garrison.

Rick didn't seem to notice him, and he leaned in for another kiss.

"Rick, we have company," Autumn whispered and Rick spun around.

Both stared at the consoler, unsure of what to say or do.

"Oh please. Don't stop on my behalf," Mr. Garrison said, taking a bite of a shiny red apple. "That was quite a kiss. Cinematic, really." He grinned.

Autumn looked at him suspiciously. She assumed she was about to get reprimanded.

"Rick and I were just, talking," Autumn mumbled, suddenly feeling embarrassed.

"Don't tell him my name," Rick whispered loudly. "He was standing in the shadows watching us kiss. The dude is creepy."

"I already know you, Autumn," Mr. Garrison said, taking another bite of his apple while leaning against the wall. "I am her guidance consoler. We just haven't formally met yet."

He reached out his hand. "Mr. Garrison."

"Autumn Kingston," she shook it, starting to relax a little.

"And you must be Rick Jacobs."

Rick nodded. "You know me too?"

"Of course! I'm your consoler too."

"Oh I see," Rick shook his hand hesitantly.

"Sorry to interrupt," Mr. Garrison said. "The gym was getting stuffy. All that teenage angst is quite overwhelming. Underage drinking and fights on the dance floor. I signed up for an *easy* night, too much to ask for apparently."

Autumn and Rick exchanged confused looks. Most teachers didn't talk to students like they were actual *human beings*. Mr. Garrison didn't speak to them like they were aliens. He was actually conversing with them.

Maybe this was why Ben called him the cool guidance consoler?

"Again sorry," Mr. Garrison said sincerely. "I'll leave you guys to get back to your *moment,* although I think I may have ruined it."

Then he smiled at them. "Oh and both of you, please come by my office next week for your mandatory introduction meeting. The more people come to my office, the less I have to hide in the shadows and spy on them," he said, grinning at Rick. Then he took another bite of his apple and headed back into the gym.

Rick waited until the guidance consoler was absolutely out of earshot before he turned to Autumn, looking utterly traumatized.

"Now that guy is *weird*. And what was with the apple? He's like a cartoon villain."

Autumn, overcome with the urge to kiss Rick, pulled him towards her by his tie, and they went back to kissing, picking up where they left off.

They had been making out for about ten minutes, when they heard voices from behind them.

Rick and Autumn parted to see Nathaniel and Mandy, standing in the doorway, mouths agape and eyes wide with shock.

"Oh my God!" Mandy's brown eyes were like saucers as her hand covered her mouth.

"Way to go Aut!" Mandy smirked, obviously unruffled.

Nathaniel, on the other hand, went from shocked to livid, in the blink of an eye.

His face scarlet and his fists clenched, Nathaniel moved towards Rick.

"I'm so sorry dude," Rick began, backing away from his angry friend.

"Is there anyone here that you *aren't* going to kiss tonight?" Nathaniel snapped.

"Autumn, I didn't realize you had feelings for Rick," Mandy said.

"Rick! Her best friend! Why would *anyone* assume that she had feelings for her *best friend?*" Nathaniel shouted. "All that talk of Rick and you being just friends, was clearly bullshit huh Autumn?"

Autumn had never seen Nathaniel so angry. When Eric kissed her, he pouted, but he didn't get this agitated.

She tried to imagine what he was feeling, and the sad part was she could, easily. He felt betrayed by Rick, his best friend. He felt like he had been stabbed in the back.

Autumn remembered the feeling well. Nikki had twisted the knife so deeply into *her* back that she thought she would never recover.

Nothing hurt worse than betrayal. Sometimes, even physical pain couldn't trump emotional anguish. It stung like a salted wound.

"Nate, calm down. It isn't her fault," Rick said, squaring his shoulders defensively. He was getting pissed now, and Autumn didn't want to see these two friends fighting over her.

Nathaniel narrowed his eyes menacingly.

"Damn right it isn't her fault!" Nathaniel roared back. "This is all you buddy!"

"Nathaniel," Autumn began but he shot her a deadly look. "Don't bother Autumn."

Then he turned back to Rick, his jaw tense.

"*You* betrayed me Rick!" he thundered. "This whole time *you* wanted Autumn. After I told you how much *I* liked her and wanted her to be my hot, sexy girlfriend!"

Mandy grunted, looking disgusted. "Oh, brother."

Nathaniel jabbed a finger into Rick's chest.

"I had this whole night planned out, and then you prance in and steal my kiss and my glory? I can't believe you man. You really are conniving you know that?"

Mandy leaned into Autumn, whispering. "Does he even know what *conniving* means or was that a lucky guess?"

Rick sighed deeply, looking beaten.

"I didn't plan this dude," he said. "It just happened."

"How do you just happen to make out with *my* date?" Nathaniel asked indignantly.

"Dude, I didn't know I liked her," Rick said earnestly. "I mean, I knew I liked her as a friend, but I just realized tonight, that she has been the one all along."

Mandy looked at Autumn, a smile spreading across her face.

"Wow. He has got it bad for you girl."

"I know but they need to work this out," Autumn said quietly. "I don't want them to stop being friends over this."

Nathaniel and Rick stood face to face, neither one speaking. Finally, Rick looked at Nathaniel, his eyes filled with sincerity.

"Haven't you ever thought you were just friends with a girl, but then you realized you wanted to be with her?"

Nathaniel looked up at the cobalt sky, like he was debating.

"Yeah. That happened to me once with a friend of my brothers. Her name was Ashley," he said.

"*Ashley?*" Mandy grumbled into Autumn's ear. "I have always *hated* that name."

"I thought we were just friends but then one night we went camping alone without Conrad, and we kissed," Nathaniel admitted. "It was pretty awesome."

Autumn looked at Mandy, who was fuming. "I bet *Ashley* slobbered."

Rick nodded his head excitedly. "See dude! And that's exactly what happened with me and Aut!"

Nathaniel sighed, looking from Rick to Autumn. "I know you guys didn't plan this, but it still stings pretty harshly."

"Sorry dude," Rick said, while patting Nathaniel's shoulder. "I wasn't trying to steal your girl."

Autumn felt her heart wrench for Nate. She could imagine the night he had planned. Dancing and flirting, topped with the inevitable goodnight kiss on the front porch. Despite his loud mouth, Nathaniel had always been kind to Autumn. She had moved to Whitan only knowing The Jacobs and Nathaniel had welcomed her with open arms.

"Nathaniel, I'm sorry I ruined tonight," Autumn said, her eyes meeting his. "I was your date. I shouldn't have run out on you."

Nathaniel shrugged, kicking a stray pebble across the pavement.

"You *did* say we were coming here as friends, so I can't be too mad. Why *did* you run out of the gym?"

"I saw *them* kissing." Autumn pointed at Mandy and Rick.

"Oh that wasn't a *real* kiss!" Mandy's cheeks went pink.

"It was too!" Nathaniel said, looking at Mandy in disbelief. "I saw it! You went at Rick like a cat in heat!" He paused, frowning. "So basically everyone here got a kiss tonight, but me?"

Rick, Autumn and Mandy exchanged awkward looks, and then nodded at Nathaniel.

"Looks like it," Mandy said matter-of-factly. "Do you feel left out Nate?"

"Yes! Actually, I do," Nathaniel said, stomping his foot theatrically. "I will not leave this dance until my lips have been kissed by a girl!"

And that was the push Mandy had been waiting for. She walked up to Nathaniel, stood on her tiptoes, grabbed his ginger hair and pulled him towards her, into a deep, passionate kiss.

Autumn watched her two friends shared a rather long kiss before Mandy pulled away, looking up at Nathaniel smirking.

"There you go big boy. Now you are part of the club."

Nathaniel looked back at her, his face flushed. "For a tiny chick you sure can kiss."

Mandy shrugged, trying to hide her delight. "Good things come in small packages, so they say."

"So am I forgiven?" Rick asked, taking full advantage of Nathaniel's blissful state.

Nathaniel hesitated for a moment before his lips spread into his familiar, bright smile. He reached his hand out to Rick, and they engaged in their traditional hand shake.

Rick let out the breath he had been holding in. "Dude, you had me so worried!"

"Man, I *was* pissed *but* you like her. I should have seen that," Nathaniel admitted. "The way you looked at her and talked about her constantly before she got here this summer. It was so obvious."

Rick crossed his arms over his chest, looking mortified. "Thanks man."

Autumn nudged Rick in his side, grinning. "Constantly, huh?"

"Oh, he *never* shut up about you," Nathaniel said. "He still doesn't."

He looked back to Rick. "I want you both to be happy. So go for it."

"I think you guys would make a really cute couple," Mandy agreed.

"I think so too," Rick said as he took Autumn's hand into his and squeezed it gently.

17

True to her word, Autumn trained religiously with Rick, Mandy and Nathaniel as they prepared to heed their new calling as monster slayers. Weeks passed, with no word on Caleb and Renee. Still, no one, not even Eric, went anywhere near the caves.

They had made a pact not to venture there until they were *all* ready.

Autumn didn't think she ever would be.

The oddest part for Autumn, was keeping the training a secret.

During the day, she was an average student, helping Rick pass tests while studying for her own. When they weren't at school, Rick and she worked together in a different manner. They sparred, lifted weights, jogged and did martial arts.

Autumn was like a double agent, harboring a huge secret that seemed unfathomable, even to her.

Rick bought a punching bag, which he stationed in his garage, where everyone practiced. Rick taught Autumn how to dodge and block, different fighting stances, and how to breathe properly during combat.

She had the least fighting experience but was progressing quickly thanks to her patient trainers. Mandy and Rick had both taken mixed martial arts when they were younger and Nathaniel had hunted with his father for years, so using weapons came naturally to him.

Rick's biggest concern was his parents asking questions about their sudden obsession with exercise. He chalked it up to Autumn learning self-defence, which mollified them for the time being.

Of course, they didn't *always* train at Rick's house. Eric's house, in all its vastness, made for a remarkable and private training ground. He had a huge backyard, with acres of land and his house was surrounded by batches of trees that shrouded it effortlessly.

Inside his giant gym, he had weights, mats and state-of-the-art machines. Plus, the lack of nosy parents puttering about was a bonus.

While everyone trained physically, Eric continued working on the spell to seal the caves and on various healing potions, in case they were wounded on the battlefield. Most nights, Eric could be found in his study or in the library, surrounded by thick piles of ancient tomes.

At times, Autumn thought this was Eric's attempt at avoiding her.

Although he insisted there weren't any hard feelings, Autumn knew he was wounded.

Their once blossoming romance wilted. After the dance, Eric had taken the news as well as could be expected. He was hurt, but he didn't want to lose Autumn's friendship. She was the one who had brought him out of his shell, and he wouldn't soon forget that.

His graciousness didn't help alleviate Autumn's guilt. She was indeed the catalyst for their end. In fact, his kindness only made her feel worse. Instead, she wished Eric would've been angrier at her, but perhaps his passiveness was punishment enough.

In the end, Autumn made the decision not to date *anyone*. She needed time to figure things out, and she couldn't do that with a guy at her side.

It was a mild, fall afternoon and everyone was in Eric's backyard training and taking advantage of the rare weather. The sun was glimmering, the wind seamlessly blowing, and the sky was a clear and vivid blue. Many trees were bare, their buttery and auburn colored leaves laid strew on the ground or blowing in the wind.

Autumn, wearing a crisp, white tank top and grey sweat pants, was sparring with Rick.

On opposite sides of one another, Autumn shuffled around Rick.

Bobbing side to side, she taunted him, before kicking rapidly, trying her best to land blows.

Rick could easily evade her, but instead he took the hit, while giving her tips as they moved around the yard.

"Aut, remember, accuracy *and* force sweetie," he instructed, as Autumn landed a shaky but impactful punch, nearly missing him.

"Don't call me sweetie," Autumn smirked, taking another shot and clipping Rick in the shoulder.

Rick, who had been positioned to punch Autumn, stopped abruptly. Autumn was set to dodge him, but she dropped her defensive stance and put her hands on her hips.

"Rick, what was that?"

Rick looked at his hands guiltily. "I can't hit you. I never hit you. You know this."

"You *have* to hit me," she said, eyes narrowing. "Otherwise, I won't learn to dodge properly, and the big bad monsters *will* wallop me. *They* don't play nice."

Rick's face went pale at the mention of his beloved being attacked by monsters.

"Don't like that option much do you?" she asked sarcastically and Rick shook his head.

"Nope."

"Alright then, we are on the same page. Are you ready?"

"Ready," Rick said as Autumn got back into her defensive pose.

"Go for it. And don't go easy on me because I'm a girl."

Autumn saw a grin on Rick's face before his fist came flying at her. She moved out of the way lithely, ducking away from him with ease.

Rick went at her again, closing the distance between them. He kicked her with a roundhouse, and she dodged narrowly. She came at Rick with a side kick, followed by a sharp jab. The kick barely landed, but she got him in the jaw with the punch.

"Whoa!" Rick said, rubbing his face. "Time out tough guy!"

He looked at Autumn, eyes welling with pride. "That one hurt! Good job!"

The hours passed and by the end of the training session, Autumn and Rick were drenched in sweat.

Rick handed Autumn a towel and a bottle of water.

She took a seat on the grass, patting her face gently with the towel as Rick plopped down beside her.

Across the yard, Mandy and Nathaniel were also scuffling. Mandy was showing off, backflipping out of the reach of Nathaniel's kick. Her tiny frame soared through the air and when she landed, she lunged at him.

Nathaniel, who wore boxing pads on his hands, was thrown backwards from the force of Mandy's kick.

"Take that!" she said, smiling smugly.

"Jeez Mand, you kick like a freaking stallion," he muttered, just barely managing to keep his balance.

Mandy, dressed in a black T-shirt and matching shorts, raised one boxing-gloved hand in the air, to demonstrate her victory.

"And the crowd goes wild as Mandy Jensen defeats Nathaniel Abrams *AGAIN!*" she yelled in a mock-sports announcer voice.

Nathaniel rolled his eyes and walked towards her.

"Alright you win, but just remember, my rifle versus your fists, now *that's* a losing battle."

Mandy chuckled, patting his shoulder affectionately. "Boys and their toys."

Autumn sat with her legs outstretched on the lawn, soaking up the warmth that became so elusive. Rick reached out to grasp her hand, and she tingled at his touch.

The sound of a door opening startled her, and she looked up to see Eric approaching them. She pulled her hand back quickly and shifted slightly away from Rick.

Eric was dressed in his usual black shirt and jeans. His chin-length, dark hair framed his handsome face, and his tan skin glowed in the sunlight. He smiled as he came towards them.

"How is the training coming along?" he asked, taking a seat beside Autumn on the lawn.

Rick squeezed Autumn's shoulder affectionately.

"She nailed me quite a few times. She definitely has the heart of a warrior."

Eric looked at Rick touching Autumn and for a moment she swore she could see the longing glimmer in his eyes, but with a blink it all washed away, and he smiled again, looking untroubled.

"I wouldn't expect anything less of you Autumn," he said almost ruefully.

Autumn studied Eric's face carefully. Even though he tried to appear bright-eyed and bushy tailed, she could see the exhaustion in the form of shadows and bags around his dark eyes. Between schoolwork, the potions and the spell, he was obviously worn-out.

"I actually came out here with news," Eric began. "The good news, the spell is nearing completion."

"Really?" Autumn's eyes lit up.

"I'm so close Autumn. I can feel it in my bones. Basically, I need a few more *ingredients*, if you will. That's the bad news. One of them is quite inconvenient to attain."

Autumn expected the ingredient to be something sinister and heinous. Still, she had to ask.

"What is it?"

"I need blood," Eric said with finality.

Rick looked from Eric to Autumn and threw his arms around her protectively.

"Don't even *think* about asking Autumn for any blood King!" he shouted.

Eric, who was now used to Rick and Nathaniel's outrageous outbursts, looked at him, unfazed.

"I don't need Autumn's blood Rick."

"You can't have mine either!" Rick added hastily.

"I don't need *human* blood," Eric said, rolling his eyes. "Otherwise, I'd just use my own."

Rick let Autumn go tentatively and rested his face in his hands.

"Fine. Go on."

"I need monster blood," Eric said as he fiddled with a large, black ring on his finger.

"The cave monsters blood."

"The lizard men?' Rick asked and Eric took his cue, reaching into his pocket and pulling out a paper.

"They are actually demons, at least according to my research."

He showed them a drawing of the creature. It had obviously been scanned from one of Eric's many tomes, and it matched the description of the *lizard men* to a T.

"Of course, the demons come in all shapes and sizes because that cave doesn't discriminate when it comes to evil," Eric jested.

"How liberal," Autumn muttered as she heard Mandy's screech echo throughout the yard.

"HI YA!"

Everyone watched as Mandy and Nathaniel, both in complete protective padding, chased each other around the trees. Mandy swung a punch at Nathaniel, and he ducked, narrowly avoiding it. He kicked at Mandy, who caught his leg and turned it sideways. She kicked at Nathaniel, nearly getting him between his legs.

"Hey! Watch where you are kicking!" he said, backing away while panting. "You could ruin me!"

Mandy stood defiantly before him.

"In the world of monsters, no body parts are off-limits," she said sharply. "Now, bow to your sensei."

"My what?" Nathaniel asked, wiping sweat from his brow with the back of his hand.

"Your sensei!" Mandy said, louder this time. "Your teacher and your instructor! Bow to *me.*"

Nathaniel looked at her in disbelief, and then he began laughing hysterically.

Mandy's nose crinkled at his amusement.

"What the hell is so funny Abrams?"

"Sorry," Nathaniel said, almost doubled over in stitches. "I don't bow to people *shorter* than me."

Mandy's face inflamed with anger. "I will remember this insolence next time we train Nate!"

Nathaniel shrugged his shoulders carelessly and began pulling off his padding. "Don't you forget it."

Mandy rolled her eyes as the two of them headed towards the others.

Nathaniel took a seat next to Rick and was joined by Mandy, who noticed Eric's grave expression.

"Who died?" she asked, before pausing. "No one did die *right?*"

Eric shook his head. "No one is dead. I was just telling Autumn and Rick, I am close to completing the spell. I just need blood for the ritual."

"You can't have mine!" Nathaniel piped in immediately.

Eric sighed, and Rick put his hands up in the air. "I said the same thing dude!"

He looked at Eric. "You need to phrase that better man. You are freaking everyone out."

"I need the blood of the monsters," Eric said, looking exasperated now. "Cave monsters. *Lizard men* as you have dubbed them." He handed the paper to Mandy, who began examining it.

"They are demons?"

"Full-fledged," Eric replied.

"We can get the blood for you dude," Rick said confidently. "We have all been training. It will be a piece of cake. Besides, we could use the practice."

"As much as I *hate* putting any of you in harm's way, I was hoping that you would offer to help," Eric admitted. "As you know, I'm not the finest fighter."

"It's alright man," Nathaniel said. "We understand. You fight like a spaz."

"Thank you Nathaniel." Eric glared at him. "As always, I love when you remind me of my flaws."

"And how I *love* to remind you," Nathaniel said, grinning.

Autumn smiled. Eric was usually a fountain of infinite patience, but even she knew there was only so much of Nathaniel's boneheaded remarks you could endure before lashing out at him.

"Now, if we are done with the childish remarks, let's get back to the grownup stuff," Eric said.

He reached into his pocket and pulled out a vial, handing it to Rick.

"I need this filled to the brim with demon blood."

Nathaniel crossed his arms over his chest defiantly. "A little demanding aren't we?"

"We need that blood Nate or the demons win!" Mandy barked at him.

"Geez, I thought you elves were supposed to be cheerful," Nathaniel said as he inched away from her.

"Guys, I really appreciate this," Eric said, ignoring Nathaniel. "I will be coming along for moral support of course and in case any of you need healing."

"Sweet, invincibility!" Nathaniel said.

"You are not *invincible* Abrams," Eric said, warningly. He was constantly trying to hammer home the idea that fighting monsters wasn't a joke. He didn't want any of them taking it lightly.

"We have been through this. I can only heal minor things. And some healing can take longer depending on the severity of the wound. So, if you break your arm out there it will take longer to heal then say a cut on your leg, and you may be out of commission for a bit."

"So avoid getting nailed," Nathaniel said, leaning back on his elbows.

"That is obvious," Eric said plainly. "Be safe. This isn't a game. This is your life."

This is your life. The words resonated in Autumn's mind, but she still couldn't quite grasp them.

Demons, magic and fighting for blood. They were playing with fire. How did *this* become her life?

18

It was a sunny Saturday morning when Autumn awoke to the sound of her cell phone vibrating on her nightstand. She reached over, eyes hooded and sleepy, to see two text message alerts on the screen.

Both were from her sister.

A SEXY GUY CAME INTO THE SPA YESTERDAY. HE WAS TANNED, MUSCULAR AND RICH. NATURALLY, HE ASKED ME OUT! JEALOUS?

Autumn chuckled to herself. At least she wasn't hiding her bragging under thinly veiled pleasantries these days.

The next message was one Autumn hadn't expected.

Seriously, I miss you Aut. Please come home for Christmas!

Although Audrina was older than Autumn by three years, they suffered the same afflictions as most siblings, and sisterly rivalry was par for the course. Most of this was due to Audrina. Autumn couldn't be bothered to compete with her sister. Audrina enjoyed it. In fact, she thrived on it. She was always vying for their parent's attention or trying to upstage Autumn in some way.

Getting as many dates as she could, had always been her go-to ace in the hole.

After putting her phone back on the nightstand, Autumn's mind began drifting, like sleepy minds often do.

She pictured her mother, in her blue and white cotton apron, baking homemade cupcakes and banana bread. Her father, in the garage, waxing his sports car while listening to oldies on the radio. Kristin and her, on the front porch, drinking tea while discussing books. Even memories of Audrina and her bickering made her heart ache.

She searched her phone for a text message Kristin had sent yesterday.

Reading your favorite book in class today and thought of you. Miss you A.

It was official. Autumn was feeling homesick.

It wasn't long before Autumn's wandering thoughts lulled her into a light sleep. She had just dozed off when she was awoken by Rick and her aunt chattering downstairs. Autumn decided she had slept long enough and got up, stretching as she headed to the bathroom.

She took a shower, brushed her teeth and put on a pair of dark jeans and a pink tunic. As she made her way down the stairs to the kitchen, she overheard Rick's voice.

"Mom, did you or dad ever go to the caves outside of town?"

The question lingered in the air for so long that Autumn thought her aunt hadn't heard him.

She realized she had stopped at the foot of the stairs, essentially eavesdropping. She felt guilty but still awaited her Aunt Katherine's response, unable to move a muscle.

"Never," Aunt Katherine said finally. "Terrible stories are told about them though. Your father and I believe them too."

"You do?" Rick sounded taken aback. "You and dad believe in," he paused. "The supernatural?"

"Yes. We both believe in bad spirits. Even if the tales are partially fabricated, I think there is some grain of truth to them. *That* is enough to keep me away."

Autumn moved from the stairs to the kitchen. It was warm from cooking and smelt of vanilla candles and freshly fried bacon.

"Good morning all," she said and Aunt Katherine turned, smiling her familiar, kind smile.

"Good morning sweetheart. Are you hungry? I made up a plate for you when I heard you in the shower."

Autumn hadn't realized it, but she was actually quite ravenous.

"Thanks Aunt Katherine," she said gratefully as she moved towards Rick, who sat at the table.

Autumn took a seat beside him, and they exchanged greetings as her aunt placed a full plate in front of her.

"Rick, why are you asking about those caves?" her aunt picked up the conversation where it had left off. "*You* haven't been there have you?"

Rick, who as per usual, was inhaling his breakfast, blinked at his mother, surprised.

Autumn began eating her eggs, silently hoping Rick wouldn't spill the beans.

Much like herself, Rick was a terrible liar, so for him to blurt out that they had been there and were going back tonight to get monster blood, wouldn't be that far-fetched.

"Nathaniel and I went there once as a goof but we never went inside," Rick said carefully.

Aunt Katherine crossed her arms over her chest disapprovingly.

"Listen, Rick. I don't want you going back there *ever*. You or Autumn," she glanced at Autumn.

Autumn felt the guilt wash over her. She hoped she wasn't next in line for interrogation.

"It isn't safe. The kids who go there are just looking for trouble," Aunt Katherine admonished.

Autumn nodded and continued eating as the phone rang, deterring her aunt's attention.

Autumn sighed deeply and Rick and she exchanged relieved looks.

It was perfect timing.

"Hello? Oh hello there," she said jovially, heading off into the other room.

Autumn looked at Rick, who was reaching across the table for more bacon.

"That was close," she whispered. Far too close.

It was exactly nine at night when everyone was finally gathered in Eric's large living room. They were getting ready to head to the caves. Autumn sat on the couch next to Rick, her dark hair pulled back into a ponytail, tapping her foot nervously.

She wondered if she would ever get used to this. Going out to the caves and hunting monsters. Being a vigilante and hiding it from her family? Would this ever become trite and ordinary? Her nerves sparked as Nathaniel, who was sitting beside Eric and Mandy, stood up.

He cleared his throat, garnering everyone's attention.

"I would just like to say a few words," he began, and he clasped his hands together.

"I just wanted to say, before we head out into the unknown, that we have just cause to be doing what we are doing tonight," Nathaniel began. "We are fighting for this town, *our* town. We are fighting for our families and the families who have lost loved ones because of those demons. We are fighting for the greater good."

"A pep talk?" Autumn whispered to Mandy.

Mandy nodded, looking bored. "Go team go."

"I understand that what we are doing, to most, would be considered foolish, stupid, even careless," he said, his face grim. "Let me say, we are not like those other weak people. We are *not* afraid. We will not be overthrown by a bunch of hideous, vile, spitting creatures! We are better, stronger and faster, and we will fight until the bloody end!" he bellowed, his fist pumping into the air.

Rick pumped his fist too, showing his support. "Here here!"

Eric looked at Autumn, amused.

Mandy rolled her eyes. "Thanks coach."

Nathaniel shot Mandy a glare and walked towards her, placing his face inches from hers.

"You see this Jensen?"

"See what?" she asked, narrowing her eyes. "The giant idiot who's in my face?"

"Do you see how negative you can be? That negativity will drag us down!" Nathaniel barked.

"You just *spat* on me Abrams!" Mandy said as she wiped her face, eyes squinted in disgust.

"You better get used to it Jensen!" he said, shouting now.

"I am here to give you all confidence! That is what battle is about!" Nathaniel said, a huge smile on his freckled face. "We will be victorious!"

Rick let out another holler as Nathaniel stood in front of them all, shoulders back and chest puffed out.

"I would like to share my story of battle with you all," he began. "It took place when my father, Buck and I went hunting together."

Mandy raised a hand. He pointed at her, like a teacher addressing a student in class.

"Yes you, the stumpy girl who I spit on."

Mandy sneered at him. *"Buck the hunter? Really?"*

"And *I* thought elves were something out of fairy tales but yet here *you* are," Nathaniel quipped.

"As I was saying before I was so rudely interrupted, when we hunt together my dad always makes sure that we have all the proper equipment. So, the important thing tonight is that we are totally prepared."

Nathaniel reached into a duffel bag he had at his feet. He rummaged through it for a moment before pulling out folded garb. He shook it out, revealing a slim black bodysuit, reminiscent of something Autumn had seen in comic books.

He held it up proudly.

"These suits are specially designed by someone my dad knows. They are made of durable yet light Kevlar. They are basically armor. Bulletproof vests are made of this material."

After Nathaniel had successfully handed out a black suit to everyone, Rick looked at Eric, who seemed to be hunting through his potions satchel for something.

"Dude you forgot Eric!" he said.

"No I didn't. He's staying in the van, safe and sound," Nathaniel said. "That way, he can heal us if we need it. If we lose our medic, we are screwed."

"And if he needs to come out onto the field and heal us, then what?" Rick went on looking panicked. "He's going to run onto the battleground without armour and get attacked while trying to save one of us?""

Nathaniel looked stumped. "Good point."

"I'll field this one Nate," Eric chimed in.

Nathaniel blew out a breath of relief. "Good because I wasn't sure how to answer that."

"First off, I appreciate the concern Rick." Eric smiled. "But I don't need to be physically close to you guys to heal you. In fact, I don't even need to touch you."

Autumn arched an eyebrow curiously. She had spent enough time with Eric to know he was gifted.

Magic was where he exceled. He studied every facet of it and read any spell book he could get his hands on.

She wondered what tricks were up his sleeve tonight.

"Remember I mentioned Arabella was scrying the night my parents died?"

Everyone nodded as Eric disappeared for a brief moment into the adjacent room. Eventually, he returned, holding what looked like a giant bowl. It looked to be empty, deep and made of wood. Etched on the bowls surface were many foreign symbols.

Eric, wearing the arrogant grin he often wore when he was about to dazzle everyone, sat on the floor, placing the bowl in front of him.

"Gather round," he instructed and they all sat near Eric as he began shuffling through vials in his satchel. Finally, he appeared to find what he was looking for. He poured it into the empty bowl and began to chant.

"Sit portae capit, magia per oculos videamus!" he called out.

They watched as Eric took his finger and dipped it in the bowl, swirling it around. The liquid began moving and rippling until an image formed in it.

Autumn leaned over the bowl and gaped wondrously at the sight.

It was an exact mirror image of her and her friends, in Eric's living sitting around the bowl.

"Whoa," Rick said, his eyes wide. "I can see *us* in there!"

"Who is that handsome ginger?" Nathaniel remarked.

Mandy rolled her eyes. Autumn watched as the reflected Mandy in the bowl rolled her eyes too.

"It is an exact reflection," Eric said. "But it isn't just that."

"So you can watch us wherever we are?" Autumn asked. The reflected Autumn's lips moved, but no sound came out. It was like watching an old, silent movie. The sight was ghoulish, almost haunting.

Eric nodded. "Better than that," he said, and he grabbed another vial out of his satchel, adding it to the mix. He swirled his finger in the liquid again and chanted as everyone watched the bowl in anticipation. Finally, after nothing happened, Rick piped up.

"What are we looking for?" Eric held up his hand and a second later Rick's voice came through the bowl loud and clear like an echo.

What are we looking for? The reflected Rick spoke.

"It talk's too!" Rick said, looking utterly bewildered.

It talk's too! The voice piped in again.

Eric said something in Latin and waved his hand, looking up at his friends, proudly.

"I made it stop for now. Mostly having a constant echo is rather abrasive."

"Especially if it's Nathaniel's voice we are hearing," Mandy grinned, nudging Nathaniel in the side playfully.

"So, I can see and hear you guys. If you get wounded, I take the appropriate healing potion and pour it into the bowl, and you will be good as new in no time. No physical contact necessary."

"That is amazing," Autumn said, looking at Eric admiringly. "You certainly have a knack."

Eric's dark eyes met her green ones, and he winked. She could tell he reveled in the praise, but he was playing it cool.

"That was *nothing* compared to what my parents could do with magics," he said modestly. "They were truly marvelous. Both were prodigies. The stories my family has told me."

After Eric's astounding demonstration, they went over their plan for the evening. Autumn, Rick, Nathaniel and Mandy would wander around the cave area and hope to find more demons. When they had a dead specimen, they would extract its blood, using a magical dagger Eric provided them, and put it into the vial for safekeeping. Eric would wait in the van in the parking lot, keeping an eye on them, ready to heal them if need be.

As time ticked by, Autumn felt herself getting more excited. She could feel the adrenaline propelling through her, as they spoke of the night ahead of them. Her fears were replaced, washed away by the thrill and power of the hunt.

The clock struck eleven o'clock and everyone, dressed in their armour, piled into Nathaniel's van.

They drove to the caves, in no rush, as light droplets of rain trickled on the windows and roof. Autumn watched the mostly darkened scenery, trying to pick out landmarks.

The silhouette of a barn and a silo on acres of deserted land, houses with long, winding gravel driveways and lights glowing in their windows. Trees swaying carelessly in the wind, miles upon miles of wires, telephone poles and streetlights, some burnt out and others flickering, close to it.

Autumn wasn't surprised. When they pulled into the parking lot near the caves, it was empty.

The wind was chilly, being late into fall, and it was dark and dreary out.

The only light came from a few streetlights in the parking lot and Nathaniel's headlights.

"Wow, this place is jumping tonight," Mandy said sarcastically as she unbuckled her belt.

"The less people out here the better," Eric replied.

Everyone began piling out of the van, preparing to gear up, but before Autumn could join them, she felt Eric reach out and grab her hand.

He said nothing for a split second, only staring into her eyes intensely. Her heart skipped a beat, and for a moment she thought he was going to lean over and kiss her.

"I know things aren't like they were in the beginning between us," he began quietly. "But my feelings for you haven't changed. I want you to know that. Please, be careful out there tonight."

"Eric, I am always careful," she began, and he touched her mouth gently with his fingertip.

"Just promise me, you will," he said his voice barely a whisper. "Because if I ever lost you, I wouldn't be able to take it."

Autumn's stomach fluttered, and she felt a rush of affection for Eric overcoming her.

She leaned into him, allowing him to embrace her. He squeezed her tightly in his arms.

"I will be careful," she murmured into his shoulder. "I promise."

He kissed her gently atop her forehead. "I will be watching over you like a hawk Autumn. That's my promise to you."

Autumn went to join the others, who were huddled around Nathaniel, who was looking through a large duffel bag. She already knew what it contained.

Nathaniel, with the help of his brother Conrad and his gang of outlaw buddies, managed to snag them more weapons.

The more Autumn found out about Nathaniel's brother, the more she felt like an accomplice to something illegal. Nathaniel had made a valid point that they couldn't be expected to fight empty handed against the creatures. It wasn't safe. They needed provisions.

"Alright," Nathaniel said getting everyone's attention. "I have your weapons here," he said, and he reached into the duffel bag. First, he pulled out a scythe with a long steel handle. The blade glinted menacingly in the moonlight.

"Autumn, this one is for you."

Autumn took it carefully, studying it. "Great. So now I'm the grim reaper?"

Nathaniel shrugged. "Considering the circumstances, I think that sounds promising."

"Mandy your nunchucks," he went on, handing them to her cautiously. "And don't use them on *me*, no matter how angry I make you."

"I can't promise anything," Mandy said, running her fingers along them deviously.

"For me, I have my rifle complete with scope, so I can hide in the trees and play sniper," he said. "And Rick brought his own item from home." He gestured to Rick.

Rick grinned and unsheathed a double-edged sword. Autumn remembered it as soon as saw it. Rick had quite the collection of swords, but this one was special. His father won it for him, for an undisclosed amount of money, at an auction in New York City. Rick had told her in an email when he got it, that his father had to outbid at least ten other wealthy businessmen for it. Rick often practiced his sword fighting with that sword, in particular, calling it his "lucky blade."

Despite having zero knowledge of swords, Autumn could see the sword was obviously well-crafted, with its glimmering dense steel blade. The hilt was adorned with beautiful ruby gems and bared an etching of a wolf on it.

"That is so cool looking," Mandy said enviously, touching the blade with her fingers gently. "I love swords, even though I'm not trained to fight with one."

"My dad won it for me at an auction," Rick held it up proudly. "It means more than anything to me," he paused before glancing at Autumn ruefully.

"Well, almost *anything.*"

The last few minutes in the parking lot were spent adjusting armor, prepping gear and stretching muscles. The ominous hooting of an owl, in the distance, rang out like a warning. Telling them of secrets it knew, secrets they dare not uncover.

Eric popped his head out one last time to wish them all luck as Nathaniel looked at his watch, clearly getting impatient. Autumn could relate. She was raring to go and damn near tempted to run across the field and leave everyone in her dust, as she raced into the dark depths.

"Alright guys, its time," Rick said finally and everyone clicked on their flashlights and began their trek towards the caves.

19

The night was quiet and eerie as they trudged along, looking for signs of anything evil. The owl didn't hoot. The rain subsided. All Autumn heard was the sound of breaking branches under feet and the wind howling its refrain.

Ahead of her, her breath was coming out in puffs.

Winter was just around the corner, waiting for the right moment to snatch Whitan in its icy grasp.

The moon hid stealthily behind sheets of thick clouds creating nothing but darkness ahead. The only light came from their flashlights as they moved along, listening for any wild, savage cries.

Nathaniel went ahead of them to take point, positioning himself to play sniper. Eric was in the van, safe and sound.

Autumn wasn't relying on her ears. She knew her body would tell her if trouble was afoot. Like an alarm system, it would warn her.

They were only minutes from the caves when the hairs on the back of Autumn's neck stood on end.

"Don't move," Autumn said, stopping dead in her tracks.

Mandy and Rick, who were on either side of her, came to a halt.

"What is it?" Rick asked, looking at Autumn through the darkness.

"I don't know *what* it is," Autumn said, her voice low. "Just that it's *here*."

She looked around, moving her flashlight slowly across the landscape.

At first, she saw nothing.

Just grass wafting in the wind, set against a black night sky.

She blinked, letting her eyes adjust and that is when she noticed it.

A few feet away, a shadowy figure perched, unmistakable.

She didn't dare shine her flashlight directly on it. Instead, she tapped Rick's shoulder, her finger touching her lips, indicating silence. Rick and Mandy followed her line of vision.

Autumn already knew what the plan was.

They attacked it together and they took its blood, easy as pie.

Slowly, they began moving in harmony.

They walked cautiously closer to it, not wanting to make any sharp, sudden movements.

The figure stayed motionless and when they got close enough, Autumn gradually aimed her flashlight at it.

"Oh my God," Autumn whispered, feeling her stomach lurch at the grotesque thing looking back at her.

Its skin was grey and hollow, and its dead eyes blazed crimson in the flashlights glow.

The creature's body was massive and burly, and it was hunchbacked like its own weight was too much to bear. Its veiny arms throbbed and tensed, and it growled, emitting a sound that sent shivers down Autumn's spine.

It had huge claws that were long and black, and it had no nose, only nostrils. As it opened its maw to growl again, Autumn saw rows upon rows of razor-sharp teeth.

"That doesn't look like a lizard at all," Mandy said, unable to take her eyes off it.

The monster watched them menacingly, breathing heavily into the night air.

Autumn wondered how intelligent it was. Was it instinct driven or did it have a penchant for death and destruction? Judging by its murderous stare, it was most likely the latter.

Autumn reached into a pocket in her armor and slipped on the night vision goggles Nathaniel had given her. Rick and Mandy already had theirs on and both were in their fighting stances, weapons in hand. Autumn followed their leads, getting her scythe at the ready.

She felt the familiar rush, as her heart slammed into her chest. The creature moved towards them, cracking its veiny neck side to side.

Then, like lightning streaking the night sky, it lunged, springing from its position and into the air, kicking directly at Mandy.

Mandy tried her best to dodge, but the blow landed. This monster was far faster than the last, and it kicked her in the leg, its large foot claws digging into her armor.

Mandy cried out and the monster growled gutturally, kicking again, closer now and with inhuman speed.

It hit her once more near the same spot, this time piercing her armor, gashing her right leg, above her knee.

The blood dripped from her leg onto the grass, and the monster watched the ruby liquid trickle down, fascinated and entranced. It licked its lips hungrily and snapped at Mandy, but she jumped back narrowly, dodging its bite.

"Mandy!" Autumn cried out, her adrenaline pumping. She rushed at the creature while it was distracted.

She swung her scythe and clipped it in the arm, below its elbow. It cried out, hissing in pain and she swung again and hit it in the shoulder.

Grunting, it leapt away, landing a few feet from her. As Rick stood posed to defend, Autumn took the opportunity to get to Mandy.

"Are you alright?" Autumn asked but before Mandy could answer the wound was sealing itself up, the bleeding desisting.

Eric. Autumn thought to herself.

"Thanks Eric!" Mandy said, looking upwards to praise her hero.

Then, her face set with determination, she looked around, spotting the creature.

It was tangling with Rick, who was blocking its attacks and slashing at it with his sword to no avail.

"It's mine!" Mandy cried and she ran at the beast, nunchucks spinning in her hands like propellers.

The creature snarled, its sharp teeth bared and its claws ready to strike.

Autumn went to Rick, her eyes still on the beast, when she heard another sound. It seemed to be coming from behind her. She felt her body tense up, and she turned around, dreading what she already knew.

Another creature, this one tall and wiry, was coming towards them. As it got closer, Autumn noticed this one resembled the lizard man they saw before. It had shiny, scaly red skin, dotted with several black spots. Its back and head were covered in spiked, black horns.

This creature didn't bother to size them up.

It charged at them, hissing ferociously.

Rick was the first to get a shot in, slicing the lizard across the chest with his sword. The lizard hissed and revealed its long, forked tongue, its bulging, frog-like eyes filled with malice. It swiped at Rick, clawing him in the arm but still not penetrating his armor.

"Nice try!" Rick said arrogantly. "Too slow!"

Autumn swung her scythe at the creature, aiming for its head, but it quickly ducked. It hissed again and sprang, its sights set on her now. Autumn was startled to see it was wielding a rusty ax.

"It has a weapon!" Rick said in disbelief.

The monsters head spun around, resting on its neck at an unnatural angle.

It looked at Rick, its lips forming a sharp-toothed grin.

Autumn felt goosebumps crawling along her arms. It was a sight nightmares were made of.

"Master trained us," it hissed. "To fight with weapons and to kill all the humans."

Autumn gaped at the creature, stunned.

It could speak ... in human tongue.

Rick looked at the monster incredulously. "Holy shit."

The creature snorted, its breath making clouds in the cool night air.

"TIME TO DIE!"

It snarled loudly, its head spinning back into place. Then it moved with lightning speed towards Autumn, ax raised above its head, ready to slash.

20

Eric watched from the van, horrified, as the battle raged on. He continued scrying, when he heard the creature speak in human tongue. It shocked him most when it referred to a *master*.

This intrigued him. He had always assumed, for lack of better knowledge, that the demons were abominations conjured by some evil magic and left to roam the caves. Now, for the first time, he saw a possible motive. The demons had a ringleader, a puppeteer.

The question was, who was pulling the strings and why?

The ax came swinging down towards Autumn, and she screamed. She waited for the feeling of rusty metal to slash through her. She waited for the pain, the agony and of course, the flow of blood.

Instead, she heard clanking as Rick's sword clashed with the creature's ax. Rick had jumped in front of her and was now pushing his sword against the ax. Rick used all his might, pushing the creature backwards through the muddy grass.

It screeched, struggling to keep its balance as Rick shoved all his weight against it.

When Rick managed to get close enough to the monster, he didn't hesitate. With a grunt, he plunged his sword into its gut. The creature cried out in agony, its face contorted in pain, and it fell to the ground, motionless.

Rick pulled his blade back out, and it seemed to shimmer in the darkness. The mix of blood and gleaming was almost blinding.

Autumn stood still, in shock, when she heard a silenced gunshot come from the bushes nearby.

The monster Mandy had been fighting, who looked rather beaten and bruised, was hit by a soaring bullet.

The ghoulish, grey creature fell to the ground, thudding. It twitched for a moment, writhing wildly then its eyes went dead and its huge body remained still.

Nate. Autumn thought numbly as Rick rushed over to her. He slipped his arms around her shoulders. She didn't even look up at him. Instead, she stared blankly at the two dead things on the ground. The two dead things that *together,* they had *killed.* The thought was absurd and surreal, and her mind couldn't fully process it.

Monsters are real. It was a fact her brain couldn't quite fathom.

Still, she didn't feel remorse. Those *things* deserved everything they got. They killed people, ruined lives and tore apart families. Eric's included.

"Are you alright?" Rick took her face into his hands gently.

He looked wild with panic, as he brushed his fingers across her cheeks lightly.

"Aut, come on honey. Are you in there?"

Like an anchor, his blue eyes pulled her back from the depths, from her own wandering despair. Her fear, and the idea that this was all a horrible nightmare she would wake up from, all of it melted away.

She snapped back to reality and nodded slowly, her eyes meeting his as he came into full focus, like a blurry image gradually getting sharper.

"I'm fine," she paused, her breath coming quick and clipped. "The ax could've hit me. I could have died."

Rick nodded, his eyes welling up. She had come so very close to death.

"You *could've* but you didn't. I would never let anything happen to you."

"Perhaps I wouldn't have died. Maybe it just would've hurt, really bad," she went on, her shoulders trembling. "The ax was dirty and so rusty and ..." she trailed off.

"You are fine. You are safe now. Take a deep breath sweetheart," Rick said gently, his eyes not leaving hers.

"It's over now."

Autumn followed Rick's instructions and took a few deep breaths.

If they were going to protect Whitan, she had to get better at controlling her fear. She couldn't let the monsters throw her off, and get the edge. The others couldn't protect her all the time like Rick had today. If he was too busy watching her back, he wouldn't have time to watch his own.

"Hey, is everyone alright here?" Mandy came over to them, looking dishevelled, sweat dripping from her brow.

Rick nodded, wiping his bloody blade on the damp grass.

"Yep we are good." He began looking around him.

"Where is Nate?"

"Present!" Nathaniel, armed with his gun, came jogging over to them from the brush.

"We won!" he said, grinning. "Go team humans!"

"Let's get that magic dagger out and collect the blood before more monsters come," Mandy suggested grimly.

"On it," Autumn said and she pulled out the magical dagger Eric had entrusted to her.

She did exactly as Eric had instructed. She put the dagger right in the first monsters grey muscled chest. She left it there until the hilt of the dagger turned from white to red and then placed the daggers tip into the vile he had given them.

The four of them watched as the dagger tip began seeping blood into the vile. The thick, murky blood filled it, until eventually the dagger was sucked dry. Autumn screwed the cap on the vile and watched as the blood inside bubbled ominously.

Not long after they had retrieved the blood, Eric came to join them and help them dispose of the dead monsters using his magic. When they were finished, and every piece of debris and evidence had been cleaned up, they began walking back to the parking lot.

"Your fighting has improved," Rick said to Autumn as they trekked along through the damp field. "I'm impressed."

Autumn felt much stronger than the last time they were at the caves, but she knew she could do better. In her mind, there was always room for improvement, and she wouldn't be satisfied until she could stand on her own without needing to be saved by *anyone*.

She looked at Rick. "I just wish I didn't freeze up when he swung that ax at me."

He took her hand into his and squeezed it reassuringly.

"I don't know *anyone* that could look into the face of death and *not* freeze up," he said. "You did amazing Aut."

"Thanks," she said, smiling weakly.

The rain picked up again, making everyone move faster.

Unsure if it was the slippery, wet terrain or just bad coordination, Autumn felt the earth slide from beneath her. She flailed wildly, trying to keep her balance, but she toppled over, plunging to the ground.

"Damn it!" she cursed.

"Autumn, are you alright?" Rick asked, reaching out his hand to her.

"I'm alright," she said, taking it. "I tripped over something."

She looked at the ground, curious to see what rock or tree branch she had managed to hit.

Her heart stopped when she saw what caused her fall.

"Oh my God," Rick began, his eyes getting wide. The others looked at the huge indent in the ground.

Autumn examined it more closely, confirming it was a giant footprint.

More than that, it was a giant paw print.

Autumn awoke the next morning with cold morning dew against her skin and birds chirping boisterously above her head.

Her eyes shot open and she immediately panicked. She recognized where she was. She was lying on her back in the field, only steps away from where the caves were.

She sat up slowly and groggily, trying to remember how she ended up here.

Eric, Mandy, Rick, Nathaniel and she had been heading to the van when she tripped over the paw print. They were examining it, and that was the last thing she remembered.

Judging by the blinding sunlight it was late morning now.

She stood up and dusted off her black Kevlar suit. She stretched and ran her hands through her damp hair.

It was cold, and she could feel the frigid air cutting through her armor and clothes, both damp from sleeping in the rain-soaked grass.

She began to walk across the field, looking for Rick and the others. She called out into the crispy air, searching the seemingly endless field, when she spotted something clustered in the distance.

She began running.

Her heart pounding, the air releasing from her lips in smoky clouds ahead of her, she ran for what felt like miles until she was breathless and had to stop.

That's when she noticed them.

Lying in the field, in varying positions, as far as the eye could see.

Bodies.

Lifeless and still, they were scattered all around her.

There were hundreds. At first, they were faceless and unrecognizable.

Autumn felt her stomach lurch unpleasantly as she rushed to the closest form, trying to decipher someone's identity.

The first was Mandy; she was torn to bits, shredded to ribbons, with her face the only part of her left intact.

Not far from her was Nathaniel, covered in acidic spit that had burnt through his clothes and skin leaving behind nothing but disintegrated flesh and bones.

Autumn ran to the other side of the field to the next body. It was Eric. His neck was clearly broken. His head was resting on the ground at an unnatural angle, and his eyes were lifeless. In his bloodied hands, he clutched an ancient book of spells.

The wind whistled loudly, whipping her black hair around her face and chilling her to the bone. She felt tears falling from her eyes, tasting like salt as they trickled from her cheeks to her lips.

Her attention was drawn to a trail of bodies that led closer to the cave mouth. She followed them along like links in a chain, like a person on a sick and twisted scavenger hunt.

The last person, whom she feared looking at most, though she wasn't sure why, had a sword skewered through them. Their body was lying limp and ragged, in a pool of vibrant red blood.

Autumn let out a terrible scream when she saw his face.
It was Rick and on his torso, written in blood were words.
Time to die.
She knelt beside Rick trembling, stroking his curls, her mind denying everything she was seeing and touching. Her screams echoed in her ears, her body racked with sobs of despair, until everything around her went black.

Autumn.
Someone was uttering her name in a singsong voice.
Autumn.
The voice sounded far away, like it was being filtered through many walls.
Autumn, wake up.
She opened her eyes and bolted upright, feeling a body next to hers.

"Whoa!" Rick exclaimed. "It was just a nightmare Autumn. You're safe."
Autumn looked around her, letting her surroundings slowly come into focus. She was in Rick's room, in his bed. Her clothes were soaked with sweat. She kicked off the covers. She was overheating.

Rick was stroking her hair softly and looking down at her with his adoring eyes.
"Are you alright?" he asked, looking concerned. "You were thrashing and muttering."

Autumn felt relief rushing over her. Rick was alive. It *was* just a nightmare, a dreadful nightmare. She reached out to Rick and clutched him tightly.

She remembered now. They had come home from their cave monster expedition and after a shower and a warm cup of tea Autumn was still pretty shaken up. Rick offered to sleep with her. She didn't decline. It all made sense now.

"You were dead," she began quietly. "Everyone was. Mandy, Nate and Eric. And there were piles of other dead bodies. Strangers. People I didn't recognize."

Rick didn't let her go, whispering gently into her ear. "It was just a nightmare."

"It seemed so real," she murmured, inhaling Rick's familiar scent. With his arms around her, she always felt safe.

"How about you relax here, and I'll go get you some breakfast?" Rick offered. "Will that help cheer you up?"

His face was inches from hers now, and she wanted to kiss him so much it made her ache. She told herself she wouldn't do this. She wouldn't give into temptation. She had chosen neither Rick nor Eric but now looking at Rick, the way he doted on her, the tenderness in his eyes. Her resolve was quickly slipping away.

Autumn could feel the electricity between them. The anticipation was palpable.

She could tell Rick felt it too.

"I am actually famished," she admitted. "I could use some carbs."

He cleared his throat, gaining his composure. "I'll run to the coffee shop. The usual then? Tea with two sugars and two milks and a bagel with extra cream cheese, right?"

Autumn nodded grinning like a fool. Rick really *did* know her inside out. This didn't help to deter her admiration. It only amplified it.

"Thanks Ricky."

"No problem," he placed a quick kiss on her forehead. "Be right back."

Since more sleep was no longer an option after her nightmare, Autumn jumped onto Rick's laptop to kill time while he fetched breakfast.

When she turned it on, the first thing she noticed was his screen saver.

It was a picture of Rick and her from the summer. She remembered Aunt Katherine snapping the photo a week after she arrived. They were on the front porch, and Rick was holding Autumn, arms around her waist from behind, as she beamed.

Both wore natural smiles. The rare kind that crinkled the corners of your eyes and didn't require force or practice. Autumn could recall the moment. She felt content and relaxed with Rick holding her, like she belonged with him.

Once the laptop finished loading up, she went on the web and logged into her email account.

The one she immediately noticed had the subject line: Miss you! It was from Kristin.

Autumn began reading it.

Hey Autumn!

I was sitting at my computer and saw the picture of us together at the "Museum of Local Art" (not its actual name, as you know). Remember the guy who took it for us? He was wearing a peach scarf and a fedora, and he kept referring to us 'aspiring models' and asked us to 'pose' for him.

We are in front of the ugliest abstract painting I have ever seen (custard yellow and diarrhea brown), and we are laughing about it (and about creepy peach scarf fedora guy).

So long story short (or short story long haha) I miss you! Obviously, there aren't many stimulating conversationalists at our school unless you count the librarian Mrs. Bilson, but she is going deaf and ignores most of us now. She doesn't even tell the students to be quiet like she used to. It is very sad and not very cliché librarian like at all.

I miss talking to you in person about good books, poems and of course cute guys (none of the transfer guys were even close to cute this semester despite my prayers).

So I was thinking. If you don't end up coming home for Christmas break (You better!) that we should do a girls weekend March Break. We could head into the city, shop and see a good play at the theatre. We could even book a hotel and maybe get a swanky room with a spa bathtub or something and spend the weekend up there?

Let me know what you think.

Miss you lots.

Xoxo

Kristin

P.S. I want some guy gossip ASAP. You have been holding out on the elusive Eric you mentioned to me! I want ALL the gory details of your torrid affair!

The next email came from her mother.

Autumn,

Please give me a call sometime this week. Your father and I want to discuss Christmas break with you.

Hope all is well since we last spoke a few nights ago. Love you and talk to you soon sweetie.

Love always,

Mom

After reading all the heartwarming emails, Autumn was feeling close to normal again. That was until she caught a glimpse of what Rick had been browsing on the Internet.

A page of search results for the query "Giant paw print Canada" filled the screen and the feeling of normalcy dissipated as quickly as it came.

Autumn began filtering through the search results.

Bears and wolves were the most common explanation but before Autumn could delve deeper into her search, Rick was at the door with breakfast.

Over bagels, she told him about the emails from her mom and Kristin. Rick offered to talk to his mom and dad about having her parents down for Christmas, so they could all be together. Autumn knew Rick meant so *they* could be together, and she was glad. She didn't want to leave him behind either. She was afraid she would miss him too much.

After breakfast, as Rick and Autumn cleaned up their takeaway garbage, Rick casually asked Autumn to go to the mall with him.

Autumn studied Rick, debating if he was being serious or not. Rick had never been one for shopping.

"*You* want to go shopping?" Autumn blinked, unable to hide her surprise. "At the mall?"

"*I* want *you* to have a relaxing day. No talk of monsters or training or spells," he said.

"We can go get you strawberry ice cream, look at the new books, pick up some fancy chocolate. All those things you love so much."

Autumn *was* in need of new reading material.

She smiled. "Okay then. Let me get showered and dressed, and we'll head out."

Autumn turned to go but Rick reached out, grabbing her wrist gently.

"Wait."

She turned, facing him.

"What is it?" she asked and suddenly Rick was kissing her.

Autumn knew she should pull away, but something drew her towards him. The harder she fought the urge to be with him, the stronger the pull was.

So she gave in and let him kiss her, on her lips, throat and shoulders.

By the time they were finished kissing, half an hour had passed.

When they finally made it to the mall, it was already packed with afternoon shoppers. Dressed in a lace tunic and jeans, with her dark hair in a braid, Autumn walked beside Rick, watching people pass by her.

A mother and father with their scowling child, teenagers traveling in packs and elderly people walking gingerly and unhurriedly, not worrying about the world rushing by around them.

Autumn remembered being just like them.

She *was once* blissfully ignorant too. Unaware of the worlds secrets, oblivious to the supernatural.

Some part of her envied their unawareness, and yet another part pitied them. They had no idea what was out there, what might come for them in the night. Once you knew, there was no turning back. There was no pretending, no evasion. Once Pandora's Box was opened, there was no closing it.

Distracted by the very thoughts she was trying to ignore, Autumn kept hoping that Eric might call and say he finished the spell. She wanted this nightmare to end.

Rick took Autumn's hand into his, as they weaved through the mobs of eager shoppers. She glanced at him, her mind unencumbered from her reverie.

"Are you alright Aut?" he asked her, nearly getting bowled over by a burly man carrying too many shopping bags.

"I'm fine," Autumn said, giving Rick her best reassuring smile. "I was just thinking about Eric."

Rick's face went instantly sour. *"Eric?"*

"Oh not *about* Eric exactly," she said quickly. "About the spell and if he's finished it yet."

"Oh," Rick said. "We just got the blood yesterday night Aut. We got home late. Give the guy time. Besides, *no* supernatural talk. We are shopping, remember?"

Autumn sighed. "I know. No more, I promise."

Rick leaned over, giving her a quick peck on the mouth. "Alright. Where to next?"

"Oh look! Jacobs got himself a girlfriend," said a familiar voice. "How much did you pay her?"

Autumn didn't need to look over to know who it was running their mouth.

Sitting at the food court, at a white roundtable, gawking at them, was Ben and two of his cronies. Dressed in their trademark varsity jackets, they were high-fiving each other and chortling at Ben's pathetic quip.

"What is the going rate on paying girls to date you these days Ben? I figured you *would* know," Autumn replied curtly.

The group of them stopped laughing. Ben grimaced.

"Girls love me sweetheart. No cash required," he boasted.

Autumn shrugged. "I heard differently Ben. Apparently, you aren't much of a catch. You are loud, obnoxious and dumb as a sack of potatoes."

Ben snorted, looking at his friends and back to Autumn.

"Don't worry babe. We can hook up anytime you like. I know you want it."

Autumn rolled her eyes, arms crossed over his chest. *"And* you're arrogant! Wow, you are just repulsive all the way around aren't you?"

Rick chuckled lightly as Ben stood up, chest puffed out like a peacock, and began walking towards them.

"No one asked *you* to speak little woman," he said.

Then he looked to Rick. "It's a shame you got to her first Jacobs. I would've wrecked that bitch and tossed her to the curb when I was finished."

Autumn sighed. She knew what was coming next when Rick relinquished her hand. He charged across the food court, weaving past the empty and occupied tables alike, rushing towards Ben.

Autumn had never seen Rick so angry. His cheeks were flushed with a heated rage. His hands were balled into fists. She wanted to chase after him, but thought better of it. This wasn't her battle to fight.

Rick could handle it himself.

Finally face-to-face, Rick and Ben began sizing each other up.

"Didn't your mother teach you to respect women Mills?" Rick asked, biceps tensing. "You apologize to Autumn *now.*"

The other two guys stood up, but Ben ordered them to sit back down.

Autumn looked around. Crowds of curious shoppers had gathered, and many of the food court patrons had abandoned their conversations to watch the show unfurl.

Ben stepped even closer to Rick, squaring his shoulders, eyes narrowed.

"The problem is Mills you are jealous. You asked Autumn out and she flat out rejected you," Rick spat. "And the great Ben Mills has never been rejected! Most girls fall all over you. It just goes to show you. Autumn isn't like other girls. She has brains."

Rick stood there, in Ben's face, smirking, victorious. Rejection seemed to hit a raw nerve with Ben because he put his hands on Rick's chest and shoved him.

And like a tree firmly rooted to the earth, Rick didn't budge an inch. Autumn knew Rick had been training hard, and this was the outcome. He was stronger than he had ever been. It gave her chills to watch him.

Autumn heard murmurs from the crowd as Ben stared at Rick, clearly surprised. He tried to shove Rick again, but Rick caught both his hands this time and began twisting his wrists.

Ben tried his best to withstand the pain, but his face was turning an ugly shade of purple, and before long he began crying out. His friends stood up, ready to close in on Rick, just as Autumn saw a figure pushing through the crowd.

"Hey! Hey! Break it up!"

She looked over and saw it was her guidance counselor, Mr. Garrison.

Rick glanced at the counselor, seemingly weighing his options, before he hesitantly let Ben go.

When Ben was free from Rick's grasp, he didn't wait around to be lectured.

"This isn't over Jacobs!" he bellowed as he and his friends took off. Autumn watched as they bolted towards the escalators and out of sight.

"Alright, everyone there's nothing to see here. This re-enactment of a teen drama show is over," Mr. Garrison said as he shooed the crowds away with a wave of his hands.

As the people all dispersed, Autumn rushed over to Rick. It was obvious he still had adrenaline coursing through him. His cheeks were red and his hands trembled, probably aching to punch Ben in the face.

"Autumn, give me a second to calm him down," Mr. Garrison implored. Autumn nodded and stepped back as the consoler forced his way into Rick's line of vision.

"Rick," he began, his voice measured and smooth. "Calm down and breathe. The altercation is over. Ben is gone. You can relax now."

Mr. Garrison spoke, and it was like a sea of calmness was washing over Rick. Even Autumn could feel the consoler's tranquility extending out towards her.

With obvious effort, Rick began breathing deeply. His eyes went from Mr. Garrison, to Autumn, anchoring to her comforting face. Minutes later, his trembling subsided and the red drained from his cheeks.

"That's it. Deep breaths buddy," Mr. Garrison coaxed.

"That's good Rick," Autumn said soothingly. She touched him softly on his chest. She could feel his heart pounding rhythmically with his breaths.

"I'm fine," Rick said but Mr. Garrison led him to a bench outside the malls movie theatre.

Rick sat down with Autumn beside him. She touched his knee gently.

"Sorry Aut. The anger, it just overcame me," he said, looking ashamed. "I have never felt such fury in my life."

"It's alright," Autumn replied. "Ben was the one who sparked that fire."

"I don't by any means condone violence, especially in public, but Mr. Mills has a history of provoking people," Mr. Garrison said, straightening his brown sport coat.

"He's had it in for me since our first encounter," Autumn explained.

"Ah, rejection can be a painful thing for a teenage boy. You probably remind him of his failure," Mr. Garrison replied casually.

"You think he'd be used to failure by now," Autumn muttered.

Rick chuckled quietly. She smiled at the counselor gratefully.

"Thanks for breaking up the fight. Everyone else seemed content to do nothing."

Mr. Garrison nodded.

"Most people can't resist the thrill of conflict, especially when they are just spectators not participants."

"I just can't believe Mills and his lackeys ran," Rick said, looking rather pleased. "Cowards."

"Anyone who believes three against one is a fair fight *is* a coward," Autumn said, frowning. "Those guys were just itching to jump in."

Rick blew a raspberry.

"I could've taken all three of them," he said arrogantly.

"Really?" Mr. Garrison said, looking intrigued. "You sound pretty confident son."

"Oh yeah. I studied martial arts and I train every day," Rick replied proudly. "They are fortunate I didn't use any of my *moves* on them. I wish I'd had my lucky sword to scare them with."

Autumn looked at Mr. Garrison, who looked back at her, and they shared a grin.

"Well, since you just mentioned a *student* and a *weapon* in the same sentence, I am going to pretend I didn't hear that," Mr. Garrison said, shaking his head.

"I should be off now. I do have some shopping to do." He reached into his pocket and pulled out a large red apple. He shined it with his shirt sleeve and grinned.

"You two enjoy the rest of the day. And try to stay out of trouble."

As he walked away, Autumn thought that lately, trouble always seemed to find them, no matter where they were.

21

Two weeks passed since operation blood retrieval. It was late November now, edging close to December and the first snowfall had already arrived. A light dusting of white snow coated the trees and grass, glimmering in the morning sunlight.

Autumn sat at her desk with Rick, large tomes sprawled out in front of them. Eric was searching for the demons master. She had offered to help him and he lent her a stack of books to go through. So far, nothing was standing out.

Christmas break would soon be upon them, and Autumn couldn't wait. Maintaining her grades, helping Rick with *his* school work and hunting, was wearing her down.

Often times she found herself walking down the school hallways wondering if *anyone* was really normal. How many of them had secret lives beyond the walls of Whitan High? She doubted any of them harbored a secret as strange as hers. Being a demon slayer was spectacularly abnormal.

Her new life came with obvious downfalls. The nightmares were continuous, and the fear before a showdown with a demon was inevitable.

However, she was becoming braver and when a creature attacked her, she no longer froze. Then there was the intoxicating thrill of the hunt. Every time she was out in the field, strapped into her armor, weapons at the ready, she was invigorated. She felt powerful and superhuman. She was addicted, and she knew that could be dangerous. Feeling super powered, when you really aren't, was a perilous mindset to have.

Every Friday and Saturday night of late, the gang headed to the caves, on the prowl for creatures to slay. Every night that passed, they found more monsters. The more they killed, the more were summoned, presumably by the master.

The demons numbers were growing and everyone, including Autumn, was training vigorously to ensure they were equipped to handle the onslaught. As the monsters accumulated, Eric began working day and night on the spell. Unfortunately, it wasn't as simple as getting the creatures blood to perfect the spell. There were more factors involved and magics that Autumn didn't understand.

Tonight, after they finished researching, Autumn and Rick were spending a monster-free night at home, snuggling on the couch and watching movies.

They craved some normality, this much she knew.

Autumn was skimming another page, not expecting to find anything, when an image caught her eye.

A full-page sketched image, next to script in Latin: *finem mundi.*

In the picture, a woman dressed in a long, white, hooded cloak stood in a cave. Her eyes glowed, a crimson color, though her face was undoubtedly, perhaps even deceivingly, beautiful. Surrounding her was the undead. Faceless creatures with black pits for eyes and gaping hallows for mouths. Their bodies were withered and decrepit. Some were hunchbacked, others upright. Many walked on all fours, like feral beasts.

Outside the cave, in the sky, was a blood-red moon. In the field, bony clawed hands rose from the ground and long talons dug deeply into the dirt.

The creatures all had something in common: They were all tethered by a rope. Some wore it around their necks like a leash, others around their waist, or ankles.

Following the rope, they all led back to two thick wooden bracelets the woman wore on either of her wrists.

Puppets on a string, Autumn thought bleakly. *Was she the elusive puppet master?*

Autumn looked at the picture again.

Upon closer inspection, the woman wore a smug grin on her red lips. The kind of grin that implied what words didn't need to say. It was the grin of victory, the grin of someone who had just won a war.

"Oh no," Autumn whispered and Rick's head jolted up from the book he was reading.

"Aut, what is it?" he asked, blue eyes filled with concern.

"Give me a sec," she said and she pulled her laptop over to her. She went to a translation website and typed in the Latin words.

Finem mundi.

When the result came up, she felt like someone had punched her in the stomach.

"Autumn," Rick said, leaning over her to see the computer screen. "What did you find?"

"This picture, this woman in a cave," Autumn pointed to the open book on the table. "The coinciding article is titled *finem mundi.*"

Rick looked at the picture, studying it for a moment, and then he looked back to Autumn curiously.

"What does it mean?" he asked. "You look like you just saw a ghost."

Autumn took a deep breath, trying her best to keep calm.

"The English translation is, the end of the world."

The end of the world.

Autumn and Rick spent the whole night analyzing their findings. Autumn called Eric, who immediately rushed over. They concluded this woman in the drawing, whoever she was, could indeed be the master. Eric also helped translate the rest of the text beyond *end of the world.*

She breeds in the darkness, she brings death.
She catches the wretched, dead souls in her net.
They will do her bidding, their fortunes sealed.
When her army is built, the layers will peel.
Death will spread, like a plague bringing its wrath.
Without refrain, swallowing everything in its path.
No one will be spared and no one will survive.
Only she and the darkness will remain alive.

Eric explained that whoever was summoning the creatures (the hooded woman they assumed) wanted to overrun Whitan and eventually the rest of the world with demons. It seemed like big plans for one person, almost implausible to pull off, but Eric said dark magics were not to be underestimated.

"What is she?" Autumn asked him. "A dark sorcerer?"

Eric shook his head, his face grim.

"I fear it's worse than that. I believe we are dealing with the queen of the demons."

When Autumn headed to school the next day, she was exhausted.

Between researching the demon queen and her incessant worrying, she hadn't slept a wink.

Apocalypse was a whole other ball game. It made hunting hell beasts seem like a picnic. Now they weren't just sealing the caves with Eric's spell. They were inevitably saving the world.

Rick had Autumn's hand wrapped in his, as they headed through the floods of clamoring students.

As soon as they rounded a corner, they saw Eric. Standing by Autumn's locker, he wore a smile so large, Autumn worried he had finally gone off the deep end. He had bags beneath his eyes, and he looked tired, but the happiness radiating from him, made his weariness less noticeable.

"Good morning!" he said cheerily as they approached.

"End of the world, demon queen," Autumn muttered. "What silver lining did I miss Eric?"

"Yeah dude, you look too happy," Rick admitted as he opened his locker.

"That is very astute of you both to notice," Eric said, not missing a beat.

"Because the creepy, clown-like grin didn't give you away at all," Autumn said sarcastically.

Eric frowned. "I wanted to let you both know. I finally got it."

Autumn felt her heart jump in her chest. She looked at Eric in disbelief.

"The spell?" she whispered and Eric nodded, grinning like a fool again.

"It was difficult, but it's finished. All the components were there. It just took some time to piece it all together."

Autumn felt happiness swelling up inside her. If this worked, everything would be worth it. All the endless training, the hunting and the time Eric spent concocting the spell.

It would all be for the greater good.

"Eric, you just saved everyone," she said, her eyes lighting up. "You just saved the world."

"I couldn't have done it without help," Eric said, pulling Autumn into an embrace. She hugged him back and when they parted, she saw Rick beaming.

"Congrats man," he said. "We were getting a little worried about you."

"To be honest, *I* was getting a little worried myself," Eric admitted. "However, I will feel even more relieved when we finally execute the plan. Even so, this is a huge accomplishment."

"And what about the queen?" Autumn asked, worried again.

She was the puppeteer, the big boss at the end of the game. Surely it wasn't as simple as casting the spell to be rid of *her*. It couldn't be that easy.

They couldn't be that lucky.

"Something tells me, she won't go down without a fight," Eric replied. "And that is exactly what we will give her."

Eric glanced around cautiously. It was getting crowded now, as students arrived at their lockers.

"We can talk later," Eric said, subtly gesturing towards the people surrounding them. "Is after school good?"

Autumn looked at Rick, who shrugged. "Sure."

"Perfect. My place and please extend the invite to Mandy and Nate," Eric said over his shoulder as he turned to leave. He smiled at Autumn, and it was the lightest smile she had seen him wear in weeks.

The rest of the day seemed to fly by and before Autumn knew it, lunch had arrived. She was headed back from the washroom, when she heard giggling nearby.

"He is so hot," a girl said. "He is ruggedly handsome. I love stubble on older guys."

"I wish he was *my* guidance consoler," her friend replied, sounding dejected.

As the girls passed by and headed into the washroom, Autumn looked over and saw a man leaning against the wall. He was smiling and nodding, while greeting the students who passed by.

It was Mr. Garrison.

She didn't know why, but Autumn sensed he was mysterious. Like her, he harbored secrets.

She ducked behind some lockers, fixing her wavy hair with her fingers, before proceeding to pass him.

"Miss Kingston," he said, looking up at her as he bit into a shiny, red apple. "Good afternoon."

Autumn stopped, raising an eyebrow at him. "Autumn, please."

He smirked at her candour. "I'm sorry *Autumn,*" he said apologetically. "I take it you don't like Miss Kingston?"

"Maybe when I'm forty," Autumn said, smiling as she tossed her hair back casually.

She cringed inside. Was she *flirting* with her guidance consoler?

"How are you Mr. Garrison?" she said cordially.

"I'm pretty good Autumn," he said, as he waved at another student. "How are things with you? You look a little tired."

"I do?" Autumn asked, her brow furrowing with concern.

Tired meant lackluster skin, bags under your eyes and sallow cheeks. Translation? Not very attractive.

"A little," he admitted. "Is everything alright?"

Autumn didn't know *how* to respond to the question. She *had* been burning the candle at both ends lately, with school and hunting. And with winter exams coming up and the spell casting, things would be getting worse before they got better.

When Autumn didn't reply, Mr. Garrison leaned in, looking worried.

"If you want stop by my office," he said quietly. "It's more private. We can talk there."

Autumn felt a sudden urge to confess *everything* to him. Maybe it was his soothing voice or his kind eyes, but she could imagine telling him the truth.

"Mr. Garrison, I hunt demons with my friends."
"Demons?" he would say, sounding unconvinced. "With what?"
"With a scythe."
Mr. Garrison would look at Autumn, his brown eyes filled with concern.
"You are delusional sweetheart. Demons aren't real. You need help."

Then she would be strapped into a straitjacket and hauled off to the loony bin where she would play chess with people who drooled and hid their meds under their tongues.

"Autumn?" Mr. Garrison broke into her daydream. "Are you alright? I think I lost you there for a moment."

Autumn looked at him, reality sinking in. She couldn't confide in him. Hell, she couldn't confide in *anyone* about this. This secret was her burden, and no one else could carry it for her.

"I'm fine," she said, trying to sound reassuring though she wasn't even convinced herself. "Like you said before, I look tired. I'm exhausted. I definitely need more sleep."

Mr. Garrison looked at her incredulously.

"Autumn," he leaned in closer, as to not let the passing students overhear.

"I know what you and Rick are going through. I hear the chatter in the hallways."

"People talk about us?" Autumn was surprised. She didn't think she merited being the subject of gossip. At least *normal* Autumn didn't. Monster hunter Autumn, now she *might* cause a stir.

"Well, everyone gossips in high school," Mr. Garrison said, taking another bite of his shiny red apple. "Students talk about each other and their teachers. That rumor mill, it grinds without remorse."

Autumn couldn't resist. She smiled coyly. "That's so true. They even talk about guidance counselors."

Mr. Garrison looked at her quizzically. "Oh?" he paused. "And what do they say about me?"

That you are smoking hot! Autumn thought.

She shrugged. "Everyone thinks you own an orchard."

Mr. Garrison chuckled lightly.

"Oh you almost had me there Autumn Kingston," he said, waving a finger as if to reprimand her. "But you can't distract me. My office, after school."

After her encounter with Mr. Garrison, Autumn went to meet up with the gang at their usual table in the cafeteria. As she made her way through the crowded, raucous room, she saw Rick, who was sitting with Mandy, Nathaniel and Eric, stuffing his face with various slices of pizza. When he looked up and saw her approaching he began waving fervently.

"Finally! You are here. I was getting worried," he said as she sat down beside him. "I thought maybe there was a demon in the bathroom."

Mandy glared at him. "Really Rick?"

"What?" Rick asked, looking bewildered. "It was a joke!"

"Considering the lives we live, please, just don't," she grumbled.

"Sorry," Rick said sheepishly as he took another bite of his pizza.

Autumn put her hand on Rick's back, rubbing it gently. "Sorry. I was in the bathroom, and I ran into Mr. Garrison."

"You ran into him in the girl's bathroom?" Rick instantly stopped chewed. "Doing what?"

"You and Garrison in the bathroom together? Juicy!" Mandy said, eyes lighting up. "Please, go on."

"No, we weren't in there *together,*" Autumn said, hoping Rick didn't notice her cheeks burning. "I ran into him *after* the bathroom and guess what?"

"He was eating an apple?" Rick mused, diving back into his lunch.

"Yes he was," Autumn confirmed as she reached into her backpack, pulling out a large chicken salad and a diet soda. "And these girls were nearby just drooling over him."

"That apple is his trademark," Mandy said, sounding as excited as the drooling girls. "And who can blame those girls? He is so sexy."

Nathaniel, who was eating a chocolate bar, snorted. "Ha. Mandy is in love with Geezerson."

"He isn't *old.*" Mandy said, crossing her arms huffily. "He's in his early twenties I bet."

Nathaniel snickered at this. "The dude has more grey hair then my dad, and he raised me *and* Conrad!"

"Streaks of wisdom," Autumn added in as Rick looked at her disapprovingly. "That is what mom always calls them."

"Older just means he is more mature," Mandy said dreamily.

Eric, who had his nose buried in his English homework, rolled his eyes.

"Are we really having a conversation about hot *faculty* right now?"

"Nope. Just hot Garrison," Mandy replied as she winked at Autumn.

"It's settled then," Nathaniel said, scarfing the last of his chocolate bar. "Mandy you can *never* meet my dad."

"So what did Garrison say Aut?" Rick interrupted, effectively halting a Mandy and Nathaniel quarrel before it could begin.

"There was a polite hello, and then he proceeded to *impolitely* tell me how tired I looked," Autumn admitted as she began spearing her salad with a fork. "He wanted me to come see him after school."

"After school?" Mandy said, her brown eyes wide with intrigue. She looked at Rick. "You better watch out Rick. He doesn't waste *any* time."

Rick glared at Mandy before turning to Autumn.

"You have been having nightmares. Is everything alright? You would tell me if something was wrong wouldn't you?"

Autumn hadn't been completely honest with Rick about how stressful her life had become. When they decided to hunt demons, it seemed like she needed some excitement. Now, it felt like she was on a roller coaster. She was either high on adrenaline or low from exhaustion. There was no happy medium.

Still, Autumn didn't want to worry Rick.

"Between school and everything else, I am a little tense. But aren't we all?" she said nonchalantly.

"Nope," Nathaniel piped in. "I don't let things bother me. I let everything roll off my back. Otherwise, I'll worry and that causes wrinkles. Wrinkles, like *old* guidance consolers get," Nathaniel said looking at Mandy meaningfully.

"I can only speak for myself when I say I have *obviously* been extremely stressed," Eric grumbled.

"If I'm stressed, I punch stuff," Mandy shrugged, pulling out a potato chip from its bag.

"You can come to the meeting with Garrison if you want," Autumn offered, looking at Rick.

"I don't know," Rick said, looking perturbed. "Something about him doesn't sit right with me."

"Autumn, if Rick is fine, you should go see Mr. Garrison *alone,*" Mandy added, grinning mischievously. "I'm sure he would love to give you some *guidance* without Rick around."

Rick grimaced, his hands clenching his soda a tad too tightly.

"On second thought," he said. "I'll go with you. I can keep you company."

"Thanks Ricky," Autumn said gratefully.

"Anytime sweetheart," he said, going back to his lunch.

When Autumn arrived at Mr. Garrison's office, the first word that came into her mind was *sad*. Or perhaps sad wasn't the word Autumn was looking for. Maybe it was bland, drab or blasé?

All of those adjectives would apply.

His tiny office, only the size of a large closet, was barely decorated and sparse, with no pictures of family or friends, not even a pet, anywhere to be seen.

Autumn sat in a chair, one leg crossed over the other, playing with the lace on her shirt. She looked up and saw the nameplate on his desk.

Ryan Garrison.

Mr. Garrison himself was quickly browsing through Autumn's file as Rick waited patiently outside the office. She peeked out the tiny square window to see Rick tinkering with his cellphone.

A few moments later, Autumn's phone vibrated. She pulled it out.

It was a text message from Rick.

Is he eating an apple? Whatever you do, don't take a bite!

Autumn rolled her eyes and put the phone away just as Mr. Garrison looked up, brown eyes taking her in. He smiled brightly. It was a nice smile, a friendly smile, the same smile that made her feel like she could tell him anything.

"So Autumn. Rick's parents informed the school you would be tutoring him."

Autumn nodded. "Yes."

"I presume you are still doing that?" he asked, jotting something on a piece of paper. "Helping Rick?"

"Yes. Rick needs help with a few subjects but mostly math. Everything else he can handle on his own."

Mr. Garrison shifted in his seat, placing his hands in a steeple. "Alright. So you tutor Rick, keep up with your own schoolwork and what else?"

Autumn looked at Mr. Garrison, suddenly unsure of what he was asking her. "Sorry?"

"What do you do in your spare time?" he said, smiling. "For fun? You do have fun don't you?"

Autumn suddenly felt like she was being questioned. She could practically feel the hot lights burning her face. She rehearsed a benign answer in her mind, leaving the *hunting monsters* part out.

"I like to read. Hang out with Rick and my friends," she replied. "I talk to my family and friends back home."

Mr. Garrison studied Autumn like she was a riddle he was trying to solve, a puzzle he was piecing together. It made her uncomfortable, and she looked at her hands.

"I'm sorry Autumn," Mr. Garrison said. "I'm just trying to get to the bottom of this. The tense girl I see in the halls doesn't seem to be having much fun."

Autumn said nothing, letting her eyes meet his, challenging him. No amount of prying or clever wordplay was going to get her to open Pandora's Box. Her lips were sealed.

"Is it the students here?" he asked searchingly. "I know it can be difficult being the new kid."

"Nope," Autumn replied. "It's nothing like that."

Mr. Garrison looked at a loss. He wrote down another note on his paper then leaned back in his seat.

"Rick's parents mentioned you were quite popular at your old school," he began.

"And I'm not now?" Autumn offered to which Mr. Garrison nodded.

"For a lack of a better phrasing, sure."

"The truth is, I was," Autumn said. "I was very popular and then I wasn't. That's how it works in high school. One day, you're the epitome of popularity then one wrong move or social faux-pas, and you are cast away like a leper. That is why I have no interest in social climbing. I am quite content with the friends I have. No matter how badly I screw up, or how far down I fall, they will be there for me. They are loyal and that trumps popularity. I had to learn that the hard way."

Mr. Garrison grinned, clearly impressed by Autumn's passionate explanation.

"You are headstrong and a born leader, all excellent qualities," he tapped his pen on his desk rhythmically. "So if it's not the other kids, what has you stressed out Autumn?"

Autumn said nothing. This was where the honesty ended. She couldn't tell anyone about her secret life. Nothing could be said about hunting monsters or Eric's spell. She couldn't explain the overwhelming urge to fight things that lurked in the shadows. She couldn't say despite her fear of death she soldiered on.

Mr. Garrison *would* ask her why. Why did *she* put her life at risk? She didn't want to give him the answer.
That it was because no one else would.

Or because it made her feel superhuman. She felt exceptional, like she had a reason for being, for breathing, for living.
She didn't walk her lonely path alone. However, not being able to tell Mr. Garrison the truth, made her feel more alone than ever.

"Autumn?" Mr. Garrison said, breaking into her reverie.
She looked up at him and saw the worry in his eyes. Did he sense she *wanted* to tell him the truth? Did he realize he had almost broken down her barriers?
Still, almost just wouldn't be enough.

Either way, she needed an answer. She needed a believable reason for acting so jittery.
"I think it's just exams," she lied, looking into his eyes with some effort.
"Really?" Mr. Garrison sounded unconvinced. "Are you sure?"

"Yep," Autumn said with as much certainty as she could muster. "Everything else is just peachy."

She forced a smile.

"Well Autumn, in that case, you have nothing to worry about. You are a straight-A student. If you keep it up, you will graduate with flying colors. Probably even make the honor roll."

"Thanks," she said gratefully. "Exams. They just strike fear in my heart."

"I understand," he said, smiling. "Only the best students worry about exams, but you are gifted. You have nothing to be concerned about. Just keep strong notes and study hard. Did you want," he was cut off by knocking on the door.

Mr. Garrison and Autumn looked over to see Rick watching them through the small square window.

Mr. Garrison waved him in and Rick opened the door, stepping inside the office.

"Can I help you Rick?" Mr. Garrison asked. Rick shook his head as he shut the door behind him.

"Nope. Just here for moral support. For my *girlfriend* Autumn," he said loudly, taking a seat beside her.

Mr. Garrison looked confused. "Alright then. By all means, join us."

"I will," Rick replied, snatching Autumn's hand.

Mr. Garrison looked at the ceiling. "Where were we Autumn? Oh yes," he reached into his desk drawer and pulled out a pamphlet.

"Its got some good studying tips. Most of them are pretty basic but I always feel better when someone leaves my office with a pamphlet."

"Oh no," Rick said. "She doesn't need any pamphlets from you Romeo."

Mr. Garrison looked stunned and perhaps amused by Rick's outburst.

"Rick, it's a pamphlet *not* my phone number."

"Oh it starts with pamphlets then its flowers and candlelight dinners," Rick said accusingly. "Come to think of it, maybe your number is written somewhere *in* the pamphlet." He grabbed it and leafed through it wildly.

Autumn nudged Rick in the arm sharply.

"Ouch!" he barked.

"Rick! What is wrong with you?" She looked at Mr. Garrison apologetically. "I'm so sorry."

Mr. Garrison cleared his throat brusquely. "Not a problem."

"I should go," Autumn said, standing up. She had never been more humiliated in her whole life.

"Yes we *should* go," Rick added. Autumn shot him a deadly glare. She looked back to Mr. Garrison, her face hot with embarrassment.

"I'm so sorry again," she said inaudibly. "And thanks for the pamphlet."

Then she turned on her heel and left Rick in her dust.

"Goodbye Autumn," Mr. Garrison called out behind her. "Come back anytime!"

Autumn raced through the empty halls, fuming and eager to avoid Rick.

How dare he be jealous, of her *guidance consoler* nonetheless? She picked up her pace and heard Rick's footsteps behind her, getting closer.

"Aut, wait up!" Rick called out.

When she finally made it to her car, she spun around. Seeing Rick behind her, grinning like a foolish child who just did something naughty, ignited the anger inside her, causing it to explode.

"What the hell is wrong with you?" she asked sharply as she opened the driver-side door. "You were acting really immature in there! You made me look ridiculous! You made *you* look ridiculous!

"I did not!" Rick shouted back.

"Oh! Very mature response!" Autumn said getting into the car and slamming the door shut. She took some deep, steadying breaths as Rick got into the passenger side. She didn't want to drive angry, so she sat there, staring out the windshield, stone-faced.

A few moments passed, and Rick reached over and gently brushed Autumn's hair away from her face. His blue eyes searched for some clemency, some weakness in her protective wall. She tried her best to be stubborn, but he always tore down her defenses, even when they were little.

"I am jealous of him," Rick admitted, his voice inaudible.

Autumn turned, facing him. She met his gaze for a second, reeling from his revelation.

"He is faculty Rick."

"All the girls swoon over him," Rick muttered. "And he seems especially fond of you."

Autumn frowned. She didn't notice Mr. Garrison giving her any extra attention.

"He does not."

"He flirts with you."

"He doesn't flirt with me," Autumn said defensively.

"He does," Rick said, looking towards his feet. "Or it looks that way I guess."

"You shouldn't say those things Rick," Autumn said, trying her best to stay calm. "If that gets around not only will Mr. Garrison be in trouble. I'll be the girl he flirted with."

Rick sighed, defeated. "I'm sorry."

"You are just being insecure," Autumn said sympathetically. She knew the feeling of self-doubt all too well. Besides, a small part of her *did* enjoy the fact that he was jealous.

"And you have no reason to be. All I want is you."

"I know," Rick said softly. "But it's not like I'm really good at anything."

"What are you talking about? You are good at things Rick."

"Like what? Fighting and hunting? When Eric uses that spell to seal the caves," Rick stared out the window like he was lost. "I won't even have that anymore. I'll be back to boring, useless Rick."

"You aren't boring or useless," Autumn interjected as she took his hand and squeezed it. "Monster hunting is something you excel at Rick but when that's over, you will go back to exceling at other things."

"Like?" Rick asked, the ghost of a smile upon his face.

"Like skateboarding, or training with your sword," she paused. "And being my boyfriend, which you do very remarkably, may I add."

Rick's lips spread into a huge smile.

"So it's official huh? We are together now."

"I tried to resist it," Autumn confessed. "But I just can't anymore."

Rick took her face into his hands and kissed her gently.

This was where she was meant to be, she thought to herself. This was home.

22

When Autumn and Rick pulled into Eric's driveway after school, Nathaniel's van was already there, and the gates were wide open. To Autumn, this was symbolic.

Eric, once a secretive, closed-off teenager, finally let her in, beyond his walls.

It could be metaphorical or literal.

Her heart swelled with joy. She had taken the chance to reach out to him and now she couldn't imagine life without Eric.

As they exited the car and headed towards Eric's front door, Autumn realized everything had finally come together.

The spell was ready. The caves would soon be sealed, and Whitan would be safe once again.

Eric's old demons would be banished with the *actual* demons.

They rang the doorbell once and were instantly greeted by the sound of Eric's voice over the intercom.

"Eric, it's us." Autumn said.

"Perfect," he replied and the intercom buzzed. Not long after, the front door swung open, with Eric behind it.

"Come in guys," he said, holding the door open. "Nate and Mand are here."

As they followed Eric into the now-familiar great room, he turned, grinning at them.

"I have a surprise for you both," he said, looking quite pleased.

"A new car? Oh Eric you shouldn't have," Rick teased.

Eric chuckled. "Do you *think* I'm loaded Jacobs?"

"You are," Rick replied bluntly. "So. What is it?"

"Rick, hasn't anyone ever told you that patience is a virtue?" Eric asked as they approached the entrance to the great room.

"Yes, but it's not my virtue," Rick admitted.

They walked into the great room where Mandy and Nathaniel sat, awfully close together, on a cream colored couch.

Autumn and Rick exchanged greetings with them, then proceeded to sit down.

Autumn loved this room almost as much as the library. The floor to ceiling windows, the red velveteen drapes and the hardwood flooring. All of it reminded her of the old-fashioned mansions they featured in movies.

"So how was your meeting with Mr. Sexyison?" Mandy asked, leaning towards Autumn eagerly.

"Can you stop calling him that?" Nathaniel said, deflated. "It's truly repulsive."

"He wanted to know why I've been stressed out. No big."

"And then he offered you a tantalizing back rub to relax you?" Mandy asked, her brown eyes wide with anticipation.

"Yes. Then the school board came and carted him away for fondling a student," Autumn said sarcastically. "Really. He just wanted answers. Answers I obviously couldn't give him."

"That's all?" Mandy grumbled, looked disappointed.

"Afraid so," Autumn replied. "The boring life I lead. Now Mister King," she turned to Eric. "The floor is all yours."

Eric who, as always, had been listening to his friends intently, smiled gratefully at Autumn.

"You are a peach sweetie," he winked at her, taking a seat in a high-backed ivory chair.

"As I told everyone, I have a surprise for you all," he began.

"And it's *not* a car!" Rick said, looking downtrodden. "I already checked."

"Oh it's *better*," Eric said, and he reached into his shirt, pulling out a necklace. Upon closer inspection, it was an oval amethyst amulet. As Eric held it up into the light, it glimmered like a thousand diamonds.

"It's beautiful," Autumn said, mysteriously transfixed by it.

"That it is," Eric said. "But beauty is only part of its appeal. This amulet was passed down in my family for generations."

"There were two. One was my mothers and the other my fathers," he explained, his dark eyes wandering to each captivated face. "Arabella, has the other. They basically allow us to use magic to communicate with one another mentally."

Autumn's mouth hung open. An amulet that made Eric telepathic? If she hadn't already witnessed the scrying bowl and Eric's other tricks, she wouldn't have believed him for a second.

"So if I wore one and you the other, we could communicate telepathically?" Autumn asked.

"Yep," Eric said, clutching the necklace tightly. "It's usually how Arabella and I communicate."

"That's one way to beat long distance bills," Autumn joked.

"It is also a tracker," Eric went on. "Say I was unconscious in the middle of nowhere. This amulet would allow Arabella to find me."

Of all the magic items Eric had shown them, this one was by far, the most interesting. Eric went on to pass around the amulet for everyone to see.

When Autumn finally handed it back to him, Eric placed the amulet around his neck.

"Watch this," he said.

His eyes closed, and the amulet began to glow. A gentle humming sound resonated around them, and the air shifted and when the glowing and humming stopped, Eric opened his eyes. Seconds later, a shadow began forming in the middle of the room.

The shadow began taking shape, lazily morphing into a large rectangle.

A bright light throbbed and it was like staring directly into the sunlight. Autumn closed her eyes and when she opened them she saw Arabella standing there, hands on her hips, the shadowy portal slowly fading around her.

Dressed in a black lace top and jeans, the matching amethyst amulet dangling down her chest and her auburn curls framing her tan face, she looked at Eric.

"You rang brother," she said flatly and Eric went to her, hugging her tightly.

"Ara," he whispered into her shoulder. "It's so good to see you."

Autumn looked around at her friends. She didn't need telepathy to know what they were thinking.

What the hell just happened?

"Likewise, Eric," Arabella went on, eyes glimmering with mischievousness. "You know I love you, but you have the *worst* timing."

Eric pulled back from her and crossed his arms over his chest defensively.

"Oh do I?"

"You do," she said, her lips spreading into a wolfish grin.

Eric rolled his eyes, obviously understanding his sister's connotation. "What's *his* name?"

"Dominic," she said, violet eyes lighting up. "Tall, dark, handsome and not at all magically inclined. Well, he does some magical things to *me* but that is a different story." She stopped abruptly, like she had just noticed the others in the room.

She smiled, amused.

"Oh how adorable. The ragtag gang is here."

"I'm sorry," Nathaniel said, not missing a beat. "But how the hell did *you* get here?"

"I teleported," Arabella deadpanned.

"You teleported?" Nathaniel repeated.

Arabella nodded. "Yes."

"You teleported?"

Arabella looked at her brother, exasperated.

"He's not the sharpest knife is he Eric?"

Nathaniel stood up, his face flaming, as Mandy grabbed his arm.

"Don't bother Nate. She would *destroy* you."

Eric smirked. "She really did teleport here. I don't have that ability *yet*, but I'm trying to learn."

"I am older," Arabella said, as she placed a hand on Eric's shoulder. "I learnt far more magic from mom and dad then you did. Don't be so hard on yourself. Everything in time."

"Besides," she said, a glimmer of pride in her eyes. "Eric learns magic quicker than any sorcerer I have ever known. The most advanced sorcerers *never* would have figured out that cave sealing spell. I cannot wait to see it in action."

"And you will," Eric said firmly. "Through the scrying bowl, at home, safe and sound."

Arabella looked at Eric defiantly. "Oh hush," she said sighing before turning her attention back to everyone else.

"Eric is worried because I am out of practice when it comes to some of my magics," she said, taking a seat in an old-fashioned wooden rocking chair.

"But you just *teleported* here," Autumn said, brow furrowed with confusion.

"Autumn, please don't encourage her." Eric said disapprovingly.

"Well, you never completely *forget* how to use magic of course," Arabella said. "But I *am* rather rusty. I barely use my magic nowadays.

I try to live as normally as possible. So if I ventured into a cave full of monsters, I would probably be more of a hindrance then a help."

"So I will be doing what I did last time. I will be watching through the scrying bowl and healing people."

"I also want Arabella alive if I should perish," Eric added in. "Then *she* can try to seal the caves with my spell."

After the hubbub of Arabella's appearance died out, everyone refocused on why they came to Eric's in the first place: Creating a plan of action for when they ventured into the caves.

By the time they were done, a couple of hours had passed. Eric ordered pizza, and they all ate while ironing out the final details. The date was set for next Saturday. As Autumn ate her pizza slice, she couldn't help but imagine the worst outcome. They were after all, heading into the belly of the beast this time. They were no longer on the outside, peering down the rabbit hole. There would be no hiding spots and nowhere to run. There were only two options for escape. They were either walking out, alive and well, mission accomplished, or they weren't walking out at all.

23

Another week had come and gone, and the weekend had finally arrived. Autumn spent her Saturday relaxing and reading, even though she wanted to train. She wanted to run for miles or spin around like a top. She had so much nervous energy to burn but she couldn't wear herself out. She had already spent all week with Rick training relentlessly in preparation for tonight.

It was time.

She sat in an armchair looking out Eric's living room window. The sky was pitch-black. The trees were swaying, and she saw nothing beyond the huge stone wall wrapped around Eric's mansion.

The one thing she could see was the pristine yard with its large, ceramic fountain and the garden, which housed withering, frail plants and dead, drooping flowers.

She was curled up under a knitted blanket, trying to fight off the terrible feeling she had since the day began.

She read from her favorite books, revisited emails from her mom, anything to keep her mind from wandering. It was no use. Her thoughts were relentless.

They went around and around inside her head like a twisted, defunct Merry-go-round.

It was a trap, an endless circle.

Would they succeed in banishing the demons and most importantly would they *survive?*

She knew the future couldn't be foretold.
She could only pray that tonight was the night that they entered the caves and destroyed the demons inside forever.

Autumn looked over at her friends.
She observed them, made random notes in her head, looking for any semblance of fear like the kind she had nestled deep inside the pit of her belly.

Eric was packing his items into his brown suede satchel. He was wearing the amulet and an expression of rigid determination. Arabella was upstairs readying the scrying bowl. Mandy was changing into her Kevlar armor.
Everyone else was suited up, Autumn included.
Rick and Nathaniel, looking light as feathers as usual, were packing up the arsenal.

Autumn felt useless, like a flat tire on a car.

She wanted to help, to do *something*, but all she could do was let the fear encompass her and swallow her whole.

She closed her eyes and tried to think positive. Everything would be alright. Things would go smoothly.
The negative thoughts were pushed aside and ignored. Everyone dead, the world overrun by monsters commanded by a demon queen ringleader.

Autumn barely heard Rick when he spoke to her. She looked up at him, only after he touched her stiff shoulders.
"Aut, we are leaving soon babe."

"Alright," she said her voice listless.

Rick moved in front of her, kneeling, his eyes meeting hers. They were filled with unease, probing her for answers she didn't really have.

"You don't need to do this Autumn. The last thing I want is you going out there when your mind is elsewhere."

Despite her despair, Autumn never *once* considered backing down. She was going to see this through, for everyone. Especially Eric.

"I am going," she said firmly. "But it's dangerous Rick. Going *into* the caves is new ground. We need to be extra careful."

"We will," Rick said reassuringly, taking her hand into his. And again he was her beautiful anchor, pulling her back from the depths.

"Nothing will hurt you on my watch," Rick said, his smile haughty.

Autumn didn't like his arrogance. Arrogance blinded people.

It tricked people into thinking they needed nobody and nothing to survive.

The truth was, life was fleeting. One minute you grasped it tightly in your palms, the next you've lost it, shattering it on the ground like broken glass.

"I don't fear for my life," Autumn whispered. "It's the rest of you. The least of my worries is *me.*"

Rick kissed Autumn's hand gently.

"Nothing is going to happen to *any* of us Aut. I promise you."

Autumn sighed, her eyes fixed on the ceiling.

She never liked promises.

As everyone headed out to the van, Autumn felt significantly better. Just talking to Rick helped her relax. She didn't need anyone worrying about her tonight. If they did, they might end up distracted and that could mean the difference between life and death.

After the van was packed up with supplies, everyone gathered around Eric. Tonight he was the leader, and they were following his instructions. The first thing he did was hand them each a vial. He instructed them to drink from it, telling them it was an anti-possession elixir. It only lasted a day, but it prevented any demons from taking over their bodies. Autumn downed it, but not fast enough. It tasted awful. The others seemed to agree, cringing as they drank the liquid back. Eric assured them it was worth the horrible taste to be immune to possession.

"Alright guys listen up. The plan is, I set up my items and do the ritual and you guys fend off the demons," Eric reached into his pocket and began handing out more vials. "This healing juice took months to create. I had some in store. If you get hurt, drink the whole vial. You each have two. Failing that, my sister will be able to heal you. However, the concoction in the vial works faster and is more potent."

"I hope this tastes better than the last one," Nathaniel muttered.

"Tonight is the night," Eric went on. "We need to keep our eye on the prize."

"As soon as I start the ritual those monsters will come for me, no doubt," Eric said warningly. "Those demons killed my family. I want them dead. Show *no one* mercy in those caves."

Autumn looked into Eric's cold, dark eyes and saw the hatred behind them. She had never seen him so vindictive and blood-thirsty. It was frightening.

Autumn had a horrible epiphany. What if Eric's cousins weren't *dead?* What if they were alive or worse, possessed by demons?

"Eric?" Autumn said and he looked at her, his lips twitching into a small smile.

"Aut, what is it?"

She ran a hand through her hair nervously. "What if we see Renee or Caleb?"

For a split-second, Eric's face betrayed him. His smile melted away. His jaw tightened. His whole body tensed. He took a long, deep breath. The tension disappeared, and he morphed into tranquil Eric again.

Eric looked into Autumn's eyes and spoke in a flat, emotionless tone.

"If they are still in that cave, they aren't human anymore. They are demons. Put them out of their misery."

It was after midnight when they finally arrived at their destination.

As they pulled into the parking lot, Autumn noticed the wind had picked up immensely, an ominous sign. It whistled outside the windows of the van, rattling it to the point where Autumn thought it might topple sideways.

As the vehicle slowed to a halt, Autumn looked at Eric. She wondered if he was scared.

Did he fear history repeating?

That he was leading his friends to their deaths?

The same gruesome death his parents were led to so many years ago.

Autumn could feel the pressure of what *she* had to do weighing on her. She could only imagine how much pressure Eric felt preforming the spell itself.

Mandy, as per usual, looked relaxed and calm. She had her small legs stretched out in front of her, arms behind her head, lounging out. Rick's knee was jiggling excitedly and for a moment, she wished she had just a little of their confidence.

As they geared up for battle, Autumn felt like she was watching another person, not herself, as she grabbed her scythe and double-checked her body armor. It was surreal and dreamlike, gathering their artillery and heading through the field in the gusting wind.

Rick had Autumn's hand wrapped tightly in his own as they walked.

She took a moment to glance at Eric. He was stoic as he moved through the tall grass, satchel in hand.

"Rick, I need to talk to Eric for a minute," Autumn began cautiously.

"Alright, we can do that," Rick said, unruffled.

Autumn shook her head. "No. Rick, *I* need to talk to him *alone*, please."

Autumn expected Rick to be jealous but instead, he just smiled indulgently and relinquished her hand.

"Take your time sweetie," he said then he kissed her softly on the cheek and went to join Mandy and Nathaniel, who were lagging behind.

Autumn headed over to Eric. He was dressed like he always was. In a long black trench coat and jeans, his dark waves falling into his face. Eric told her he always wore something black. He said it was to remind him of two things. That he was still in mourning and that he had a mission to fulfil.

Looking out into the blank night sky, the one without stars, the one brimming with possibilities good and bad, he seemed deep in thought.

"Eric," she said, feeling almost guilty pulling him from his contemplation.

He looked over at her, the usual warm smile on his handsome face.

"Is everything alright Autumn?"

"Eric," she began, walking in step with him. "I'm not going to sugar-coat this. You look like shit."

"Shit?" Eric said, smirking slightly. "I hope this isn't your way of flirting."

"I am just saying. You want us to believe in this cause, that we will win this battle but your body language says we are already in body bags."

Eric averted his eyes. He said nothing, just kept his pace, slow and deliberate, avoiding her gaze.

"What is going on?" she asked quietly.

Eric never held back. Even when the truth stung like salt sprinkled on a fresh wound, he said what was on his mind. She *needed* to do the same with him.

"What aren't you telling me Eric?"

Eric's eyes met her own.

"From the comfort of my house this all seemed like a great idea but now, being out here, in the moment, I just realized something. I shouldn't have dragged you guys into this. This is mine and Arabella's revenge to take. You guys shouldn't have to risk your lives for people you didn't even know."

Autumn reached out and grabbed Eric's forearm gently.

"We know *you* Eric. What kind of friends would we be if we weren't willing to fight off a few demon beasts for you?" she said, trying her best to lighten the mood.

Eric chuckled slightly. "*This* goes above and beyond friendship, especially when the friend is the so-called prince of darkness."

"I never thought you were the prince of darkness," she said, squeezing his arm gently. "Maybe a court jester," she trailed off.

Eric rolled his eyes but still grinned. "Very droll Autumn."

"All joking aside, we *want* to help you. Though selfishly, I think Mandy and Rick just *enjoy* fighting things," Autumn said, as she looked up at the sky.

The moon was shining, vibrant and full against the pitch-black sky. The wind hadn't relented and it whipped in Autumn's face violently, making her tear up.

"My parents wanted to save this town and look where it got them," Eric said bitterly. "And they were far more powerful than me. I am an amateur." He paused and smirked. "And I'm arrogant. To believe a sorcerer like me can pull this off."

"Like you said Eric, I didn't know your parents," Autumn said, choosing her words carefully. "But I *do* know we believe in you, and we wouldn't be here if we didn't."

"People aren't safe in Whitan as long as those demons are lurking," she went on. "As long as people explore those caves, everyone is at risk. And if that demon queen has her way, the evil will spread like a virus. First here, then the next city, then the next. Personally, I think a world ruled by a demon queen and her loyal cronies, sounds mighty terrifying."

Eric reached out and took her hand into his.
His hands were ice cold.
Cold hands warm heart, her mother always said.

"Autumn you don't have to do this," he said finally.
"Do what?" Autumn asked.
"You don't have to pretend you *want* to go into those dark, dank caves and possibly never come back out. You don't need to embrace death like it's a long-lost friend."

When Eric said this, a vicious shiver crept down her spine. It wasn't breaking news to her. All night, all day, she had felt death near her, like it was breathing down her neck, like it could reach out and grab her at any moment.

"I'm not scared to die," she said, her voice quavering.
"I'm scared I'm going to live and everyone else will die."

Eric shook his head in disbelief. "You are always thinking of other people Autumn. Just promise me one thing," he said. "That you will fight until the very *end,* no matter what happens tonight."

Autumn looked at Eric's grave expression.

"Eric, what are you saying?"

"I'm saying," Eric said without hesitation. "If anything happens to me or anyone else in there, tell me you *will* keep fighting. You will get the hell out of those caves, and you will *never* look back."

Autumn fought back the tears that threatened release.

She wasn't going to cry. She refused. There was nothing to cry over yet, she would save her tears for now.

"Nothing is going to happen to you or anyone else Eric King," she said firmly.

"We are a team. We are going in together, and we are leaving together. There is no other way."

When Eric and Autumn were done talking, they rejoined the others and continued their trek towards the caves.

When the caves appeared, looming and murky, a thick fog began to envelope them. It was the kind of fog that made the world look surreal, and made everything hard to see.

Rick grabbed Autumn by the hand, guiding her along.

"Stay close guys," Rick instructed. "This fog is dense."

As they moved closer to the cave mouth, the fog began to thin out and eventually it dissipated. Autumn looked at it, taking it all in. The terror-inducing cave. She was finally face-to-face with it. It looked different than the last time she had seen it.

The jagged rocks of the cave were interlaced with rotting vines and lifeless plants. From the mouth of the cave seeped a foul, rust-colored liquid onto the arid, patchy, russet grass that surrounded it. Coating the caves edge was a thick, black, tar-like substance.

"Okay, it's go time," Rick said and the wind seemed to die down a little as they began gearing up.

Eric had his satchel. Rick pulled out his sword. Autumn had her scythe in hand, Mandy was lightly swinging her nunchucks and Nathaniel was baring a handgun.

"Everyone, just remember to be safe and watch out for each other," Rick said. "If you need help you holler. No playing the action hero in there."

"And above all else, keep the monsters away from Eric. If they get to him, the ritual will be ruined."

"Alright! Let's do this!" Nathaniel said, his gun-free hand pumping in the air.

"I'm ready," Mandy said, her eyes bursting with excitement.

Autumn could feel her blood pumping and her heart thudding in her chest. The adrenaline was pulsing through her, urging her to begin, like a race runner awaiting the shotgun start.

It may not have been *her* parents who died in the caves, but this cave had stolen people's families and friends. This cave was the reaper. This cave was the demise of lives.

The demons had to die.

"Alright, so a summary of the plan," Eric said as he began examining a vile in his hand. "I set up the items and you guys take a position to guard me. Everyone watches each other's backs and when you see something, no hesitation. You kill it."

"And remember, be precise. We want those monsters down for the count as quick as possible," Rick added. "That way if there are a lot in there, we won't get overwhelmed."

"Aim for the head, heart or other vitals because this is the *nest*. I expect there to be loads of beasts inside."

"So, are we good to go now dude?" Nathaniel asked, looking to Eric, who was readying his vials for the spell.

"As ready as we'll ever be. Let's get in there," Eric said.

So the five of them headed towards the cave mouth, into the dark, into the unknown, unsure of what exactly was waiting for them, on the other side.

24

It was pitch-black inside the entrance to the cave, and Autumn felt she was being devoured by a mammoth beast. The pungent smell of blood, filth and moss overwhelmed her nostrils as she slipped on her night vision goggles. Everyone had to wear them. The cave yielded no light, and they had to be able to see where they were going and what was coming.

"It stinks in here," Mandy declared as they moved through the cave gingerly. The many ridges and rocks that made up the cave floor made quick movements difficult. That and not knowing the layout of the cave held them back. Autumn didn't mind. She was in no rush to dance with death.

"Demons live here," Nathaniel said bluntly. "Were you expecting it to smell like roses?"

Mandy sighed and looked at Eric. "How deep do we have to be?"

"There's no specific depth," Eric replied. "But I would rather be further from the opening in case someone comes by."

"Funny that, I feel more comfortable *near* the opening," Mandy quipped.

Autumn looked around her, observing her surroundings, committing everything she saw to memory. She investigated every nook and cranny in sight, though she wasn't sure *exactly* what she was looking for.

Demons? Dead, rotting corpses? Renee and Caleb's lifeless forms? The thought *had* crossed her mind.

Instead, all she saw were pieces of scrap wood, crinkled, withered leaves, mud and other random litter that had found its way inside.

The further they ventured into the cave, the worse the smell of rot and decay plagued her. She fought the urge to throw up, her stomach squirming in protest.

Be strong, she chided herself. *There is no turning back.*

Minutes passed before Eric found a suitable and stable location. He began inspecting a small alcove in the cave. He looked around, examining the area thoroughly before turning back to them, appearing pleased.

"This is as good a place as any," he said and he kneeled on the ground and began unpacking his items.

"I should scout ahead," Rick said to the rest of them. "See what's shaking."

Nathaniel stepped next to him, his handgun at the ready.

"Not without backup buddy."

"Nathaniel is right. This cave has many passages and hidden areas. You could get lost," Eric said, sounding mildly distracted. "Go together."

Rick's lips formed a pout. "Yes sir."

He turned to Autumn. "I just want to get an idea of the path ahead. I will be right back. I promise."

Mandy shook her head disapprovingly.

"That is exactly what they say in the horror movies before they croak."

Rick narrowed his eyes. "No one's dying."

Not being at Rick's side made Autumn uneasy, but she didn't argue with him. If anyone here could get themselves out of a jam with their exceptional fighting skills, it was Rick.

"Alright but please, be careful Ricky," Autumn murmured.
Rick kissed her on the forehead gently.
"Always sweetheart."
Nathaniel looked at Mandy, shuffling his feet. It was obvious he wanted to say *something*, but he couldn't get the words out.
"Mandy, I want to say something too," he began sheepishly.
"Don't," she warned him. "Just get it done Nate."

Autumn watched gloomily as Rick and Nathaniel plodded off together.
She watched until they faded into the distance, becoming minuscule and fleeting, like specks of dust in the light.

Eric continued setting up his items. He lit candles, sprinkled powders and hauled out a giant tome that looked to weigh at least five pounds. He flipped to a bookmarked page then grabbed a red ornate box. He went on pulling out vials from his satchel, setting them beside it.

Autumn watched, lost in Eric's endeavour when she heard the jolting sound of footsteps pounding across the rocky floor. Hard, fast and spirited, they were headed her way.
Autumn looked out into the darkness, eyes wide with panic.
"Did you hear that?" she asked and Mandy nodded.
"Footsteps."
Suddenly, the footfalls grew louder and closer and before long Rick and Nathaniel appeared, running towards them swiftly, their faces frozen in terror.
"THEY SAW US!" Rick bellowed, through sharp, quick breaths.
"THEY ARE COMING!" Nathaniel added.

When they finally stopped, they looked at the girls, both catching their breath.

"We tried to be stealthy, but they spotted us," Rick said. "They are headed this way."

"We need to draw them away from Eric *now*," Autumn said, gripping her scythe so tightly she felt her fingers cramping up.

Eric, who had finally finished setting up for the ritual, stood up, his face lined with concern.

"You guys, please be careful."

"We will. The same goes for you," Autumn said.

Knowing full well this moment could be hers and Eric's last, she reached out and hugged him tightly. He hugged her back, his warm breath against her neck.

"I want you to know," he whispered. "You are the best thing to come into my life. You make me stronger and braver Autumn. Without you, I wouldn't be *here* now."

"Stuck in a dark cave full of bloodthirsty demons?" Autumn offered back weakly.

"Finally finishing this battle," he replied, his eyes meeting hers. "You were the catalyst. You helped me move forward. You gave me the will to trust people again. I thought there was nothing for me in that school, no one worth knowing, but you helped me see I wasn't looking hard enough."

Eric kissed her softly on the forehead, his hands gently gripping her face.

Autumn closed her eyes, wanting to stay here, in the alcove with Eric, forever.

When she opened them, Eric was looking at her, his eyes filled with adoration and something else.

Something hidden, something fragile, possibly something he wasn't even aware of.

Was it love?

She wasn't sure, but either way, she leaned up, and kissed him on the cheek tenderly.

"Good luck Eric," she murmured, fighting back tears again. They stung her eyes and she wanted to let them flow, but it still wasn't time to cry.

Not yet.

"Be safe," she said.

Eric went on to reiterate words of caution to everyone before retreating back to his semi-circle of burning candles. He didn't dare to say good luck, because luck had nothing to do with it.

Luck was too fleeting and too fickle.

Luck was a charm, a winning lottery ticket, an item of clothing that helped win the big game.

To live or die, that was their choice to make.

They had to fight. They had to win. Losing wasn't an option.

Losing meant dying, and no one was dying tonight.

Autumn and the others began running.

Against the relentless terrain, they zipped along. Their leg muscles stretched, and their hearts pounded. Beads of sweat formed on their foreheads and trickled down their cheeks.

They were attempting to cut the creatures off before they discovered Eric in the alcove.

They rushed into the darkness, running towards the commotion, towards the sounds of wild beasts screeching and growling. They should've been running the *other* way. Autumn had always run away in her nightmares.

Tonight she was jumping in.

Everyone was geared up, their weapons ready to be unleashed, as they sped along, eyes meticulous and watchful.

"How much further until we hit the jackpot?" Mandy asked impatiently.

"They weren't that far ahead," Rick said as he moved cautiously but quickly along the jagged rock floor.

"Oh shit!" he grumbled.

Autumn glanced at him quickly. "What is it?"

"They are drawing us into the cave," Rick said as he dodged past a large cluster of rocks. "They know the deeper they bring us in, the harder it will be to escape."

"I hate to admit it," Mandy said bitterly. "But it's crafty. And we are playing right into their hands."

"We have no choice Mandy. We have to keep them far away from Eric," Autumn said.

There weren't any arguments because everyone knew it was true. Tonight, they were Eric's bodyguards, and their objective was to take out as many creatures as they could.

So into the fray they went, no looking back.

Everything seemed to move in slow motion when Autumn saw the first wave of creatures descend.

It was like she wasn't even there, like this was happening to someone else. She was just watching from outside herself. One moment they were running through the empty and still caves.

Next, they were staring down three monsters.

They stood barrier-like, solid as the rocks surrounding them, blocking the path ahead.

Noises escaped them, a series of guttural sounds and grunts.

The night vision goggles made them even more terrifying.

Their huge bulging eyes, flat noses, and tiny fleshy mouths.

They stared at Autumn, Rick, Mandy and Nathaniel, hungrily, acknowledging them with stone-cold eyes.

Tonight the pesky demon hunters became the prey.

Autumn watched in horror. The beasts began to screech, the sound reverberating off the walls. It was almost deafening, like sharp nails on a chalkboard. Their jaws began cracking and dislocating, revealing gaping pits that replaced mouths. All along the circumference of the holes were teeth. Sharp, pointy teeth exposed and ready to rip them all to shreds.

25

E ric was mixing potions wildly, his hands steady, sweat dripping down his brow.

He could hear the vile shrieking, the sounds of creatures unleashing wrath on his friends, on *her*, his beloved Autumn, but he couldn't think about it. He couldn't do anything to help her.

He had to focus on the task at the hand, every minute, every second counted now.

Every minute he wasted they were closer. She was closer, to getting hurt or worse.

He couldn't live with himself if anything happened to Autumn.

Eric mixed the ingredients faster, keeping his hands stable and his movements deliberate.

There was no room for error tonight, no second chances to get it right.

Eric reached the last vile when he felt something strange. The energy around him was shifting. Being a sorcerer meant having heightened senses. Eric didn't even need night vision goggles to see in the dark. His sight was so sharp and keen. He could feel, smell, see, taste and hear things tenfold.

The only way he could describe it to those who weren't imbued with magics, was the surrounding air became heavy. It was like in the summer, when it rained. Eventually, it stopped and the sun came out, soaking up the water from roads, grass and sidewalks, leaving behind humidity.

The thickness in the air was similar to what he could feel when magic was being used nearby.

His brown eyes scanned the alcove, searching for the source of this new energy. Suddenly, there was a crackling sound and Eric felt enormous power surging around him.

The last time he felt this amount of power, his mother and father had been alive.

He hated himself for even considering it, but his heart was heavy with hope.

Could it be? Had they returned to him in his time of need and reckoning?

He saw a shadow moving towards him, heard shoes clicking on the canvas of rocks.

"Who is there?" Eric asked, just as the shadowy being stepped forward.

It wasn't his parents.

Eric should've known better. They wouldn't be here after all these years. He scolded himself for being gullible, ridiculous and stupid. He *knew* their return was impossible.

When she walked into the alcove, Eric didn't recognize her.

Whoever she was, she was stunningly beautiful. With flawless alabaster skin, full lips and piercing catlike eyes of ruby. She was surely one of the most gorgeous women he had ever seen.

She wore a hooded red cloak over a black lace and velvet dress. On her wrists were many golden bangles, and her neck was adorned with long shimmering necklaces with different colored gemstones on them.

Despite her appearance, Eric knew there was something dark lurking inside this woman, something wicked. His father always said that evil often came in the form of something unbelievably beautiful.

"Eric King," she spoke, her voice low and sultry.

Eric's heart thumped in his chest. She knew who he was?

"How do you know who I am?" Eric asked.

She chuckled throatily.

"I know everyone in this sleepy little town," she said mockingly. She pulled down her hood revealing long straight black hair streaked with red.

"So you know me," Eric said, his eyes narrowing. "Now tell me who *you* are."

The woman made a *tsk* sound and wagged her finger, scolding him.

"Now, now. Manners young one. You wouldn't want me to get offended would you?"

Eric stood up and dusted his pants off with both hands.

"Do you mind? I am kind of busy here." He gestured to the ornate box now filled with various ingredients.

The woman chuckled, deeply, heartily like Eric truly amused her.

"And therein lies the problem Mister King," she said. "This cave is *my* domain. Those demons are *my* followers. So I *cannot* possibly let you continue the spell. If I did, all my hard work would go to horrible waste," she said, pouting as she placed her hands on her hips.

"And we wouldn't want that would we?"

Eric's body went rigid, as fear crept across his skin. Something about this woman was pulling him in. Her lilting voice and unmatched beauty made him want to know her, to learn everything about her.

While at the same time, her commanding posture and glowing eyes of ruby pushed him away like a blinking sign, warning him she was danger incarnate.

Then it hit him, like being sucker punched in the guts.
It was *her*.
The woman Eric had been researching, the master.
She was the queen of demons.

"You look astonished," the woman said, almost sadly. "In case you *really* don't know me, I will introduce myself. I am Bianca. Also known as The Demon Queen."
She bowed formally then lifted her body back up, grinning wickedly.

Eric had no words. There had been very little information in his books about her but what Eric did find out wasn't good.
Much like his family, she came from a family of witches. That he remembered. In the history books he had, mostly consisting of witch ancestry, heritages and family trees, her family were one of the first to settle in what became Whitan in the 1900's. Bianca's age, vast knowledge, and her lineage of fire sorcery, made her a deadly foe.

"Why are you doing this?" Eric asked, eager for the knowledge and to keep her speaking. He needed the time to hatch a plan, to figure out his next step. "Why this town?"

Bianca blinked at him, looking stunned. Was she not used to people inquiring about her motives? Surely someone who had lived as long as her, through as many decades and centuries, had garnered some curiosity from people?
"Certainly you have no interest in my life's tragic tale," she said flippantly.
"Truly, it isn't a novelty. All the usual components are there. Betrayal, bitterness and sweet revenge. A story with much similarity to yours actually."

"Do tell," Eric said, his eyes entranced by her while his mind ran through the best ways to get rid of her. He wasn't foolish enough to fight her directly. He knew it was a losing battle. She was stronger, older, and more skilled than him. He wouldn't last one round against her magics. He needed some way to outsmart her. He needed to use his brain not his magical brawn.

She shrugged. "Fine. I will tell you. After all, the story is anything but dull, and I have nothing but time. You see, it was my mother who planted the seed that would inevitably doom this town into the hell hole it is now," she began. "She decided though she was a witch, she wanted to marry a normal man, a human man. My father, you see, wasn't a warlock. He was a noble and honest working man, who managed to woo my mother with his good looks and boyish charm."

"Much to my grandparent's chagrin and protest, she decided to follow her heart and ended up marrying him. Unfortunately, he had no idea she was a witch and when that came out … let's just say father lost his mind. He thought she was a demon, a woman possessed, a deviant, a *monster*."

Eric listened intently, in spite of himself. The story was intriguing, and it wasn't something he would likely ever read in the historical magic books. However, it was more than that. There was something about the way she spoke, the sadness in her voice, that reminded Eric of himself.

Bianca's face contorted with pain as she recalled the agonizing memories.

"My father, who was apparently scared out of his wits, the pathetic swine he was, told the wrong people of my mother's *affliction*. Mind you, this happened right in Whitan before it was known as *Whitan* of course. However, I digress," she said, ruby eyes flaming with scorn.

"So, much like in the movies, the townspeople rounded up a lynch mob. They were intent on burning my witch of a mother at the stake. I was only young when it happened, but even I could feel the revulsion and hatred in the air, the fear my mother felt as they tied her upon the pyre as everyone watched her, feverishly anticipating her demise."

"My father wanted to take me with him, to keep me from my grandmother. But it was her that came with mother's brother, a warlock, to rescue us. Together, they saved us but when we tried to flee, the town's people wouldn't have it. They began attacking us, with no regard for even a young child like me. They threw their rocks; they swung at us with their shovels and pitchforks, all the while calling *us* the evil demons. My family had no choice. It was either run or fight back. My mother didn't want to hurt anyone in the town, despite their animosity towards her. They were people she had grown to know and care for. So though my grandmother and uncle wanted to stay and stand their ground, we turned to escape. Just as we went to leave, a rather ferocious and ambitious villager managed to stab my mother quite literally in the back with a pitchfork."

Bianca averted her eyes from Eric's, and he swore he saw dark, ruby tears trickling down her face. But when she met his gaze again, there was nothing but cold, hate-filled eyes staring back at him.

"No amount of magic, no caliber of it, as I'm sure you know, can bring back the dead. So my sweet, gentle mother died that night. Not a death of flames like many an honorable witch had in days past, but at the hand of a man who didn't even have the decency to look her in the eyes while he stabbed the life out of her."

"And so my path for revenge was laid before me. I started studying the dark magics and in turn, I began summoning dark creatures to terrorize this town. Hence, my notoriety as Queen of Demons. They do my bidding, like puppets on strings."

"But it is more than that now. The revenge became bigger than me. Power begets power, and I became well," she paused, looking thoughtful. *"Thirsty* for it. So I spent centuries becoming more and more powerful and decided eventually it might be nice to conquer the world."

She looked up at the cave ceiling wistfully.

"But I was never in a rush. One day at a time as the saying goes. As you've probably noticed, age means nothing to me. Magic cannot bring back the dead, but it can prevent one from dying."

She stared at Eric, awaiting his response. He hated himself for feeling *any* compassion for this woman who had cursed this town and killed his family, but he couldn't help relating to the loss and bitterness she felt.

Still, it changed nothing.

His mission was still the same.

"I understand how it feels to lose loved ones better than most," he replied, looking at her watchfully. "But these people are not the ones that killed your mother Bianca. You know that much."

"And so the old adage goes, we pay for the sins of our fathers," she said curtly. "Revenge is a dish best served cold. I could go on, but you get the idea. Now that story time is over, you need to go or else," she trailed off before grinning wildly. "Well, you know the rest, I'm *sure."*

"Or else what?" Eric asked, feeling his jaw tighten. He wasn't dense. He had no way to stop her should she decide to attack him, but he wouldn't go down without a fight. If losing his parents had taught him anything, it was to be courageous even in the face of impending death.

"Eric, I know the fate of your parents," she said grimly. "I also know you thirst for revenge, much like me but I can't let you ruin this."

She outstretched her arms indicating the cave walls surrounding her.

"I have built this empire of darkness and pure, perfect evil. I don't intend to give it up until this town is nothing but a rotten, festering hole in the ground. So, you can take your friends and leave willingly, or I can pick you all off, one by one, starting with *you*."

Eric hadn't forgotten. Arabella was watching from the scrying bowl but even her magic was no match for Bianca's. This was his battle and his alone. So he did what his mother and father would have wanted him to do. He fought against every instinct that told him to run and never look back. He ignored the voice of reason that said Bianca was too powerful, and she *would* end him.

Then he looked her in the eyes, not one muscle in his face betraying him, his voice unwavering and his head held high.

"I'm not going anywhere Bianca," he said firmly.

Bianca looked surprised for only a mere second before a sinister smile spread across her lips.

"Well then, let the games begin."

26

Autumn watched with terror as one of the creatures crouched and sprang upwards, leaping at her, eyes feral and venomous. It glided at her through the air, snarls escaping its throat.

"Autumn, watch out!" Rick bellowed.

"I got this!" she reassured him.

She positioned herself. Feet rooted to the ground. Her scythe gripped tightly in her hands.

She swung at the beast, hoping to slice it when it landed, but she missed and it clawed at her, nicking her armor but not penetrating it.

Autumn glanced around her. The three monsters had suddenly become eight and Rick was fending off two by himself, slashing at them with his sword. Mandy was being cornered by another and Nathaniel was firing off shots at the one nearest him.

Autumn swung her scythe again, this time connecting. The scythe slashed through the creatures arm, carving through scaly skin and muscles.

The demon screeched, eyes glowing with rage as dark liquid spewed from the gash in its arm. She pulled her weapon back, and it lunged at her, its mouth foaming, ready to sink its teeth into her but she was ready for it, and she jumped. She landed to the side, crouched, as the monster rushed past her.

It looked around, its head whipping side to side. It spotted her by the cave wall and charged at her.

Autumn stood up and swung her leg out sharply. She kicked, slamming it into the stony cave wall.

As her monster struggled to move, Autumn checked on the others.

A creature slugged Mandy in the jaw, but she was tough as nails. She could take her licks.

"You little shit!" she barked, swinging her nunchucks, letting them gain momentum before she flicked her arm out and whacked the beast in the face. Its head whipped sideways from the impact, and the creature growled.

"It stings doesn't it?" she said before landing a roundhouse kick in its guts.

Nathaniel had already managed to put one monster down, showering it with bullets until it was nothing but pulp.

Rick slashed at two slobbering monsters with his glinting sword. He moved like a whirlwind, his blade dancing back and forth quickly, cutting them lithely and fluently.

The monster Autumn was fighting stood up, cracking its muscles and adjusting its neck. It stared her down, shrieking with rage, and it charged at her again. Its sharp claws struck her, shredding her in the side.

Autumn felt the sharp, rigid, talons tear through her armor and into her flesh. She let out a yelp as the creature kicked her with its clawed feet. Autumn tried to dodge, but it hit Autumn in her guts, sending her flying into the cave wall.

She felt the stones jutting into her body and the impact as she hit the solid rocks, hard and fast. Her body slumped to the ground with a thump, and her vision became hazy.

I can't fade away when they need me, she thought to herself.

Still, her body didn't want to cooperate, and when she tried to get up, it felt like she weighed tons. The wind had been knocked out of her, and she gasped, hardly breathing as her lungs struggled to take in air.

"AUTUMN!" she heard Rick's alarmed voice.
Her head was spinning now. He sounded like he was miles away.

She blinked, waiting for her vision to stabilize. When it did, she saw Rick was trying to get to her but the demon he was fighting wasn't making it easy. It blocked his path, swinging at him ruthlessly.

Autumn tried to reply, to let him know she was alright, but no words came. She was still gasping for air while trying to stand up.

The sound of growling shifted her attention and she saw the creature that had kicked her was coming to finish her off. Another demon was next to it, watching her ravenously. The first one rushed at her, its forked tongue flicking out. It was thirsty, for her blood, for her essence, for her life.

"NATE!" Rick called out. He was blocking the creature clawing at him with the steel of his sword.
"HELP HER!"

"I got it Rick!" Nathaniel said. Then bullets rang out. The monster took one to the head and collapsed to the ground limply. Nathaniel shot at the other beast but missed. It continued charging at Autumn who had managed to get some air back into her lungs. She was standing up now, bracing herself for another round.

The demon kicked at her again but she dodged this time. She used her free hand to punch it, using as much force as she could muster in her weakened state. The beast took the hit as Autumn swung her scythe, aiming for its head.

The dazed demon tried to move, but it was too late. Swiftly, the scythe came at its neck, and Autumn watched as its head was severed against the razor-sharp blade. She slashed repeatedly until the cranium finally toppled to the ground. The headless body stood in front of her, unmoving, before crumpling onto the rocky surface.

Autumn breathed in and out deeply, her heart pounding. She wanted to collapse onto the ground and call it a day, but she couldn't. She wasn't done yet. Not even close.

"Aut?" she heard Nathaniel calling out to her. "Are you alright?"
He was headed towards her, gun at the ready, sweeping the path as he moved.
"I'm fine!" she said, when out of the corner of her eye, she saw movement.
Another demon appeared, seemingly out of nowhere.

This one moved faster than any of others, and Autumn was in its line of destruction. Swinging at her wildly, a mix of limbs and claws came at her in all directions. She dodged and blocked as best as she could but the fury of blows struck her. She felt her arms, hands and face getting slashed.

Mandy struck a final blow to her monster, whipping it in the back of the head with her deadly nunchucks. Rick, who had finally killed his two creatures, rushed over to Autumn.

Autumn kicked the monster swiftly and sharply in the chest sending him far back enough to stop the onslaught of blows. It moved towards her again and punched her, growling and spitting.

Autumn took its punch in the shoulder and swung her scythe, missing. The demon whacked her again, this time nailing her in the mouth with a mighty uppercut.

Autumn's teeth rattled from the power of the blow, but the pain was nothing to her now. She was running on adrenaline.

She tasted blood and looked at the monster.

"Is that all you got?" she asked, her eyes steely.

She hacked her scythe at it, nailing it right in the chest. It screeched, stumbling backwards while clutching its torso. Autumn swung again, slashing its stomach. Dark black fluid spurted from its belly, and the creature went down, twitching for a few moments before it stopped moving all together.

Autumn doubled over, hands on her knees.

All the demons were dead.

Everyone looked at each other wordlessly, like if they spoke, they might wake the dead lying scattered at their feet.

Mandy cleared her throat.

"Is that it?" she asked, breathing heavily. "Weak."

Perspiration dripped all over Autumn's body and her wounds throbbed, stinging as the sweat trickled into them.

"I think so," Autumn offered, taking time to catch her breath.

Nathaniel wandered a few steps ahead to investigate with his gun pointed and ready. Rick went over to Autumn.

"Is everyone alright?" he asked, touching Mandy's shoulder tersely as he passed by her.

"I'm all good," Mandy said, keeping her eyes fixed on Nathaniel.

Rick stood next to Autumn, his eyes tracing over her wounds.

"You were amazing sweetheart," he said, touching her face gently. "But you are hurt. Drink the healing potion."

Autumn examined her boyfriend. He'd taken a few hits himself but nothing too serious.

"No way. These are minor injuries. It's a waste."

"Take mine then," Rick said, reaching into his Kevlar bodysuit, but Autumn refused.

"I'm fine. When Nate gets back we should go check on Eric and see how he's doing."

"Aut, come on. Take it," Rick pleaded.

Mandy sighed impatiently.

"I love you both but this is no time for a lovers quarrel," she said. "We need to rest up quickly and keep clearing the cave out."

"Guys!" Nathaniel's voice interrupted, echoing down the passage. He ran towards them, wiping sweat from his brow. He looked like he had just seen death itself.

Autumn's stomach tightened into knots.

"They're coming," he whispered. "Listen."

Autumn listened carefully. She could hear it. The distinct sound of thudding and pounding against the cave walls, footsteps coming towards them and claws scrapping against stones.

More were coming.

An army of demons was on its way.

A bolt of lightning formed in Bianca's hands, and she hurled it at Eric. He used a blocking spell to create a barrier and it disintegrated.

At this moment, Eric was thankful his nagging but protective sister had taught him some useful instantaneous spells, or else he wouldn't stand a chance of surviving.

"Clever boy," Bianca said, eyes glimmering with excitement. "Let's see how well you handle this next one!"

She raised her hand, and the cave lit up with bright, intensely burning fire. The flame rested in her palm and in its glow, Eric saw Bianca's face staring at him, eyes maniacal, grin wide.

She closed her eyes, focusing and Eric watched with a mix of awe and horror as the flame became bigger and bigger until it was a huge ball of fire ready to swallow him whole.

"Don't worry Eric. I will be sure to tell your friends, before they meet their maker, how you were incinerated to death," she said cruelly. "Or should I let them discover your ashes *before* I kill them?" she chuckled hysterically. "So many choices!"

Eric knew well enough that his magical barrier wouldn't block flames of that capacity. It could barely handle the lightning shots. He just wasn't strong enough.

He couldn't dodge it. It was too huge, and he wasn't going to beg her for mercy. He only hoped someone would save his friends when he was dead, that Autumn would be spared. His precious, darling Autumn.

"Give my regards to mama and papa King!" Bianca screamed. And she launched the fireball at him.

He would be with them soon, his parents, his uncle, Renee and Caleb. He would be with them, wherever they were, and he could finally find the peace he had been seeking.

He closed his eyes saying a silent prayer as the fireball hurtled towards him.

He could feel its heat, growing stronger and closer, like he was a candle made of wax, about to melt under the flames. He prepared himself for the anguish and the pain. He felt the sweat trickling down his neck and face.

Suddenly, he heard a whoosh, like a strong wind blowing around him. His hair whipped wildly, and he felt his face cooling down.

Unexpected but powerful energy overtook the air around him. He recognized it as surging and throbbing magical prowess.

It enraptured him, and he opened his eyes just in time to see someone standing next to him.

Her hair was long, waved and white blonde. Her eyes were large and blue, her skin porcelain. She was clad in a white lace dress and for a moment, standing there, she looked almost angelic.

Angel or not, this woman had just saved his life.

27

Autumn and the others were being hit by an onslaught, a full-on assault.

Dozens of demons marched towards them, almost rhythmically, like militant soldiers, ready for war.

It was an eerie and nightmarish sight. Autumn had to fight to keep her eyes open as she watched with horrified fascination. She could feel the goosebumps spreading across her arms, the shivers emanating down her spine.

Autumn looked to Rick. He looked back at her, jaw tensed, eyes determined. If he was scared, he wasn't showing it.

"Rick," she began but a scraping noise from above shifted her attention.

Demons, moving on all fours were crawling along the cave ceiling above her. Their eyes glowed red and yellow in the darkness, taunting her, tempting her to flee, but she wasn't going anywhere.

She was going to see this through to the end, even if it killed her.

"Guys we need a plan *fast!*" Mandy said.

"Incoming!" Autumn said as a swarm of bats with deformed, scabbed wings soared through the air. Enormous, furry spiders boasting *more* than eight legs scurried along the jagged cave rocks, their beady, black eyes alert.

"The plan is, don't let them overrun us!" Nathaniel snarled as he cocked his gun.

"There are too many!" Mandy bellowed as Nathaniel began letting out shots, trying to spray them with bullets. Some hit the ground but for every demon he took out, five more seem to come out of the woodwork.

"We can't just give up!" Rick roared as he got his sword ready. "We fight!"

Autumn knew Rick well enough to see through his fearless façade. Even he couldn't deny the cold hard facts. They were outnumbered. As always, Rick was tenacious. He wasn't going down without a fight. He stood back to back with Autumn, a technique he taught her. Together they moved, working their way through the mass of demons.

Fighting is like dancing, Rick once told her. *You need to find your own rhythm, your own style, and own it.*

Autumn remembered this when they separated. She used her scythe to chop at a huge demon who was trying to run her through with a pike.

She missed and the creature tried to stab her, but she managed to knock the pike from its grasp with a hearty kick. It clanked to the ground, and with the demon caught off guard she swung her scythe at it again. This time she sliced through its side. As she got ready to swing again, she heard a gunshot. The demon collapsed to the ground, and she headed over to help Rick.

He was tangling with a beast so tall its head grazed against the cave ceiling. It thumped along, trying to stomp Rick out with its mammoth feet. Rick dodged it with ease, jumping up and slashing his sword upright through its throat.

It gasped and stumbled backwards, blood gushing from its gullet, as it crashed into the boulder wall, sending rock debris flying everywhere.

Rick waited for it to get back up, but it didn't. Instead, it lay still and lifeless, buried under the pile of rocks.

Nathaniel shot at the monsters on the ceiling and the ones directly around him. Autumn knew when it came to targets, Nathaniel rarely missed.

Another creature from the ceiling jumped to the ground, and Mandy captured it in her grasp. This time she bypassed her nunchucks, instead grabbing the creature by the head and breaking its neck.

They went on like this for what felt like hours but when Autumn looked around she saw the steady stream of hell beasts wasn't slowing down.

They were coming in droves now. As they overwhelmed them, Rick pushed Autumn back out of harm's way. He looked at her and she saw it, for the first time, in his ice-blue eyes.

She saw the fear.

He was scared now and in a last bid to save her, he would stand in front of her and die first.

They weren't going to survive.

This was the end of the line.

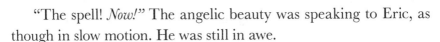

"The spell! *Now!*" The angelic beauty was speaking to Eric, as though in slow motion. He was still in awe.

In awe of her saving his life, of her power, of her presence.

Bianca was shooting off spells. Her hands created fire balls and lightning shots alike but to no avail. There was a barrier blocking them, keeping Eric and the angel safe, like they were in their very own protective bubble.

This angel was indeed a sorceress.

"Who are you?" Eric asked, instantly realizing that this wasn't the time or the place.

Still, foolishly he yearned to know. He wanted to know *everything* about her. He never betted on anyone in Whitan saving his ass, especially a powerful sorcerer. Anyone who could go toe-to-toe with the demon queen had to have some serious magical prowess. Eric could practically see the waves of energy, radiating from this woman.

"My name? That doesn't matter," she said, smiling ever so slightly. "What matters is that you complete your spell."

"And what about Bianca?" he asked, kneeling before his box, getting ready to continue the ritual.

The woman's eyes were stony.

"You leave her to me. You will be protected in here."

Eric watched as she teleported out of the safety of the bubble. Finally, she was face-to-face with Bianca. The demon queen held her fire, her eyes taking in the mystery woman, sizing her up.

"Oh lucky me," Bianca said, lips curled into a sneer. "The dogs let you come out to play did they?"

The woman chuckled. "I didn't come here to engage in witty banter hell bitch."

"Then why did you come?" Bianca asked, eyes flashing with rage. "To try to screw up my wonderful plans I suppose? Or to aid him," she pointed to Eric. "The pathetic fool and his friends while they try to stop me?"

The angelic woman didn't smile and there was no mirth in her voice, only cold hard truth.

"Why I thought you knew Bianca," she said bitterly. "I came to kill you."

Though he wanted to, Eric didn't have time to watch the battle unfurl, he didn't have time to focus on this mysterious woman whom he owed his life to. That had to wait. He had a spell to cast. So he sat down on the rocks and began to chant, silently hoping that his friends were still alive.

Crowding around them, the cave was heaving with monsters now, breathing their rancid breath into the air, eyes glowing with hunger and malice. They were surrounded and the demons closed in, moments away from taking their victory.

Snuffing out lives would be their prize.

Autumn had always wondered when or how she might die. She never imagined it would be in a cave full of hideous demons with Rick at her side.

Her mind raced, full of abstract thoughts with a similar thread. A life lost.

She would never hug her mother again and smell her sweet and familiar vanilla perfume. She would never again learn how to repair a car with her father. He was the one that taught her everything. How to ride a bike, how to count, how to drive.

She wouldn't hear her sister ranting about her terrible dates or her string of boring part-time jobs, or go shopping with Kristin at Teddy's Bookstore downtown.

She would never marry Rick, go to college, or become anything more than a buried, rotting, corpse tucked into the earth for eternity.

She imagined what life could've been like for her and the others if they hadn't wandered into these caves. If they hadn't been too big for their britches, thinking they could destroy what no other humans could.

Still, she would never ever, not even now, moments before the throng of demons devoured her, regret trying to help Eric.

She looked at Rick in front of her, and pulled him to face her. Tears flooded her eyes.

"I need you to know, before," she trailed off unable to say the words aloud. "I want you to know I love you."

Rick's ashen face, contorted with anguish. He wanted to save her. He wanted to make it all go away. He couldn't. Death was coming from them, and they couldn't outrun it. She was right all along. Luck had nothing to do with it. They made their beds and now they were going to lie in them. Their gravestones had been carved, their fates sealed, the moment they arrived here tonight.

"Don't you dare say goodbye to me!" he said, frustration contorting his features. "You are going to live through this Aut. I will protect you until the end. Even if I die, you aren't going to. I don't know how yet, but I will make sure you live."

With renewed determination, Rick turned away from her and lunged at another monster, sword raised as he fluidly hacked its head off.

Autumn knew it was fruitless. The fleet of creatures came at them without refrain.

They didn't have a prayer, not a hope of surviving this.

Autumn closed her eyes, for only a split second. She yearned to keep them closed forever. She didn't want to see anyone die. Still, she reluctantly opened them.

She watched as Rick and Nathaniel fought on, determined and unyielding.

Then she heard something.

A low growling, followed by wild, piercing, howls that reverberated off the walls.

Fear ripped through her.

What awful creature was coming now?

The sound was coming from behind her, meaning whatever it was had to have passed by Eric at some point meaning Eric could be ...
Her brain had to stop there.
She wasn't going to let herself wander into that realm of thought.
Instead, she looked behind her, holding her scythe tightly in her hands, waiting for whatever was coming to rear its ugly head.

The howling came again, this time louder and much closer. Even the monsters seemed to take notice, some staring in the direction of the commotion.
"What the hell was that?" Mandy asked as she swung at a creature with her nunchucks.
Rick, who kept slashing at the demons, grimaced.
"More monsters?" he offered wryly.
Then something stepped out of the shadows.
Autumn's pulse quickened.
Whatever they were, they were colossal and there were at least three of them that she could see.

28

Autumn blinked because she couldn't believe her eyes.

She had to be delirious. She was hallucinating for in front of her stood three giant wolves.

One was the color of chocolate, the other grey with white flecks and the last jet black.

The strange thing was, they didn't walk on all fours like wolves.

Towering and massive, they were walking upright on two sinewy, furry legs. With pelt covered faces, snouts and hypnotizing wolf eyes, they bared their teeth and razor-sharp talons as they moved gracefully through the cave.

Despite being petrifying, Autumn recognized there was something majestic about them, something benign.

She felt like her feet were rooted to the spot as she watched them in wonder.

They growled, looking only at each other, almost as though Autumn and the others didn't exist.

Autumn lost her breath as the black wolf jumped, soaring through the air with grace and flourish.

Rick, who was still slashing away at the horde with his mighty blade, watched as the jet-black wolf landed smack-dab in the middle of the demons and began tearing them limb from limb, howling riotously.

The chocolate one and the grey one weren't far behind their comrade. They followed it into the fray, jumping into the swarm of beasts, biting, tearing and hacking without restraint.

With their massive frames, quick reflexes, sharp teeth and claws, the demons, no matter what size they were or what weapon they brandished, were no match for the burly, skilled wolves.

It took a moment for Autumn to realize that the wolves were on their side. They were here to demolish the demons too. The wolves had taken over the battle, monopolizing the fight.

She took a deep breath, finally relaxing.

They were saved.

Apparently, luck *was* on their side tonight.

"Aut, did I get hit in the head?" Rick asked. "Are those wolves real?"

"Yes." Autumn nodded, eyes fixated on the creatures. Demons were real. Magic was real and now the *wolf man* was a confirmed myth too.

It was overwhelming how much was actually true.

Rick and Autumn watched in awe as the wolves battled on. The way they moved with such precision and speed, despite their size, was truly a sight to behold.

Autumn was impressed.

"What *exactly* are they?" Rick asked.

"Our saviours," Autumn quipped. "Seriously, they look like oversized wolves to me."

Autumn watched as the black wolf spotted a red-eyed bat soaring along above it. Like a predator hunting prey, it launched into the air, trapping the bat in its mouth. The wolf landed back on the ground, crunching on the mammal, looking satisfied.

"Yum," Mandy joked as she approached.

"Well that was a close call," Nathaniel said, wiping the perspiration from his forehead. "The werewolves saved us just in the nick of time."

"Werewolves?" Mandy asked, looking bemused. "You think they're *werewolves?*"

"Well, they definitely aren't White Fang," Rick replied, rolling his eyes.

Everyone watched on, enthralled and astounded. The wolves were cleaning house now, taking out the masses of demons, making Autumn and the rest of them look like the rank amateurs they were.

Autumn was completely engaged in watching the wolves, so distracted that she didn't even see the cave rocks moving and shifting. Beside her, a secret passage way in the wall was opening up.

By the time Autumn had turned around to see the skeleton-winged demon, it was too late.

It had her in its deadly grasp, and it was preparing to fly away.

29

This moment, this memory, would haunt Autumn for a lifetime, if she didn't die first.

This demon was unlike the others.

It offended all her senses.

It omitted a rancid smell that Autumn couldn't identify but inhaling it was enough to make her want to vomit.

Its eyes flamed red like an inferno.

Its mouth was thick and rubbery. Its flimsy skin was translucent, revealing its emaciated torso. Its nose was flat with only nostrils and attached to its gaunt, frail, frame was a long, spiked tail that whipped back and forth.

Then there were its wings. Large and skeletal, flapping with a disgusting cracking sound, they looked almost like twigs, bony and breakable.

The last thing Autumn heard was Rick screaming and after that, everything was a blur.

The demon was clutching her in its bony hands, sharp nails digging into her soft flesh.

It clutched her throat and began choking the life from her with one skeletal hand.

Autumn felt its claws digging into her throat, like tiny razorblades slicing into her skin.

She wanted to cry out, but she couldn't.

She couldn't breathe. She couldn't move. She was a porcelain doll, beautiful, delicate and ripe for the smashing.

She saw its eyes, burning into hers, taunting her. It relished the imminent thrill of victory, enjoyed watching the light in her eyes slowly being snuffed out.

Autumn thought her life might flash before her eyes, like all the near-death stories foretold, but it didn't. Instead, she saw her life as it might have been.

She was the valedictorian at her graduation. Her parents were spectators, brimming with pride.

She was wearing a white lace gown while marrying Rick on a beach.

It was warm and the sun was setting. The ocean waves crashed in her ears, the gilded sand was cool on her bare feet.

All the things she would never have, at least not in this lifetime.

This was the end for *her,* but the others would survive.

That's all that mattered.

She heard Rick's cries, as they faded into the distance, Mandy's screams of terror and Nathaniel's futile gunshots.

All of it sounding like it was coming through a stereo with dying batteries.

She was breathless.

Her vision started to blur, and everything began to fade out.

She couldn't fight it anymore. Death would be far more enjoyable then the pain of sharp claws digging into her flesh and being asphyxiated by bony, merciless hands.

So she let the warm and inviting calm wash over her, like a gentle tide. Then she welcomed the blackness as it enveloped her.

When Autumn awoke, she was being cradled. She was surrounded by heat and the feeling of utter safety, though inexplicable.

She could smell the heady scent of pine and the freshness of the outdoors and feel fur softly cushioning her body.

Was she alive?

Blackness was still all she saw but surely death wasn't this beautiful, this blissful?

Had she been saved? It was the only thing that made any sense to her now.

Her throat ached. Her wounds throbbed.

She attempted to open her eyes, anxious to see her knight, but her lids felt so heavy, so tired.

She felt movement, as though she was being carried somewhere. She had to open her eyes, had to see her destination and her hero.

It took all her might and will, but she opened them. When she did, she saw she was being held by the wolf, the grey one to be exact.

It was holding her gently in its furry, muscled arms, being careful not to claw her with its long nails.

Its eyes, expressive unlike any animal she had ever encountered, stared down at her, looking utterly relieved to see her awaken.

A rush of affection for this creature came over her.

This wolf saved her life.

"Thank you," she whispered, unsure if it could even understand her. "For saving me."

The grey wolf cocked its head sideways, looking back at her in silence.

"Autumn!" Rick called out, garnering her attention.

He, Mandy, Nathaniel and the other two wolves, were finishing off what appeared to be the last of the monsters.

Still in the grey wolf's grasp, Autumn noticed the steady flow of demons had puttered out and all that was left were hordes of dead creatures scattered all over the cave floor.

Autumn watched, still against the wolf's chest, its heartbeat pounding steadily and comfortingly, as the other wolves tore through creatures succinctly and ruthlessly. Teeth barred, claws slashing, muscles tensed, showing no remorse.

Rick was going hit for hit with a creature wielding a large axe. The axe hit his sword and his sword the axe, clinking and clanking, as they moved around in an odd rhythm, almost like they were dancing.

Nathaniel was shooting off his gun diligently, his eyes focused and his aim true.

A demon with yellow eyes and a horned hide swung a huge fist at Mandy. She ducked, avoiding the punch, and swung her nunchucks into the creature's jaw.

The grey wolf, with its heartbeat still thudding in her ear, snarled at the other wolves.

They gave it their attention for a moment then went back to combat, unperturbed.

Autumn searched for the demon that had almost killed her, and she spotted it, a few feet away. It had claw marks riddling its body. Its neck had been snapped, and its frail wings were smashed into pieces.

The battle raged on, faster now.

The wolves obviously wanted this night to end as much as Autumn did.

It didn't take much longer for them to clear the area. When they were done there was nothing left but bodies, piles of them and body parts, scattered haphazardly along the cave floor. Autumn tried to block out the gore and focus on the victory but for some reason, she couldn't look away from the disgusting scene.

Once the coast was definitely clear, the wolf looked at Autumn. She smiled at it, wanting so badly to reach out and stroke the soft, grey pelt on its nose.

Instead, she uncertainly touched its arm. She smiled again as the wolf placed her onto her feet gingerly. She thanked it once more.

"Are you alright?" Rick asked, as he ran over to Autumn, his blue eyes filled with alarm.

Autumn looked down at her arms. They were cut up and bloodied and muscles she didn't even know she had ached and throbbed. Her throat was sore both inside and out.

"I will be," she murmured, as she pulled out the healing potion Eric had given her, downing it.

Almost instantly her skin began to tingle. She watched as her wounds began to seal up and her skin patched itself over. The inside of her throat prickled like she was drinking a warm cup of tea.

Rick reached out and touched her face, stroking her cheek tenderly.

"I thought you were dead. I tried to get you, but I wasn't as fast as …"

"As the wolf," Mandy offered. "We all tried to get to you. That winged demon came out of nowhere."

Autumn glanced over at the wolves. They were snarling and growling back and forth, obviously their means of communicating.

She wondered what they were saying and what they knew about the caves when she caught a glimpse of something approaching. The wolves glanced up, ears perked, as it drew nearer.

Moments later, another large wolf stepped through the darkness.

With fur the color of pure white snow, it wore a long purple robe adorned with intricate symbols and gilded tassels. It carried a metal staff which had masses of fur and a golden wolf head atop of it.

The white wolf took a quick look at Autumn and the others. It moved past them, heading towards the group of wolves. They began growling and snarling again and when they were finished the white wolf reached into a pocket in its robe. It pulled out a chalky powder and began sprinkling it atop the piles of bodies.

When it was done, the other wolves formed a circle. Autumn watched, feeling like she was witnessing something precious and private as the snowy wolf raised its staff into the air and began howling. The other wolves joined in, and together they howled, creating noise so loud it was almost deafening.

"What are they doing?" Nathaniel asked, looking puzzled.
"I think it's a ritual," Autumn said.
"A ritual to do what?"
"Probably *that*," Mandy chimed in.

Autumn looked over and saw the corpses in the cave evaporating before her very eyes.

It was like they were ghosts. Simply melting away into thin air, traveling into another realm.

The howling stopped abruptly, but the white wolf continued to snarl and growl while swaying its staff side to side over the remains.

When all the monsters were gone, and every last inch of the cave had been cleansed of debris and filth, the wolves began their exit.

Autumn wished there was some way she could thank them for their aid, some way to show them her gratitude. Instead, she just watched as they stomped off, silently wondering why they came tonight, of all nights, to this God-forsaken cave.

The only one that turned back to look at her, was the towering grey wolf.

30

"All I remember is doing the ritual while *she* fought off Bianca."

It was Saturday evening, one week after Eric's spell had been cast. He was recounting his adventure to Arabella and the others. After the cave was empty, he used the spell to protect it from evil returning to it.

"She was amazing," Eric gushed. "This woman used magics I have never seen before. She had all the elements mastered. Most people can only use one or two, max, but she was fluent in using earth, wind, water and fire magics."

Autumn felt a tiny tug inside her stomach whenever Eric's beautiful savior was mentioned.

She had been replaced by this mysterious, nameless woman who had pulled Eric from the scorching coals of death. She hated to think she was jealous, but a small part of her was.

"She finished off Bianca and just left me there," Eric said. "I have to find her and thank her."

He winked at Autumn knowingly and she frowned. She couldn't help but think he was enjoying making her jealous a little too much.

"So this beautiful sorceress basically saved your ass, and I saw none of it because that demon bitch used her magics to impede my scrying sight?" Arabella interrupted with a smirk on her face.

"Exactly," Eric said, looking wistful. "You really missed out Ara. I have never seen anything like it before."

"You mean *anyone* like *her* before?" Arabella teased.

Eric rolled his eyes while crossing his arms over his chest defiantly.

"I never said a word about *her,* specifically, just her magical talents."

"Eric, you have told this story every day since we left the caves," Rick said, as he took a chip from the giant bowl on the coffee table and flipped it into the air. He caught it in his mouth, looking proud.

"Face it dude you are smitten," Mandy said as she looped her arm through Nathaniel's.

"Can I go on with the story?" Eric asked, ignoring the jabs from his friends.

"Why? It always ends the same. The pretty witch kills the evil demon queen. Everyone lives happily ever after," Arabella muttered, looking mildly bored.

"Well not *everyone* Ara," Eric said, looking sullen. "I wish I could've saved Renee and Caleb."

"I just wish they weren't stupid enough to get themselves killed in the first place," Arabella said bluntly. "They were never my favorites, but they didn't deserve to die."

"Says the woman who just called them stupid," Eric said, looking at his sister, displeased.

"I can hardly call them smart now can I?" she said, throwing back her shoulders haughtily.

"Besides, no one actually found their bodies. Maybe they ran off together to some place where bonking your cousin is legal."

Eric frowned, preparing to chide his sister but the sound of a clanking glass distracted him.

Nathaniel was standing up, holding his flute of champagne into the air.

"Everyone, I have some words," he began, cheeks flushed from the alcohol.

Mandy sighed deeply and took a swig of her drink.

"I told you not to let him drink," she muttered under her breath to Eric, who looked rather amused.

"I want to say that what we did to help Whitan, is probably the *least* selfish thing we will ever do," Nathaniel said, his face solemn. "I can't speak on behalf of you guys, but I have always admired superheroes. They constantly put their cities, their people, their families and friends, before themselves. Why? Because that is what a *true* hero does. I never imagined that I would save anything in my life, let alone the people in this town."

"Watching you all that night, I was proud to have friends who are so brave and selfless standing with me on the battlefield. You guys didn't care what risks you had to take to help Eric on his mission."

He paused, looking around the room, misty-eyed.

Autumn had learnt that compassion, and sentimentality came to Nathaniel naturally.

Mandy, not so much.

"This toast is to you all. Eric, you faced the fears you've had for years. Rick, you fought like a noble knight with your sword. Autumn, you went in there with very little training and still killed it. And *you* got the closet to that awesome grey ninja wolf. And Mandy, even though you are tiny, I have never seen anyone filled with so much rage."

Mandy looked at Autumn and sighed exasperatedly, but she was wearing a huge smile.

"And?" Arabella asked, eyes narrowed at Nathaniel.

Nathaniel looked at her, his brow furrowed with confusion.

"And what?" Nathaniel asked, dumbly.

"Didn't you forget to acknowledge someone?" she coaxed.

Nathaniel looked thoughtful before shrugging his shoulders.

"Nope. I don't think so."

"Me!" Arabella said, her fists clenched and her eyes ablaze. *"I was helping you know!* Before that demon queen messed with my magical mojo!"

"Oh yeah!" Nathaniel said, his eyes brightening like a light had flickered on in his head.

"And this toast is for Arabella too. For watching over us from the *safety* of a living room."

Arabella looked at Nathaniel, unimpressed. "Touching. I will have those *exact* words scribed on my tombstone when I die."

"Awesome!" Nathaniel said obliviously before going back to his speech.

"So as I was saying. We were all superheroes that night. Even if we needed saving by the wolves, or some really smoking hot witch, we still didn't back down. We kicked demon ass. We made Whitan a safer place to live. As the saying goes, we went, we saw, we conquered. So to us," he raised his glass once more. "And the many new adventures that hopefully lie ahead."

Everyone raised their glasses then took sips of Eric's expensive and imported champagne. The sound of applause filled the large room, and Nathaniel bowed before sitting back down.

The many new adventures that hopefully lie ahead.

Autumn wondered what Nathaniel meant by this. Though somewhere deep inside herself she already knew. She had been warned by Eric, when Rick became obsessed with training and vigilantism, that he knew his plight.

"Even though I was never a vigilante per say," he had said. "I know the addictiveness of power. Doing magic, the temptation is there every day. So I can see how enticing it is, to want to be more than just the average person, to want to spurn change, to make a mark in our world."

"And you think Rick will have a hard time walking away from this?" Autumn asked. It was almost foolish. After all, she knew Rick better than anyone. She knew seeing evil lurking in the shadows of the world had changed him. He would see the immoral not as something to ignore, but something he *would* change.

"I think all of you will have trouble being normal teenagers after this," Eric had said. "It isn't something you can just tuck away and forget. The world of the supernatural has been revealed to you. You can't just close your eyes to it now."

It was the feeling of Rick's hand on hers that brought Autumn back from her reverie.

"Aut," he said, sounding miles away. He pulled her back yet again. Her precious anchor.

"Are you okay?" he asked gently. "Have you had too much bubbly?"

He grinned. It was the familiar Rick smile she had loved her whole life.

"Try not enough," she joked and took another deep sip. One thing she could say for the expensive imported champagne was it made everything seem a lot less terrifying in its wake.

"What are you thinking about?" he asked her, leaning over to kiss her cheek.

"You look lost."

Rick usually had a knack for reading her thoughts, so much so it was uncanny, but not tonight. They were *all* different people now, in some way, shape or form. They were all wild cards. Their stories had begun, but many pages were still left blank.

"I was just thinking, about what Nate said. About having more *adventures,*" she began almost cautiously.

Rick's eyes sparkled with excitement at the mere mention of adventures, and Autumn instantly knew Eric's prediction had come to fruition.

Rick was hooked on the hunt.

"I was thinking the exact same thing as him! We could go out and save *more* people!"

He paused, looking at her, blue eyes bursting with hope.

"Why? Were you thinking the same thing Autumn? That it isn't over yet? That we have so much more left to do?"

Autumn wanted to say something to deter to him, because she knew what they did was dangerous. Death had brushed against them so close she could still feel its bony hands on her throat.

Still, she couldn't look into the twinkling blue eyes she had stared into since her youth and tell Rick this.

She couldn't crush his dreams, not yet, not tonight. So instead Autumn just smiled and took Rick's face into her hands.

"I don't think it's over Ricky. Not by a long shot."

About the Author

Sabrina Albis was born in Ontario, Canada, and began writing in her childhood. In college she majored in print journalism and wrote for the school newspaper. After graduation, she worked as a freelance writer for a variety of newspapers and magazines before pursuing a career as a novelist. She lives with her husband and their cat, Martin, in Canada.

Printed in the United States
By Bookmasters